'Heartwarming, emotional and full of community spirit. I couldn't put it down' **Amanda Prowse**

READERS LOVE DEBBIE MORRISON!

'An absolute delight to read – a beautiful story of family, loyalty, and self discovery'

'This gripping novel will take you on an emotional rollercoaster'

'Perfect for fans of compelling women's fiction'

'A must-read for anyone seeking an engaging story with relatable characters and unexpected twists'

'Incredibly refreshing . . . I found it hard to put the book down'

'An entertaining fiction novel that raises so many important, real-life issues'

'Packed with suspense and drama that will keep you hooked until the very end'

Also by Debbie Morrison

The 'Perfectly Imperfect' Duet:

A Perfect Algarve Villa
A Perfect Chelsea Townhouse

The Brambleton Series:

A Perfect Devon Farmhouse
A Perfect Devon Pub
A Perfect Devon Christmas
A Perfect Devon Manor

A Perfect Devon Farmhouse

Debbie Morrison

PROSPERINA
PRESS

First published in the UK in 2025 by Prosperina Press
This edition first published in the UK in 2025 by Prosperina Press

9 7 5 3 1 2 4 6 8

A catalogue record for this book is available from the British Library.

ISBN (PB): 978-1-0686884-6-1
ISBN (E): 978-1-0686884-9-2

Cover design: Hannah George (illustration) / Cherie Chapman (design)
Text design by Ellipsis, Glasgow

PROSPERINA PRESS

Prosperina Press,
Grenville House, 9 Boutport Street,
Barnstaple, Devon, EX31 1TZ

In loving memory of "Sir" Frederick,
the inspiration for Stop-it.

"I aspired to be the person my dog thought I was. Turns out, he was more than happy with the muddled, biscuit-giving version of me."

— *Anon.*

One

On a Monday evening, in a compact flat in South London, a tall woman lay sprawled on the sofa, her laptop angled against a cushion. Her short straw-coloured hair was slightly straggly, as if a trip to the hairdresser was imminent. The sash windows were open, letting in a warm June breeze along with the smell of a neighbour's late-night barbeque. Someone had burned the sausages.

She reached down for her own meal and forked in a mouthful of tandoori paneer tikka masala. Indian was her favourite cuisine. It had also been Guy's.

Glancing up from her screen she noticed the pulsing glow of light from cars, streetlamps and houses long since converted into flats. It was never dark in London, not like the deep darkness of her rural Devon childhood, where torches always hung in readiness from hooks on the pine kitchen dresser.

Her phone pinged. She glanced at the screen and chuckled. Someone had posted on the *Brambleton Gals* WhatsApp group. It was Rianna. Most people knew her as 'Anna', but she used her full name for her work as an architect, believing it conjured a ring of glamour.

> Can't believe you're off on Sunday! If it rains here for one more day, I'm coming with you!

Clare let out a long, deep sigh. After five long years without Guy, she was used to travelling solo, but it still hurt. Seconds later, the screen lit up with a string of emojis from the third group member, Trish. There was a picture of an umbrella, clouds, and then a monkey hiding his face behind his hands. Clare responded.

Five days to go! I'll send some sunshine your way. xxx

She dropped the phone and returned to her curry. She missed her friends, but she could never understand why Trish and Anna had wanted to stay in Brambleton instead of escaping Devon the minute they were old enough, as Clare had. She pictured her childhood home, Orchard Farm, a pretty farmhouse nestled among rolling meadows where Jersey cows roamed, munching contentedly on lush grass. She remembered her father holding her up in his arms so she could stroke the ears of a milker. Like Guy, he too had died in an accident before his time. Clare had been eleven when she lost the first man she loved, and nearly forty when she lost the second. She would never love another.

She pushed the memories away, as her mother had taught her to do after her father died, diverting her mind by choosing a few emojis to reply to Trish and Anna. Neither had come to London recently and Clare hadn't been back to Devon in seven years, not since that row with her mother. What her mother had said then was wrong, and she had compounded that sin under the guise of a condolence letter when Guy died. But time had eroded the spiky edges of Clare's anger, and she was beginning to think she might be ready to patch things up. She would add '*ring Mum*' to her task list, and if there was time, she might even visit her before she flew to Spain on Sunday.

Clare pulled up a file marked *Sabbatical*. For the last five years she had been too wrapped up in her work to contemplate planning a holiday.

But in January the senior partner had urged Clare to take a year off, sweetening the suggestion by offering to pay 50 per cent of her salary. Carefully planned to eke out her savings, the adventure would start in Spain and take her across Europe before heading east, culminating in a two-month journey through India.

A bus screeched to a halt outside pulling Clare from her daydream. She finished her curry, then composed a letter, her fingers dancing across the keyboard, loving the reassuring clickity-click sound of the keys; she felt like a medieval champion on a white horse, galloping to rescue a distressed damsel. Clients didn't understand the protections provided by employment law, but they didn't have to. Clare and her colleagues did. And Clare relished taking on powerful employers on behalf of the underdogs.

Clare saved her work, then picked up her to do list, crossing off '*finish letter for Jenkins case*'. She ran her eyes down her tasks:

- Hand over work notes
- Finish packing
- Clear bedrooms to storage
- Find white goods manuals
- Spare keys
- Clear out fridge

Her mortgage company prohibited renting, so at the end of June two trainee solicitors were moving in as 'flat sitters' and would reimburse Clare for the utility bills.

She tossed the list aside, collected the used takeaway containers and in three strides was in her tiny galley kitchen. She flicked on the kettle, and as she caught sight of her suitcases by the front door, a shiver of excitement shot through her. Her year-long adventure would take her to continents she'd never visited. When she was younger, she couldn't afford long-haul jaunts, and then she'd met Guy and there were more important claims on her holiday time. He had been a rally driver, and while her colleagues had lazed in pampered luxury in far-flung destinations, Clare had spent her holidays at racetracks, listening to the high-pitched whine of finely tuned engines, frantically searching for Guy's number on the bonnets of cars hurtling towards her. This adventure would take her to all those places she might have visited if she hadn't been his most loyal fan.

Clare pulled open the fridge, revealing the breakfast she had purchased on her way home from the office – a single yoghurt beside a punnet of strawberries – and a small container of milk, which made her think about her mother's dairy herd. Cindy's passion was her orchard, but the farm's income came from milk. She imagined her mother jogging across the farmyard, a black Labrador lolloping in her wake. The dog's name would be Jet; their family's labs were always black, and always called Jet. In her mind's eye, her mother had a spanner in one hand and a hammer in the other. Farming was a life of fixing things: fences, equipment, old vehicles. After her father died, her mother had mastered those skills and tried to teach her daughter too, but tools didn't sit naturally in Clare's hands. She shuddered at the memory of her mother showing her how to change a tyre. Clare liked instruments she could master, like law books.

What her mother did teach her though was how to recover from life's upsets, no matter how traumatic, by keeping busy. Living that mantra helped both women after Clare's father died in a farming accident, ensuring task lists were always long and never allowed space to dwell in the past. After he was buried, mother and daughter never discussed him again. Clare sighed.

Her mother was good at compartmentalizing. Would she welcome a phone call from Clare? She wondered if her mother was ready to heal their rift. After seven years, how would she react to her daughter getting in touch properly, not just the stiff 'seasonal greetings' cards they exchanged at Christmas? Maybe Clare shouldn't rush things. After all, she had her hands full with her sabbatical on the horizon.

The kettle clicked off and Clare's hand hovered over the milk, then switched to a bottle of wine. There was just enough left for two glasses, and, with a pang of longing, she thought of the many times she used to come home from work and pour a glass for her and Guy. He preferred beer but was forgetful about restocking the fridge; she smiled, he was forgetful full stop, always fetching himself a beer or a sandwich without bringing anything for her.

Her phone rang. She glanced at the kitchen clock – ten past nine. Odd. She ran to answer, seeing the screen flashing on the sitting room table. It wasn't anyone in her contacts list. It was too late for a cold call, probably a wrong number. She answered warily.

'Hello?'

'Clare?'

She struggled to place the voice. It was a woman, vaguely familiar. Was it a former client? It wasn't too late for a business call. 'Speaking,' she said in a formal tone.

'Clare, are you alone?'

She clutched at the phone, her stomach churning, but the voice was gentle, caring. 'Who is this, please?'

'It's Ivy.'

'Ivy!' Mentally, she visualized her mother's best friend. Ivy was short, famed for being precisely the height of a badminton net: 5 ft 1 in. And if asked for a word to describe the recently retired vicar, Clare would have chosen 'rotund'. She was stocky, with a round open face, and frequently wore billowing, tent-like dresses which accentuated her girth. Why was Ivy calling at this hour?

'Clare, I've got some bad news. This is going to come as a terrible shock. I'm so sorry, there's no gentle way of saying this, but your mother died earlier this evening.'

'What?' Clare slumped on the sofa.

Ivy spoke slowly, gently as if to a child. 'Cindy died before the paramedics arrived. I'm so very sorry. Is there someone I can call to be with you? A friend?'

Clare went completely still. Her mind was blank. She dredged around it for anyone in London she could call on. She had workmates she occasionally met for drinks on a Friday night, but no one to share such intimate news with. After Guy had died in a horrific crash at a rally, she'd lost touch with their social circle. They were his friends really and, like him, petrol heads. She didn't blame them for his death, but they were a constant reminder of the sport which killed him.

'Clare, are you still there? Take your time. I'm here. I won't hang up. Before Cindy died, we said the Lord's Prayer together . . .'

Clare suspected the prayer was more of a solace to Ivy than Cindy; her mother worshipped the orchard, not God. Clare tried to focus on what Ivy had told her. Her mother was dead. That couldn't be right. Ivy must be mistaken. Mentally she envisioned her mother manhandling cows from the milking parlour into a meadow, dressed in her trademark blue overalls, splattered with stains, the once-dark colour long since faded from repeated boil washes. Clare could see the rolling hills, the gentle swaying of the cows, hear their clomping hooves and soft snorts as her mother chivvied them through the gate. How could such an active woman die so suddenly aged seventy-four? She closed her eyes in an attempt to block out the memory, feeling the soft pricking of tears on her eyelids. Ivy's soft voice interrupted her thoughts. 'You need to come home. Is there someone who can be with you tonight, then you can catch a train in the morning?'

'No.' she croaked.

'Right,' said Ivy forcefully. 'There's a late train from Paddington at ten o'clock. I'll meet you at Tiverton Parkway.'

Clare swallowed the lump in her throat, but her face crumpled, and she bit hard on her lip to stop the tears. Her mother was dead. They hadn't spoken for the past seven years, but still Clare felt an empty numbness descend like a dark Devon night.

Clare realized Ivy was saying something else. 'She asked me to give you a message. Hang on . . . I wrote it down.'

Had her mother told Ivy she regretted their estrangement? If Cindy had confided in anyone, it would have been Ivy. Clare spoke in a breathless rush. 'What did she say?'

The line fell silent, then Clare heard a rustle of paper being unfurled, a gravelly cough and finally Ivy's voice. 'She said, "Tell Clare, I'm sorry. She's a smart girl. She'll sort this out."'

Two

A sharp keening howl woke Clare at dawn. She flopped onto her side, dragging the duvet over her head and clamping it around her ears. The barrier barely muffled a high-pitched squawk. It sounded like a cockerel. What was that doing in London? Clare threw off the covers, feeling a knot form in her stomach. Her eyes closed, and a dull, empty sensation settled on her chest as the events of last night came flooding back. She was in Devon, on her mother's farm, but her mother was gone.

She swallowed her tears. The howling and squawking paused, replaced by the soft gentle trill of the dawn chorus. Listening to the gentle beck and call of the birds, a tentative smile spread across her face – she had missed this tranquillity. The peace was shattered by another sharp squawk and Clare remembered Ivy's warning last night that the cockerel – Captain Hilts – and the hens would need feeding. She glanced at the time – 5.30 a.m. Early even for her. She would feed them. She didn't want to give Hilts any excuse to misbehave. She forced herself out of bed and walked down the corridor to the bathroom.

Already formulating a task list in her mind, Clare stepped gingerly into the dusky pink bathtub of her childhood. She needed to feed the animals, register her mother's death and arrange the funeral. Struggling to adjust the height of the shower head, which was too low, she mentally added '*find Mum's will*' to the list. She tugged at the mechanism, but it seemed locked solid, so she fiddled with the taps, causing a spurt of water hit her chest, as if someone had fired a water pistol. She turned off the tap and removed the shower head. Her nose wrinkled. A thick scum of limescale covered the surface. Her mother should have modernized the bathroom decades ago. She wasn't adding that to her list. She would muddle through with baths – she wouldn't be staying long. She added '*find the accounts ledger*' to the list, feeling a quiet sense of control. If she itemized everything, it would be like the charts she used to draw as a child to mark off the hours until the start of school holidays. She could tick everything off and escape back to London. Reluctantly she added '*delay sabbatical by a week*'– she would get the travel agent to change her flights.

A wailing noise cut through her thoughts. First chore, console that dog. Last night, he had seemed fine while Ivy was there, but after she left, he wouldn't come inside. Clare assumed he had settled down to sleep in one of the barns.

Dressed in jeans and flat felt boots, Clare walked into the kitchen and contemplated the cream-coloured Aga. It dominated the room, sitting at right angles to a fireplace, a sofa and saggy armchairs ranged in front of the empty fire grate. Decades ago, Clare had done her homework lounging on those seats, her mother bustling about offering slices of homemade lemon drizzle cake or mugs of tea. A lump formed in her throat. She couldn't face food or drink right now.

In front of the Aga, where a modern kitchen designer would have built an island, was the same kitchen table Clare had eaten at every day until she left for university, still carpeted with copies of *Farmers Weekly*, and a two-inch jumble of letters. Her mother had liked the physical side of farming, not the paperwork. She strode across the huge grey flagstones, noticing parts of the grouting had worn away. It was lucky her mother hadn't copied other farmers by diversifying into bed and breakfast. Unlike her spotless London flat, this kitchen would fail a health and safety inspection.

She opened the back door, and the view hit her like a warm shower on a cold winter's day. In front of her were rolling fields separated by ancient hedgerows of pollarded beech trees. The meadows were filled with rich, deep green Devon grass spiked with vibrant wildflowers – the vivid yellows, soft purples and bright whites of buttercups, clovers and daisies. Groups of trees framed both sides of the picture. Beyond the furthest field, the sun was rising over the sea casting a shimmer of mauve and pink on the horizon. There were no cows in the fields, which struck Clare as odd. Maybe a neighbouring dairy farmer had already collected them for milking. Mentally she pencilled '*find a dairy hand*' as an early chore; she wasn't taking over the herd.

To one side of her was the farm's namesake, an orchard. She caught a glimpse of a sheltered tree still with thick pink and white blossom hugging its branches like a multi-sleeved fluffy jumper, but she turned away abruptly as if someone had hurled a bucket of cold water at her. Birds were warbling, the air was warm and smelt so much cleaner than London. A drowsy calm seeped through her body, competing with her jangling nerves

A dog started barking. Sitting beside her mother's Land Rover was a small white dog with a black patch of fur circling one eye, like a thick smudge of badly applied liner. It wasn't a Labrador, nor was he called Jet. Ivy had told her that Stop-it was a year-old miniature bull terrier. He was the height and weight of a young lamb, but stocky like a ram. Clare crouched to the animal's height, trying, and failing, to catch his eye.

She held out an encouraging hand. 'Stop-it . . . Come, boy.'

The dog shifted his bottom.

'Come on, boy. We're both upset. Come inside.' She moved towards the animal. His hackles rose. Clare backed off.

Giving Stop-it a wide berth, she walked to the chicken coop. According to Ivy, Clare needed to be vigilant with the rooster. Her mother had named him 'Hilts' after the character in her favourite movie, *The Great Escape*. Hilts had a habit of hovering by the gate and if her mother inadvertently left the gate ajar, he would make a dash for it. Cindy used to dispatch him to solitary confinement for his escape attempts and occasional misogynistic habits.

The hens swarmed towards her, a brown sea of clucking, chirping happiness. Their pen was a fenced area the size of a tennis court. It was scrubland but chicken paradise, especially compared to their former home in an egg factory. The birds could roam and scratch and peck at bushes and wildflowers all day. In the centre of the enclosure was a wooden henhouse, the size of a garden shed, and in a corner sat a much smaller one, shaped like a kennel but with ventilation slits in the sides – *the cooler* – for when Hilts misbehaved.

She spotted the galvanized dustbin, which contained the grain, and her hand was on the gate, when she realized she didn't know how much to feed them. She felt her lip start to tremble, and pulled up her mental task list for comfort, adding that query. She counted the flock. She'd google the quantity of feed.

Back inside, the empty room was lonely after the clucking chickens, giving her a pang of longing for Guy. He'd have jollied her out of this melancholy mood. She couldn't find a Wi-Fi signal and concluded the system needed rebooting. When she was last here, seven years ago, the router had lived on the pine dresser, wedged into place between the farm's accounts ledger and the first aid box. Both the router and ledger had since moved. Clare scoured the room, uncovering multiple packets of cigarettes – *was that what had killed Cindy?* – alongside stacks of old newspapers, drawers so full they were jammed, and cupboards stuffed so full of junk that the doors wouldn't shut. She discovered a thick folder marked *Bills* – she didn't want to open that – and a bundle of letters from APHA, the Animal and Plant Health Authority. She knew she was looking in unlikely places. Secretly, she was keeping an eye out for evidence that her mother had wanted to heal their rift, but her search revealed neither a router nor any half-written letters of apology.

It was a long shot. The last time her mother had sent a letter to Clare it had not gone well. Cindy had written to her after Guy had died and Clare's heart had softened after reading the first few lines. Cindy had said that she was sorry for Clare's loss, saying she of all people understood how difficult it was to lose someone unexpectedly. She had also apologized for upsetting Clare two years earlier, but not for what she'd said. If only her mother had finished the letter there. If she had, there might have been a reconciliation. Instead, Cindy had told her daughter to come back to Devon 'now there was no reason to stay in London'. Clare could still remember her hands shaking with rage as she'd read those words. Didn't her mother understand the importance of Clare's career? London wasn't just about Guy; it was about being an exceptional lawyer – using the law to stand up for those who needed it most. Clare wrote a scathing response asking her mother not to contact her again. She hadn't needed Cindy's brand of sympathy.

Clare decided to search the lounge. A hint of pine-scented air freshener lingered. Her eyes fell on the ancient brown sofa. There was a dent at 'Cindy's end', closest to the kitchen, and Clare clung to the door, hearing her mother's voice: 'I'll get us a slice of cake and mug of cocoa for supper. Then let's get you off up to bed.'

She shut the door firmly on the memory.

Outside, the dog had abandoned his post. The Land Rover was glinting in the early morning sun. It was decades since Clare had driven a car, but she would have to get to grips with it. The bus to Barnstaple had been unreliable when she was a teenager; now it probably didn't run at all. Attached to the Land Rover was a twelve-foot trailer, but she suspected it wouldn't be difficult to unhitch. There must be a YouTube video. If only she could find the bloody router.

She yanked at the car door, letting out a smell of stale cigarette smoke. Clare pressed her eyes shut, but the tears still threatened, and an image formed of her mother wearing her blue overalls, arms around the steering wheel, cigarette dangling from the corner of her mouth. Clare let out a soft moan, rubbed her eyes and clambered onto the seat, leaving the door wide open. The key was in the ignition. She ran her hands over the gearstick and round the steering wheel, familiarizing herself with the controls before turning the key. The engine whined, coughed and then died. She tried again. Then a third time. It finally spluttered into life and the car juddered. She heard a yap and turned to see Stop-it in mid-air. He landed in a heavy lump on her lap, then scrambled over her onto the passenger seat, his claws digging painfully into her legs. A dog harness was attached to that seat belt. Clare snorted; Jet had always travelled in the boot.

Depressing the clutch, she put a hand on the gearstick, trying to recall where first gear was, remembering driving lessons with her mother's calloused hand covering her own, forcing the stick into position. Clare sighed; she didn't feel ready to rake through memories. She removed her hand and peered at the stick, but decades of use had worn away the illustrative diagram. It was useless. Clare crumpled over the steering wheel, picturing her neat London flat with its reliable Wi-Fi, the Tube a ten-minute walk away, and those suitcases packed and ready in the hallway

She felt a warm breath on her hands and opened her eyes, looking straight into black mournful ones. Stop-it's muzzle lowered, his tongue poked out and he licked her hand, before crawling into her lap. She wrapped her arms around him and for a few minutes cuddled his warm furry body, nuzzling her face into his neck. Then she pushed herself upright and wiped her eyes. She scratched his head. 'Oh, you are a gorgeous dog, aren't you! You're right. I can't fall apart just because I can't get the car into gear. I'm a fighter not a quitter. Let's get you inside and we'll have breakfast together.'

Jumping out of the car, she gave herself a stern talking to and consulted her mental list. Tidying up her mother's affairs wouldn't take long. She might have to cancel the first two weeks of her adventure, but her sabbatical was an entire year. 'Come on, Stop-it.'

The dog didn't move.

Deciding everything would feel much better after a cup of tea, she filled the kettle and placed it on the Aga's hot plate. It was cold. She knelt and peeked in at the pilot light but there was no flame. Clare gazed at the Aga at a loss for what to do. She wanted Guy's arms around her, telling her that he would sort everything out. He would have known how to unhitch a trailer, and driving the Land Rover wouldn't have challenged him. After a few minutes, she crawled upstairs and, fully clothed, collapsed on the bed, pulling the duvet up over her head to block out the bright sunshine.

A knock on the bedroom door woke her. She shuffled upright, running her hands through her hair. After decades of cropping it as short as the stubble left over from harvesting wheat, she had decided to grow it during her sabbatical, and hadn't been to the hairdresser for a month. The door opened and Ivy's stout figure appeared, a tentative smile creasing her round face. 'How are you feeling?'

'Shitty.'

'That's grief kicking in.'

Dear Ivy, she had plenty of experience of grief. She'd been the Brambleton vicar for decades, coping with a diocese which, like her circumference, had gradually expanded. Ivy spoke gently. 'Did you sleep okay?'

'No.' Fuzzy monsters had filled Clare's dreams, chasing her down dark alleys.

'You should take something to help you sleep for a few nights. Come on, let's get you up and dressed.'

Clare tossed the duvet off. 'I've been up once already but I . . . I don't know what to do . . . how much to feed any of the animals . . .' Her voice started quaking. 'The dog won't come inside.'

Ivy spoke in a reassuring, soothing voice. 'Let's go downstairs for a cup of tea.'

Clare groaned. 'We can't. The pilot light's gone out.'

'I'll sort it.'

Clare trailed in the vicar's wake, feeling like a teenager tempted downstairs for a restorative chat after being dumped.

Stop-it was in the kitchen, crunching his way through a breakfast bowl of kibble. Clare threw up her arms. 'How did you get him inside?'

Grinning, Ivy picked up a small tin. 'This lives by the back door. Watch.' She shook the tin. It rattled as if full of stones. The dog shot over and sat, nose twitching, tail sweeping from side to side. Ivy removed the lid and scattered a few treats at her feet. 'He'll do anything for a biscuit!'

Ivy showed Clare how to light the pilot light, made tea, and then they took their mugs outside. 'Who's looking after the dairy herd?' asked Clare.

Ivy put her mug down on a windowsill. 'Don't worry about that; let's feed those hens,' she said striding off. Depositing her own tea, Clare ran after Ivy, calling out 'I need to write all this down, so I don't forget.'

They fed the hens, then the two pigs. Ivy showed Clare where to find fresh straw and where to dump the soiled bedding.

Back inside, Clare wished she was starting her travels, not stuck in Devon. She didn't want to spend her sabbatical farming. Ivy passed Clare a fresh mug of tea, saying gently, 'the funeral is pencilled in for three weeks' time.'

'I can't find Mum's will.'

'You won't. It's with the lawyer, and he's reading it on Monday.'

Clare shook her head. 'This isn't a movie. Lawyers don't read wills.'

'They do if it's specified.' Ivy gave her a sympathetic look. 'That's what Cindy wanted. She wanted the lawyer to be on hand.'

'Why?'

'You'll find out on Monday.' said Ivy turning away.

That's an evasive answer thought Clare, wondering which lucky farmer's second son had inherited the farm. He probably knew who he was and would most likely be the person who'd collected the herd. Her mother would have wanted the lawyer to dissuade Clare from contesting the will, but Clare wouldn't do that. She didn't want or need her mother's money.

'The reading's in Exeter. Let's take the train from Barnstaple,' said Ivy. Clare's eyes narrowed.

'You're invited?'

Ivy smiled and nodded.

It must be Ivy who would inherit the farm, thought Clare. She couldn't think of a more worthy recipient. After Clare's father died, Ivy was a regular feature of farm life, especially on Sundays when Cindy would prepare a roast dinner timed to fit in around the multiple services Ivy presided over.

'Just the two of us?' asked Clare.

'Yes,' said Ivy, pulling Clare into a hug. Now Clare was certain Ivy would inherit. 'Do you know where she kept the farm accounts? They used to be on the dresser.'

Ivy released her and disappeared, returning with a handwritten ledger. 'I'll make another pot of tea while you take a look.'

Clare opened the book. Her mother's neat spidery writing filled the pages. She squeezed her eyes shut for a moment, then opened them and flicked through the pages. There seemed to be a lot of minuses and not many pluses. Wanting to ensure she wasn't expected to do the milking Clare asked, 'Who's looking after the dairy herd?'

The kettle whistled drowning out Clare's voice.

'The apples will need harvesting in the autumn,' Ivy said.

Clare was about to repeat her question but stopped. Ivy might not want to reveal who the helper was. She might know about her inheritance, have a contingency plan for the milking and have already implemented it. She hoped whoever it was knew what to do with apples too. Autumn was three months away. Clare would be in Jordan by then, marvelling at Petra's lost city and enjoying a Wadi Rum desert tour. She asked where the router was.

'Gone. Your mother used to walk Stop-it into the village to buy cigarettes and either use my Wi-Fi or Trish's on the way.'

'Why?'

Ivy looked a little shifty, which struck Clare as odd, but she hadn't seen Ivy for seven years, maybe she was reading too much into the woman's body language.

'Was it the smoking that killed her?'

Ivy spoke softly. 'It was a heart attack.'

'What?' Cindy was fit and active. The family had no history of heart disease. 'How?'

Ivy took her time replying. 'Possibly stress.'

'*Stress?*' Had Cindy been dwelling on their rift? Was Clare partly responsible for her mother's death? 'What was she stressed about?'

Ivy turned away. Did she know? Clare tried a different tack. 'What did Mum mean by her message to me?' The other woman's back stiffened. Clare waited, but there was no reply, and she decided not to press. There would be plenty of time to probe on the train to the will reading on Monday.

Ivy plonked the teapot on the table. 'Why not come for supper at the pub on Friday, there's a group of us going.'

Recalling plastic baskets of microwaved scampi or chicken and chips, she declined Ivy's invitation. Anyway, she didn't want to socialize, especially not with strangers badgering her about why she'd not visited for years. Cindy had always batch-cooked, so hopefully there'd be something in the freezer.

By Thursday Clare had cancelled the first two weeks of her sabbatical. Sitting at the kitchen table, she glared at her chores list:

- Prep for traveling – see London list
- Land Rover
- Descale shower head
- Lower shower head
- Register death
- Sort out Mum's bedroom
- Get Stop-it to eat kibble
- Rehome dog
- Buy more chicken food
- From where?
- Check freezer stocks and plan meals

She heard the door open; it was Ivy, 'How are you getting on?'

She felt like she was out of her depth but wasn't going to admit it. 'Do you know where I can buy chicken food?'

'I can't believe Cindy would have let herself run low. Have you looked in the barns?'

Clare heaved herself upright. 'Tea?' she offered.

'No thanks; tea is not the answer to everything.' Ivy walked towards her, scooping Clare into a hug; it was good to feel someone's arms around her. 'What you need is to get out,' said Ivy decisively. 'Come to the pub tomorrow night. It will do you good,' she coaxed.

'Let me think about it,' said Clare noncommittally.

'Trish and Anna will be there.'

She wanted to see her friends, and wasn't sure how full the freezer was. 'Oh, all right.' If she ate out tomorrow, it would be one less meal to worry about.

Three

At five thirty on Friday afternoon the treat tin rattled and Stop-it bounced inside. Clare hooked him to a lead and, with her arm at full stretch, jogged towards Brambleton. For centuries the village had been a remote hamlet of thatched fishermen's cottages hugging a natural bay on the North Devon coast, all defiantly facing the sea. Then, in the sixteenth century, an aristocrat, newly enriched by Henry VIII's dissolution of the monasteries, built Brambleton Hall and the settlement spread upwards, bridging the gap between the two livelihoods of the sea or the squire. While the Hall still dominated village life and remained the largest local employer, most of the villagers' livelihoods now depended on tourism.

There was no pavement, so with the June late-afternoon sun warming her bare arms, making her skin tingle, Clare and Stop-it walked along the side of the road, each step taking them closer to the gates of Brambleton Hall. The grass banks teemed with mauve-coloured poppies, pale blue cornflowers and oxeye daisies, which always reminded Clare of fried eggs. They reached the closed gates of the estate and stopped. She looked through the bars, admiring the spaced-out mature oaks and majestic copper beech trees, their dark purple leaves swaying in the breeze.

Horse chestnut trees lined a long straight drive which bisected the park, their overhanging branches creating a tunnel of greenery which she imagined led to Brambleton Hall. She knew the current owner, Richard Hastings, but she'd never been inside the house itself. She last saw Richard when she was in her twenties and she and Trish had been working behind the bar of the village pub. Clare recalled him as an arrogant, brash, entitled toff. Richard once introduced Trish and Clare to one of his chums as 'village girls', who worked in 'my family pub'.

Two pretty cottages flanked the entrance. They had well-tended gardens: both lawns were neatly mown, the box hedges clipped green headboards for borders filled with matching peonies and lupins. She wondered with a smirk if the lodge house leases specified the variety of flower and the required height of the grass. Richard Hastings wasn't the type to leave such important matters to the whim of a tenant.

Clare tugged at the leash and walked downhill towards a house which wouldn't look out of place in a fairy-tale. Built in the Gothic revival style, it had a steeply pitched roof, ornate bargeboards and pretty chimneys. From a distance, it looked like one dwelling, but Clare knew it was four separate cottages: Numbers 1 to 4. The almshouses, the precursor to social housing. In the late 1960s, after Clare's grandmother died, her grandfather had purchased all four. He moved into one, enabling her parents to take over Orchard Farm, and let out the other three, selecting tenants connected to the village. Twenty years ago, her mother had sold them back to the family who'd built them. Above the pointed arched doorways of the middle two houses, the name of the Victorian altruist – Samuel Hastings – was inscribed.

One of these middle houses was occupied by Ivy, the other by Mr Thompson, Clare's former primary school teacher. Both cottages were in need of repair, their woodwork cracked, chipped and bubbling. In contrast, the end pair of cottages were smartly painted, and beside their doors were slate boards, renaming them Rose Cottage and Jasmine Cottage. It was ironic that two properties designed for the homeless now operated as holiday lets for the wealthy.

Behind the houses was the vastness of the Hastings' 5,000 acre estate. Clare could hear the low rumble of a tractor. Squinting, she spotted the machine threading its way across Hastings' land, leaving hillocks of mown grass. As a child she had loved riding in the tractor, cocooned safely between her father's arms as he cut haylage, inhaling the sharp yet sweet scent of the newly cut grass. He died when she was eleven, a tender age for Clare to learn how to compartmentalize grief.

Ten minutes later, she dragged a reluctant Stop-it away from a lamp post towards a white, low-slung building, the last property in the village, perched like a full stop: the Smugglers Inn. Beyond it the harbour wall reached out, a protective arm shielding Brambleton from Atlantic storms.

She breathed out and ran a hand through her hair as she gazed down at the sandy beach, dotted with lazing bronzed bodies. People sat beside picnic hampers, stretched out on towels, or relaxed in deckchairs beneath sun umbrellas anchored in the sand. In the sea, tourists bobbed about. A woman stood, shook sand off her towel, stowed it in a bag, then did the same with her partner's before they left the beach hand in hand. Clare wished it was as easy for her to pack up and leave. Still, the warm Mediterranean Sea awaited her.

Clare turned back to the pub, with its quaint wooden sign hanging above the entrance. It looked like it hadn't changed at all in the past seven years. She pushed open the door. Inside, the sun blazed through open windows, lighting up the low-beamed ceilings, rustic wooden furniture and the polished dark oak bar. Customers sat at an assortment of well-worn wooden tables on plush, high-backed chairs, or among a warren of cosy nooks and booths. Each was lined with ancient wooden settles, once practical for the rough working clothes that had sat on them, centuries of use having carved imprints into the seats. Historic black and white photos adorned the walls, telling stories of the area's heritage: pictures of gap-toothed farmers, fishermen and tousle-haired children. It was easy to imagine the lantern-lit tavern as it was in the seventeenth or eighteenth century, to almost hear the snatched conversations between smugglers and customers haggling over the price of a barrel of French brandy.

In front of the bar was a crowd dressed in shorts and T-shirts. All the bar stools were occupied, and waiting staff were dashing about with loaded trays. There was a gentle hum of conversation, punctuated by hearty laughter and the clinking of glasses. Clare sniffed, smelling the same combination of sea air and suntan lotion, she used to moan about when she worked there with Trish. Someone had spruced the pub up since those days. She ran her eyes over the space, seeking her friends.

'Clare!' shouted a female voice. She tracked the sound down to a nook where Anna was standing, waving. 'Over here!' Anna called.

Anna was tall with long fair hair tugged back off her forehead, coiled into a bun and secured on her head with a large, practical clasp. It gave her friend's face a pinched look, which disguised her real beauty. Apart from special occasions, Anna always tucked her hair away. Clare sometimes thought it was because Anna was so wrapped up in her job as an architect that she forgot to let it loose after finishing work.

Dragging Stop-it behind her, Clare threaded her way through the crowd to a table where Ivy, Trish, Anna and her husband Roger were sitting with another couple she didn't recognize. A woman with a small shiny face and her partner, who had a mop of frizzy ginger hair. Clare smiled and concentrated as Ivy introduced her, but a background burst of laughter blotted out their names. Fearing they'd assume she hadn't been listening, Clare didn't ask Ivy to repeat herself – she was unlikely to meet them again.

'What are you having?' asked Roger. He was a tall man, with sandy-coloured hair and a pencil moustache, which gave him a military air. Roger worked from home doing something frightfully intelligent for insurance companies, which together with Anna's income from her architect's business earned the couple enough to afford to live at Anna's lovely childhood home, the Old Rectory, with its five acres of gardens. 'The other women are drinking prosecco, but if you'd prefer something else?'

'It's the same brand I serve at Prosecco and Prose,' chirped Trish. She had the physique of a whippet, with lean elegant limbs, a pretty face and mournful tawny eyes beneath a curtain of dark hair. Clare responded with a smile. Trish never struck Clare as an entrepreneur and had surprised Clare when a decade ago she'd set up a café-cum-bookshop.

Clare suddenly realized how exhausted she was. 'I'll have an espresso martini, please.'

Someone snorted. Clare cringed, a flush sweeping over her cheeks. The two strangers were both smirking. 'I can ask Rose,' said Roger stroking his moustache, 'but that sounds like a London drink to me.'

Clare shuffled her feet. 'No drama. I'll have what everyone else is drinking.'

Anna patted the seat beside her. 'Saved you a spot.' Clare sidled over, grateful for Anna's protection. Next to Anna, she couldn't see or be seen by either of the two strangers. 'Come here you,' said Anna, folding her into a hug. 'It's great to have you here, even in such sad circumstances. How are you?'

Clare wasn't going to answer that one. Her stomach felt like someone had put it on a spin cycle. Other than work dos, or with Trish and Anna, she hadn't been out for a drink, let alone a meal, since Guy had died five years earlier. She preferred take-aways to the idea of sitting alone in a restaurant, worrying if people at adjoining tables would think she was eavesdropping.

'I'm fine,' she said breezily.

'Is there anything Roger or I can do to help?'

'If you know anyone who can unhitch a trailer send them my way, please.' Clare smiled grimly. Trish was leaning across the table for a kiss, straining to get close enough.

Clare reached out and kissed her friend's cheeks, saying, 'This has changed a lot since you and I worked here.'

Trish laughed. 'That was yonks ago, but some things don't change.' She pointed an elegant hand at the bar, 'There's Sam. Remember him? He used to hang around when we worked here.' She giggled, then added, 'He was always flirting with you.'

Hearing the name, Clare's nostrils flared. Sam was Richard Hastings' younger brother, and in her opinion, they were both as snobbish and rude as each other. She glanced across the room at the man chatting to Roger, his back towards her. He was over six feet tall with broad rugby player's shoulders and hair a distinguished iron-grey colour, but there had been flecks of grey even when he was in his twenties. Trish was right. Sam had been a flirt. He'd even kissed her once. Clare had told Trish about that, but not what had happened the next day, which was far too humiliating to share.

Even with his back towards her, she could tell Sam had aged well. His hair hadn't thinned, his stature was still upright, like a soldier. He turned her way. His bronzed face spoke of an out-door lifestyle, his jawline hadn't slackened, and his smooth face suggested a peaceful life. But where once had been chiselled cheeks, there were now faint laughter lines. Sam had always been popular for his carefree approach to life. But then it was easy to be happy if you were born into the rich Hastings family and had your future lined in goose down for you.

'And you also know that man Sam's having dinner with,' said Trish.

Sam's companion was looking Clare's way. Mentally she tightened his facial features, painted his white hair blonde, rolling back twenty years of ageing and recognized her primary school teacher, Mr Thompson. It was the tie which gave her the last clue. He always used to wear one, even if he was taking a games lesson.

Roger was walking back to their table, a clean glass in his hand. She hoped Sam didn't follow him – he was the last person she wanted to run into after the way he'd treated her. Roger poured Clare a glass of prosecco.

Trish winked at her. 'You know, Sam is divorced. No one special in his life . . . And he's loaded.'

Clare blushed and took a gulp of fizz. She considered telling Trish what had happened the day after Sam kissed her, but realized she was being silly. They were not starry-eyed youngsters anymore. She kept her tone light. 'He was never serious about me, just messing around. My, it's busy in here!'

'The food is exceptional,' said Anna. 'It's come a long way since chicken in a basket. Rose, that's the landlady, has really revitalised this pub. And ask Roger – the wine list is amazing, Rose's husband George is the chef, and he's a bit of a wine buff. We thought we'd just have the bar menu tonight, if that's okay with you?'

Talk turned to a party everyone seemed to be attending, which was being held at Brambleton Hall. 'Come! I'm sure you'd be welcome. After all, we were all at school with the host,' said Anna.

'He's got pots of money,' said the man with the frizzy hair. 'He holds it in a walled rose garden. He's got a butler too.'

Clare laughed. 'Tricky Ricky? Hope he's mellowed since he was at school.'

Anna huffed. 'He's just hiked Ivy's rent by over 10 per cent.'

'What?' exclaimed Clare, throwing Ivy a concerned look. 'The dirty rat, bathing in champagne paid for by the toiling masses. Can he do that?'

'Good point,' said Trish. 'You should have a look at the lease.'

'I'm not a property lawyer.'

'But you're a lawyer. You'll work it out,' said Trish.

Clare felt herself go hot. She didn't want to get drawn into village politics. She'd be gone in a few weeks. 'It's not my field.'

Next to Clare, Anna stiffened and exchanged a furtive look with Trish. Clare told herself to ignore it. Ivy wouldn't need to worry about rent after Monday. Ivy would soon be living at Orchard Farm. Roger came to her rescue. 'Quite right,' he said, stroking his moustache. 'Little spats can split a village. Best to keep out of it. I do.'

'Let me buy another bottle of prosecco,' offered Clare, squeezing past Anna.

Skirting past Sam Hastings, Clare walked to the far end of the bar and tried to catch the landlady's eye.

Rose was soon in front of her. 'What can I get you?' she asked in a business-like voice. Physically there was nothing remarkable about Rose. She was of average height and build, with practical short brown hair.

'I'm with Trish and Anna. A bottle of the same prosecco they ordered, please.'

'You're their lawyer friend, aren't you?'

She replied warily. 'Yes.'

'Can I ask you a question?'

Clare nodded. Rose blew out a breath, her lips vibrating. 'Can a landlord hike your rent by 20 per cent? We can just about afford it, but it's a serious dent to the profit.'

Clare's eyes flickered to the far end of the bar. She didn't have to ask who the landlord was, or how he had learned the pub could afford such a massive rent rise.

'It's not my field, but just say no – 20 per cent is egregious.'

'I can see it from his perspective,' said Rose, placing Clare's prosecco in a plastic wine bucket. 'I've got friends renting in Barnstaple and all their landlords have increased the rent to cover their mortgages.'

Clare raised an eyebrow. 'I hope they don't expect to see the other side of that coin. Landlords won't be lowering rents when rates fall. Anyway, interest rates don't affect the likes of Tricky Ricky – he inherited everything. He doesn't have a mortgage.'

Rose stroked her lips between finger and thumb. 'Do you think he's trying it on?'

'Yes. Make a counter-offer. The worst he can do is say no.'

'But if he throws us out, we're homeless. We live here too.'

Clare drew breath, then released it slowly through clenched teeth. Hastings had Rose pinned over a barrel. He was greedy, hiking everyone's rents, but it sounded like he was a canny businessman, picking a level he judged they could afford.

Back at the table, Clare topped up glasses and squeezed back in to sit next to Anna.

'Will you come to the drinks party then?' asked Ivy, beaming across the table.

Still irritated with Hastings' plans to gorge on the pub's success, Clare spoke in a sceptical tone. 'Why are you all going? He isn't inviting you because he wants you to enjoy yourself. You're just adornments.'

'Adornments?' said Anna, tinkling with laughter. 'At my age I take that as a compliment.'

Clare chuckled. She'd missed being a threesome with her mates. They so rarely came to London. She would enjoy their company while she was here. 'I don't like the host or his brother.'

Anna snorted, then said 'I don't think anyone other than his family *like* him. We go because it's a village tradition, not to see Richard.'

'And because the booze is free-flowing,' added the frizzy-haired man. 'Come and join us. You'll have fun and meet heaps of people.'

It was a generous, inclusive voice and Clare warmed to him. 'But I'm not part of the village. I'd feel like an intruder.' And anyway, she didn't want to meet heaps of people.

'You are. You live on your family farm,' said Anna bluntly.

It was a logical, practical response from an architect and made Clare smile.

'Do you ever regret not returning to the farm?' asked Anna.

Clare shook her head. Much as she deeply regretted not healing the rift with her mother, London was where she could be useful, and she had always been determined to go there. Maybe if she hadn't fallen out with her mother, she might have learned to love the gentle rhythms of a farming life, but it was too late for what-ifs. Clare was a London lawyer who had worked hard all her life and had earned her sabbatical.

Buoyed by the group's spirit, Clare took a swig of prosecco then, feeling amicable, she smiled at Ivy and said, 'If you give me a copy of your lease, I'll take a quick squint at it.'

Four

On Monday, Clare rose early again thanks to Hilts and breakfasted on a single slice of toast. She had made two but Stop-it had refused his kibble, again, his beseeching eyes making it clear that he would prefer to share her breakfast. The dog's name was apt. Stop-it was better at training Clare than she was at training him and seemed set in his mildly irritating ways. 'Lord alone knows what I'm going to do with you!' she said, feeding him the last crust of toast. Would Ivy take him on, along with the farm?

Outside, she fed the animals, noticing a section of sagging fencing in the pig enclosure. She gave it a gentle nudge. It would last another two weeks, and after that it would be someone else's problem. She might not be arriving in Seville today as planned, but she would be jetting off soon enough. A horn tooted and she jogged back to the house, grabbed her bag and slid into the passenger seat of Ivy's little car. 'How are you today?' asked Ivy.

'Umm,' said Clare, turning to stare out of her window. She could hear a pair of pigeons cooing to each other, their low echoing calls reminding her of childhood games in the woods. She fastened her seatbelt and asked about train times.

Once on the train, Ivy arranged her billowing dress then sat opposite Clare. Her face was one large round smile as she settled herself and took out a book.

Listening to the train rattling along the Tarka Line, Clare

looked out of the window, seeing the outskirts of the town fade, replaced by fields of sheep, their white coats contrasting with the deep green of the grass. She wished she was walking among the animals, listening to their soft bleats, not on her way to say a final goodbye to her mother's farm.

Ivy looked up from her book. 'Why not tell me what's on your mind? Talking can be helpful,' she suggested.

Clare didn't answer. She wasn't ready to share her complicated mixture of regret, guilt and loss, each one a painful burden, but together a crushing weight which left her mute. She shook her head and stared out at a green wooded valley with a stream meandering through it. It seemed dark and a little foreboding, reflective of her spirits. Her mind flitted from her mother to Guy and then to her father. She was a widowed orphan. Gosh that sounded sad. Clare tried to shake off her mood, telling herself that today she was simply learning the extent of her task list and once she'd ticked it off, she would close that part of her mind and scamper back to London faster than Stop-it dashed to the treat tin. She spotted a pair of walkers hiking along the riverbank. Soon she, too, would be off on her adventures.

Across from her Ivy was engrossed in what Clare spotted was a Jackie Collins novel. Had Cindy confided the contents of her will to her best friend? Orchard Farm with its 400 acres and period farmhouse, although tatty, was probably worth over £4 million. What would Ivy do with such wealth?

'Ivy, did Mum tell you what was in her will?'

Ivy marked her place with a ribbon, looked up and her face split into a sympathetic smile. 'No.' *You're in for a surprise then*, thought Clare. Why *did* Ivy think she had been invited today?

'What did Mum mean? You know, when she said, "Clare will sort it out"?'

'I don't know, my love, but she was convinced you would.'

How could Clare sort anything out with her mother dead?

'Are you going to tell me why she was so stressed?'

Ivy dipped her head. Was it money? Was her mother worried that Clare would be upset she'd left the family farm to Ivy? Clare didn't need or want money, and she wasn't about to swap city life for a farm. That had been her mother's dream: that Clare would tire of London, return to Brambleton, marry a farmer and take over the dairy herd and her mother's beloved orchard. But Clare loved her job and the buzz of London life.

'Tell me, please. Why was Mum stressed?'

Ivy raised her eyes. 'I think we may be about to find out.'

At the lawyer's, the receptionist showed them into a board-room which, with its small round table and walls lined with hardback copies of the Law reports, reminded Clare of her own.

A trim bespectacled man, who Clare judged to be about the same age as herself, walked in and introduced himself as Percy Wilson. 'I am sorry for your loss. She was a fine woman.'

Clare smiled, acknowledging the condolence. 'Unfortunately, we fell out.'

'I know,' said Percy, taking the seat opposite her. 'She told me. She said you took after your father – too proud to take advice or to compromise.' He raised his eyes at her, his mouth twitching into a smile. 'I'll leave you to assess how accurate that description is.'

Clare paused. She rarely thought about her father, and Cindy had hardly ever talked about him. She didn't recall him being stubborn, but as a child, she hadn't really thought about her parents' characters.

Percy steepled his hands. 'The will is quite straightforward. She left the small Georgian writing desk to you, Ivy.' His eyes flashed at Ivy. 'She told me you often wrote your sermons there while she cooked dinner for the three of you.'

Clare was transported back decades to laying the dining table for special Saturday dinners, with classical music playing softly in the background and Ivy hunched over that Georgian desk, books propped open on the floor around her feet. Percy turned his gaze Clare's way. 'What's left goes to you.'

Clare's hand flew to her mouth 'Me?' she mumbled. What would she do with all that money? Her eyes narrowed and she said in a shaky voice, 'But I'm not a farmer. I live in London. Besides, what do you mean *what's left*?'

Percy started tutting. 'Yes, I had a feeling you wouldn't know; that this was why she wanted me to explain the contents of her will.'

'We hadn't spoken in seven years, so no, I don't know. What do you mean?' she demanded, her eyes flying between the lawyer and Ivy.

'Your mother wasn't a businesswoman.'

Clare felt her throat constrict. She never asked herself how her slightly muddle-headed mother had managed the money side of farming. 'She was never much good with numbers,' said Percy. 'She kept going when milk prices slumped, but she still employed the same number of men to work for her.' Clare knew; she'd drafted their employment contracts. 'But she didn't adapt, and she did something I think she regretted.'

With a stab of guilt, Clare turned to Ivy. 'So that was why she sold the almshouses? To prop up the farm?'

Ivy nodded. Percy blew out a long breath. 'I wasn't referring to that.'

'What did she do?' she asked. Hearing the criticism in her voice, she winced.

'She sold land,' replied Percy.

In the farming world, that was a cardinal sin. Surely, her mother couldn't have gotten into that much debt. 'Right,' said

Clare slowly, feeling a rush of shame at the thought of her mother struggling alone. 'How much land and which part of the farm? Is there a map?'

'She sold a hundred acres, about five years ago.'

'A quarter of the farm! Why didn't she tell me she needed money?' And why hadn't her mother asked Clare for advice? But Clare knew the answer to that one; it would have been when Guy died.

'It's worse than that,' said Percy. 'She borrowed too, pledging another 300 acres as security. Unfortunately, with farm incomes plummeting, Brexit and the rural farm payments drying up, your mother got into arrears.'

Clare sighed. 'How much? If the estate hasn't got the cash, I've got reserves.' Ring fenced for her adventure, but not yet committed.

'It's too late for that,' said Percy gently. Clare's heart started pounding. Why was this man giving her the soft-gloved touch? 'Recently, that land was seized and sold.'

'Hang on,' said Clare, placing both hands on the table. 'This doesn't make sense. Decent farmland is worth £10,000 an acre. She can't have owed £3 million.'

'She didn't.'

'Then what happened?' she asked, a sinking feeling in the pit of her stomach.

'It smells a bit odd, but I gather from asking around that the man she did the deal with—' His nose twitched as if he was about to sneeze. 'Well, let me put this delicately . . . he's a bit *wide*, and paid just a fraction of the land's true market value.'

Clare's eyes popped open. She switched her gaze to Ivy, who was clutching the cross at her neck. 'She didn't . . .' Clare looked at the lawyer. 'She didn't sell to Tricky Ricky?'

Percy's eyebrows furrowed. 'Richard Hastings?'

'The monster,' said Clare. No wonder her mother had been stressed. 'So, all that's left is the orchard and the land surrounding the house? About thirty acres?' *This explained the absence of the dairy herd*, thought Clare.

'Yes, but I'm afraid the house is mortgaged too.'

Her head jerked forwards. How much worse could this get? 'To Hastings?' she asked.

'No, one of the banks, but she was in arrears.'

Clare lacked the strength to speak. How had Cindy got into such a financial mess? She should have guessed from the state of the farmhouse, with its ancient kitchen, the same battered furniture in the sitting room, the upstairs bathroom with its clogged shower head. She turned towards Ivy. 'I don't understand. What was she spending her money on? Where's it all gone?'

Ivy shrugged, equally shocked.

Percy wriggled in his chair. He spoke gently: 'For decades she put money into the farm and never took any out.' He fidgeted with his stack of papers. 'She was spending over £100,000 a year of capital. We advised her to stop farming and sell up, but she wouldn't hear of it. I'm sorry, but you don't have much of an inheritance. The mortgage is over £500,000.'

'I don't want any of her money,' said Clare defiantly, 'I've a flat in London and, like you, I'm a lawyer – employment law. Is there anything I can do? '

Percy shook his head. 'There was nothing illegal in what Hastings did. Immoral, but not illegal.'

'How much is the mortgage in arrears?'

'About £100,000.'

Clare's jaw dropped. She felt light-headed, dizzy. She swallowed, trying to concentrate on the enormity of what she'd learned. Her mother owed over £600,000. She had her travel savings, but to repay her mother's debts, she would have to refinance her flat.

Percy was speaking, but Clare was too stunned to take anything in. She saw a knowing look flash across his face as he poured her a glass of water. Percy would recognize shock; he was used to delivering both good news and bad. Realizing her mouth was dry, she gulped the water down, the mundane act calming her. Why hadn't her mother seen sense? But it was always all about the farm, especially that orchard, Cindy's refuge which she lavished attention on like some gardeners did with their roses. Her parents had planted most of those apple trees together, and her father's ashes had been scattered there.

Clare bit her lip. 'It might take me a while to come up with the funds.'

It wasn't just the money. Sorting out her mother's affairs would take far longer than she had delayed her travels by. Clare wasn't leaving Orchard Farm anytime soon. She heard her mother's voice in her head: *'Tell Clare, I'm sorry. She's a smart girl. She'll sort this out.'* Cindy had been apologizing for losing the farm in a poor business deal, not for their rift, and she expected her daughter to fix the problem. Although exasperated with her mother she hoped she could live up to her expectations.

Clare asked Ivy to drop her in the village, so that she could walk towards the harbour and think things through. Squinting up at the sun, she stepped down onto the beach, removing her shoes and burying her feet in the warm sand, hoping the calming waves would still the vein throbbing at the base of her neck. Hastings was evil; her mother had been desperate, and he had seen an opportunity to buy her land cheaply. He may not have intended to ruin her financially, but he wasn't bothered. He'd taken advantage of a vulnerable elderly woman. The hateful man was also trying to gouge Ivy and the pub's landlady by hiking their rents. That was wrong. Clare was no stranger to the abuse of power. She'd met employers who manipulated staff into resigning, or who cut corners on health and safety costs at the expense of employees' welfare. But this was one man riding roughshod over so many lives. The village seemed to be in his unscrupulous grip– Ivy, Rose, her mother. Tricky Ricky was a ruthless unethical businessman.

Her legal training kicked in and she told herself to accept facts; until Percy obtained grant of probate – which he estimated would take six months – Clare couldn't sell the farm and was facing a monumental financial challenge. If she remortgaged her flat and emptied her savings account, she could cover her mother's debts. Just. But on her reduced salary, Clare wouldn't be able to afford the additional costs for long. Until the farm sold, she would have to live frugally and delay her travel plans. Sadly, the sale could take months.

With the wind gently tousling her hair, she gazed out over the vast expanse of the sea, an endless blue merging with the sky in a distant, hazy line. The rhythmic sound of waves lapping against the shore filled the air, her thoughts drifting away with each swell surging towards the beach. It was a soothing beat which reminded Clare of Guy letting the engine gently idle before a race. Shielding her eyes from the glare, Clare stared at the tranquil beauty and wandered towards the water.

'Hey, careful there,' said a cultured voice she recognized from her youth. A voice honed at vast expense at the boarding school he had attended after Year 6. Just inches in front of her stood Sam Hastings. He was barefoot, looking comfortable with his tanned limbs on display, and she couldn't help noticing he looked as fit as a man a decade younger.

'Everything okay?' he asked. 'You're not really dressed for a beach walk.'

She looked vacantly at her business suit. 'No, I . . .'

Sam laughed. It was engaging, carefree with a hint of sexiness.

Clare remembered it from her evenings working at the Smugglers Inn in her twenties. Back then, she'd thought it was the most attractive sound she'd ever heard. Now she peered at Sam, trying to see if the mirth reached his eyes, but a pair of aviator-style sunglasses concealed them.

'Why not take off your jacket?' He walked behind her and helped ease it off, then took her shoes and bag from her. 'I heard why you're here, and I'm sorry. Cindy was a fine woman and a good neighbour.'

'Thanks,' she mumbled.

'Come for a paddle. The water's warm.'

She raised an eyebrow. 'It never used to be.'

'That's because you used to be taking a dip after sunbathing – it's just the contrast.' His voice was gentle, soothing her restless mind. She reminded herself that just because he'd been cruel to her in their twenties didn't mean they couldn't be civil to each other now.

'Why not!' she said, offering a guarded smile.

She rolled her trousers up to her calves and he led her towards the water where they stood silently in the damp sand, letting the waves break over their feet.

'It's good to see you again, Clare.' He spoke softly and she recalled again how much she used to like his voice. 'There's a party up at the Hall on Saturday. Why don't you join us? Your mother used to come every year.'

She wasn't going. 'I heard it's your brother's party.'

'He won't mind if I invite someone. There'll be over a hundred guests.'

'I expect I'll be too busy, but thanks for the invitation. I must get going,' she said, reaching for her shoes. He held out his arm and said, 'Why not hang onto me while you put those on.'

With one hand on his arm, she steadied herself. His skin felt warm and the muscle firm. Liking the solidity of it, she swiftly reminded herself his brother was the village bully and Richard's greed may have hastened Cindy's death.

Walking up the hill, Clare heard the clank of metal on metal and glanced up. Outside the almshouses was a lorry. Shirtless men with nut-brown torsos were dumping scaffolding poles and planks on the roadside. She squeezed between the lorry and the fencing, opened the latch on Ivy's gate and rang the bell.

The door opened, revealing a room crowded with furniture. Where would Ivy put her mother's bureau? Taking a closer look, Clare realized it was deceptive. There was only a two-seater sofa, a rocking chair and a square footstool covered in dark brown fabric, all squashed into less space than her London lounge.

'That was a shock this morning,' said Ivy. Then she spoke over her shoulder: 'Fred, get the kettle on.'

'You knew, didn't you?'

Ivy's lips pursed. 'Not exactly. I knew she was short of money, but not how short and she didn't tell me what she'd done.' Clare pointed behind her at the pile of poles and boards. 'Good news?'

Ivy grinned. 'Looks like it!'

Clare closed the door shutting out the noise. Above her she noticed pretty, exposed beams, but her eyes settled on the walls, where paint was blistered, and in areas strips hung in curls as if someone had used a paring knife. Thank goodness Hastings was sorting the problem before winter. She followed Ivy to the kitchen where a man wearing a yellow tie was filling a kettle. It was Mr Thompson, her former primary school teacher and Ivy's neighbour.

Ivy beamed at Clare. 'We've been moaning to Richard Hastings about the damp for years, but it's like talking to the proverbial stop sign. Time for tea?'

'So, what's he agreed to do?' asked Clare.

'Eh?' said the man.

'Don't be vain, Fred,' said Ivy, pulling mugs out of a cupboard. 'Put your hearing aids in.'

'I still think of you as Mr Thompson,' Clare said.

His eyes twinkled at her. 'Call me Fred. Everyone else does.'

'He's not agreed to anything yet,' said Ivy, 'but the scaffolders have been told to put it around all four cottages, so he must be doing something.'

'Don't bank on it,' muttered Clare. 'Mum should have done the work years ago, when she owned these houses.'

'Your mum had a heart of gold,' said Ivy, 'but she was a farmer, not a landlord.'

And she wasn't much better at being a farmer, thought Clare.

'We're too reliant on amateur landlords,' said Fred, fiddling with one of his ears. 'Not sure it's the right model. Providing housing should be a social contract, a bit like being a teacher. We wouldn't outsource teaching kids to people who just fancied having a go, would we?' he added.

'Tea or coffee?' offered Ivy

Clare shook her head. 'I haven't got time for either. If I don't walk Stop-it, he'll take revenge by destroying something. I just called in for your lease.'

Ivy's eyes lit up. 'I'll get a copy.'

When Ivy showed her out, she hugged Clare. 'I know it looks bleak. Losing your mother must bring back memories of your father's passing too.'

And Guy's. But Clare wouldn't think about any of them now. She would compartmentalize her losses and concentrate on keeping busy. Clare clutched Ivy's lease to her chest, feeling a calmness seep through her – she had work to do.

Back at Orchard Farm, Clare viewed the house as a prospective buyer might. Although a sale couldn't complete before probate was granted, a buyer could exchange contracts and pay a deposit, with completion occurring on grant of probate. She hoped that would happen soon; until she had a dollop of money, she couldn't afford her adventures. But to achieve that, she must spruce up the house and get it on the market. Clare tugged at a tangle of ivy snaking over the back door. It came free, dislodging a shower of mortar. Underneath, the brickwork was a gorgeous honey colour. If she cleared the ivy carefully and gave the bricks a scrub it would look lovely.

Inside, she grabbed a pen and paper and went from room to room scribbling. The list ran to two pages. Clare dropped it on the floor and sagged into a chair, curling her knees up to her chest and circling them with her arms. She dragged herself upright again – it was going to be a lengthy process, and she needed to get cracking if she wanted to avoid spending the first six months of her sabbatical in Brambleton.

Five

To do:

- Delay travel plans
- Organize second charge loan on flat
- Repay Mum's arrears
- Complete works on farmhouse
- Find estate agent
- Get Stop-it to eat kibble
- Rehome Stop-it, hens and pigs

Clare staggered to bed long after midnight and slept fitfully. At 5.30 a.m. Hilts woke her. She groaned, flopped onto her stomach and pulled the pillow over her head. If she were in Madrid as planned, she would be enjoying a lie-in right now. The muffled sounds of the cockerel managed to filter through, so she tossed the pillow aside, got up and stumbled to the bathroom. The mirror's reflection was not kind, highlighting the blue bags under her eyes and hair which looked like a child had been wielding the scissors. She ran herself a bath, squirted the remains of a bottle of bubble bath into the water and clambered in for a long soak.

An hour later, still wrapped in a towel, she moved the kettle onto the hot plate in the kitchen. Someone knocked on the back door. She spun round, as the door suddenly opened, and Sam

Hastings walked in. She clutched the ends of her towel, wrapping it tighter. 'H— h— hello,' she stammered. *What was he doing here and why did he think he could just walk in?*

'Hi. I gather from Roger you've got a trailer problem. Want me to take a look?' He grinned. 'After you've got dressed?'

He focused his piercing eyes on her. They really were stunning, and unlike her own, his steel-grey hair gave him a distinguished look. Clare wrapped her towel close and shuffled Ivy's lease under a copy of *Farmers Weekly*. 'I don't think there's anything wrong with the trailer. It's operator error.'

He laughed and she couldn't help but smile. It was such a welcoming, cheerful sound. 'Sorry, I thought you'd be up early.' He made it sound like an apology, not a criticism. 'If you throw on some clothes, I'll show you how it's done.'

She clattered up the stairs. In her bedroom she kicked aside yesterday's soiled jeans, pulled on a pair of pristine denim overalls and rushed into the bathroom clutching her make-up bag. She picked up her perfume and stopped. In her head, she could hear her mother's voice chiding her: *Clare Hetherington, just what are you playing at?* She replaced the bottle, squirted hair mousse onto her palms and smoothed down the worst of the spikes.

Downstairs, Sam was playing with Stop-it. She picked up a notebook and pen, pulled the keys from their new home on the pine dresser, next to the torches – she hoped she was away from Devon long before the clocks changed and she might need one of them at night – and trying to avoid looking at him, went outside.

In the space of a few minutes, Sam had unhooked the trailer. He then spent twenty minutes showing her how to reattach it, explaining where the electrics plugged in and how to check the trailer indicator and brake lights worked, while Clare scribbled copious notes.

'Now do it yourself while I'm still here to help,' he said. 'I'm surprised your mother never taught you.'

Clare grasped the trailer hook and unwound it. 'After Dad died, we had farmhands,' she said. 'And by the time I was old enough to learn, I had my nose glued to a schoolbook.'

'Nearly there, I reckon,' Sam said. He was so close she could smell him: a mixture of apples and a spice she couldn't identify, but which made her think of beaches lined with palm trees. Clare unplugged the electrics, lifted the trailer hook free, twisted it to one side and lowered it to the ground.

'Now rehook it,' he said.

Laughing, Clare said, 'I won't be doing that I'm only here a few . . .' she stopped, the word 'weeks' had been on the tip of her tongue, 'months' she whispered, 'but really, I can't thank you enough.'

'You can thank me by coming to our party,' he said.

'I'm not big on parties.' She didn't add that she hadn't been invited to a party in five years, except for the office Christmas ones.

'I'll make sure you enjoy yourself.'

Was he asking for a date? Why was she resisting? His brother had pots of money, there would be buckets of champagne, and Ivy, Trish, and Anna were all invited. She shook her head.

'Go on. Say you'll come,' he said, more forcefully.

She chewed at her lip, then said, 'If you help with one more thing, I'll come.'

'What's that?' he asked grinning.

She pointed to the Land Rover. 'Can you show me how to get this monster into gear?'

That evening, she emailed her travel agent instructing her to cancel everything booked for the summer: she would start her adventure in Istanbul. She defrosted one of her mother's pies, put it in the Aga and went to feed the chickens, the pigs and finally Stop-it. He sniffed at the kibble and slunk off.

By nine, she was hungry. Clare took her pie outside, where the sun was fading over the fields, settling a pink glow across the horizon. She drank in the beauty. But there was a sour aftertaste – Hastings had taken advantage of her mother, most of that land should still belong to Orchard Farm. She sat down on a hard garden chair, unfurled Ivy's lease, took a bite of pie and started reading. Something solid brushed against her legs. She peered down. Stop-it had brought her a cushion clenched between his jaws; one corner was chewed apart, and a trail of feathers snaked back to the door. She removed it with a laugh, placed it behind her back and picked up her pen and the lease.

As Clare read, she sensed a familiar surge of adrenalin. The lease was so one-sided. The bully versus the underdog. She got up, poured herself a small glass of wine, dropped the remains of her pie into Stop-it's open jaws and reread the lease line by line. An hour and a larger glass of wine later, her scribbles covered the pages. She had to finish this by Saturday. There might be an opportunity to speak face to face with Tricky Ricky at his party. Hastings was responsible for Clare spending the first few months of her sabbatical in Brambleton; she would enjoy pitting her skills against him.

She took a sip of wine and picked up her phone, scrolling to the *Brambleton Gals'* WhatsApp group.

> Hey, girls. Think I might join you at the party on Saturday if that lift's still on offer, Anna? X

She picked up her glass, heard a ping from the phone, took a sip and read a message from Trish:

Sam told me he dropped round to help you with the trailer. Is this a date?

Clare tapped her response.

Of course not!

Then she drained her glass. She wasn't going to the party to see Sam. She wanted to spend time with her friends and speak to Tricky Ricky. That was all.

Later that week, Clare shut the door on the last of the three estate agents and sat at the kitchen table to amend her master chores list.

- Decide and appoint agent
- Repaint bedroom
- Fix kitchen floor tiles
- Sort garden
- Replace missing apple trees
- Probate list
- Small repairs list

The last chore was a fudge – the small repairs she had identified ran to two pages. The principal problem was there was only one candidate for these jobs and Clare didn't want to do any of them. What she did want to do was soak-up Madrid's culture, which was where she should be But at least at the weekend she would be spending time with her friends, this time at Hastings' expense.

On Saturday morning, after a decent night's sleep and a slick of make-up, Clare hunted for a suitable party outfit. She found a floaty gauzy dress she must have left in the case when she hurriedly repacked for Devon. Looking in the mirror, she ran a hand through her hair. It still unnerved her to feel soft strands of hair rather than bristle. She flattened her hair into shape with some mousse and did a quick twirl in front of the mirror. Much better than the last time Sam had seen her.

Roger and Anna drove her to Brambleton Hall and escorted her to the walled garden. Roger was wearing a blazer, which emphasized his military look, and for once Anna's hair was loose, falling in an elegant sheen of dark blonde. As they tramped closer to the party, Clare heard the rise and fall of voices and the occasional tinkle of laughter. She smiled, sensing that shiver of anticipation she used to experience when the taxi dropped her off near the rally team's base on a Friday night. Today, she would enjoy herself.

Stepping inside, the beauty of the garden struck her. It was a bit grandiose for her taste – like its owner, pimped to impress, but she could tell how much work had gone into nurturing the stage for Richard's party, and she doubted it was the host who'd been manning the hoe. The garden was divided into quarters, each framed by neatly clipped knee-high box hedging, then wide pea gravel pathways. Each quadrant contained a different colour of rose – pink, yellow, white, and red – all underplanted with billowing bunches of yellow Alchemilla mollis, white frothy clouds of gypsophila and purple fronds of Nepeta. Between the outer pathways and the brick walls were strips of lawn so finely mown they looked like green velvet.

It was so manicured she wished she'd brought Stop-it to bounce over the box hedging and push it out of shape, squash plants and scatter mulch onto the pathways. She stifled a giggle, imagining him with his nose wedged down a hole in the lawn, his front paws clawing at the turf to reach a tempting smell.

Elegantly clad guests stood on the paths and lawns and uniformed staff were circulating with silver trays of drinks and canapés. In one corner was a brass band belting out *Hey Jude*; it all looked terrifically English.

Roger picked up two glasses of Pimm's, passing one to Clare, the other to his wife. Clare drank, letting the gingery taste linger before swallowing. She disliked Pimm's but was pleased that was what was being served. It would prevent her from getting carried away and ending up squiffy. After all, she had work to do.

Clare's eyes circled the guests, and she spotted her quarry nearby, standing with an attentive female audience. Physically, Richard Hastings was very different from his brother. Where Sam was tall and lean, Richard, at only five foot six, was four inches shorter than Clare. He wore a dark suit, white shirt and a green tie patterned with pheasants. He was standing sideways to her, his stomach bulging unattractively over his waistline. His hair was black – no premature greying for the elder brother – but it sat atop a pinched, florid face. Richard's complexion was that of a Victorian gentleman fond of his post-dinner port.

Clare chewed at her lip. She had learned early on in her career that she did her best work when she stopped her personal feelings intruding on the professional. This time it wasn't easy. Some wealthy people recognized that inherited wealth brought responsibilities, and were generous, like Hastings' nineteenth-century ancestor Samuel, but not Richard. Samuel Hastings had built houses for the homeless and hadn't tried to rob his tenants.

Clare felt a hand on her arm.

'No,' said Anna.

'But—'

Anna gripped Clare's arm, her fingers digging into the bare skin, and steered her towards a wooden bench. 'This way,' said Anna. 'There's Fred. And don't be rude to Sam.'

'He's not the one I plan on being rude to!'

It seemed like Fred's suit had been bought to grow into. The sleeves were too long, the jacket stood proud of his shoulders and a belt secured bunches of spare fabric at the waist. Today the tie was a vibrant purple. He was talking to Sam, who in chinos and a button-down shirt, was the most casually dressed man at the party. 'Hi,' said Sam, smiling, 'thanks for coming today.'

She returned his smile, trying to decide if Sam's had been flirtatious.

'Good growing day for your mother's apples,' said Fred, sliding up to make room on the bench for the two women.

'How is Cindy's crop?' asked Sam.

Clare didn't want to talk about apples. She still hadn't been into the orchard. She couldn't – the ghost of her mother still stalked those trees, cigarette in mouth. The orchard was where they'd had their terrible row.

As if sensing her discomfort, Anna diverted the question by asking Sam how his own crop was and explaining to Clare that Sam made cider from his.

'I thought you had holiday cottages' said Clare.

'I do. Cider started out as a hobby, but I've got the bug now. I think I spend more time on that than I do running my cottages.'

That's because you don't need to earn a living from either, thought Clare.

As Clare adjusted the sleeves on her dress, she glanced furtively at her toned arms. All those expensive personal training sessions had been worth it. With a pang, she thought of the hotels she'd carefully selected for their top-quality gyms. She had lost most of Europe, but she'd be away in time for the Eastern part of her adventure. At a resort she had booked in Thailand there was a treadmill with a view of the sea. She'd enjoy running on that.

The heat of the sun rippled through her. 'I love this weather.'

'Me too,' said Sam. 'Summertime is funner time.'

Clare smiled. That was something he used to whoop as an eight-year-old child playing on the beach.

'Are you having fun today or are you on hosting duty?' she asked, looking straight at him. He was undeniably good-looking.

'I took a decision a long time ago to allow fun into my life. It's always there if you look for it.' He took off his glasses and looked straight into her eyes, his startlingly bright eyes radiating warmth, making her feel both hot and cold at the same time. She was sure he was flirting and took a gulp of Pimm's to steady her nerves. Clare tried to think of a witty response, but her flirting skills were rusty. She returned his gaze, angling her body towards his. 'Want to show me how?'

He replaced his glasses and took a pull of his drink. *Oh, Clare*, she remonstrated with herself, *that was cringingly obvious*. He's certainly not interested in you; he must have every single woman in Devon chasing him.

Thankfully, Fred came to the rescue.

'Did you have a chance to look at our leases?' asked Fred.

Sam spoke tersely. 'Fred, I told you – rents have gone up everywhere. I can't ask my brother to make an exception just because you're a mate.'

'But 10 per cent,' said Clare. 'Is that fair?'

'What's this got to do with you?' asked Sam frostily.

She felt her insides shrivel. Even now after twenty years he blew hot and cold. She felt just as confused and silly as she had done after he'd kissed her in the pub, and then made her feel like dirt on his shoe. She excused herself and got up to talk to Ivy, vowing to abandon memories of her schoolgirl crush.

Today the retired vicar wore a long pink batik kaftan, and a straw hat wound with a bright pink scarf, the ends draped like two skinny pigtails on either shoulder. There was a smile on Ivy's face and her tinkling laughter soon soothed Clare's temper. How does she do it? Clare asked herself. How is this woman permanently happy?

'It's kind of Richard to include me,' said Ivy.

'Anyone would invite you, Ivy.'

The other woman chuckled. Clare picked up a warm filo parcel baked to a golden hue from a silver platter held temptingly close. She took a bite. It was a mixture of smoked chicken and crunchy pine nuts, held together by a creamy filling. She held her other hand out to catch the flakes of crisp pastry, mumbling, 'When's your cottage being renovated?'

'It's not. He's just repainting the front doors and window frames.'

Raising her glass to her lips, Clare said, 'He's not a very generous man, is he.'

'Richard is generous when it's in his interests to be *seen* to be generous,' said Ivy.

'What do you mean?'

'When I needed money to repair the church organ he donated thousands of pounds, but he made sure the entire village knew what he'd done.'

'I see,' said Clare thoughtfully.

'People are rarely perfect, Clare.'

'Hmm,' muttered Clare.

'You know the saying; if it ain't broke, don't fix it? Don't strive for perfection in everything you do. Sometimes it's best just to find a way to live with an uncomfortable situation. Your mother did.'

Clare frowned. 'What do you mean?'

'I probably shouldn't tell you. I don't think anyone else knows . . . well, apart from Richard.' Clare held her breath. 'When your mother was on the parish council, after he bought the almshouses from her, Richard tried to get permission for rather large extensions to the end two houses.'

'The renamed Jasmine and Rose Cottages?'

'Yes.'

'And let me guess. Mum wasn't keen and told him so.'

Ivy nodded. 'He went to see her, basically tried to bribe her, offered her ten grand to give him permission, said he'd *underpaid* for the almshouses originally and wanted to put things right.'

'Wow. He didn't understand who he was trying to corrupt!'

'No,' said Ivy, wagging her head. 'She turned him down and persuaded her fellow councillors to vote against him. That's why she resigned from the council. She didn't think it was right to expose him, but equally she knew she'd be unable to consider any future applications by him impartially.'

Clare asked herself if, when Hastings took advantage of her mother's penury, he had viewed it as revenge for her spurning his bribe. Had Cindy's morals cost her most of the farm and maybe her life?

Over Ivy's head, Clare noticed a man with short, neatly trimmed raven-black hair and a flushed shiny face. The most striking thing about him was his clothes. He was wearing a sweeping black tailcoat which reached his knees, pin-striped dark grey trousers and a green waistcoat with brass buttons that gleamed in the sunlight. He could only be the Hastings' butler. He carried himself with an air of calm, dignified, discreet power, like a head teacher quietly patrolling the school corridor. Briefly she wondered what it would be like working for someone as unpleasant as Hastings. Richard would bend employment laws to suit himself – she doubted the butler took his holiday entitlement and suspected Richard's interpretation of a day off was sending the man into Barnstaple on an errand.

Ivy introduced him. 'This is Magnus. Now here really is someone who needs your help.'

'In what way?' asked Clare, noticing beads of sweat covering Magnus's forehead, making her want to offer to mop his face. Clare felt sorry for him. He must be wilting in this heat.

'In winter he's colder than me. Richard only turns the central heating on for the three winter months, regardless of the temperature. If we get a cold snap, Magnus here is expected to either freeze or use electric fan heaters, which he must pay for.'

'He's very generous to me, madam,' said Magnus deferentially, as if referring to the king. Magnus was holding a jug of Pimm's. His hand looked sweaty, and the sight of his damp collar stirred Clare's fighting spirit. 'Is this true, Magnus?'

'I don't like to complain.'

'Would you like me to?'

Magnus looked flustered. His hand shook and he shifted the jug, holding it between both hands. 'Please don't,' he said.

Was this man frightened of his employer? She allowed her glass to be topped up, then, clutching the cool glass to regain an even keel – she knew better than to take on a fight without her emotions in check – she strode towards her host, the crunch of her heels on the pea gravel chiming with her scratchy mood. Clare hadn't spoken to Richard in decades. First, she would watch and listen for clues, then leverage his vanities and weaknesses like she did with her opposition in a legal case.

She joined the fringe of Richard's admiring coterie, feeling a bit like a teenager on the edge of a fan club, waiting to thrust an autograph book forward. For a few minutes, she adopted an interested expression, listening to Richard explain the family history behind the silver goblet he was drinking from, who the silversmith was and how the village benefitted when the Hastings family donated a larger matching piece to the church; apparently that chalice was still used for Sunday communions.

'We Hastings always look after our village.'

She washed away the sour taste in her mouth with a gulp of Pimm's. Brambleton wasn't his village. He owned a lot of buildings, and he cast a pall over many of the residents, but that didn't mean he owned it. Richard was still talking. 'I like to do my bit.'

Clare stepped forward and said politely, 'But surely you could do more?'

'And you are?' said Richard coldly.

Of course, Richard wouldn't remember her. The last time he'd seen her, she was a 'village girl' pulling pints in his 'family pub'.

'Clare Hetherington. Orchard Farm.'

'Ah. I knew your mother,' he said, his face flushing a deep shade of red. Richard took a sip from his goblet, eyeing her over the rim. 'What did you have in mind? How would you like to spend my money for me?' He spoke in a superior tone, convincing Clare he was looking down his nose at her.

'Well, I'm a lawyer, and I think you might look at better terms for your tenants.'

He wafted a hand at her, dismissing her comment in the same way she could imagine him instructing Magnus to leave a room. Time didn't seem to have improved his manners.

'No need. They're all happy,' he said, taking a gulp of his drink.

Watching his red neck pulsing as the liquid slid down his throat, Clare was reminded of Hilts and bit her cheek to stop herself from laughing. 'Are they?' she asked.

'None of my tenants complain.' Richard lifted his goblet, which glinted in the sun. Clare felt her hackles rising.

'Only because they don't dare. It doesn't mean they're happy.'

'It's not my job to make them happy,' said Richard dismissively. 'It's a business.'

She bit back a retort. She'd never treat a client with such callous indifference. 'I think most of us providing a service want our customers to believe they've been well served. I certainly do. Tell me, if there was a way of making them happy at no expense to you, would you do that?'

He rolled his eyes at her. 'Why do I sense that what you are about to suggest will be presented as something which won't cost me anything, but will end up being expensive?'

'They're good tenants, pay rent on time, don't give you any hassle?'

'Yes', he said, drawing out the word, forestalling the moment she could make her suggestion.

'Give them longer leases. Next time make them three years instead of just one. Give them a sense of security. Fred and Ivy have both devoted their lives to this village.' She dug deep, concerned her next words might stick in her throat, but experience told her this was the way to secure her goal. Richard didn't treat tenants as equals. He was living in the nineteenth century dispensing charity to villagers who doffed their caps and lived in awe of his power. 'Brambleton is your village. Have some compassion for their plight.'

'And if I did that, it would make them happy, would it?' His eyes locked onto hers as he took a long pull of his drink. This was going much better than she could have imagined. She'd been worried he might summon Magnus to escort her off the premises.

'Yes.'

His brow wrinkled. 'And if I did this . . .' e was looking at her, his eyes narrowed, making her think he might agree, that she'd touched his human side, '. . . you think they would be grateful?' he said thoughtfully.

'Yes.' She nodded. 'Yes, I think they would.'

'Okay then.'

She took a gulp of Pimm's, hiding her smile. She didn't want him to see her surprise. 'You'll do it?'

'Remind me. I'm far too busy to remember tedious details about every property I own. Magnus will give you my email address.'

She shook his hand. It was clammy. She looked into his eyes, which had a cold, calculating menace to them. Why had he agreed? And why so quickly? She asked herself if he had an ulterior motive and a shiver ran down her spine. She hoped she hadn't just made a huge mistake.

Six

Early on Wednesday morning, Clare woke without Captain Hilts' help. Outside her bedroom door, she discovered Stop-it curled up, his muzzle cradled beneath a front paw. She leaned down and scratched his neck, then crossed to the bathroom. Inside, there was a new shower curtain – a present from Trish – patterned with cheerful yellow sunflowers. She pulled it back. The shower was now set a couple of inches higher thanks to Roger and a can of WD40. The shower head gleamed, as Anna had taken it away and soaked it in descaler. Her friend had returned it together with a Wif-Fi hub and a prepaid contract for six months as a 'welcome back' present. It was a thoughtful gesture, but she wouldn't need it nearly that long. She thought briefly about where she should be right now: exploring the Sistine Chapel.

She trotted downstairs, the dog following, and prepared her breakfast, toasting three slices of bread. She wanted two for herself. In the farmyard, Hilts announced Clare's approach like a herald trumpeting the arrival of the king. The rescue hens clucked, fluttered their wings and darted obediently to the patch the cockerel indicated. All were a golden-brown colour and, to Clare, impossible to tell apart, so she had named them all Vera after Vera Lynn.

Clare scattered a few vegetable peelings. Hilts ran forwards scavenging in the dirt. She stalked around the rooster and tipped the rest of the peelings directly in front of the hens. Hilts dashed over, crowed at Clare and flapped his wings, keeping the hens behind him. Thinking the girls weren't very empowered, dancing to the rooster's tune, Clare wagged a finger at the captain. 'Behave!' she scolded. 'You're as bad as Richard.'

She ground her teeth together. Just thinking about Richard made her hackles rise. Yesterday, she had sent him an email so he couldn't wriggle off the hook over Ivy and Fred's lease extensions. She wrinkled her nose. Something about the way Richard had so readily agreed on Saturday worried her. It wasn't logical. Either he'd lied and wouldn't do it, or there was a hidden reason for his acceptance. But she couldn't think of one. She couldn't dwell on that now. She must focus on prepping the house to go on the market.

It was sunny, so she decided to start outside. She knew she would have to get into the orchard, the grass probably needed mowing, but she couldn't face that yet.

Clare slathered sunscreen on her exposed limbs, collected secateurs and a flexi-plastic tub with one handle missing – thank you Stop-it – and surveyed the garden properly.

The lawn resembled the rougher edges of a golf course, with mounds of dirt beside holes dug by the dog pursuing tantalizing smells. There was a border where a rose bush, peonies and lupins competed for space with nettles, docks and buttercups. The telltale heart-shaped leaves of bindweed curled around the struggling plants. According to the estate agents, this bull terrier playpen needed transforming into what they referred to as 'a stunning mature garden.'

Dragging her bucket behind her, she advanced on the solitary rose bush. Unlike Richard's perfectly formed tea roses, this was an old-fashioned English variety, and getting closer, she could smell its perfume. She cupped a bloom in her hands, inhaling the scent. The flower crumpled, petals tumbling to the ground like confetti – just like her adventure seemed to be unfurling. She was clinging on to the lifeline of an early sale; if she could exchange by the end of August, she might still make it to that hot air balloon ride above Cappadocia in central Turkey.

She unwound the constricting bindweed. Behind her she heard Stop-it's snuffles, ignored him and snipped at the dead roses, letting them fall in a pile by her feet. Finished, she reached for the tub. It wasn't there. She spun around. Her bucket was ten feet behind her, the remaining handle secured in the dog's jaws. 'Stop-it!'

He replied with a low-throated encouraging growl, his tail wagging furiously.

'Drop.'

He cocked his head to one side, his eyes challenging her. She didn't have time to play, so turned her back on him, trying to ignore the sound of ripping plastic as she returned to her task. Something butted into the back of her knees. She looked down at her trug, now without handles. She grasped at his collar, but her hand closed on air as the dog darted away.

'This looks like a good game.'

Recognizing Anna's voice, Clare stood, stretching her arms over her head. Anna rearranged her hair clasp. 'He does love to play, doesn't he?'

'I don't have time to play, and he's got boxes full of toys.'

'He's bored! He can't throw his own ball.'

'Fancy a cup of tea?' Clare offered. 'I could use a break.'

'No thanks. You're reminding me how much there is to do in my own garden.' Anna leaned her elbows on the fence. 'I just called around to say congratulations.'

'What for?' asked Clare.

'I've just come from Prosecco and Prose. Ivy was there.'

'There's nothing to congratulate me about Ivy being in *there*. That's where she delivers pastoral care.'

Her friend smiled. 'She's had a letter from Richard's lawyers. Fred has had one too. He's offering to extend their leases at a fixed rent, for – wait for it – *five* years.'

Clare straightened her back. There was something bothering her. She still couldn't work out Richard's motive and didn't think he did anything unless it feathered his own nest.

'Oh, I shouldn't think me prodding him made any difference,' she said.

'You think that do you?'

Clare waved a hand dismissively. 'He'd probably already decided to do it. It makes sense. They're good tenants. You didn't say anything linking the lease extensions to me, did you?'

'No, but—'

'Good.'

Anna shook her head. 'Why won't you take the glory? This is a terrific result.'

'And that's all that matters. Let's not brag. We don't want to give Richard any excuse to change his mind. Let him take the credit for his generosity.'

Anna gave her a withering look. 'We are talking about the same landlord, aren't we? The one who's trying to jack up Rose's rent?'

That was what was bothering Clare. Extending those leases would fix the rent, albeit at a higher rate, for five years – an odd move for a man who seemed keen to piggyback on Rose's efforts. Unless it really was because Clare had asked. Had he made so much money from her mother that his conscience was telling him to give a bit back? Maybe he did have a better side.

Seven

Three weeks after she had died, Clare's mother was laid to rest. Clare stood in a pew numbly singing hymns and murmuring prayers, then sat listening to Ivy deliver a touching eulogy about Cindy and her love for Brambleton and the orchard. Ivy had suggested that Clare make the speech, but she couldn't – not after seven years apart. Some of Ivy's anecdotes brought a smile to Clare's face; a few had her biting hard on her cheek to stop the tears while she desperately scrolled through her mental to-do list as a distraction.

She managed to make it through the wake and the villagers' condolences without crying, and the following day threw herself back into running the farm and clearing up 'Cindy chaos'. She spent hours chivvying the garden into shape and driving box loads of clutter to charity shops.

A few days after the funeral, Clare was in the kitchen washing straw off warm eggs when she heard a rat-a-tat on the door. Through the frosted glass top half, she saw the smudgy outlines of three people. The door opened and in walked Ivy, Fred and Anna. Ivy wasn't smiling, and why was Anna, with her busy architect's practice, here at 10 a.m. on a weekday?

'What's up?' asked Clare, trying to sound cheerful.

'Can we come in?' asked Ivy.

Clare felt her jaw tighten. They already were in. She looked pointedly at her watch.

'I've brought cake,' said Ivy, placing a hand gently on Clare's arm. 'Your mother's lemon drizzle recipe.' Clare let out a soft sigh. 'I'm not sure I've time for cake, Ivy. I'm quite busy.'

Fred took a seat at the kitchen table, slung his tie over one shoulder and shunted the neat stacks of correspondence with APHA into a single pile. Clare frowned, collected her paperwork and rearranged it back into date order on the pine dresser. 'Please, don't touch those.'

'I'll put the kettle on,' announced Ivy. 'Every crisis needs tea.'

Clare raised her voice: 'Crisis? What crisis?'

Anna gave Clare a hug murmuring, 'I think you'll want tea when you hear what he's done.'

Deciding to ferret out the reason for the impromptu tea party, Clare asked, 'Who's done what?'

'Richard,' said Anna, shaking bunched fists as if having a tantrum. Clare squinted at her friend. Her hair hung loose. What was so dire her friend had forgotten to secure it in a clasp? 'He's going to start doing eggs,' said Anna.

Clare let out a short laugh. 'There's nothing quite like a newly laid free-range egg, but I'm having difficulty picturing him cleaning out the henhouse.'

'Not like you do eggs,' said Ivy softly.

Clare swallowed.

'He's applied for planning permission for a battery hen farm,' said Anna. 'Wants to house 40,000 chickens.'

'40,000?' said Clare, an image of rows and rows of Veras crouched in their own waste clouding her mind. 'Why does he need so many and where's he going to put them all?'

'Right by our cottages,' said Fred. He removed a knife from

its home in a wooden block and passed it to Ivy, who sliced the cake into thick wedges.

Clare dragged her eyes away from the crumb-coated knife and looked at Anna. 'You're the architect. Can he do that?'

Anna let out a long sigh which disturbed Clare. It wasn't a reassuring sound. 'Depends if his land is classified legally as *agricultural*.'

Clare snorted then said, 'There's nothing agricultural about his land. He's got plenty of tenant farmers, but he doesn't grow anything in his own fields except grass.'

'It might still be classed as agricultural,' said Anna

'And Brambleton Hall is a farmhouse?' Fred chortled.

Clare's eyes tracked Fred. He dropped the dirty knife end on into her sink, making Clare wince, then pulled at her kitchen towel roller in the same way Stop-it tugged at his rope toy, unfurling a ten-foot length which he bunched in his hands. Clare darted over and ripped the paper free before he could unravel any more, then picked up her knife and examined the end for damage.

'Well, thanks for letting me know,' she said.

'We're not just letting you know,' said Ivy, wrapping pieces of cake in paper towel and passing them around. 'We need you to help.'

Clare took her time wiping her knife clean and returning it to the block. 'Help?' she stuttered.

'We must stop him,' said Ivy.

'Yes, you must,' said Clare.

'Not us,' said Ivy gently. 'You.'

'I won't be here. Besides. I don't know anything about planning law.' She bit into her slice of cake. It was moist and sweet with the sharp tang of lemon she remembered so well from her childhood. She chewed, pushing memories of her mother to the back of her mind. 'Anna this is one for you.'

'I'm not a lawyer. I know a bit about planning, but this is more about the law – procedures, evidence . . .' said Anna.

'No' said Clare, 'absolutely not.' She had her hands full. She didn't have time to become an expert on planning law.

'Please,' said Ivy. 'He listens to you.'

Clare laughed grimly. If this was why Richard had offered to extend Ivy and Fred's leases, hoping to buy their support for his planning application, he had underestimated them.

'We'll all help,' said Fred, scrunching up his spent paper towel and dropping it into a bucket labelled *Compost*.

'Can we talk about this another time?' asked Clare, transferring Fred's rubbish to the bin.

'That'll compost down,' said Fred defensively.

'It's got sugar on it,' said Clare.

'I don't think you understand,' Anna said. 'This won't just affect the almshouses. They will suffer most, but the whole village will share their pain. How many holidaymakers are going to put up with the smell and noise of an intensive chicken farm? There'll be traffic jams from lorries collecting eggs and delivering feed. And what's going to happen to all the waste?'

Clare's thoughts vacillated between fixing her pig fencing and the implications of what Anna was saying. She didn't like the sound of waste from 40,000 birds. Richard would not be as diligent with chicken poo as she was.

Her eyes fell on her piles of APHA letters. 'There'll be regulations controlling waste from that many birds.'

'And you trust him to comply, do you? This is the man who conned your mother out of the farm,' said Ivy.

'What's this?' asked Anna sharply.

'Another time,' muttered Clare. Her instinct was to help, but this time it was impossible. It wasn't just that she didn't understand planning law. Planning battles took months, sometimes years, and she wasn't staying in Brambleton that long. She was flattered they'd turned to her, but she wasn't getting tangled up in village politics. And she wasn't interrupting her adventure to dispense advice from a sunbed. They would have to sort this drama without her.

From the door came a frantic scratching noise, followed by a long, low whine. Stop-it could smell guests.

'Shall I let him in?' asked Ivy. 'He's quite partial to lemon drizzle.'

'He's quite partial to anything unless its kibble. Leave him where he is,' said Clare.

'Please help us,' said Fred again.

Clare looked from Ivy to Fred. They'd both devoted their lives to the village, and in return, Richard was going to ruin their retirement.

'We need someone to spearhead the fight,' said Ivy.

Fred pointed a finger at her in mock Lord Kitchener style: 'This village needs *you*.'

The scratching started again. The door shook, banging against the architrave. Clare gave a half-hearted shrug and opened the door. Like the dog, Richard's motive was greed – and she didn't trust him to follow the rules either.

Promising to think about it, Clare said goodbye and strode to the pigpen, trailing a bag of straw. Ivy and Fred assumed that she was a miracle worker. Often, in her clients' eyes she was, but like every magician, the secret was in the preparation. Clare knew every piece of legislation, every tribunal decision and, from experience, understood how employers would react to being accused of breaking the law. That combination explained her success. Clare knew nothing about planning law, nor anyone who specialized in that field. She'd never accepted a case unless she'd been confident she could win, and she had an inkling that people's trust in her ability to solve this problem was unfounded.

Rounding the corner, Clare heard snuffling noises. Two hairy black pigs with white snouts, feet and tail tips rested their front trotters on the top rung of their fence, their snouts twitching. Cindy's Berkshires: a rare, hardy, outdoor breed that, unlike pink pigs, weren't prone to sunburn. She opened the gate, and shooed them towards an oak tree, then leaned into the pig ark and scraped out the soiled bedding. She thought about the impact an intensive chicken farm would have on Orchard Farm. If the run-off from 40,000 birds seeped into the Shire river, it would contaminate her borehole. Would it affect her mother's apple trees? She still hadn't been into that orchard; the grass would definitely need mowing: she must get in there. One of the pigs snorted, reminding her of her task list, and she went to fetch a length of wood to shore up the fence, wishing there was a simple way of fixing the planning problem.

By the time the fence was repaired, she had decided to investigate. Armed with a slice of Ivy's cake, a mug of tea and her laptop, Clare settled on the patio. Surfing the net and reading about intensive farming, she began feeling light-headed. Run-off often contained pathogens, antibiotics and hormones, which would devastate the orchard, deterring bees and affecting the soil's pH levels, inhibiting nutrient take-up and damaging root structure. She couldn't let this happen. The orchard was her mother's legacy. Maybe she could appeal to his better nature, like she'd done with Ivy's lease? To do so, she would need to prepare thoroughly.

In the early evening, she discarded her third mug of cold, undrunk tea and switched to white wine. She had finished researching the background law to a planning application and pulled up the North Devon Council's website, found Richard's planning application and downloaded the site plan. A shiver ran through her; it would be enormous. The documents referred to a 'shed', but that innocuous term masked the scale of a building which dwarfed the almshouses, looming above them like a cat over a cornered mouse. Stepping into their back gardens would be like walking onto an industrial estate.

The application sought permission to erect a shed to house poultry, up to 40,000 birds. According to Ivy, when Cindy's rescue hens had first arrived, they were skittish and wary of human interaction. Some had no feathers, others displayed blotchy red patches of skin from parasitic infections. One had arrived with a broken wing, and they were all skeletal, their muscles weakened from an inability to exercise in their cramped living space. Clare wasn't a nimble mathematician, but it wasn't difficult to work out that Richard's birds would have roughly the size of an A4 piece of paper to themselves. The hens would lead an entirely unnatural life. There wouldn't even be a cockerel.

She trawled through the documents and discovered that Hastings had considered, but rejected, several potential sites closer to Brambleton Hall. *What a surprise*, thought Clare. She read something called an Environmental Impact Assessment, which reassuringly concluded there was nothing to worry about. The report claimed there would be no unpleasant smell. No increased noise. No impact on the surrounding soil or watercourse from waste. Surely adding 40,000 birds that close to a river and a village would do all those things? The stench of ammonia would be horrid, the noise disruptive and the river contaminated.

She refilled her glass and took a sip of the chilled wine. The report reminded her of the slick responses she would get to her letters alleging corporates had breached their employment responsibilities – it was a bit *too* reassuring. Her instincts told her she'd stumbled on something, and she returned to the Hastings' site plan.

There was a second area with hatch marks on it. Clare recognized it as the field next to the village hall where the villagers parked. But that was earmarked as the site for another shed for storage and parking for lorries. Where were the villagers supposed to park? She suddenly thought of the annual Brambleton Agricultural Show, held every August – the chicken factory would be precisely where the main show ring normally stood.

The site plan stopped at the road in front of the almshouses, but Clare mentally sketched in the surrounding landscape. Below the lane was the River Shire, then the harbour and the beach. A sense of foreboding fell over her. No one would want to drive past that eyesore to reach the little beach or eat their picnics with the stench of chicken waste filling the air. Could the Smugglers Inn survive? What about Prosecco and Prose? The villagers supported both businesses in the lean winter months, but they made most of their money from tourists. She massaged the back of her neck. It was stiff and unyielding. And who was going to buy Orchard Farm with this threat hanging over it? Cursing, she closed the website. Hastings must be stopped.

She tossed back the remnants of her glass. The wine was warm and tasted sharp. Clare checked her itinerary. Today she should have been on a day trip to Tuscany, probably rounded off with a crisp glass of Pinot Grigio. She groaned. To fund her travels, she needed to sell the farm. If she wanted to salvage her adventure, she must solve the planning problem. Getting away from Brambleton was like extricating herself from quicksand and she was sinking further into its depths. She sighed, got up, found her to do list and reluctantly added 'fight planning application'.

On Sunday evening Clare stopped outside the Smugglers' Inn, staring at the harbour wall jutting out in its protective arc. If only it could defend the village against Richard's onslaught. It was low tide, exposing dank streaks of seaweed on the sandy beach. A gust of wind whipped up the scent of samphire, an earthy, sweet smell, which evoked a powerful memory of laughing with her mother as they nibbled on the sweet tendrils of bright green seaweed they had gathered earlier that day. She wondered how Cindy would have reacted to Richard's plans if she was still alive.

Inside, the pub was busy. She recognized most of the people at the bar, including the couple she'd met a few weeks earlier. The man with the frizzy ginger hair offered to buy her a drink.

'Thank you, but I'm meeting some friends.'

'Another time,' he said.

Rose was behind the bar, pulling a pint. She plopped it on the bar and waved. Clare was itching to know how Richard had responded to her suggestion of not raising the rent, but in front of the landlady, his bar stool angled to one side, was Sam. Opposite him, looking slightly less comfortable on a stool, sat Fred. Clare took a deep breath. If they were going to take on Tricky Ricky, she must warn Fred to be careful around Sam.

She found Anna and Roger in a cosy nook, kissed her friend on both cheeks then sat.

'When I walked past Ivy's house I could feel the onshore breeze,' Clare started. 'It's going to blow the stench of those birds directly at her, but with 40,000 birds, won't it drift back down to the rest of the village?'

Roger ran a hand over his face and groaned. Anna shot him a swift look then said, 'Of course it will.'

'It's not just the smell,' said Clare. 'It's the run-off. Lots of us rely on boreholes. I was looking through Mum's records and last year she spent £25,000 installing a new soakaway system because the old one was too close to a tributary of the Shire. Her sewage wasn't allowed to leak into the water system, but who's going to make sure his poultry don't contaminate it?'

'Good point,' said Anna. 'We can't let that happen.'

'Don't be so dramatic,' said Roger, 'No one's going to let him pipe untreated poo into the river.'

'No,' snipped Anna. 'Only water companies are allowed to do that.'

The couple were looking in opposite directions.

'Did you read the EIA?' asked Anna.

Clare glanced at Roger, but he was still staring at the bar. She shook her head. 'I tried.'

Roger's head swivelled back. He huffed. 'It's just a few chickens. It's his land. Let him do what he wants with it.'

'Pfft!' said Anna. 'You were saying, Clare?'

'The report says adding 40,000 birds will have no impact.'

Anna snorted. 'Go figure.'

'What's that supposed to mean?' asked Clare.

'The expert was hired to reach that conclusion. So, they have,' said Anna.

'Are you saying they lied?'

'They didn't lie,' snapped Roger.

Anna rounded on her husband, glaring at him and said, 'I've read the report, which is more than you've done, Roger.'

Clare held up her hands. 'Enough.' She turned towards Roger. 'I'm getting the vibe you're in Richard's camp.'

He cupped his hands round his pint glass. 'Wrong. I'm not in anyone's camp. I just don't want to see this village split between Richard's supporters – and don't kid yourselves,' he said, his eyes darting between the two women, 'he will have his supporters – and the anti-camp, which I would prefer Anna not to be a fully paid-up member of.' He lifted his glass, took several gulps, and then banged it back down on the table like a full stop.

For a few moments Clare let the charged atmosphere cool. Roger was right. Richard was the biggest local employer and the next largest was his brother. Not everyone would be against Hastings' plans. Roger topped up the women's glasses, then excused himself to fetch a fresh pint.

Anna spoke rapidly. 'What I meant about the EIA is that the report points out North Devon is agricultural. Farmers spread muck to fertilize fields, which smells pretty rank if you're not used to it. But the life blood of this village is tourists, and they won't come if it stinks of ammonia.'

Roger had bent over, sipping his drink to a safe level to carry before he started walking back to the table. Anna spoke rapidly: 'I'm just saying the assessment only paints part of the picture.'

Roger put his drink down, then pulled a couple of packets of crisps from his pockets. Clare picked one up. 'I'm starving. I haven't eaten yet.'

Anna laughed. 'That's because there aren't twenty restaurants within walking distance of you. Once you run out of Cindy's pies, you'll have to learn to cook. I hear what you're saying . . .'

Clare spotted Sam heading their way. 'Shh,' she said. But Anna was in her stride: 'You're right to be sceptical about the EIA.'

'Evening, Roger. Ladies,' said Sam, nodding to each in turn. 'Are you talking about my brother's new business venture by any chance?'

'None of your business.' said Clare archly, earning her a sharp look from Roger.

'Evening, Sam,' said Roger. 'How's the holiday season going?'

'Pretty good thanks.'

'Your cottages are upwind, so you won't be affected by his new model farm, will you?' said Clare sarcastically.

'But my brother's two holiday lets will though.' said Sam, crossing his arms. 'He's a smart businessman, so he must think the impact is minimal. Have you looked at the EIA?'

'I think the Council is staffed by sensible Devonians, who'll see through Richard's report, commission their own and learn the truth,' said Clare.

A thoughtful expression crossed Sam's face. 'If they dare,' he said. 'The Council know Richard. They won't risk a legal fight; they haven't the funds.'

Clare clutched at her wineglass. 'That's outrageous! Your brother shouldn't be able to threaten his way into getting planning permission.'

'He's not threatening. He's just in a powerful position.'

Roger stood up, scraping his chair legs across the floor. He pointed a finger at Anna. 'This is what I warned you would happen. It will destroy this village, pull us apart.' He tossed back his pint, banged it on the table, glared at his wife, Clare and finally Sam, before stomping out of the pub.

Sam rolled his eyes at the women and followed him. Clare waited until she couldn't see Sam anymore, then said, 'Hateful man, interrupting our evening to come and gloat. Upsetting Roger.'

'I think Roger is responsible for upsetting himself. He wants this to go away.'

'Hopefully, it will,' Clare added. 'I checked, and if that field isn't agricultural land, the Council will refuse permission.'

Anna rolled her eyes. 'He's not a farmer.'

An image of her mother's orchard filled Clare's mind. She couldn't let Hastings ruin those trees. 'Then we can see this off. We must stop him.'

'Glad you're onside,' said Anna. 'What's the plan?'

'It's quite simple,' said Clare, 'I'll call the Planning Officer and tell them they can't grant permission because the site isn't agricultural land.'

Clare could shoehorn that into her schedule before she left Brambleton.

Eight

To do:

- Contact Planning Officer
- Arrange meeting
- Finalise second charge loan
- Repay mum's debts
- Probate
- Farmhouse repairs
- Estate agent
- Make Stop-it eat kibble

Before making her own breakfast, Clare fed the hens. She loved the way they greeted her, with their soft chirrups and gurgles of pleasure. It was like being hailed a powerful deity, just for turning up to dole out grub. She wondered how Guy would have reacted to the hens; he hadn't liked animals. The first weekend she had brought him to meet her mother, Guy had shrunk away from Jet. Perhaps that was why Cindy didn't warm to him; her mother always maintained that a dog was an excellent judge of character.

After completing the early morning chores, Clare called the Council, asking to speak to the Planning Officer. He was in a meeting. She left a message, but two hours later he hadn't returned her call, so she called again, left a second message, then went into Brambleton.

It was a gloriously warm, sun-drenched morning. If she were in London, she would be hiding in her office, soothed by the cool air conditioning. Thinking of her little cubicle reminded her that every Monday morning she had been stuck in back-to-back departmental meetings – the Planning Officer was probably suffering the same fate.

At Prosecco and Prose, the terrace was crammed with tourists lounging in the dappled sunlight filtering through the trees. Some were hunched over maps and guidebooks, while others basked in the warmth, soaking up the sun and ambiance. Laughter and lively conversation filled the air, blending with the clink of cutlery. She heard her mother's voice in her head: *you don't need a proper holiday; a change is as good as a rest!*

It didn't matter if Clare spent part of her sabbatical in Devon, she would still return to London refreshed.

She went inside, entering a long, low room filled with comfy high-backed velvet chairs, each with their own reading spotlights. Beside every chair was a table just big enough for a small plate and a drink. There were larger tables displaying books, with signs advertising their genres. To Clare's left was a second room full of rows of floor-to-ceiling bookshelves, and on her right open bi-fold glass doors led out to the terrace. A gentle breeze blended the aromas of freshly brewed coffee, pastries, bacon and suntan lotion. Mentally, Clare added a whiff of ammonia and pictured the terrace empty of customers; that factory would decimate Trish's business.

There was only one other customer inside, who was quietly reading a book, a pot of coffee and a plate of toast on the table beside him. Sam Hastings. His hand reached for his mug but he didn't look up. She suspected he was here to eavesdrop. Well, she'd give him something to listen to.

Clare strode to the bar. She wanted to shake this problem off.

It was clouding her mind, making her moody. Two waitresses rushed in, slapping order slips in front of Trish, who glanced up. She flicked her curtain of hair over one shoulder 'Howzit?' she asked.

'Don't ask,' replied Clare. She ordered a coffee.

Clare looked up into her friend's hazel eyes, seeing the compassion radiating from them like a comforting hug.

'What's up?' asked Trish.

Before she could stop herself, Clare vented her frustration that the Planning Officer wasn't returning her calls. Trish shifted her eyes to Sam's table and whispered, 'Keep your voice down.'

But Clare refused to tiptoe around the village, dodging Hastings' spies. 'It's the arrogance of the man. Richard bangs on about this being his village, but he's got no respect for it.'

'Shh!' said Trish, turning her back on Clare and fiddling with the coffee machine. The hiss of water matched Clare's mood, and she spoke in a voice loud enough to reach the enemy. 'You can't build a chicken factory on a park.'

Trish spun round, her eyes wide. 'It's not Sam doing this. He's my best customer. Please keep your voice down.'

'He won't get permission,' Clare exclaimed even more loudly. 'His land isn't a farm. To get—'

A male voice cut her off. 'You won't win that way.' Clare turned, her eyes boring into Sam. His face was down, as if reading his book. How could he sit there knowing what his brother was trying to do? Clare spoke confidently. She might not be a planning lawyer, but she knew more about this than Sam Hastings.

'It's binary: no farm, no permission.'

Sam chuckled. It infuriated her that his laugh was so endearing. She had an image of the pair of them as eight year olds in the school nativity play, with Sam cast as Joseph, while she played Mary. At that tender age, Clare had convinced herself she would marry her fellow actor, but now she believed that dream would have turned into a nightmare – no wonder he was divorced.

Without raising his head, Sam said, 'It's a farm.'

'It's not enough to be surrounded by farms. The site he wants to put this monstrosity on isn't farmed,' Clare said.

Sam used a finger as a place marker, closed his book and looked at her. His piercing blue eyes seeming to mock her.

'It is a farm,' he said softly. 'The entire Brambleton Estate is legally a farm. All these estates are farms.'

'And Brambleton Hall is a farmhouse?' she shot back.

He nodded. 'Yes. Quite a smart one, but a farmhouse nonetheless.'

'Tell me what your brother farms then,' said Clare indignantly.

'Well, it used to be handouts from the EU. Every landowner who registered as a farm used to get an RPA –a rural payment allowance. That stopped with Brexit, but he's got his RPA number, so that site is classified as a farm.'

Clare had a sinking feeling that Sam was telling the truth. She felt stupid. She may loathe him, but Richard was canny and wouldn't have spent money on an EIA without checking for simple impediments like she was clutching at.

'Talk to Bill Matthews,' said Sam.

Clare frowned. 'Who's that? Why would I want to talk to him?'

'He's the local councillor. He's a good guy. He'll give you a reading on how he thinks the Council will approach this.' Sam took a sip of coffee, his face crinkled into a smile and his blue eyes focused on her. Clare felt the nape of her neck going hot and her breath grow shallow. She couldn't decide what was irritating her most: that she found him attractive or that he was showing up her poor preparation in front of Trish.

'Bet your brother's got him in his pocket.'

'If you don't like the way my brother does business, do something about it.'

Seeing her hands quivering, she hid them by crossing her arms. 'I don't think I'll take the advice of a Hastings.'

He laughed and despite herself, she smiled – it was such a disarming sound. 'I'm my own man,' said Sam, pouring coffee into his mug. 'I don't always do what Richard wants.'

'And nor does the village,' said Trish. 'He's going to have a fight on his hands. Clare will take him on, and she always wins.'

Spurred on by her encounter with Sam, the following morning Clare persuaded Anna and Fred to join her in sounding out the village. They worked their way from cottage to cottage, leaning over garden fences, ringing doorbells, rapping knuckles on windows. No one knew about Hastings' plans and revealing them often elicited the same response. 'Well, that's Tricky Ricky for you. Guess we'll have to learn to live with it.'

By noon she was exhausted and wishing she was in London, where most houses had been converted into flats. There were probably fifty households on her own street. Clare strode away from another house, throwing her hands into the air in frustration. Why were people just accepting this? They were treating Hastings like a medieval feudal lord, who could do whatever he wanted. Outside the village hall, Anna suggested splitting up, and although that would have made them three times faster, Clare resisted. She didn't want to be labelled as the Londoner who was stirring up the village.

Clare spotted a young woman in overalls who was squatting

in front of a door, sanding it down with a power tool, and suggested they speak to her. A *Sold* sign stood in the garden.

'Lovely day for a spot of DIY,' said Fred.

The woman turned off the machine and introduced herself as Gina. She glanced fondly into a pram next to her, its hood up, protecting the occupant from the sun. 'My partner and I have just moved in. We've been saving for five years for a place like this.'

As Gina chatted about her plans for the house, Clare's eyes flickered between the garden, with a view of Richard's proposed site, and the sleeping baby with its tiny head flopped to one side, breathing in the pure Devon air. There was a waft of honeysuckle. Clare let her eyes wander, tracking down the scent to a trellis attached to the side of the house, where the clashing pink and orange flowers were wilting in the sun.

'Do you know what's possibly happening over there?' Clare asked, pointing to the fields beside and above the village hall.

'Oh yes,' said Gina, smiling. 'We know all about the Brambleton Agricultural Show. My husband's going to take that Monday off. We want to become part of this village, support its traditions.'

She spoke proudly, making Clare's heart clench. She didn't want to shatter this woman's idyllic life. Clare gave Anna a sideways look. 'You tell her.'

When Anna revealed Hastings' plan, Gina's face drained of colour. She swayed and reached out, clutching at the door. Clare followed Gina's gaze out to the fields. Bales of hay were stacked up waiting for collection, and birds were jabbing beaks into the ground, searching for titbits in the newly cropped grass. It was hard to picture a factory replacing that view. Gina spoke in a shaky voice. 'Forty thousand birds? I can't believe this.' Gina wiped a hand down her face. 'Why didn't it show up on the local searches?'

'He's only just applied,' said Anna. 'You'll probably get a letter in the post soon. You are quite close.'

'It's going to affect our value.'

Fred was shuffling his feet.

'I think it will damage house prices in all of Brambleton,' Anna said.

Maybe not the Manor House or Sam's holiday cottages, thought Clare.

Gina's face darkened and she pointed at the pram. 'Ben's only six months old. I don't want him breathing in fumes. My sister lives in the Wye Valley. That's Chicken Factory Central. She says the ammonia fumes are bad for kids' health.'

Walking away, Clare felt the same surge of injustice which had always spurred her on in complex employment cases. Gina and her family didn't deserve this. Anna spoke in an excited voice about the strength of local opposition. 'It's something the Council consider before granting planning permission.'

Clare pulled a face. 'But it's not local opposition, is it? People don't like his plan, but no one's suggested doing anything about it.'

'Because most people haven't thought this through,' said Anna. 'The village doesn't understand how this will affect them yet.' She waved her arms. 'Everyone is going to take a hit to their wallets.'

'Not everyone,' mumbled Fred. 'And most will still be in a better position than Ivy and me.'

'Yes,' Anna nodded in agreement. 'The almshouses will be the most affected.'

'That's not what I meant,' said Fred waving his arms the same way Anna had. 'If all these people didn't have so much housing wealth, Ivy and I might be able to afford our own homes.'

Fred delivered his speech without bitterness, but Clare spotted a haunted look in his eyes and tried to imagine what it would be like to rent all your life in a village of rich homeowners.

'Ironic really, isn't it,' said Fred. 'Here I am, fighting what I know is morally wrong for the village, protecting the value of everyone else's houses and risking an eviction notice for my efforts.'

At least Clare could put his mind at ease there. 'No, he's just offered to extend your leases for five years.'

Fred laughed. 'Heard of Section 21?' he asked scornfully.

Clare considered Fred's words. Richard hadn't signed the new leases yet, and under Section 21, he could evict a tenant with just three months' notice. But he wouldn't. 'He's not going to evict you. He won't find it easy to replace you as tenants when he's applying to build a factory a stone's throw away.'

'You think that do you.' Fred said. 'There speaks the voice of the house owner.' This time, his voice was bitter. 'They'll be queuing up. Those are *houses*. With gardens. Near an excellent primary school. He'll have hundreds applying and he knows it. You could rent a garden shed in this village if it had running water and electricity.'

She didn't think even Tricky Ricky would risk the public relations backlash of evicting the former vicar and a man who'd taught at the local primary school for forty years, but she didn't want him to worry. 'Fred, I hadn't considered that Richard might throw you and Ivy out. We'll fight him without you.'

'You will not!' he said defiantly. 'I won't be cowed by that man, and I know Ivy won't either. I've always stood up against a bully and I'm not stopping now.'

Anna patted Fred's arm affectionately. 'The challenge is that no one thinks he *can* be stopped.'

'Why not organize a briefing session at the village hall?' said Clare. 'Invite everyone and explain his plans. If people see how much this will affect their lives . . .'

'Exactly,' said Anna. She cast a fond look at Fred and added, 'Fear of loss is a great motivator.'

'More powerful than desire for gain,' added Clare, stirred by her friend's enthusiasm. 'Let's take the monster on.'

If Fred and Ivy were prepared to risk their homes, the least she could do was offer her time.

Nine

Later that afternoon, Clare called her travel agent to rejig her travel plans once again. It was hard to imagine that she'd ever expected to be in Rome last week, and Athens right now. Now it was unrealistic to think she would be anywhere but Brambleton before the new year – she couldn't afford to travel until someone paid a deposit on the farm, and who would do that with Richard's chicken factory looming over it like a storm cloud on the horizon? She couldn't even return to her own flat; having given notice on their own accommodation, the flat sitters were both sofa surfing until Clare got up to London and cleared out that spare bedroom.

With a heavy heart she pulled up her online banking portal. Her reduced salary easily covered her mortgage, but once the new second charge loan kicked in, she would have less than two hundred pounds a month to live off. She winced, closed the screen and went upstairs to clear out some more of her mother's clothes.

Moments later she ran back downstairs, grabbed her computer, and within thirty minutes was admiring her handiwork:

Free range eggs for sale: £5.00 a tray or £3.00 for a dozen

She downloaded a picture of some happy looking hens, then printed off the notice and took it, along with her eggs and a rinsed-out yoghurt pot to the front gate.

The first occasion Clare that laid eyes on Richard since learning of his scheme was at Thursday evening bridge club. She was with Anna. Neither had expected to see him, both calculating it was too soon after his plans became public for him to show his face. But what Clare didn't know, and Anna had overlooked, was that most of the bridge players didn't live in the village.

Inside the village hall were several square tables covered with felt tablecloths, each surrounded by four chairs. Red plastic 'bidding boxes' sat on the tables, enabling players to bid silently, avoiding any claims of cheating by subtle changes to a bidder's tone of voice or pointed clearing of throats. There was a card marked with an 'N' showing the position of the north-sitting player, who was required to keep score. Typically, the pairs sitting north–south remained at the same table all evening, while after playing a few rounds of pre-dealt cards, the east–west pair moved to a different table. Every time players switched tables, the cards also moved, in a different direction, and by the end of the evening, every pair would have played the same hands. The competition would produce a winning north–south partnership as well as an east–west one.

Richard and his partner were already occupying a north–south position. Clare scowled at her friend and muttered, 'Bang goes our relaxing evening.'

Anna gave her a small smile. 'Come on. We'll get through this together.' She then whispered, 'He's not with his usual partner. You'll like his stand in, Mike; he's only been playing a couple of years, but he's charming, has an accountancy practice in Barnstaple.' Clare wasn't reassured; Mike could be Prince Charming himself, but that wouldn't make up for Richard. In a tart voice, she said, 'If I'm forced to sit at the same table as Richard I might—'

'If we grab another north–south position, we probably won't meet them.'

The room filled up. The club chair, Penny, stood and spoke. 'I'm directing, I need to be north, and with her dodgy hip, I don't want to ask Shirley here to have to move,' Penny said, indicating the woman sitting north at Penny's table. 'Please could someone else in a north–south position volunteer to switch to east-west?'

Clare stayed silent. With a feeling of dread, she saw Richard's partner, Mike, reach around for his jacket. Clare winced as the pair walked over – Richard less enthusiastically than Mike – and swapped seats with Penny and her partner.

Concentrating on the cards, Clare soon forgot about Richard. The evening passed quickly. The powerful hands were mostly north, and as the south player, Clare ended up as dummy, laying down her cards face up and silently following Anna's directions. As players arrived at their table, Anna introduced Clare to each new east–west partnership. Everyone was friendly; there were several retired doctors and other professionals, who seemed to divide their time among the bridge table, the golf course and lots of charity work.

The last two boards arrived and with them, Richard and Mike. Clare snatched up her cards and arranged them into suits. Mike was the dealer, and reached into his bidding box, placing down a wodge of cards and bidding two Hearts.

'That's weak,' said Richard.

Clare's hands clenched around her cards. Richard shouldn't explain his partner's bid unless the opposition asked for clarification.

When the bidding stopped, Richard was dummy, like Clare

had been frequently that evening, and laid down his cards, a triumphant expression on his face. His hand hovered over his exposed cards.

Clare folded her own cards together, desperate to remind Richard he was supposed to be a dummy – not a coach for his partner. Mike was staring blankly at the exposed cards.

Richard picked up the Queen of Hearts.

Clare folded up her cards, slammed them on the table and jabbed her index finger at Richard. 'No,' she said firmly. 'You must keep your hands away and only select a card when instructed to do so by your partner.' Her heart was racing. The sheer arrogance of the man. She fixed her eyes on his, and for a few moments they stared at each other like chess masters before a championship final. Then Clare raised her arm. 'Director.'

Finally, Richard broke eye contact. 'There's no need to do that,' he said. 'It's just a game.'

'With rules. As dummy you must follow the declarer's directions. Not play the hand for him.'

Mike was examining his cards, seemingly unable to meet his partner's eyes. Anna had her own cards raised, covering her face like a fan. Clare wasn't backing down. Penny came to the table, and doing her best to keep an even tone, Clare explained events, all the while aware of the tension hanging over the table like a rain cloud threatening to burst. Why was she complaining? She wasn't surprised to discover Richard cheated at cards. Someone who planned to devastate the village for his own selfish gain would stop at nothing to win at everything he did.

Richard ignored rules. In the planning battle, he would have an equally powerful hand to play as he had tonight. The difference was, when it came to his sheds, he would select who fought on his side with more care than he chose tonight's stand-in bridge partner. She thought of her own team. Ivy and Fred were well meaning, but they were no match for Richard. Anna was compromised by Roger's stance on the battle. Was Clare going to be fighting alone?

Later that evening, squeezing out a tiny blob of night cream from the travel-sized tube, Clare's thoughts were channelled on revising her to do list. How could Hastings be defeated? Was there a local bigwig he would listen to? Should she contact the local MP? Would villagers be up for a fight, and did Richard even care what they thought about his plans if they were? She massaged the cream into her face. Was she destined to spend months on the warpath instead of on a sun lounger? She flicked off the bathroom light and trudged to her bedroom. If Brambleton stood up against Hastings, Clare would try to persuade the Council to veto the application. She reached for a pad and pencil by her bedside, scrawling down:

- Draft notice for briefing meeting
- Contact Planning Officer
- Arrange to meet them
- Reread EIA
- Get up to London
- Farmhouse repairs

Once this was over, she could put the farm on the market and finally get away.

Ten

Clare arrived at the village hall panting – in London she would have been able to catch a cab if she was running late. The notices advertising the planning consultation had been up for a week. Counting ten cars in Richard's field, she wondered whether those drivers realized how difficult it would be to use the hall if Hastings won. Given the narrow road, on-street parking would be challenging.

Inside, it was busy. There was a gentle hum of conversation, but no laughter. People were fidgeting, chewing their fingers and tapping their feet. Clare recognized the same atmosphere she'd experienced at employment tribunals. She helped set out another row of chairs, all the while hearing the fire door hiss open to admit more people. Shortly before 7 p.m., Anna arrived with Ivy and joined Clare in the front row of seats. 'Where's Roger?' whispered Clare.

'Not coming,' replied Anna.

'Has Richard got to him?'

'No. He wants it all to go away. Like he said in the pub, he doesn't want the village to split.'

'It's too late for that,' said Clare. She gave Anna a pained look. 'Roger's not trying to stop you fighting this, is he?'

'No,' said Anna, settling herself back in her chair. 'He knows he can't.'

By seven o'clock, most of the seats were full and people were standing at the back of the room. Searching for faces she wanted to see, Clare realized there was a three-way split. Those in favour: Richard, his brother and their hangers-on; the wishful thinkers like Roger, and those against. But within the latter group were a silent opposition who, with Richard as their landlord, couldn't risk publicly opposing him. She wished she could paint in the missing faces of Trish, Rose and her husband George. Prosecco and Prose, the Smugglers Inn and the village shop – also run by Rose and George – were the three focal points of the village, and Clare was concerned that people might take their absence tonight as support for Richard.

Clare put her hands on her hips and a hush fell. She felt the same surge of adrenalin, which rose within her like a powerful wave, lifting her as she walked into an employment tribunal. She looked out at the sea of faces, picking out the few she knew, realizing with a pang that her mother would probably have known everyone.

'Thanks for coming,' she said. 'This is serious. Our village is being threatened.' She paused, not for effect, but because she realized the implication of what she'd just said. She was accepting her role as the person who would spearhead this battle. At this rate, her whole sabbatical was going to be spent in Devon.

Clare was outlining Richard's plans when she heard the door creak open. Hoping it might be Trish or Rose, she glanced over. Sam. *Blast!* Richard wasn't brave enough to come himself, so he'd sent his spy. Everyone liked Sam. No one would question why he was here. Sam didn't fool her, but she would be unpopular if she tried to ban him, so she held her tongue. He put up a hand in apology, and mimed a creeping, walking action, his shoes squeaking on the floorboards, further fanning the flames of Clare's temper. He walked in front of the audience, took

Clare's vacant seat and threw her a smile, which she didn't respond to. He wasn't winning her over that easily.

She returned to her speech, aware of Sam's eyes on her just a few feet away. He stretched out his long legs, placed his elbows on them and leaned on his arms, as if emphasizing how much he was concentrating. He was grinning at her, toying with her, like he used to when she worked in the pub. Convinced he was trying to distract her, she scolded herself: be professional. It's not the first time you've encountered a good-looking man at work.

'Now I've explained everything, let's have a show of hands. Who's against this idea?' asked Clare. A sea of hands shot up. Clare threw a triumphant look at Sam. She'd like to see Richard's face when his brother reported the strength of feeling against his plans. 'So, what do we do? Any ideas?' asked Clare.

'Form an action group,' said Anna.

Ivy's hand was up. She was waving furiously, like a schoolgirl confident they could answer a tricky question. Clare nodded.

'We must ask ourselves if this is ethical. We don't want to split the village.' Clare felt her heart sink and wondered if, given Sam's presence, Ivy – wary of Section 21 – didn't want to be seen as anti. Was she about to lose Fred's support too?

'I don't agree with his ideas,' said Ivy, 'but Richard has as much right to his point of view as we all do.' Clare struggled with her temper. As always, Ivy was being generous and Clare was trying to refrain from countering that as Richard didn't give a damn about them, why should anyone in the village gave a damn about him?

'He doesn't give a fig what happens to my business,' shouted a male voice. 'How many people will want to buy an ice cream to eat on a beach that stinks of chicken shit? Why should I care about his views?'

'But we must act ethically,' said Ivy.

Clare used a measured, lawyerly tone. 'I don't think *he's* acting ethically, Ivy. Richard is threatening our way of life, and in a lot of cases, our livelihoods.'

'And our property values,' piped up a woman's voice. Clare tracked the voice to the speaker, recognizing Gina from last week. Gina had the baby strapped to her chest in a sling.

Clare saw backs straighten, heard a few sharp intakes of breath. Several hands flew up to cover mouths.

'What about the chickens?' shouted someone from the back. 'He doesn't care about the chickens. That's not ethical, Ivy!'

'Or what happens to their waste. I'm on a borehole . . .'

There were so many people speaking at once, it was impossible to decipher what anyone was saying. Clare's heart sank. She could sense their fear, but she needed people to concentrate and agree an action plan.

She lifted her voice. 'Let's do this one at a time.' As she waited for quiet, she was irritated to notice Sam smiling. How she would love to drag him to the door and eject him. Yes, he was going to enjoy reporting this part of the meeting: lots of angry people, but chaos, no plan.

'We're all tense because we're frightened. Most of you rely on tourists and this would be damaging. Some of you are more exposed than others.' She looked pointedly at Sam. His cottages were further up the hill and unaffected by the sight or smell; his orchard wouldn't suffer the fate which awaited her mother's.

The meeting lasted another twenty minutes before Clare wrapped it up. Wanting to show that there was a plan, she said, 'Here's what I suggest we do. We form an action group to investigate how we can get Richard to change his mind. Anyone with time to help please have a word with me or Anna after the meeting.' She was keen to cement Anna to the cause.

People started gathering coats and bags and crowding around

the exit. Sam remained sitting, smiling, his eyes raking through the crowd. She wanted to wipe that cocky expression from his face. Sam would be off to report on the meeting and he would have noticed certain influential villagers were absent. His wretched brother had parts of Brambleton by the throat. But as a lawyer, she accepted the facts: she could only fight with the weapons available, and that didn't include Rose or Trish. She would set the action group to work, then get up to London to pack up her flat.

Eleven

To Do

- Name for action group: Brambleton against Richard's Factory?
- Objectives
- Approach Richard?
- Meeting with local councillor
- Draft a campaign leaflet
- Work on Farmhouse – see list
- Orchard
- London flat
- Stop-it/kibble

Three days after the village hall briefing, the action group gathered together on Orchard Farm's patio. The night sky provided a velvet backdrop for the stars, and for a few minutes Clare stood looking at them, trying to remember the constellations her parents used to point out to her on clear evenings. Clare hadn't thought about stars for decades – she didn't notice them in London as it was never dark enough. She wondered whether the stars were as clear from the Greek islands she was missing – she would make a point of looking upwards on the rest of her trip. Not wanting to chew expensive electricity, she switched on a string of fairy lights she'd found on special offer in the supermarket, adding a festive air she wasn't sure matched the occasion.

First to arrive were Ivy and Fred. Ivy was a win, given her influence, but her presence was a mixed blessing. Ivy was Richard's tenant, and Clare didn't like the idea of Ivy publicly resisting his plan. Her ethical stance would also require careful handling. Fred too presented multiple challenges. He was also a Hastings' tenant but in addition was a friend of Sam's and might inadvertently leak their ideas to the opposition.

Fred arrived carrying a shopping bag and Ivy a cake. Clare led them outside, where Ivy cut slices of cake, explaining that several villagers including Gina and her partner were keen to be involved, but couldn't join evening meetings. 'They've all got young children,' explained Ivy. Anna puffed in late, gave Clare a hug, whispering that Trish was going to help 'but off stage,' she said with a wink. 'Sorry, but I can only manage an hour tonight.'

'It's not that long an agenda!' said Clare.

'Good,' said Fred, fiddling with his ears. 'Need to give the dahlias an evening drink of water.' He flinched. 'Wretched hearing aids have just given me a dollop of static.'

Clare sat with her back to the pockmarked lawn. Repairing the grass from Stop-it's exploits was like dealing with an overactive mole – as soon as she filled in one set of holes, he dug another. The women sat on either side of Clare, with Fred and his shopping bag opposite them on a rattan sofa. Ivy picked up her agenda and frowned.

'Before we start, can I raise something?' said Ivy.

'Me too,' said Fred, forcefully.

Guessing she didn't want to hear what Ivy wanted to say, Clare smiled at Fred.

'You need to change the name – it can't be BARF!'

'Fine,' said Clare, fishing around for alternatives.

'He refers to it as a shed,' said Anna, 'so maybe make it BARS?'

'You need to add an F before the S,' said Fred.

'What does the F stand for?' asked Ivy.

'It ends in –ing. I'll let you fill in the three letters between the F and the –ing' said Fred chortling.

Clare exchanged a look with Anna who was trying to hide a grin. 'I understand the sentiment, Fred, but the acronym will appear on official documents. I think it's best to be professional,' she said, as she ticked off item number one on her agenda.

Ivy was wriggling. 'I'm a bit concerned about setting up an action group without giving Richard a chance to explain his position.' *Not again!* No one would laugh louder than Richard if he could hear Ivy dithering about the ethics of trying to stop him. Any minute now, Ivy would suggest they invite him to future BARS meetings just to be fair. 'I don't like going behind someone's back,' Ivy finished, wringing her hands.

'Which brings us neatly back to the agenda,' said Clare. 'We'll circle back to item two, but I agree with Ivy – I think someone should go and speak to Richard. Ask him to reconsider and suggest an alternative use for that field.' She stopped. Fred had his little fingers in both earholes, a bemused expression on his face. 'Everything okay, Fred?' asked Clare.

His eyes wavered at her.

'Hearing aids working?' asked Clare a little louder.

'Eh?' said Fred, poking at his ears.

Clare raised her voice, 'I was suggesting someone should try and convince Richard to change his plans from eggs, maybe—'

Fred sat back against the sofa, his eyes wide. 'No need to shout.'

Clare took a breath. In ten minutes, all they'd achieved was a name. She lowered her voice. 'He could plant soft fruit – strawberries, blueberries, raspberries. Maybe set up a pick-your-own section, which could be popular with the holidaymakers. They can be very profitable.'

'Hard work though. Very labour-intensive,' said Fred. 'All that pruning and irrigation, and soft fruit is mostly hand-picked.'

Clare hadn't realized that. As a teenager, the harvest just happened while she was at school. She hoped there was a machine that picked apples, and that her mother had one. Her eyes misted over. Until now, she hadn't accepted the practical implications of spending months in Devon – she would be harvesting; she must become a farmer. She would have to slay her ghosts and get into the orchard. Mentally she added '*Check mower and locate machine to pick apples*' to her farm task list, and then tuned back into the conversation.

'There must be a machine that picks soft fruit,' mused Fred.

'Technology must have cracked that one,' said Anna.

Clare ran her hands down her face. Her activists were veering off course like tourists following a sat nav down a blind alley.

Anna popped the last of her cake into her mouth and mumbled, 'Maybe a robot . . .'

Clare held up her hands. 'It was just an idea. It's his land. I don't think we care what he does provided it doesn't affect the village. Do we agree someone should go and see him?'

'Yes,' said three voices in unison.

'Who?' asked Clare.

Silence. There was a rustling sound. Clare glanced towards the noise. Stop-it had his nose wedged in Fred's shopping bag, his tail wagging faster than a set of windscreen wipers in a storm. Anna piped up, '*You're* the best person. You're the farmer with all the ideas.'

Clare wasn't a farmer, and more importantly, she didn't want to go. Of all of them, she would elicit the worst reaction

– Richard had her earmarked as a troublemaker. 'Not me. I'm the newbie.'

Anna shot Clare an apologetic look. 'I haven't got time, and I don't think we can ask Ivy or Fred to be the spokesperson.'

Clare was listening to Anna with one eye on Fred's shopping bag. There was a bit too much snuffling going on for her liking. She sighed. 'All right, I'll go. I must warn you though, I'm not convinced he'll see me with an open mind, so I suggest we have a backup plan. Which brings us to our next agenda item. What is our objective? What does BARS want to achieve?'

'Get him to reduce the scale,' said Anna.

'Or nudge it back up the road,' suggested Fred.

'And make sure he's dealing with the waste properly,' added Ivy.

Clare shook her head at them. 'Too tame. Even if he halves the number of birds, it will still ruin Brambleton, and he's not going to move it up the hill. That puts it closer to the Hall. We need to get it stopped.'

'Compromise is always best,' said Ivy.

'You can't compromise with a bully,' said Clare. Stop-it's nose emerged from Fred's shopping bag. He had a new toy; Clare reached over to remove the banana from his mouth. It was covered in visible puncture holes. She tossed it and gave an apologetic look at the owner.

'Do you think we can stop him?' asked Ivy.

'How?' asked Fred, staring at his damaged banana.

'By convincing the Council to refuse permission,' said Clare.

'We had a brilliant turnout at the village hall,' said Anna. 'We need to get everyone to formally object.'

'How do they do that?' asked Ivy.

'They write to the Council asking them to reject his application for a specific reason.'

'Because their houses will drop in value?' said Fred sarcastically.

'No,' said Anna. 'That's not grounds for the Council to refuse permission. They can only reject this on planning grounds.'

'What are they?' asked Clare.

'It's a short list,' said Anna. 'I've spoken to someone who does this for a living and apparently the best grounds for refusing permission on this sort of thing are . . .' She paused, opened a notebook and started reading. 'Noise,' she glanced up and added, 'both from the birds and from the increase in heavy goods vehicles. He's going to need lots of those with 40,000 birds, getting feed in, eggs out. And then there's the visual impact of the shed . . .'

'Don't call it a shed,' shouted Fred. 'A shed's what I store my garden tools in. That building's the size of an airport terminal.'

'Let's call it what it is,' said Clare. 'A factory. This is an industrial process, it's not farming. Sorry, Anna, you were saying.'

'Visual impact,' Anna continued. 'And that's the point – this will alter the look of the area, turn it from a rural landscape into an industrial one.' She dipped her head again, then added, 'Smell and impact on the watercourse.' Anna looked up from her list.

'Right, so that's what we put in the leaflet,' said Clare scribbling down the last words.

'Has everyone read the EIA?' asked Anna.

'The what?' said Fred.

'Here,' said Anna, passing out copies. 'EIA stands for Environmental Impact Assessment. It's a report by experts which examines the theoretical impact the chickens would have on the surrounding environment. Take a look.'

For the third time, Clare flicked through the document. It was full of jargon and legalese. She glanced up at Ivy's furrowed brow and then at Fred, who was using a finger to trace a line under the words, a confused expression on his face. Two intelligent, well-educated people were struggling to understand the document. Was the Council any better at deciphering the weasel words of Richard's expert?

Anna got up, her eyes glued to her watch. 'Must dash.'

'Hang on a tick,' said Clare. 'I thought we were going to start drafting a leaflet.'

'I'm sorry,' said Anna, throwing Clare an apologetic look, 'I must go. And anyway, I haven't a clue what to put in the leaflet.'

'Nor have I,' said Fred, rising to his feet. 'I must see to my dahlias – night-time feeding's best.'

'Not one for me,' said Ivy. Anna was backing away, stuffing her notebook in her bag.

Clare sighed again. 'I'll have a crack at it and circulate something for comments.' It was going to be a late night. She would find somewhere to curl up and pretend she was in London.

Once the others had left, Clare poured herself a glass of wine, flopped on the sofa and surfed the net, intending to approach the task like a new case. Initially, she jotted down all the negatives about Richard's plan, smiling when she started a second page, then ranked them in descending order of nastiness. Top of the list, in contrast to the reassuring conclusions of the EIA, was the environmental impact. The waste would cause air and water pollution. Next on her nasty scale were health risks from ammonia fumes.

She added smell and poor animal welfare, which reminded her of Ivy's stories about the state the Veras had arrived in. Clare refilled her wine glass, then downloaded photographs. She winced at the images of hens in cages, peering forlornly out of bars, thousands of skeletal birds cramped so close together they couldn't move. Bright lights lit up the space all day and all night, mimicking sunlight to encourage laying. These exhausted looking hens had never seen daylight, roosted in a bush at dusk or wriggled in a dust bath on a warm summer's day.

After a couple of hours, Clare had a first draft and a mounting sense of anger. She allowed her true feelings to spill out into the document – it was only a draft – all the pain, hurt and fury at what Hastings had done to her mother was translated into biting accusations of Richard's evil intentions. It would never pass the legal test of verification, but it felt good to write. She drained her glass and for a laugh sent the draft to Anna:

Would love to circulate this version!

Then, wanting to be inclusive, she sent it to Ivy and Fred, too, promising to circulate the real version later that night.

She took a gulp of wine, imagining herself in her London office drafting a document. This leaflet was going to be circulated throughout the village, and before it was she needed to satisfy herself that everything it said was correct; that statements – especially those critical of Richard – were supported by hard evidence. A blog or news article wouldn't be sufficient.

Clare switched to coffee and started backing-up her claims, reluctantly striking out some allegations, toning down the language and inserting phrases like 'Some people experienced in the field of . . .' and 'It's possible that . . .'. Then she attached her revised draft to her BARS email tag, asked for comments and hit the send button with a sense of triumph.

First strike!

In the morning, she would attack again – she was going to visit Richard.

Twelve

Thinking that the earliest she could turn up for an unscheduled meeting with Richard and hope to find him receptive was ten o'clock, Clare decided to spend the early morning finding a way to make her shrunken farm profitable. If Richard's shed went up, it would make Orchard Farm less attractive as a home, and her only hope would be to try and sell it as a business.

The solution wasn't free-range eggs. She planned to supplement her meagre income that way, but without industrial scale production like Richard was proposing, selling eggs was not a money-making venture.

She steeled herself to seek inspiration for the farm in its namesake, but with a hand on the orchard gate, one look at the branches clustered with fruit brought the memory of her last ever conversation with her mother flooding back. She snatched her hand away as if stung by a bee. If only Guy was with her. She wanted to bounce ideas for the farm off him – not that he'd been a great listener, unless the topic was himself or cars. Her father, on the other hand, had been a good listener.

Her father had risen every day at 5 a.m., had a single cup of strong tea and gone milking, returning for a breakfast of two poached eggs on toast at precisely 9.30 a.m. Guy had been a maverick who ordered pizza for breakfast and ate Weetabix for dinner. In the evenings, she sometimes got home from work to find him waiting in the street. He'd bounce towards her, smother her in kisses, and announce he'd hired a sports car for the day and was whisking her out for a late-night drive in the country.

Clare reached into the pig's treat bin, fishing out a handful of the tiny apples her mother must have thinned from the orchard and scattering them over the fence. The pigs rushed off, squealing, falling on the fruit and gobbling greedily.

She raked out the soiled pig bedding, heaping it into a wheelbarrow to deposit in the manure pit, which Ivy had shown her that first morning nearly six weeks ago. It was a concrete-lined set of bins that ensured the farm waste could rot down without run-off leaching into the soil. Unlike Hastings, her mother had been passionate about protecting the environment.

She examined the section Closing the gate on the pigs, she still had no idea how to make the farm profitable, but she knew she had to find a solution. Escorted by Stop-it, Clare trudged to the old milking parlour, a vast barn on the edge of the shrunken acreage. She rested her arms on the fence, gazing at the land now owned by Hastings. For generations, from spring to autumn, the fields had been full of Jersey cows happily grazing in the meadow grass. Now the grass was knee-high, thick and tufty, and she could see ragwort sprouting its deceptive yellow flowers. Hardly inspiring. Clare turned away in disgust. Hastings wasn't using that land and wasn't caring for it.

She strode to the barn and opened the door. It was virtually empty – there was no milking equipment and no railings to separate the animals. The silence was unsettling. This had once been the nerve centre of the farm, where her father had slept when the calves were due. It should be echoing to the gentle hiss of milking machinery. What could she do in here? The place was dry, the floor was level, and it was away from the farmhouse – maybe some sort of events venue? Conferences? Weddings? Something rustled in the straw-strewn ground. Stop-it dashed forwards and pounced. There was a frantic snuffling noise. He pounced again, then returned, but his prize was merely a piece of rope; he waggled it excitedly.

'Not now, boy,' she said dismissively.

She spotted a storage unit in a corner, beside a large Rotavator – what did her mother need that for, she wondered. Had she planned to prepare the soil for vegetables? Clare wandered over, the dog following closely, eager for her to play tug with his newest toy. 'Stop it!' she scolded. Next to the Rotavator was a hunk of metal shaped like an anchor, which Clare assumed was an old part from the milking machinery. She switched her attention to the shelves, which were crammed with so many cardboard boxes it looked like a city skyline packed with towering buildings. Clare pulled one towards her, which was surprisingly heavy, as if it contained books. She lifted the flaps. It was full of bottles. Intrigued, Clare pulled one out, recognizing her mother's spidery writing as she did so:

Cindy's Cider '23

Now this was interesting. Her mother had made apple juice, and never drank alcohol, so why had she started to make cider? Clare lugged a box back to the house, leaving the barn door open for the dog.

There was a spring in her step; if this cider tasted good, it could be a neat solution. She could earn a bit of cash selling last year's vintage, and if she made cider again this year, it would demonstrate the farm was viable as a business. *Cindy's Cider* was quite a catchy name too. There was a minor obstacle to her plan. Clare needed someone else to try it, as an overindulgence in scrumpy as a teenager meant she now retched at even the smell of cider. But the only cider expert she could think of was Sam Hastings, and she wasn't about to ask for his help.

Carrying a second mug of tea and a banana – her first breakfast had ended up in Stop-it's bowl – Clare went upstairs to change for her visit to Hastings. She chose a business suit she'd worn to represent clients against unscrupulous employers. After all, she was defending the villagers, most of whom were no better equipped to fight than her clients. Brushing her hair, she realized she had worn the same suit to her mother's funeral. She would draw strength from that and try to protect her mother's legacy – the orchard. She closed her eyes, vowing to finally get in there tomorrow. She must if she was going to become a cider maker.

Fortuitously, the gates to Brambleton Hall were open. Clare turned in, past the imposing gate lodges with a fluttering feeling in her stomach, shot down the drive and pulled up in front of the Hall. She took a moment to consider the house. It wasn't a classic design; centuries of architects had tinkered with the building, none constrained by concerns about symmetry. The walls were faced with grey ashlar stone and the ground floor windows were double height, each with nine glistening polished glass panels – eighteen panes per window: they must take an army to keep polished. She guessed the house had started out as a classic Tudor manor, with the original great hall at the front and two right-angled wings for private reception rooms. At some point the left wing had been converted into the entrance. Now it displayed a porch in front and an impressive triple-storey extension on that side. Indented from the original dining hall, the extension virtually doubled the length of the building. She concluded that the house was like its owner – a formidable force. Her hands felt clammy, and she ran them down the sides of her trousers.

In her mirror, she saw the front door was open. Magnus, in his butler's uniform, was standing like a soldier on ceremonial guard. In this heat? Wasn't there a summer uniform? Hearing his footsteps crunch over the gravel towards her, she reached for her handbag and shuffled out of the car.

'Good morning, madam,' said Magnus. 'Is Mrs Hastings expecting you?'

Clare offered the butler a smile, but his face was impassive. There was no sign that he recognized her from their conversation at the summer drinks party.

'It's not Mrs Hastings I'm after. It's Mr Hastings.'

'Ah. Do you have an appointment?'

She shook her head. 'I was hoping he could spare me ten minutes. Have you thought any more about my discussing the heating of your cottage with Mr Hastings?'

Briefly the butler closed his eyes. 'I would be grateful if you did not do that, madam.' Magnus shook his head, as if reminding himself of his duties, widened his eyes and spoke. 'And who should I say is calling?'

She gave her name. The butler nodded. 'This way please, madam.'

Inside, he pointed to a pair of leather library chairs positioned either side of a stone fireplace. 'Please take a seat and I'll see if Mr Hastings is available.' Clare did as she was instructed, choosing the chair closest to the front door. Magnus was wearing soft shoes which seemed to glide silently over the polished flagstones. She watched his departing back until he disappeared, leaving her gazing around the entrance hall. It was as long as a tennis court, but only a third as wide, which gave the illusion that ceiling was lower than its twelve-foot height. The walls were lined with wood, painted a soft fawn colour, and decorated with what she knew from her days studying Tudor history for A level was called 'bolection moulding'. The technique created little frames, which looked like a series of blank canvases. Some of the uppermost squares were painted with coats of arms, splashes of bright yellow, red, blue and gold.

The ceiling was painted in the palest pink and covered in fine cream-coloured plasterwork, but it lacked elegance and looked slightly crude. There were plate-sized oblongs of interlocking cornicing with a single small rose in the centre, but the shapes weren't uniform. Some were fatter, some longer, as if a group of artists had produced their own interpretation.

As the minutes ticked by, it occurred to her that Richard probably never admired his entrance hall, and suspected the beauty was lost in a haze of familiarity, in the same way she dismissed her own entrance hall in London. That thought reminded her she needed to shoehorn in a trip to pack up her flat. She would take a couple of days off and enjoy a few Indian takeaways when she was there. Her mother's stock of prepared meals was dwindling.

As she waited, she sat asking herself what it would be like to live in such an enormous house. Would it be fun, intimidating or would you just live in the kitchen like most families? She heard purposeful footsteps, then Richard Hastings, dressed in a jacket and tie, appeared at the end of the hallway. Magnus stood a deferential distance behind him.

'Good morning, Ms Hetherington. Sam told me to expect a visit.' At the mention of Sam's name, Clare felt herself tense, but told herself to keep calm. After all, she had known he was spying. 'What can I offer you to drink? Magnus, I'll have tea. And for you?' he asked, inclining his head her way.

'Tea works for me.'

'India, China or herbal?' asked Magnus.

What was this charade? They both knew she wasn't here on a social call. 'You choose,' she said neutrally.

'Let's do this in my study,' said Richard. Clare followed him into a second hallway. This one was triple height, its walls lined with heavy gilded pictures of what she assumed were generations of Hastings' ancestors. Richard pushed open a huge wooden door. She scurried after him, catching the door as it was closing. Her quarry marched on ahead, leaving Clare gawping at the room she found herself in. An intricate painted wallpaper covered all four walls. It depicted Chinese figures pursuing everyday activities: hoeing, fishing with spears, men with a pole over their shoulders, pails of water balanced on either end. The colours had been muted by the passage of time, but the impact wasn't lessened. How long had this hung here? Richard was letting himself through another door and she rushed to catch up.

By the time she entered yet another spectacular room, Richard was already sitting behind a desk, his elbows propped on the leather top, hands cupping his chin, a determined look in his eyes. 'Take a seat,' he said, making it sound like an instruction and indicating two carved wooden armchairs in front of his desk.

Clare sat, squashing her handbag onto the seat beside her. She took a moment to admire her surroundings and gather her confidence. It wasn't like any study she'd seen before, and she suspected he had chosen the location to project power. Twenty feet above her hung impressive plasterwork – there were elegant birds with what looked like fish suspended from their mouths, sheaves of wheat and fat cherubs. 'What a beautiful room,' she said. 'It must be inspirational to work in here.'

'I've never sought inspiration in here. This is my study because it's at the furthest extremity, cut off from the rest of the house.'

'Well, it would inspire me,' she said.

A sour expression crossed his face. 'That's because you don't have to grapple with the cost of maintaining it,' he said.

She didn't want to antagonize him further, so simply thanked him for seeing her.

He nodded.

'I think you know why I've come,' she said.

There was another nod.

'Your brother will have told you that feelings are running high in the village. What you're proposing will have major implications for a lot of people.'

He arched his eyebrows but maintained his silence. In a peculiar way his refusal to engage, far from making her nervous, was steeling her backbone. She had plenty of experience dealing with prickly opponents, and now selected her words carefully. 'I've come to ask you to consider an alternative form of farming.'

He gave the self-satisfied smile of someone waiting for the first opportunity to say no. 'Like growing apples?' he asked, a hint of sarcasm in his voice. 'That may work for Sam, but not for me.'

No, she thought, he was an impatient beast. He wouldn't be prepared to wait years for apple trees to mature. She kept a neutral tone in her voice. 'What about soft fruit?'

'Nah. Overrated. I'm an egg man myself.'

'Have you ever kept chickens, because you see I have.' She gave a little laugh, a picture in her mind of Captain Hilts stuffing his craw. 'They're a lot of work. Rewarding, but time-consuming.'

'I've done my research,' Hastings said, and his look warned that he was confident of his position.

She tried again. 'I don't think they're very lucrative.'

'Experts have pored over my business plan,' he snapped. 'I don't need you to comment on my profit forecast.'

His tone disturbed her concentration, and her next words came out more rushed than she would have liked. 'Can't we work together? As a village? People have come up with lots of interesting ideas for those fields. What about a campsite?'

'Nope.'

'Or a pick your own? Fields of strawberries . . .?'

'Eggs.'

'There's a lot of money to be made selling pumpkins for Halloween. Children like to come and choose their own . . .' She tailed off, disturbed both by the look of power projected from those dark eyes and the contrasting sound of her own voice, which seemed whiny, desperate and feeble. She took a breath, trying to rejuvenate her fighting spirit, and said in the same voice she used to scold Stop-it. 'Have you thought about how this will affect the village?'

'I've worked hard all my life. I've had to. I don't lead the same lackadaisical life my brother does – he was always the favourite. Unlike you and your group of rabble-rousers, I'm not speculating about what will happen. I've paid for an expert to check there won't be any impact on the village.'

She wanted to retort that he'd done nothing of the sort. That he'd merely paid someone to reach his preferred conclusion. Clare couldn't look at his supercilious smile and glanced away. 'Is there anything I can say or do to encourage you to reconsider?'

'Frankly, no. I think you'll find this is all being overblown. People don't like the idea because they're frightened of change. You're from London; you don't understand rural life. They'll get used to seeing the sheds and we'll all move on.'

She had to connect with his human side. There must be a way. The seconds ticked away, then she said, 'But what about parking for the village hall? You play bridge. There must be forty cars on Thursday nights. How are we going to park forty cars in the road?'

'You exaggerate. There will only be thirty-nine. Magnus will chauffeur me there and back.'

She heard a door creak and Magnus entered, as ramrod straight as an officer carrying the regimental colours, holding a tray with an elaborate silver tea service. While the butler poured, Clare inhaled, then slowly let her temper flow out with her breath. She tried to think of something which might persuade Richard to reconsider, but her mind was as blank as Magnus's deadpan expression.

She drank her tea, listening to Richard boast about his plans. Seeing him had been a waste of time. He wouldn't engage because his mind was made up. The only solution was to persuade the Council to refuse permission. She must convince them before Richard and his 'experts' sealed the deal.

Returning to the farm, she noticed a tray of eggs had been taken from the table by the gate. She trotted over and found a folded bank note in the honesty pot. She plucked it out, savouring its crisp smoothness; this represented the first tiptoe out of the mess that she blamed Hastings for creating. Behind her, Stop-it gave a rumbling growl. She turned. He was shaking a toy secured in his jaws. She fondled his ears, then pushed past him, drawn to a large cardboard box on the doorstep. She felt the toy graze the back of her trousers. 'Not now, boy, I've a mountain to climb.' On the box, written in felt tip, was a message:

I thought you might find a use for these. Trish
xxx

Clare lifted the flaps; inside were pots of paint, rollers, paint brushes, sandpaper and tools she had never even seen before. What was her friend thinking? Clare didn't do DIY. She carried the box inside and upstairs to her mother's old bedroom. When she had more money, she'd pay someone to come and redecorate.

Then, determined to finally slay those ghosts, she marched outside to the apple orchard.

She stopped at the gate, forcing herself to let in the memory of the last time she'd spoken to her mother. Seven years ago, Clare and Guy had returned to Orchard Farm after discussing their wedding plans with Ivy, each tripping over the other's words as they chattered excitedly. Cindy had met them at the gate, wearing blue oil-stained overalls. Clare had hidden her irritation. Her mother had been wearing those overalls since Friday, not even changing when Clare had attempted to cook a nice dinner on Saturday night and laid the dining room table. Clare squeezed Guy's hand, whispering, 'Sorry, I don't know what's wrong with her this weekend. Why don't you pack up the car and I'll make an excuse for us to get away early.'

There was an answering squeeze, which sent a wave of happiness pulsing through her limbs, and for a moment Clare questioned if it was simply jealousy eating her mother. Was she lonely? Was seeing Clare wreathed in happiness forcing Cindy to confront her own solitude? Her mother juggled a packet of cigarettes. She pulled one out, lit it, took a long drag and let smoke trickle out sideways. With forced jollity Clare said, 'We've had such fun. Ivy's fine with the idea of having the wedding rings delivered down the aisle in a miniature remote-controlled rally car.'

'Could we go for a walk, please?' said Cindy, looking directly at Clare. 'Just the two of us.'

Clare dropped Guy's hand. Her heart was pounding; there was something wrong. Was her mother ill? Had smoking finally caught up with her? She fell into step beside her mother, breathing in the familiar smell of tobacco smoke that clung to those overalls. 'What's on your mind?' asked Clare.

Her mother released the catch on the gate to the orchard, and ushered Clare inside. She took another puff of her cigarette, this time letting the smoke escape through her nostrils as she spoke. 'I love you, Clare, and it's because I love you that I have to say this.' Clare didn't reply. She twisted her engagement ring round and round with her thumb. She had a nagging suspicion this concerned Guy. 'He's not right for you.'

'You barely know him. This is only the second time you've met him.'

'I know he's not the one. You are your father's daughter; you work hard and play fair. He's the opposite. He's scrounging an easy ride off you and when the novelty is over, you'll regret it.'

Hot anger pulsed through Clare's veins. Cindy had been outside all weekend. She'd made no effort to get to know Guy, simply made a snap judgement based on prejudice. 'I make enough to support us. He's a talented driver, unlikely to make money, but we don't need it. He brings other things to our relationship.'

Her mother ground the butt of her cigarette beneath a heel, picked up the stub and tucked it in a pocket. 'He'll break your heart.'

Clare's mind clouded with a fog of rage; her hands bunched into fists. 'He's different; that doesn't make him unreliable. Not every driver drifts from one rally to the next picking up women along the way.'

'But what's the hurry?' said her mother, pulling out another cigarette. 'Why are you rushing into this wedding when you've only known the boy six months?'

'He's not a boy,' Clare said through clenched teeth. 'We're both in our mid-thirties and anyway, I know my own mind.' Her mother struck a match. The rasping sound fuelled Clare's temper, and she forced herself to count to ten before saying in a conciliatory tone. 'Didn't you know Dad was the one for you when you met him?'

'Exactly,' said Cindy triumphantly. 'I'd known him all my life. He courted me from afar.' A smile came over her mother's face. 'I thought he wasn't interested, but then he plucked up the courage to ask me out and . . . well, the rest is history.'

Clare smiled too, recalling her parents' happy marriage; a bit too dull and predictable for her, but it had worked for them. Then, like a hidden knife, her mother lunged for Clare's heart. 'That's why I know Guy isn't serious,' she said, her voice soft but firm. Her mother waved her arms out wide, taking in the rows of trees heavy with fruit. 'Your father and I loved the same things; we planted most of these trees together.' Cindy bent down, picking up a windfall apple from the grass and holding it to her nose. 'This orchard was just as special for him as it is for me . . .' She paused, her fingers brushing gently over the apple's smooth skin, before looking up again, her eyes distant, full of memory. 'That's why I scattered his ashes in here. Right here, under these trees.' She exhaled slowly, as if releasing a long-held breath. 'Come back down to Devon. You'll find the right man for you. I'm sure he's here.'

'So that's what this is about? The farm? You want me to find some farmer's boring second son who won't inherit and marry him? That's *your* dream, and in case you hadn't worked it out for yourself, it's *not* mine.'

Cindy shook her head and repeated her words. 'Don't marry him. He'll break your heart.'

Clare backed away and started running. She heard her mother calling after her. 'I know you. He's not the man for you.' Clare heard footsteps pounding behind her, the rasping, heavy breathing of the seasoned smoker, and picked up her pace. She could see Guy sitting in the car, their bags on the back seat. He glanced up and a look of alarm flashed across his face. Clare shot into the passenger seat, yanking at the seatbelt so sharply it jammed.

She looked up, saw her mother's crumpled face and said to Guy, 'Drive. Just get me away. I don't ever want to come back here again.'

Clare didn't tell Guy what had happened. She never told him, and he never asked. Clare made her choice and that left no room for a relationship with her mother. They were married in a registry office so had no need to come back to Devon. For years afterwards, apples didn't feature on Clare's shopping list; the taste sent her somersaulting back to that row. She took a final look at the trees now, swaying gently in the breeze, then without entering the orchard she turned and trudged back inside.

Clare spent the afternoon finalizing the campaign leaflet. None of the other BARS activists had any comments, so she tinkered with the words and then emailed it to a colleague, Sally – a defamation lawyer – asking her to cast a careful eye over it. Richard was in a feisty spirit, and she didn't want to be accused of libel.

On Friday evening, with the green light from Sally, Clare strode to the village armed with hundreds of leaflets in a shoulder bag and Stop-it secured to a lead. She started at the top of the village, pushing one through each of the old almshouses' letter boxes, then she came up with a better idea and headed for the Smugglers Inn.

It was only six thirty and customers were sparse. Behind the bar, Rose was polishing glasses as she chatted to Sam and Fred. When Clare walked in, all three looked her way and Fred leaned over on his barstool and reached down. 'Come here, boy,' he clucked. Clare let the lead fall slack, and the dog ambled over to the outstretched hand.

'Don't feed him any crisps please, Fred, he'll get fat.' Clare stood with her back to both men and beckoned Rose over.

'Do you mind if I leave a few of these here and next door in the shop?' she asked, dropping half her leaflets on the bar.

Rose put down her cloth. She picked up a leaflet, ran her eyes over it, then put it back. 'Can't you leave us out of this?' she asked, rubbing at a glass so vigorously Clare was concerned it might crack.

Sam spoke: 'I think Rose is in a tricky position. My brother is her landlord.'

Clare rounded on the eavesdropper. Tonight his hair didn't look distinguished, and his eyes didn't seem dazzling. There was nothing attractive about this man. He was cut from the same arrogant cloth as his brother and enjoying basking in the family's power, just like he'd done all those years ago when he had just used her for fun.

'I know that, thank you,' she said, turning her back on Sam again and dragging Stop-it sideways, distancing him from the enemy. 'Yes, the Hastings family are nasty enough to find a way of moving you on if you were to publicly oppose them. I won't put you in that position, Rose.' She snatched up the leaflets. 'Come on, Stop-it.'

Banging the door shut behind her, Clare turned her face to the sea, letting the wind whip into her face, driving salt into her eyes and making them smart. How could she fight a family who controlled this village as tightly as a feudal lord, punishing anyone who opposed them?

She could only hope that the man she was meeting in half an hour would have the answer. Further up the hill, Clare's luck improved. Trish was preparing for the evening crowd, her slim arms transferring trays of muffins and scones to the kitchen, returning to the counter bearing savoury treats. She looked up from her task, a steely look in her hazel eyes. 'I see you got my message: I'm going to help on the QT. My business is doomed if he gets permission; if those are the leaflets Anna told me about, leave me fifty to start with.' Trish flashed her a warm smile. 'I knew you'd see this off.'

The door opened and in walked a man so tall he had to stoop to get through the doorway. He wore knee-length shorts, a washed-out T-shirt and a battered straw hat which he removed to reveal short salt and pepper hair.

'That's your man,' muttered Trish.

'Bill Matthews?' asked Clare.

'That's me,' he said, tossing his hat onto a corner table. 'Your local councillor at your service.' Trish took their order, and Clare took the opportunity to pull a leaflet out of her bag. He waved it away. 'I've already seen one,' he said, patting a pocket. 'Very punchy! Very brave. Very quick. I'm impressed.'

She smiled. She wasn't expecting or seeking praise, but she'd worked hard on those words, and Bill had got hold of a leaflet astonishingly quickly.

'Look, I'm on your side,' he said.

She lifted her hands in despair. 'So why hasn't the Planning Officer returned my calls?'

'There's no point. He can't tell you anything you want to hear. But the good news is, I've escalated the matter. It will be heard by the full Planning Committee.'

This sounded promising. She chose her words carefully. 'How do we ensure that they make the right decision?'

'The most important thing you can do is to make sure the parish council vote it down.'

Clare hadn't thought about the parish council, not since she learned from Ivy that it had been the catalyst to catapult her mother and her farm onto Richard's radar.

'Right. I'll get onto it.' she said, taking a gulp of wine. 'Do you know who the councillors are and when they meet?'

'Once a month. There's a website. Find out when the next meeting is, and I suspect this will be on the agenda.' He sank the rest of his wine and reached out for his hat. 'They'll be a bit cagey but try speaking to them in advance. They're mostly farming stock. It took them a while to trust me – I don't farm. But your family's farmed for generations. Oh, and get a big turnout. There's nothing like a big show of voters to help a councillor decide which way to jump!'

'Maybe I should start with the chairperson?'

'I don't recommend that.'

'Why not?'

'It's Richard Hastings.'

Clare let out a soft moan. She would be willing to bet that Richard had cajoled or bribed every parish councillor into his pocket. She only hoped enough of them were as principled as her mother had been.

Thirteen

In London, Clare stuffed a month's worth of post under an arm and carried her overnight bag up the stairs. She unlocked the internal door to her flat, letting out a blend of mustiness from the old wooden floors and the comforting aroma of brewed tea. She tossed the post on a table, then wandered from room to room, unscrewing locks and pushing up sash windows. Soon, there was a warm breeze blowing through the flat, the sound of honking traffic and wailing sirens, and she felt an inner peace at the familiarity of being at home.

In the kitchen, which seemed narrower than she remembered, Clare secured her task list to the fridge with a magnet Guy had given her for their first wedding anniversary: *Trust me I'm a barrister.* She gave a wry laugh. He'd never cared about the difference between a solicitor and a barrister.

'Same difference,' he had said. 'Lawyers! You all charge through the nose and by the hour.'

This to Guy was an insult. If you charged for your time, you were prevented from being a free spirit by the ever-present demands of billable hours. At points in her career, she had been inclined to agree with him, but for the next ten months she wouldn't have to worry about charging anyone. She did, however, have to manage her time carefully. If she wanted to attend the parish council meeting, Clare had just two days to pack up the flat and gorge on her favourite takeaways.

Clare started in the spare bedroom, which no one had used for five years; it had been Guy's home gym. Being a rally driver required stamina, strength and quick reflexes and when he was separated from his beloved car he trained to improve his reaction times. It was also where Guy and his co-driver refined and memorized pace notes.

The room had never previously struck her as small but comparing it to the one she'd slept in for the last couple of months, today it seemed cramped. She opened the wardrobe. The sight of cardboard boxes piled in a precarious stack in the space for hanging clothes was like an arrow to her heart. She sagged onto the bed. She should have done this years ago.

After Guy died, lacking the strength to decide what to keep, Clare had sold the gym equipment, replaced it with a bed and bundled everything else into these boxes, stuffing in clothes, toiletries, maps and Guy's notes. Unable to separate keepsakes from junk, she'd sealed it all up together.

Clare shook open a bin bag, pulled out a box at random and delved into the past. Half an hour later, the rubbish bag was bulging, and a small collection of papers and trinkets lay on the duvet. She picked up a glossy brochure - a hotel on the Isle of Wight where they had stayed when Guy competed in a rally there. He'd won, and that night they'd joyfully celebrated with champagne, the thrill of his victory electrifying the air between them. They had lingered at dinner, hands brushing and later they'd made love. She held the brochure a moment longer before setting it aside, then rifled through the rest of the pile, dispatching crumpled maps and scribbled pace notes into the bin liner beside her. As she worked, a photo slipped free, fluttering to the floor.

She bent to pick it up. It was Guy with a much younger red-haired woman. She flipped it over, recognizing Guy's squiggly handwriting:

Hannah and me.

She frowned. Who was Hannah? Was she the girlfriend of another driver? She couldn't recall ever meeting her. She peered more closely. There was a look of awe on the woman's face – she must have been one of Guy's groupies. *Well, there'd been plenty of those*, she thought. Clare had gotten used to them early on in the relationship; it was something you learned to live with if you were dating a good-looking rally driver. So, what was unnerving her about this one? She couldn't put her finger on it, but something told her to be wary. She dropped the photo into the bin bag thinking it was odd that this was the first photo of one of his groupies she'd found.

She got up off the bed and smoothed down her blouse. She still had to clear out all of her belongings; she didn't have time to comb through the rest of Guy's stuff. She would take it all back with her to Brambleton

Clare wiggled the last box into the footwell and shut the door. The boot was full, and the back seat piled so high she would have to rely on her wing mirrors. Clare joined the queuing traffic on the South Circular. Being stationary was irritating, not just because it delayed her journey, but also because it allowed her mind to wander, and she kept seeing that photo of Guy with 'Hannah'. What did it mean? Maybe she wasn't a groupie – just a friend of his co-driver or the sister of another driver? But if so, why had Clare never met her?

Maybe Hannah had connections with another more successful rally team and Guy hadn't mentioned her because he didn't want to get his wife's hopes up? But that couldn't be it. Guy was supremely confident in his talents; he would have told her if there was a sniff of a lucrative transfer.

To distract herself, once she was on the motorway, Clare pulled into the inside lane and called her travel agent on her hands-free phone, asking her with a heavy sigh to cancel the rest of this year's bookings. She had barely thought about her sabbatical in the past week – she had been so busy with BARS, but vaguely recalled she should be somewhere in Croatia now. She finished the call and told herself the glass was half-full – she had only cancelled the first six months of her trip. Then she consulted a scribbled list taped to the dashboard and, using her voice command, started calling the five parish councillors. The first three didn't pick up, but the fourth call was answered by a woman with a strong North-Devonian accent: 'Pat Mayhew.'

'Pat, my name's Clare Hetherington. I wanted to talk to you about the upcoming parish council meeting.'

'Ah, I knew your mother. She was a fine woman. What's on your mind?'

'Chickens.'

'Umm.'

'Can I ask your views on the planning application?'

There was a snort. 'I won't talk in advance of the meeting, but if that jumped-up— If he thinks we're all going to roll over and vote in favour just because he's in the chair . . .'

A smile spread across Clare's face, and she thanked Pat for her time.

Traffic whipped past the car while Clare thought about how Cindy would have reacted to Richard's plans. Her mother would have been apoplectic if he'd even hinted that unpaid service on the parish council entitled him to preferential treatment. Feeling confident, she called the final name – Hazel Jones.

For a second time she was lucky: her call was answered, and Hazel was happy to talk about chickens. But that was when Clare's luck ran out. Hazel pointed out that the chicken farm would provide three permanent jobs, and, in Hazel's opinion, if people didn't like the sight and smell of farming, they shouldn't move to the countryside. No prizes for guessing which way Ms Jones planned to vote. That was one in each corner – to win, BARS needed two out of the other three councillors to stand up to Richard, who wouldn't be able to vote.

It took another four hours to reach Brambleton. To keep her mind off Guy, Clare repeatedly called but failed to reach the other councillors. She would have to wait another night to discover their views.

Fourteen

All day, Clare's chest felt tight. She had set aside the morning to pay her London bills, but quickly realized her finances were so dire that she would have to contact the suppliers and arrange a monthly repayment schedule. Unable to face that task, she ended up outside repairing the lawn. She picked at a sandwich for lunch, pulling out the cheese filling and dropping it into Stop-it's snapping jaws, and by the evening, for once, she was glad she didn't eat alone, scraping a virtually untouched omelette into Stop-it's bowl.

Washing up the frying pan, Clare could feel her hands shaking with nerves. What was going to happen tonight? She hadn't been able to reach any of the other three councillors. Until she'd spoken to Hazel Jones, it hadn't occurred to her that people unconnected to Richard might side with him. Now she was worried that farmers would share Hazel's view. Most farmed dairy herds. She recalled her parents in the milking parlour, working as a close-knit team, her mother diligently hosing away slurry while her father encouraged the herd back outside the barn. As a toddler, Clare had played with Jet on a ledge made from hay bales, and didn't recall being disturbed by the smells or sounds of farming. But farmers were probably fed up with townies whingeing about run-off from slurry. Why should they pay thousands to dispose of waste when water companies pumped raw human sewage into the sea with impunity?

At six o'clock it started raining. Looking at the damp, dreary sky, Clare gave a soft groan. People wouldn't come out in this weather. They couldn't summon an Uber like you could in London. It was still spitting at six thirty, when Clare wrapped herself in a raincoat, pulled up the hood and set off on foot. Striding towards Brambleton Hall, several cars passed her, kicking up spray which splashed onto her coat. She trudged on, viewing the dirty water as a small price to pay for a big turnout, and pushing to the back of her mind the nagging fact the village hall was at the top of Brambleton, and there were plenty of other places those cars might be going.

Rounding the last bend, Clare plodded downhill keeping her eyes on her destination. There was a trickle of people. At the entrance, she took a breath and went in. The clock in the outer hallway told her there were still five minutes before the scheduled start time. She pushed at the inner door, letting out a buzz of voices, walked in and gasped. There must have been 200 people. All the seats were full and there were so many people standing she couldn't see a space for herself.

At the far end of the room was a table where five people were talking among themselves. There was a forced air of purposefulness to the group, as if each was conscious of performing in front of an unexpected audience. An empty chair at the table seemed to wink at Clare. The chairperson was missing.

Clare stayed where she was and leaned her back against the wall. Beside her, the door creaked open. There was a ripple of noise, and she craned her neck to see who it was. In the doorway, dressed in a suit and tie, stood Richard. A slow clap echoed round the room. Someone started hissing and the noise swelled. Richard's face coloured and she wondered if it was due to embarrassment or rage. He rolled his eyes and marched to the long table, taking the empty seat, spoke briefly to the woman on his right, then rose again. The crowd settled. Richard's voice was calm, but there was a hint of warning in it.

'As the Chair of Brambleton parish council, I'd like to extend a warm welcome to you all. We meet once a month; the dates and times are displayed in the village shop and outside on the noticeboard. It's the first time I've seen most of you here,' he said, making it sound like a reprimand, 'and I assume you aren't familiar with the protocol. We conduct business without interruptions. At appropriate points there will be an opportunity for you to speak, but if you disrupt proceedings, you will be . . .' He paused, running his eyes over the crowd, then rested his gaze on Clare for a moment before he finished, '. . . ejected.'

Clare reflected on the words he'd chosen. Not 'asked to leave', but 'ejected'. Far from being rattled by his reception, it looked like Hastings viewed it as a challenge. Clare had a fleeting image of Captain Hilts chasing down a hen and wished she could banish Hastings to the cooler.

Richard steered his fellow councillors through the tedium of village problems. There was a detailed discussion about a troublesome pothole on the main road close to Richard's entrance gates. Apparently, that stretch was built above a spring, so no sooner was it repaired than the water worked its way through the tarmac.

A woman spoke and Clare recognized her voice: Pat Mayhew. Clare took a closer look at her ally. She was slim, well-dressed with neat grey hair swept off her face and tied in a ponytail. She wore glasses and a pair of long earrings. Pat's confident air suggested a career in the police or military, where she was used to commanding respect.

'We could solve this permanently by shifting the road, moving it a few metres to the right,' she said.

'I don't think the budget would stretch to a bypass,' said Richard.

'It would be a minor diversion, a few metres; hardly a bypass. And in the long run,' said Pat, still looking directly at Richard, 'it might prove less expensive.'

'You don't know that' he said defiantly. 'The spring might run for some distance, and this is just the current weak spot. The water might just work its way up elsewhere if we move the road.'

Pat shook her head, making her earrings swing. 'Simple to get someone to investigate where the underground water is.'

'So, you're a water diviner now, are you, Pat? Let's move on,' said Richard.

Undefeated, Pat asked. 'Do you think the owner of that land would object to selling it?'

Richard glared at Pat, making Clare smile. Everyone knew who owned that stretch of land – it was a sliver, lost in the rounding of the estate's acreage. Why was Pat goading Richard? Was this the warm-up act to Hastings' planning application? Clare hoped the three councillors she *hadn't* spoken to were as feisty as Pat Mayhew.

Pat offered to call the Council to ask if they would consider her idea. Richard tapped his pencil on the table, the sound mimicking his irritation, but gave in. Pat sucked in her cheeks – Clare suspected to hide a smile – and wriggled in her seat. *Pat Mayhew, 1 – Richard Hastings, 0*, thought Clare. The village was fighting back.

'Moving on,' said Richard, a note of frustration in his voice. 'Now we come on to planning applications. Tonight, there are two, both agricultural. I will remain in the chair for the first, then I will absent myself in favour of Hazel Jones for the discussion of the second.'

Clare huffed quietly to herself. Hastings had planted a councillor who was in favour of his application in the chair. 'Has everyone had a chance to consider the first application?'

Papers rustled, plans unfolded, and Richard invited the applicant to speak. A man in his forties, with the ruddy complexion of a farmer, stood up. He looked about as relaxed as a child waiting to see the dentist, and spoke in a slightly shaky voice, explaining why he needed an extension to his milking parlour. Poor man thought Clare. Rotten luck his application coincided with Richard's. None of the councillors had any questions and heaving a huge sigh of relief, the man flopped back into his seat.

Richard addressed his fellow councillors. 'It's important to support the farming community, as we're a rural economy. I'm in favour. Who else?'

Five additional hands went in the air.

'Right, I'll pass the baton to Hazel,' said Richard. 'I'll wait by the door in case you want me to answer any questions.'

He walked towards Clare, his arms swinging. There was a triumphant look in his eyes that made her back stiffen. He knew every one of those councillors, had served alongside them for years. Richard would know how to sway them. Had he bribed any of them like he'd tried to bribe her mother? Was this already stitched-up? At the door he paused, and Clare held her breath, waiting for a cocky taunt. His eyes narrowed and he looked her in the eye, seemingly reluctant to break away. He grinned and opened the door. Slowly it hissed shut, but she was conscious of his presence and suspected he'd be listening in from behind the door.

Like actors readying themselves for a key scene, the councillors were fidgeting, wriggling and toying with their papers. One of them pulled themselves closer to the table, her seat scraping noisily on the floor, then she spoke forcefully. 'I'm assuming the chair for the next agenda item.'

So, this was Hazel Jones, thought Clare. Although not as trimly turned out as her opposition, Hazel looked every inch a match for Pat Mayhew. She was as short as Ivy, with thick, curly black hair that covered her ears, and she wore a sweatshirt, loose trousers and trainers. But Clare wasn't taken in by the casual appearance. She had spoken to the woman. Hazel was a farmer, and Clare recognized the same determined look in those eyes that used to be present in her mother's. Hastings had a strong backup; Hazel wouldn't give up easily.

'An application by Mr Richard Hastings,' said Hazel, her dark eyes darting at each of the remaining councillors before circling the audience as if warning them all to behave, 'to erect a shed.'

There was a rumble of voices, then from the back of the room, a man spoke. 'That's not a shed, that's a factory.'

The room erupted into laughter. Hazel shouted over the noise. 'Quiet.'

As if on cue, a baby started crying. Hazel muttered something under her breath, then said. 'The council must be allowed to discuss business without interruptions.' She shook out a sheaf of papers, arranging one on the table and anchoring it with water glasses. 'This is a site plan. It shows where the two buildings would be erected, and you were all sent a detailed report which concluded that there would be no negative environmental impact from the erection of these buildings.

'Rubbish!' shouted the same male voice.

'Final warning,' said Hazel, her eyes darting round the crowd like a sheep dog searching for a wandering charge. 'One more peep out of anyone and they'll be outside.' She turned to the councillors. 'Richard has kindly arranged for one of the experts who conducted the research to be here this evening to answer any questions.' Hazel waved a hand at a man sitting in the front row who rose. 'This is Peter Roberts.'

Clare thought that the best way to describe Peter was 'boffin'. He was tall and slightly stooped, with wispy grey hair, a thick moustache and wire-framed glasses. Peter wore smart trousers and, despite the heat, had a V-neck jumper on over his shirt and tie.

'I have one,' shouted the man who'd interrupted twice already.

'Quiet!' snapped Hazel. 'The matter is not yet open for general discussion, only for councillors.'

'I have a question,' said Pat, her earrings dancing as she waggled her head. 'I'm at a loss to understand how you conclude 40,000 birds won't result in,' – she ran her fingers over a line in the report – 'and I quote . . . "*any noticeable adverse smell*".' She raised her head, sat back and crossed her arms. 'I reckon they'll be able to smell them in Barnstaple.' There was a ripple of laughter. Clare decided to try to catch Pat after the meeting and co-opt her into BARS.

Richard's expert appeared unfazed. 'This is a farming district. People are used to the smell of animals.'

'I might be,' chirped Pat. 'We farm dairy. But my sister doesn't and nor does the rest of the village.'

For a moment, Peter chewed his lip, his moustache shifting like whiskers on a wary animal, but he didn't have an answer to that one.

'What about waste?' said Pat. 'I notice the plan is to invest in a storage facility and produce fertilizer. How can we be sure that it's done properly? Where's the oversight coming from?'

Peter spoke confidently, making Clare think that waste was his speciality. 'Mr Hastings has to follow industry guidelines,' he said, then spoke in a droning voice that reminded Clare of sitting beside her mother as a child listening to a cattle auctioneer. Peter talked about the regulations covering waste management. They sounded marvellous, but Clare was itching to make him answer the question Pat had posed – who was going to ensure Hastings stuck to these rules? She bit her tongue, convinced Richard would have warned Hazel who the chief troublemakers were. Hazel wouldn't hesitate to remove Clare.

Peter was summing up and Clare wished he had a less monotonous voice; it was difficult to concentrate in the heat. She ran a hand around her throat, using her fingers to open the neck of her blouse. Peter drawled on. Clare decided he was not the sort of man you'd want to end up sitting next to on a long train journey. 'All of those tests would be conducted periodically to ensure the safe management.' Clare yawned, stretched her hands over her head and glanced at her watch. In the middle of the crowd, she spotted Ivy, her head lolling on her chest. To Clare, Peter's words sounded hazy. 'He's also investigating installing an anaerobic digester.'

Clare gave a start.

'A what?' asked Pat, suddenly sitting as bolt upright as Stop-it did whenever Clare sat down to eat.

'It's a machine that will convert all of the manure into electricity,' said Peter, beaming. The crowd erupted. There were shouts of 'What next?' and 'He can't do this to us.' People started stamping their feet. Hazel stood, her hands on her hips, her eyes tracking across the crowd. 'Quiet! Or I shall have this room cleared.' She waved her hands at the audience, but it seemed to fan the flames of anger, and the noise rose.

Clare imagined Richard, impotent behind the door. She turned, saw his face smudged against the glass and a smile crept over her own. Pat and the woman sitting next to her were shaking their heads, muttering to each other. Clare was desperate for Pat to quiz Peter further. What were the implications of having an anaerobic digester in that field? How big was it? Was it noisy, smelly, dangerous? Was this Richard's secret goal? She didn't trust him to look after hens properly; she certainly didn't want him in charge of a gas field.

In the centre of the crowd, Fred rose, waving a fist at Peter. 'You're going to install a gas factory yards from where I live,' he shouted.

Peter went completely still. His eyebrows furrowed and his voice faltered as he spoke. 'It's just an early thought and it would be . . . the subject of a separate planning application.'

Hazel ran her eyes slowly and purposefully over her fellow councillors. 'Anything else for Richard's expert?'

There were no further questions from the councillors. Hazel glanced around the room uneasily, then invited questions from the floor. 'One at a time. Raise your hand if you would like to speak.'

A teenager was the first to catch Hazel's eye. Clare judged him to be about fifteen. The youth was tall and slim, with long limbs. He spoke to his shoes, but he spoke from his heart, asking the councillors to think about the environmental damage Richard's project threatened. His voice wavered as he spoke about mutual respect for animals, saying humans had a responsibility to use their power fairly, to allow animals to live as natural a life as possible, not exploit them to maximize profits. Clare turned but there was no face pressed against the glass. Concerns for animal welfare wouldn't make Hastings change his mind. The boy finished and the audience clapped.

Ivy spoke next, 'What Terry just explained so eloquently, is that this is a question of ethics.'

Clare's mind wandered and she let her eyes circle the room. People were nodding and muttering. For over an hour Hazel batted away villagers' questions, but Clare noticed the tightness in people's eyes, the hardening of features. Hazel could dismiss their concerns as petty and irrelevant, but that wouldn't dispel the anger. She spotted Bill, wearing his battered straw hat, jotting notes on a pad. He was listening, and he would surely detect the resentment and fear in these voices.

When Fred asked what was going to happen to the Brambleton Agricultural Show, Hazel suggested that Richard answer. Clare opened the door. As if controlled by a switch, heads swept from left to right, tracking Hastings as he stalked past. Someone started hissing, then someone booed, and the crowd took its cue, stomping their feet and booing like a pantomime audience when the wicked witch came on stage. Richard's face went scarlet – Clare hoped this time it was from embarrassment, not rage.

Fred repeated his question.

'I'll find another site somewhere on the estate,' promised Richard.

'But it will be further away from the village,' said Fred. 'Not so convenient. Why not put the shed somewhere else?'

'Because he's a greedy bugger,' said a North-Devonian accent, eliciting splutters of laughter and another rush of colour to Richard's face.

Anna rose and asked a technical question about the scale on the site plan.

'Um . . . Peter, one for you, please,' said Richard.

A flush crept up Peter's neck. He cleared his throat but didn't answer.

'Well?' said Anna.

Had Anna stumbled on a weakness? Was there something underhand about Richard's scale?

Hastings glared at his expert. Peter averted his eyes. 'I'm not an architect.'

'I am,' said Anna stridently.

Hazel saved her ally. 'The Council will investigate that.' Clare's eyes darted to Bill and a smile swept over her face – Bill was scribbling on his notepad. 'Any further questions?' asked Hazel.

Clare raised her hand. 'Like many others here tonight, my family has farmed here for generations. There are plenty of viable options for that land which Richard could be encouraged to explore such as a campsite, or fruit farming.' Her speech earned her a scowl from Richard.

Peter answered. 'A thorough investigation was done before settling on this scheme. There's a detailed business plan and extensive discussions have taken place with the local Council. This is the best plan, and it will provide employment for three people full-time.'

There was a round of huffs and snorts, then a male voice piped up, 'He's got more folk employed pruning his roses.'

'That's enough, Wilf!' shouted Hazel. 'Now, are there any further questions before we vote?'

There was a collective shuffling of feet, several harrumphs and snorts.

'The matter is now closed,' said Hazel. 'Richard, if you could absent yourself again, please.'

A hush fell. Hastings marched past, looking like a child sent off to detention. The doors closed behind him and Hazel spoke. 'Councillors, how do you vote? I'm in favour.'

'Me too,' said a male councillor.

'I'm against,' said Pat firmly.

Clare chewed on her knuckles. She couldn't look at the two remaining councillors. To defeat Hastings, both had to follow Pat's lead. The first, a young woman, slowly shook her head. 'No, I'm against this Hazel.'

Clare swallowed. The room was so quiet she could hear birds singing outside the open windows. In the middle of the room, Ivy's eyes were shut and her hands clasped in prayer. The seconds ticked past. The last councillor spoke. 'I don't think this is right for the village.' Before the woman could formally vote, the crowd cheered and stamped their feet. A smiling Bill pocketed his notepad, and Clare felt a surge of pride.

She hung back, watching people stream out of the hall. Several saying they were going to the Smugglers Inn. Bill shook hands with everyone who'd spoken. He was a shrewd operator. She waited until the room emptied, leaving just the officials gathering up papers and chatting. Clare thought about speaking to Pat but decided not to tackle her in front of Hazel. She pushed open the door. Richard was blocking the exit to the street, standing with his arms crossed and his legs set slightly wider than his shoulders, like a bouncer outside a nightclub.

'Don't think you've won,' he said. 'This isn't even the first battle. It's just a skirmish in a very long war.' He stormed off.

She shuddered. In her legal work, she often met employers reluctant to admit defeat, but she'd never seen such a sore loser. She suspected his anger stemmed from an arrogant assumption the parish council was in his pocket. Hastings blamed her for tonight's decision, and she suspected he would get his revenge. She had to stay one step ahead of him. Through his brother, Richard was spying on BARS, so it was only fair if BARS spied on Richard in return.

Fifteen

It was gone nine and the light was fading fast when Clare turned through a pair of glossy white metal gates, about a mile outside Brambleton. Shortly afterwards, the drive forked. A wooden sign listing four cute-sounding cottage names pointed to a spur road. Guessing those were Sam's holiday lets, Clare chose the road marked *Private*, her headlights picking out a well-managed orchard, once again reminding her she must get into her own, then a cider barn and finally a large farmhouse.

The curtains were open, and she could see someone leaning over a hob. Her stomach rumbled. She hadn't eaten since lunch. From his height and build, she assumed it was Sam. He looked up and his eyes screwed tight, as if trying to identify the unfamiliar vehicle outside. She sat drumming her fingers on the steering wheel, uncomfortable at disturbing his dinner, but also concerned that he might have recognized her car. She didn't want him to think she had lost her nerve. He was halfway across the kitchen, so she got out of the car and marched to the porch, telling herself to pretend that this was a business pitch. With her finger on the bell, the door opened.

'Hi,' said Sam. His blue eyes flashed straight at her. She couldn't detect any hint of curiosity in them. Didn't he want to ask what she was doing here? 'Come in. Can I offer you a glass of wine?'

He spoke in a gentle husky voice which made her feel welcome, as if he had been expecting her. She ran her hands through her hair. Maybe this was a mistake. 'I don't want to disturb dinner. I'm sorry, it's quite late. I thought you'd have . . .'

'Don't apologize. Most people have eaten by now. One of my guests had an accident. What about that glass of wine?' he said.

'Go on then.'

She followed him down a corridor decorated with cheerful, bright pictures of local scenes: Exmoor with an enormous herd of wild deer; a long sandy beach which she recognized as Saunton Sands.

The kitchen was bigger than Clare's entire flat. It was modern, spotlessly clean and smelt of spices. Her stomach growled, and she closed her jacket, trying to mask the sound. 'I should go,' she said.

'Have you eaten?' he asked, making her blush: he must have heard her tummy. 'I'm batch-cooking, so there's plenty.'

She sniffed appreciatively, then asked what he was cooking.

'Maa ki dahl.'

She smiled at him. 'What?'

He returned her smile, his eyes met hers and she dropped her gaze and ran her hands through her hair. 'It's basically slow-cooked black lentils,' said Sam.

She was here to infiltrate the enemy. What better way than sharing a meal? She wasn't here to fight, nor, she warned herself, to flirt. 'Go on then.'

He fussed over her, making her feel less like a spy and more like a blind date, showing her where the toilet was, asking if she wanted to eat inside or, as it was so warm, would she prefer the terrace? 'Kitchen's fine,' she said plonking herself down at the breakfast bar.

'Red wine or white?' he asked.

'You choose.'

He opened a bottle of white wine and poured two glasses, pushing one her way, then turned away. She took a sip and watched his back. He pulled out an ancient-looking cast iron pot from the oven – the sort that still filled her mother's cupboards. He set it in front of her and lifted the lid, releasing a spicy aroma that made her mouth water, before ladling two large bowlfuls, sprinkling on a brown powder and adding a swirl of yoghurt.

'Tell me what you think,' he said, nodding at her bowl. She dipped in her spoon, stirring the yoghurt, and took a mouthful. It was delicious: perfectly seasoned, an incredible blend of spices. She dropped her spoon. 'Where did you learn to cook like this?'

'My mother. She taught both of us. I find spices fascinating.'

That made her smile. Guy hadn't been interested in food. He viewed it as fuel, something humans needed to survive, just like his car used petrol. He cooked nothing more elaborate than toast. Not that she was much better. That would have to change: the freezer was nearly empty.

She glanced around the room, at the bottles of neatly labelled herbs and spices, the stacked pots and pans all on display. 'This kitchen has a sort of masculine feel to it. Did you design it?'

He nodded. 'I've redone it since I got divorced.'

Clare slid her chair closer to the counter and took another spoonful of food. She stole a furtive glance at him. 'Sorry. I'd heard it hadn't worked out.'

'Laura wasn't a Devonian. She couldn't take the wet winters. She thought she could learn to love country life, but she was a city girl at heart, and we just drifted apart.' He took a gulp of wine. Clare didn't speak, wondering if the wound was still raw. Sam turned those eyes on her, making her body tremble. She blinked and spooned in more lentils. 'It was a while ago now. I'm over it,' he said.

'Me too,' she said thoughtfully, wondering if she was ready to try again. She wasn't sure, but if she was, it wouldn't be with a Hastings. 'How long have you lived here?' she asked, changing the subject.

'I inherited the cider farm from my father fifteen years ago.'

Clare frowned. She'd worked and saved for years to scrape together the deposit for her flat. She forced a laugh and said, 'Lucky you.'

While they ate, she talked about the London life she missed, and he told her about his four luxury holiday lets. That spur road culminated in four sleek timber-framed cottages facing the sea. He told her they had previously been barns converted under Class Q permitted development.

'What's that?' she asked.

'It allows farmers to convert some agricultural buildings into residential units without having to apply for planning permission.'

She seized her opportunity. 'I thought you'd have been at this evening's meeting.'

'I didn't think I'd enjoy it.'

Of course, it was his night off. His brother was on duty.

'Your brother didn't enjoy himself very much.'

He gave a faint huff. 'Richard is big enough and ugly enough not to care if people like him.'

She waited until she could see his face before speaking. 'I think he expected them to vote it through.'

'And they didn't?'

He seemed surprised. There was a quirk of a smile round his lips, but she was sure Richard would have been on the phone to Sam immediately after the meeting.

'No,' she said smugly, 'it's been refused. Everyone's gone off to the Smugglers Inn to celebrate. '

'Piece of advice,' said Sam. 'Tempting though it is, don't back him into a corner. If he's cornered, he'll fight harder.'

She felt herself bristle but was careful not to react. He was as cocky as his brother, thinking he could manage BARS's tactics with a few innocent-sounding tips. She hid her feelings by finishing her meal. With each mouthful she reminded herself to pretend he was a client – she didn't like all her clients, but she was never rude. She must treat Sam the same way. Some of his tips might be useful. She just had to sift out those designed to lead BARS astray.

'If you were in our shoes, what would you do?'

He didn't hesitate, which made her suspect he'd been told by Richard to plant the idea, probably with Fred. 'I'd commission my own EIA.'

She laughed. 'Why?' she asked, taking a gulp of wine. 'Won't the Council do that?'

He looked at her with an intense expression of concern. For a bizarre moment she was catapulted back to their kiss over twenty years ago. It had been sensuous, both firm and tender, and for years afterwards was the benchmark against which she'd assessed each boyfriend. She shook her head, reminding herself not to get carried away. Sam may have been a good kisser, but his true character was revealed by his cruel actions the following day.

'Don't count on it, Clare.,' he responded. 'The Council probably can't afford one.'

'Nor can we,' she said, then bit her lip. She hadn't wanted to let that slip and blamed her mistake on the wine. He offered her more food, but she patted her stomach, and he collected the dirty dishes, rinsed and stacked them in a dishwasher, then pulled the bottle of wine from the fridge. She put her hand over her glass. 'Thanks, but I'm driving.'

'What do you think Richard will do about the parish council?'

'Ignore it.'

Clare laughed. Richard couldn't do that, but she accepted Sam wouldn't reveal her brother's tactics. She would have to wait for his next move.

It wasn't long before Richard launched a counterattack. It came through the post, in the form of a lawyer's letter. Clare unfurled the single page from a London firm. The first thing she noticed were the words 'without prejudice'. She'd often used them herself. It was a legal term used to encourage open and frank discussions between disputing parties, allowing them to explore resolutions, knowing their statements could not be used against them if negotiations failed and litigation started. As if the Hastings family knew how to compromise!

Clare chuckled as she read on:

> Our client has reason to believe that you are the author of a libellous leaflet which you have been actively circulating in, and around, the village of Brambleton. Mr Hastings requires you to cease immediately and will be seeking redress and substantial damages for the harm done to his reputation.

She folded up the letter, thinking he may be a decent bridge player, but unlike his sibling, there was no finesse to Richard – he attacked with a full-frontal assault. This was textbook aggressive use of the law. As if she'd be so stupid. Didn't he know she was a lawyer? She scanned the letter and sent it, together with another copy of the leaflet, to her colleague Sally, seeking reassurance that Richard didn't have grounds to complain.

Outside, she strode to the orchard and leaned against the gate, drinking in the view. A gentle breeze rustled through the branches. She concentrated, but she couldn't hear another sound. It was a tranquil spot. Scrappy – the grass was calf-height – but peaceful. She unlatched the gate, then froze, turned, and, leaving the gate unlocked, jogged off to the chicken run.

Captain Hilts was chasing down a hen. His prey squawked and flapped her wings. Clare unlatched the gate – didn't that boy understand 'no'? The cockerel had his claws on the hen, pinning her down. Clare rushed over, tugged him away and glared at the rooster. He lowered his head and slunk towards the cooler.

Rescuing the hen made Clare feel better. But who would rescue her? Earlier she had spoken to Pat Mayhew, who was too busy to help BARS. Increasingly, Clare compared the action group to Dad's Army – they meant well, but relying on them to beat the Hastings brothers? To quote Private Frazer from that series, 'They were all doomed.'

She checked the laying boxes – six eggs. Clare rubbed the straw off them, adding the eggs to a tray. With this laying rate, by the end of the month, at £5 a tray, her emergency cash jar would have swelled to £55. For someone never previously short of money, it was an odd sensation to be counting pennies in a jar. She asked herself if that's how Guy had felt, perennially short of money, never able to buy a round in a pub, always borrowing twenty quid, promising to reimburse her. He never did; he spent all his money on cars, either his own or hiring flashy ones.

With interest costs quickly eroding her reduced salary, Clare needed to progress the cider selling idea. She closed the gate on the hens. Strolling back to the farmhouse, she gazed out to the distant sea and the dumpy little Devon fishing boats bobbing across the waves. The beach would be teeming with tourists. August was the peak month. As a child, she had loved this time of year, playing hide and seek in the fields, Marco Polo in the sea and helping her mother prepare for the Brambleton Agricultural Show. That must be soon.

She would enter her mother's cider. It would be the perfect opportunity for someone to taste it. If it won a prize, Trish and Rose might stock it, which would be handy cash and also illustrate the farm's potential. An additional ten acres, on the right root stock, would produce a healthy apple crop within four years. Although not for her. She would return to her old London life, but the idea would appeal to someone. She went inside to make a cup of tea.

Before the kettle boiled, the door opened.

'Hi. Anyone home?' called out Fred. His shock of white hair appeared and beneath it, today's tie: pink. Behind him stood Ivy, dressed in blue overalls, just like Clare's mother. 'We won't get in your way,' said Ivy, beaming at her. 'We just want to sort out your kitchen floor tiles for you.'

'Why now?'

'Fred's a dab hand at DIY. I'm just here to mop and clean.'

'I'll grout today, then come back and seal them tomorrow,' said Fred, turning and leaving the two women.

Ivy took both Clare's hands in hers. 'It's Fred's way of saying thank you, for what you're doing for everyone.'

Fred walked back in, carrying a large tub and a trug of tools.

'Fred, this is very kind, but you don't have to do this.'

'And *you* don't have to take Richard on. Everyone does what they can. I'm not a lawyer. Anyway, I find the sight of these tiles offensive.' He tucked his tie into his shirt, pulled out a set of overalls and stepped into them, pulling the zip up.

Offering to make them tea, Clare was secretly delighted. That was one more tick on her to-do list.

*

Spurred on by Fred's activities, the following day Clare tackled the boxes she'd brought from London. She sat on the bed, scraped a hand through her hair, unbuttoned the top button of her blouse and tipped out the first box, her fingers raking through the contents of what looked like Guy's old sock drawer. There was nothing that sparked any interest, and the second and third boxes were equally uninspiring. The fourth revealed his wedding ring, which she let fall to the bed, then the scrapbook he used to scribble down ideas. She picked it up, flicking through, picturing Guy, helmet on, striding to his beloved rally car that in the end had killed him. She closed her eyes on the memory, then tossed the book high in the air, watching it land next to the ring. A postcard fluttered out from between the pages and dropped onto the floor. She reached for it, her fingers scrabbling, connecting, but it slithered out of her grasp. She picked it up again. The postcard was a map of Devon, the surrounding sea a stylized Caribbean blue. Someone had circled the town of Torquay in bright red ink. She flipped it over.

> Remember what we did here? When are you next alone in the West Country? Hannah xxx

Clare welled up. Occasionally Clare had suspected Guy of being unfaithful, but had never been confronted with evidence, so had buried her husband's possible guilt with him.

She squeezed her eyes tight, thinking of her mother and the rift she'd never repaired.

Now, finally, here was evidence which suggested her mother might have seen Guy for who he really was. Clare liked to think and, when asked, always said she'd been happily married, but the truth was more complicated. She picked up Guy's wedding ring, running her fingers over the cold metal, recalling not the early days of their romance, when she'd buzz the flat doorbell and find their front door open, Guy waiting with a chilled bottle of wine, but those later months, before he died, when they spent more time apart than together. Guy was 'at a rally', 'pacing a course', or 'away practicing', mostly in places too remote for Clare, a newly minted partner at her firm, to join him.

She juggled the job she loved with the man she adored, catching sleeper trains to spend Saturday at a rally, before an early Sunday start to get home, or surrendering Friday nights to depressing departure lounges. Claiming that he made enough sacrifices for his sport, Guy refused to compromise his career for his wife. All the efforts to sustain their relationship came from Clare. She understood his career came first, just like hers did, but that didn't explain why he rarely called or messaged when she couldn't join him. Maybe women like Hannah were the real reason. Clutching the card, Clare clattered down the stairs, out into the fierce sunshine, hearing her mother's voice shouting at her: '*He'll break your heart.*'

She ran into the orchard and collapsed in a crumpled heap. Her body convulsed with sobs. For a long time, she lay crying, shedding tears for a marriage that she had always persuaded herself had been tragically cut short. In truth, how much longer would she have ignored that nagging feeling that Guy was being unfaithful? She sobbed for the loss of her parents and her blind stubbornness which had prevented her from healing the rift with her mother. Cindy had seen through Guy, recognized him for what he was.

She sniffed as her tears subsided, and lay watching the branches swaying in the breeze, the fruit clinging to them, new life growing in front of her eyes. She felt the spiky grass rough against her bare skin, but stayed where she was, as a peaceful, comfortable feeling settled over her. Clare heard the gate clatter, saw a flash of dirty white fur, before Stop-it landed on her chest, winding her. She sat up laughing, pushed the dog aside, dried her eyes with the end of her shirt, then ripped the postcard into little pieces, before stuffing them into her pocket. She would not sully this sacred space with Guy's betrayal.

Clare charged back inside, Stop-it hot on her heels, his paws thumping up the stairs behind her. She dragged out every bag and box she'd brought from London, tossed each one into the Land Rover, then shot off into Barnstaple. How dare he! *How dare he!* After all she'd sacrificed. Hot tears pricked at her eyes, but she was too angry to let them flow. She screeched to a halt at the municipal tip, leapt out, grabbed the first box and charged up the steps like a rugby fly half heading for the touchline, before hurling it into the tip. It crashed open, spewing maps, socks and pants among the discarded rubbish. Guy had been just as careless with Clare's love. He hadn't cherished her as he'd promised to.

By the time the last bag had been tossed into the skip. Clare felt light-headed with relief. It was like closing a chapter on her life. Finally, she had said goodbye to Guy and the misery he had inflicted on her.

Sixteen

The annual Brambleton Agricultural Show was always held on a Monday towards the end of August. Legend had it that the sun always shone for at least part of the day. For over 200 years, the Hastings family had paid the setup costs, enabling entry fees to fund prizes. Local radio had been plugging the show for weeks, and over the weekend, as the preparations unfolded, in Prosecco and Prose, the pub and the village shop it had been the subject of fevered excitement and speculation: which farmer's animals were in top condition? Whose plants, cakes and crafts would win in the show?

By Sunday evening, a row of tents peppered the field next to the village hall, together with stalls displaying farm machinery, solar panels and quad bikes. There was also a large marquee which housed the food and drink stalls – precisely where Richard wanted to build the chicken factory – and a smaller one, next to the main show ring, with its fabric door shut and a sign attached: *Private Party*.

On a bright morning, Clare rose early and, after tending to the animals and walking Stop-it, she ambled along the roadside, passing stationary trailers and horseboxes. She heard bleating and squeaking from within and glimpsed spotlessly turned-out sheep, pigs and cows. The smell of freshly hosed down animals evoked memories of sitting beside her mother as a child, towing a couple of dairy cows behind them. There was always a lemon drizzle cake in a plastic box on the back seat.

Clare reached the head of the queuing traffic, where an army cadet was barking orders at frazzled-looking entrants attempting to park. She paid her fee and wandered across the grass, past advertising banners fluttering in the gentle breeze. There was a persistent sound of generators, the smell of frying food and the scratchy sound of someone commentating over a Tannoy system. Very little had changed since her ten-year-old self was racing around the stalls with Trish and Anna.

A cloud of smoke billowed from a tent advertising barbequed meat. It was next to a jade-green van with *Mole Control* stencilled on the side – she hoped that wasn't the meat on offer. The van promised to clear moles from farms or gardens, which made her think of Stop-it and his garden antics. Once the farm was on the market, she'd somehow have to prevent him from digging up the lawn.

She passed farmers calming meticulously groomed cattle, sheep, pigs and poultry, no doubt dreaming of ribbons and rosettes. Spectators milled around, shouting encouraging remarks.

Clare reached the main ring, where sheep were being judged, each one harnessed and tethered to a white-coated owner, like a large pet dog. Most exhibitors wore straw hats and ties. This was an important day, and casual dress wasn't appropriate if you were exhibiting. Even her mother had discarded her blue overalls on show day. The judge was running her hands over the hindquarters of a large Suffolk, the black head and feet contrasting with its butterscotch body. It was a lovely animal. The judge moved on to a Devon and Cornwall Longwool, the coat hanging in elegant tufts like a shaggy jumper.

'My money's on the Suffolk,' said a male voice behind her. Sam.

The judge picked up a rosette and marched towards a black and white sheep. 'It's going to be the Jacob,' announced the Tannoy. 'And the reserve is . . . the Suffolk. A round of applause for all the exhibitors, please.' Clare clapped loudly, watching the sheep being led out of the ring and over to a series of gazebo-covered pens erected to shield them from the sun.

She kept her voice light-hearted. 'I used to come every year as a child. It was always a fixture in Mum's calendar.'

'If I recall, you usually won the girl's sack race.' She smiled, surprised by Sam remembering her in this way. He laughed. 'You always left the others trailing.'

Her brow furrowed. Why was he being so friendly? She decided not to mention the year she'd seen Richard bribing someone to trip the fastest youngster in the boys' race. She didn't want to poison the atmosphere.

'I was a lot taller than most of the other girls. Still am.' She looked his way, wanting to check his reaction, before saying, 'I had a legal letter from your brother. You can tell him to save his money.'

A look of alarm crossed Sam's face, but he didn't fool her – he was probably just disappointed the letter hadn't spooked her. 'What sort of a legal letter?'

'He claims my leaflets are libellous and defamatory, but I know what I'm doing.'

His eyes narrowed. 'Be careful. He doesn't waste money on lawyers' letters. He must think he's got a good case.'

She looked at him askance. Sam knew every move his brother made. He was a decent actor, though. He did look genuinely concerned. She decided to change the subject.

'I found some of my mother's cider.'

'She knew how to grow an apple.' He looked thoughtful for a moment then added, 'She was always telling me she planned to get into cider-making. I'm pleased she finally tried.'

'Do you make your own or does an expert do it for you?'

'I make the base cider, then someone makes and bottles the final product to my recipe. I'd love to do that too but it's quite a big investment. I already have an apple press, but I would need to buy vats, testing equipment, a bottling system. I might take the plunge next year. I'd love to stay and chat, but this has reminded me that I've left *my* cider entry in the car,' said Sam.

She watched him as he walked away, waving and calling out cheerily to people he passed.

Why had her mother been confiding her business ideas to Sam?

The entrance to the long marquee revealed rows of trestle tables resting on coir matting. Inside, it was hot and airless, exacerbated by the heaving crowd. It reminded Clare of the London Underground in summer – she didn't miss that. People were moving slowly, inspecting everything from freshly harvested produce to handmade crafts and jars of honey. At one end of the tent, Rose and her husband were behind a pop-up bar, serving drinks in plastic cups. Trying not to push, Clare made her way down the tent, stopping to sample a few artisan cheeses and to chat with a woman selling home-cured bacon and sausages. Had that been her mother's plan for the pigs? At the bar, she caught Rose's eye and asked for a glass of lemonade.

'That's on the house,' said Rose, waving away Clare's card.

'Thanks.'

'You can thank Richard.' At the mention of his name, Clare's fingers tightened around the plastic cup. Rose bustled past, handing a man his change as she said, 'His lawyer told me the lease will be renewed at the existing rent.

'The rent's staying the same for another five years?'

'Yup.'

'We suspect he doesn't want any more grumbling while he's

after this planning permission you're fighting. You've saved us a fortune.'

With mixed feelings, Clare gave Rose a thumbs-up. Part of her was pleased for Rose. She had stood up to Richard and won, but that victory came at a price. Richard had sacrificed his gain from that lease for a greater prize. Rose would now not object to Hastings' plans until her new lease was signed. Clare would lay odds that there would be a plethora of reasons that this would take months, and while it languished, a key influencer was offside.

She drank her lemonade, marred by the bitter taste of being outplayed. She was up against a wily fox, and unlike her, his resources and influence were both vast.

Outside the marquee, the show ring was being set up for a horse jumping competition. Marshals were manhandling fences into position, and children were pacing the course, assessing the jumps for the best route, spotting the ones which might alarm their mounts. Despite the heat, the junior riders wore jodhpurs, knee-high black boots and protective jackets.

Clare spotted Bill Matthews, his straw hat towering above the crowd. He was shaking hands and slapping people on the back, seemingly comfortable despite not being from farming stock. This was a perfect opportunity for him to be out meeting voters. She heard him commiserating with someone for coming second. Then he caught her eye and came over.

'This is an important event for you isn't it, Bill.'

He gazed around the crowd, smiling. 'I'm here because I love everything this show represents. It's the essence of rural life. Shows us at our best.'

'And our worst,' she replied.

He nodded. 'You mean the competitive spirit?'

'I don't mind that. It's human nature to want to win. But it's unattractive when someone cheats.'

He gave a soft chuckle. 'I know who you're referring to, and I'm afraid I've got some bad news on that front.'

She stiffened, feeling her heartbeat quicken. She thought she'd delivered what he asked for. The parish council had said no, and people were lodging objections. 'What's that?' she asked.

'It's not in the bag.'

'But surely, the strength of local opposition . . . I've counted forty formal objections on the planning website. There's only six in favour and they include Richard and his wife, Cora. Isn't that and the parish council's view enough to see this off?'

'Not sure,' he said, clicking his tongue. 'It's the cuts. This is about money and Richard has a whole lot more than the Council. If we reject his application and Richard appeals, we must defend our decision, and we don't have the budget. Worse, if we lose on appeal, we'll have to pay his costs.'

Despite the heat, a chill shot through her. After all their hard work, the Council would still grant Richard permission to build his monstrosity.

He patted her on the shoulder. 'Chin up, eh? You can always appeal.' Then he strode off.

She watched him work his way through the crowd, doffing his straw hat at people, the breeze ruffling his salt and pepper hair. This wasn't Bill's fault, but he was a politician and knew how to navigate this jagged terrain better than her. She had a sense he had encouraged her to show the strength of feeling in the village prematurely when the real battle would be the appeal. Was Bill calculating that with its blood up, the village would ride to the rescue and fund an appeal when the Council granted Hastings permission?

She tried to recapture her earlier relaxed mood. She watched but didn't take in the horses or the riders as they sped around the ring, clearing jumps. The commentator announced an interval while the marshals prepared the course for the next competition. It was a lovely, cheerful voice praising all the youngsters who'd just competed, and encouraging the crowd to clap. She recognized the voice, but couldn't immediately place it, then realized it was Sam's.

Clare turned and walked away. She'd had enough of the Hastings family for one day.

The horticultural side of the show was inside the village hall. The room buzzed with excited chatter and cackles of laughter. People were jesting about who'd won and vowing to do better next year. She wanted to shake them. Didn't they realize that if they didn't get their act together, there may not be a show next year? She dawdled her way around the vegetables, home-made jams and cakes, her eyes alert for the cider class. Judges had already left shiny rosettes for the top three entries in each category. Ivy had won first prize for her lemon drizzle cake, the category her mother had won most years, though even when she'd outgrown the sack race, the day had been about Clare. They'd always collected Cindy's rosette and prize money together on their way home.

Beside vases of dahlias, the vivid orange and purple flowers the size of small dinner plates, she met Fred fussing over his entry. 'Did you win?' she asked.

'I did,' he said, a note of pride in his voice.

Next to the dahlias were the roses. Clare bent over the winning flower, which was perfectly formed, its petals just bursting open. She sniffed, but there was no perfume. She glanced at the entrant's details: Brambleton Hall. What did that mean? Was it Cora Hastings, Richard or one of the gardening team?

'Shame they gave it to a tea rose – not an old-fashioned variety,' she said.

Fred rolled his eyes at her. 'His gardeners will have been

watching that bud closer than a team of doctors monitoring a patient in an intensive care unit.'

She laughed. 'And haven't you been tending your dahlias as closely?'

He tutted. 'I bet that rose has been in and out of a fridge or the glasshouse, fed on pipettes of goodness knows what to ensure its petals are just at the point of unfurling.'

Recalling there was a trophy for the exhibitor who won the most classes, she asked who'd won it.

Fred huffed. 'Prize-giving soon, so we'll find out then, but it'll be Brambleton Hall. It always is. It's a con. His gardening team divvy up the categories and one of them enters every class as Brambleton Hall. Everything from jams and cakes to flowers and veg. No one else can do that.'

Clare laughed darkly. 'What do you think would happen to the head gardener if he lost?' She smiled to herself, working through wording she would use if instructed to draft a clause for an employment contract, which defined losing the trophy as gross misconduct. 'Why doesn't someone change the rules? It's a village show; it's supposed to be for amateurs, to capture the pride and spirit of a rural community. It's not the Chelsea Flower Show.'

Clare had attended the event in Chelsea three months earlier; it was her firm's annual corporate hospitality event. She smiled inwardly, imagining inviting guests to Brambleton instead of Chelsea, expecting them to watch sheep being judged, not admire small, staged *show gardens*; to cruise stalls selling tractors and animal feed, instead of classy jackets and expensive secateurs. She asked herself which show she admired most, but Fred's hushed voice interrupted her thoughts. 'Look out. Hastings alert.' Then he said cheerfully, 'Hi there, Sam. Good turnout for the family show.'

'It's the *village* show, Fred. We just pay for it,' said Sam.

Clare turned to leave, but the room was full, and she didn't want to push past people. Sam stood beside her, so close she could see the fine hairs on his arms and she couldn't help but imagine what it would feel like to have them wrapped around her. She remembered his arms as powerful and strong when all those years ago they'd had their disastrous 24-hour romance. She shook herself and turned away. 'Are you exhibiting?' asked Sam.

She turned towards him. 'I've slightly bent the rules – I've entered some of my mother's cider.'

He grinned at her. 'You realize you're talking to one of the judges. There were a lot of entries, some of them very good. How did you do?'

'I haven't checked, but I presume your brother won.'

Chuckling, he shook his head. 'Nope. Everyone around here knows I'm the cider man. Besides, there's no trophy on offer.' He winked at her.

She couldn't help herself from spitting out, 'He's a greedy bastard, isn't he.'

'You know that's not what I meant. He's my brother . . . and he's standing behind you, waiting for the prize-giving.'

Clare blushed, and not wanting to give Richard the satisfaction of seeing her embarrassment, didn't look round. She noticed no one was laughing anymore. The voices weren't excited or jolly. There was a tension in the air similar to that at the parish council meeting. Clare rested her bottom on the table behind her, watching Pat Mayhew shunting people aside, clearing the area around a small table with polished silver trophies – presumably Magnus had buffed those up.

Pat raised her hands, and the room fell silent. 'Mrs Hastings has kindly agreed to present this year's prizes,' she said.

In contrast to the T-shirt, shorts and sandals of the audience, Cora wore a startling emerald-green silk dress and heels so high and spikey that Clare wondered how she'd reached the Hastings' private tent without getting stuck in the grass. Cora's hair had that shiny, glossy 'recent trip to the hairdresser's' look, and a pair of sunglasses held it off her face. As Clare watched Cora smile and shake hands with the winners, she realized that she was well cast as the 'lady of the manor'. Like all talented actors forced to perform in front of a slightly awkward audience, she seemed oblivious to the atmosphere. This time, it didn't seem to affect Richard either. He stood beside his wife, beaming and clapping as she presented the prizes.

Two men and a lady Clare didn't recognize, but who Cora seemed to know, won repeatedly – Clare guessed they were Richard's gardening team. This was what BARS was up against. Richard wasn't bound by professional ethics like the BARS team was. He would bend and twist the rules to his advantage. She eased her way past the crowd. She couldn't stand here and clap for a cheat.

Walking back to Orchard Farm, Clare replayed her conversation with Bill. Something was missing from her approach. Bill had been trying to communicate that to her earlier. What was it? Scuffing her feet in the dust like a recalcitrant child, she tried to see things from Bill's perspective. Clare pictured herself advising a client and felt her chest tighten. She'd been stupid. Years preparing for legal tussles should have taught her that to steel the Council's backbone, BARS must counter Richard's EIA.

At the farm gate she emptied the honesty pot, briefly enjoying the weighty feel of pound coins in her pocket but scolding herself. She had allowed Hastings to present his case professionally while she bodged her own, naively assuming that village sentiment would be enough to sway the Planning Committee. This was her fault, but worse, there was no time to fix her mistake – the deadline for the decision was Friday.

Seventeen

Morning task list:

- Clean hen enclosure
- Ditto pigs
- Restock both feed bins

On Friday morning Clare rose before Hilts summoned her, exhausted from a fitful night of tossing and turning, like a candle flame flickering in a draft. She awoke with an uncomfortable feeling in her chest: she hadn't felt it for decades, but she knew what it was – exam results day. Today, the Council would officially decide if Richard could build his factory.

She went outside, where the clear blue Devon skies heralded a gorgeous summer's day. The dew was heavy on the grass, sparkling in the sunshine like fireflies resting on emerald threads. It was difficult to envisage receiving bad news on a day like this. She heard a twig crack and turned. A red deer emerged from the woods, its ears twitching, its nose pointing Clare's way; then it trotted across the field, barely twenty feet in front of her. Magical, she thought, wondering if the rangers on the African safari she was supposed to be visiting at the end of the year would get her as close to wildlife.

After feeding the animals she spent four hours tidying the pig enclosure, then cleaned out the henhouse and heaved a bag of grain into the feed bin. She heard a squeak and glanced up. Bill Matthews was pulling the front gate shut. She dropped the lid on the bin and ran moist palms over her trousers. Was Bill coming to break the news personally? She studied his face, hoping for a hint. He wore a serious expression. This didn't look like a good news story. Her mouth felt dry.

'Hi,' she croaked, then she cleared her throat. 'What news?'

He shook his head.

She swallowed hard. At least he'd had the courtesy to come and tell her. She closed her eyes, struggling to get her breathing under control, listening to his footsteps coming closer. She had been right – without a contradictory EIA, the Council couldn't refuse permission. When she opened her eyes, Bill was standing in front of her. He looked stern, as if something weighty was on his mind. He was twisting his neck and rubbing it as if it was sore. 'The meeting is this afternoon,' he said.

Relief flooded through her. Then she asked herself why Bill was here. He took off his hat, tapped it against his chest, then his eyes drilled into her. 'Have you got the funds to fight this?'

She hesitated but didn't look away. A Vera was making a satisfied squawking noise. Clare had learned that this was the hen celebrating laying an egg. Richard's chickens would never make that cheerful sound. If she said yes, would that encourage the Council to reject Hastings' plans, knowing BARS would pay to defend the decision if Richard appealed? Or would it have the opposite effect, allowing the Committee to grant permission for the factory, knowing the village had the funds to appeal? She scraped a hand through her hair. Either way, it boiled down to the same thing.

Stuttering a little, she said, 'I— I am confident we will raise the money to fund an EIA.'

She didn't know how, but they had to.

'Right,' said Bill, thrusting out his hand. She shook it. His was a firm grip and she tried to keep her own hand steady. 'I'll do my best,' said Bill. 'The decision will be later today.'

'Call me, please – whatever the decision is.'

He nodded. 'I'll call you.'

Unable to concentrate on farm chores, Clare drove to Barnstaple with a short shopping list and a £10 note. She collected a trolley, then replaced it with a basket and, without looking at anything on display, strode to the fruit and veg area. Her hand hovered over the different punnets of strawberries – the cheapest was over £1. She gently shook the container. There were less than ten berries. She sensed somebody behind her and not wanting to be an obstruction, walked away, thinking Richard should have taken her advice and gone into soft fruit.

In the vegetable aisle, she told herself to select seasonal produce. What was in season at the end of August? There was a man waiting for her to choose. She tossed a packet of asparagus into her basket and ran her eyes over the other greenery, then removed the asparagus from her basket – it was from Peru and cost more per stem than the strawberries. In her peripheral vision, she noticed the man was still behind her. She spun round to see a figure scurrying off past the pineapples. A shiver ran down her spine. Had someone been following her? Clare prowled up and down, calculating the cost of produce. She chose a cabbage, some loose carrots and a few courgettes. She would have to work out what to do with them, but it was a start.

The rest of the day passed in a frenzied bout of DIY. She watched three different YouTube 'How-to' videos, then threw dust sheets over the bedroom furniture, dug out a ladder and Trish's box of paints and rollers, chose a cheerful yellow and began painting. There was something soothing about changing the beige tones of her childhood bedroom to a vivid, sunny yellow. She wished she could alter the mess the Hastings family was creating in her life as easily.

At five o'clock, having painted the last corner, she washed the roller and checked her phone. But there were no missed calls. Surely the meeting was over by now? Was Bill too embarrassed to call? She was carting the ladder downstairs when her phone vibrated in her back pocket. Clare stumbled down the final steps, propped the ladder against the wall and reached for her phone, surprised to see her hands were shaking. The screen was alight: *Bill Matthews*.

In a scratchy voice she didn't recognize as her own, she crossed her fingers and answered. 'Hi, Bill. What did they decide?'

'The decision will be posted online later today. Don't speak to anyone about this until you've read it.' Her heart was racing. There could only be one reason for his warning. 'Richard's application was rejected,' he said.

Tears welled up in her eyes. 'Oh, Bill. That's fantastic,' she spluttered, feeling almost light-headed. 'Well done.' She gushed out her thanks.

'We expect him to appeal,' said Bill. 'You must assume he will, and don't rely on us to fight this. We'll defend our decision, but we can't pay for expert reports. We're relying on you.'

'Yes.' She wanted to sound more convincing and hoped the excitement in her voice masked her lack of confidence. 'How long before he appeals?'

'He has six months.'

That bolstered her confidence. Then Bill shattered it. 'But I know that man; he likes a scrap, so he'll attack much sooner. If I were you, I'd assume you'll need an EIA before Christmas.'

Less than four months. That didn't leave long for BARS to raise the funds.

*

That night the Smugglers Inn was full, and everyone wanted to buy Clare a drink. After three large glasses of wine on an empty stomach, Clare had convinced herself that Richard wouldn't appeal, that she'd sell the farm by Christmas and catch the last half of her sabbatical; she was already anticipating her journey through India. She felt strong hands on her shoulders and glanced up into Sam's dazzling blue eyes.

'Congratulations.'

'Shank you,' she mumbled.

His smile faded. 'Clare, when did you last have something to eat?'

She laughed and danced a little jig. 'Who needs food when you've got wine!'

'Come on, you. Let's get you fed.'

He took her by the hand. She loved the feeling of his warm fingers enclosing hers and she squeezed. He squeezed back, sending a thrilling pulse coursing through her body.

At the bar, he made her eat the burger and chips he'd ordered for himself. 'Unlike you, I had lunch.'

'Is he very, very cross?' she asked, grinning round the sides of the burger. She took a huge bite, trying to recall the last time she'd eaten.

Sam rolled his eyes. 'Let's put it this way – I wouldn't like to be Cora for the next few days.'

She giggled and speared a few chips. 'Horrid man, threatening to ruin the village.'

'Planning battles bring out the worst in people. And I'm afraid he's not done yet.'

She took another bite of the burger, chewing and considering what he'd said. He was right, but tonight she didn't want to talk about Richard.

She picked up a chip and held it out towards Sam. He leaned

forward. His eyes locked on to hers, then gently he brushed the chip aside and drew even closer.

'There she is – our saviour!' hollered Roger, pushing between Sam and Clare. 'My round!' he said. Suddenly Anna was there, hugging Clare tightly.

Roger insisted on buying a bottle of champagne. 'Thank goodness that's over. Cheers, everyone,' he said, clinking glasses. Ivy and Fred appeared, and Roger poured more champagne, leaving Clare fumbling to recapture what Roger had interrupted – had Sam been about to kiss her?

Sharp squawking woke Clare at dawn. Overnight, someone had turned up the volume on Hilts. Each drawn-out crow echoed through her brain, making her temples throb. She felt groggy and thirsty, and as she moaned, pulling a pillow over her head, she caught sight of her sleeve. She sat up. She was still wearing yesterday's clothes. Why? Had she made a fool of herself? She had a cloudy memory of flirting with Sam, eating his burger, a fleeting moment where it felt like they might kiss, but then everything became blurry: everyone was laughing, there was dancing and a lot of drinking. She couldn't recall how she had got home. Did Anna and Roger drive her back? She rubbed her eyes, lay back down and groaned. Last night was the blowout the village needed to release tension, but Richard wasn't beaten. They must start preparing for an appeal . . . just not today.

She caught the sound of a car engine, followed by Stop-it's barking, and a voice drifting up from downstairs. The dog replied with an excited yowl. He knew the visitor; probably Ivy, popping in to check on her. Clare glanced at her wrist – six o'clock! She winced, then heaved herself upright and staggered to the bathroom, peeling off her clothes and stepping into the shower.

Five minutes later, wrapped in a towel, she flopped back onto the bed, her head pounding. There was a knock on the door. She sat up, tucking the towel tightly round her. 'Come in, I'm decent,' she called.

The door opened. A mug appeared and her mouth salivated.

'I hope that's tea,' she said.

Sam walked in, grinning. She wanted to duck under the duvet. She ran her fingers through her wet hair, pushing it into shape, then folded the towel more tightly around herself. 'How are you feeling this morning?' he asked.

'Did *you* bring me home?'

'No one wanted you to leave, but by nine you were looking a bit shattered, so I persuaded Anna to help me.'

Clare ran her hands over her face, 'Tell me the worst. What did I do or say? Who do I need to apologize to?'

He laughed. 'No one. Well, you were shockingly rude about my brother, but he doesn't know that.' He plonked the tea on her bedside table, then added a packet of painkillers. 'Drink, take two of those, then go back to sleep. I used to help Cindy with the animals when she was poorly, so I'll do the morning rounds and then take Stop-it for a walk.'

She ran her tongue round her parched lips and reached for the mug. She thought about resisting his offer and saying she was perfectly capable of looking after her own animals, but her throbbing temple turned the words into a simple, 'thank you'. Sam left. Watching the door close and collapsing back onto the bed, Clare was too grateful for the extra sleep to ask herself why he had been so chummy with her mother.

On Bank Holiday Monday, Clare washed her hair and found a lipstick. She dressed in clean jeans and a floaty top, collected a dozen eggs and drove to Sam's. Approaching the farmhouse, she spotted him strimming around the base of an apple tree, reminding her she must do hers before the crop started falling.

She parked, and for a few moments sat watching. She had imagined he paid someone else to do the hard work, just like his brother did. Clare picked up her present. It was only a dozen eggs, but she could sell them for £3, and that was a hefty chunk of her current weekly shopping budget. She hoped that he would appreciate the gesture. She got out and crossed to the orchard. He was wearing a protective visor and ear defenders, so she walked in a circle until she was standing in front of him and with her fingers clamping the lid shut, waved the box of eggs.

He jumped, then switched off the machine, raised his visor and knocked his ear defenders aside.

'Hi,' she said. 'Didn't mean to startle you. I brought you some eggs to say thanks for being my gallant knight in shining armour on Friday night.'

He tutted. 'You didn't need to do that. It was my pleasure.' He took the box, but he was looking at her, his blue eyes steady, seeming to peel away her inhibitions. She dropped her gaze, and he spoke gently. 'Thank you. Your mother's chickens lay the best eggs in Devon. I love them. Can I offer you a drink?'

'Hmm. Kind of gone off wine.'

He laughed, sending a fluttery sensation through her. 'What about a pot of tea?'

She smiled at him. 'That would be lovely, but I'm interrupting you.'

He shook his head. 'I was about to take a break anyway. Come in. We'll have it on the terrace.'

They walked side by side. She glanced down at his hand, recalling him holding hers on Friday night. Inside, her arm brushed against his and her breath caught in her throat. He led her out to a patio teaming with pots of lavender, spent snapdragons and flowering herbs. She sat listening to the bees buzzing in and out of the flowers, the afternoon sun warming her skin, trying to remember what she'd been doing on the August Bank Holiday Monday last year. Eventually she recalled vaguely planning to head for the Notting Hill Carnival but missing it because she was up to her ears in a fresh case.

After ten minutes and no Sam, Clare went to investigate. Smiling, she stepped into the kitchen saying, 'How long does it take a man to make a pot of—?'

'What are you doing here?' snapped Richard.

Startled, and determined not to show it, Clare said, 'I was looking for Sam.'

Richard's chest was puffed out and his face pinched and red. 'He's not here.'

Clare ran her eyes over the kitchen as if Sam might be hiding under a bar stool. Richard stepped closer to her. He smelt powerfully of cologne as if he'd showered in it, making her want to gag. 'I know who you all are, and I've got every one of you in my sights. I'll pick you off one by one. I don't know why you came here today, but you can piss off.'

Clare was stunned. Sam must be in league with his brother after all. He'd inveigled her into his house deliberately to embarrass her, reeling her in only to slap her in the face, just like he had when they were younger. Feeling her cheeks flush with hot anger, she glared at Richard, then stalked outside to her car.

Eighteen

To do:

- Fundraising
- Investigate experts for EIA
- Sort garden
- Repairs list
- Replace apple trees
- Find YouTube video – how to get dogs to eat kibble

Following her encounter with Richard, Clare had convened a BARS meeting for Tuesday. They gathered in Fred's back garden, which was a stark contrast to Orchard Farm's. The recently mown lawn was flat with no divots, and there was a weed-free channel separating it from a border which was dominated by Fred's champion dahlias. Geraniums and spiky pale purple lavender fronds were interspersed throughout. The bed was smothered with a blanket of mulch.

Fred and Ivy were lounging on deck chairs. Ivy's long floaty dress spilled over the side of the chair. Her arms were folded in her lap, her face tipped up to the sun. Beside her, Fred wore a short-sleeved shirt and a dark green tie, which made his hair seem a snowier white. Anna and Clare sat on pine kitchen chairs, with a view past Fred's little garden shed to the field Hastings wanted to build his factory on. It looked horribly close.

With her eyes shut, Ivy spoke in a lazy drawl. 'What's this meeting for? Haven't we just won?'

Clare handed out copies of the agenda. Ivy folded hers in half and fanned herself. Fred let his slip to the lawn. Anna released her hair, wound it into a bun, released it again, then recoiled it and secured it with the clasp.

'What is it?' asked Clare.

Anna chewed her lip. 'Isn't this premature? A bit defeatist? Shouldn't we wait and see if he appeals?'

'Exactly,' said Ivy. 'The Council had good grounds to reject it.' Ivy spoke a little triumphantly. 'The Council are the experts, and it wouldn't be right for Richard to challenge them.'

Clare took a deep breath. Richard was a cutthroat, slippery devil unfettered by anyone else's opinion. It was important for village morale to have Ivy on BARS, but it was tough accommodating her noble stance – a bit like taking on a Russian dictator when constrained by the medieval spirit of chivalry. Mentally, she imagined herself in shining armour, holding a sword and pointing it at the Hastings brothers, shouting, 'Do you yield?'

'Sadly, I don't think Richard Hastings adheres to your high moral standards,' Clare said.

Ivy sat up and gave her a wounded look. 'Oh, ye of little faith.'

Clare rolled her eyes at Anna. Ivy and Fred were lounging in the sun as if the war was already won. It wasn't. All her instincts told her Richard was preparing to appeal already.

Clare spoke tersely. 'The Council are not the experts. They are the regulators, and they stuck their neck out for us.' She directed her words at Ivy, who was looking her way. 'The experts wrote Richard's EIA. And that's the point – we need our own to refute his, because . . .' Ivy's chin was trembling. Clare swallowed, then softened her tone, 'If, and I accept there is a chance he might not do it, but *if* he appeals, the Planning Inspectorate won't be so kind to us.'

After Clare's outburst, there was a strained silence. Clare debated apologizing but decided not to. She shouldn't have spoken sharply, but they needed to understand the facts and start taking this seriously.

'How long has he got to appeal and what's the process?' asked Fred.

'He has until the end of February,' said Anna.

'How much does an EIA cost?' asked Ivy.

Anna answered. 'It's expensive. There are lots of people involved.'

'Sounds like we need to start fundraising. What's the target?' said Ivy. Mentally Clare sent up a little cheer.

Anna explained about the different experts involved and talked about site visits. There was no mention of cost. Clare willed her friend to answer the question. After five minutes, Clare interrupted. 'It sounds complicated, but what do you think it will cost? How much do we need to raise?'

'Um,' said Anna.

For a quarter of an hour, Anna, Fred and Ivy debated the fundraising target. Clare kept her eyes shut and mouth closed, itching to tell them to discuss the *how*, not the *how much*. Fred reminisced about raising money for the school playground. Clare sat on her hands wanting to interrupt and ask how he'd done it, but pleased to discover the village was used to contributing to good causes.

'And we raised thousands for the organ repair fund five years ago,' said Ivy.

'How?' Clare looked from one to the other of her friends, and telling herself to speak patiently asked, 'What did you both do?'

The pair exchanged a look.

'Richard was very generous.' said Ivy.

Clare raised her eyes at Fred. He nodded. 'Same for the playground.'

'Well, he's not going to help here, is he?'

'There are some rich doctors who've retired close by,' said Anna. 'Roger met them playing golf. And Wilf's daughter is married to an accountant – we went to their wedding. When was it, Ivy? Four years ago?'

'No, I think it was five. Nice lad. Works at the hospital. Can't recall what he does there.'

'Let's stick on message. How do we raise this money?' Clare asked.

'But how much are we trying to raise?' asked Fred.

'Specifically,' said Ivy.

'Does it matter?' said Clare. 'It doesn't sound like we are in any danger of overreaching the target, whatever it is, as we haven't come up with a single idea to raise a pound yet.' She could feel her heart racing and noticed Ivy and Fred wriggling in their deckchairs. She took a breath and spoke gently: 'Please, let's agree on some ideas and get cracking.'

'Well, I always like to know the target,' said Fred. 'In my experience, the first questions people ask are how much and what for?'

'I agree,' added Ivy. 'When I—'

'Right,' said Clare.' Let's just say it's £5,000. Anna, can you get estimates so we can revise that number if I'm wrong? Ideas, please. I'll take notes.'

'That's a big number,' said Fred.

'Exactly,' said Clare. 'Now, ideas please.'

Fred offered to do a sponsored sky dive, saying he'd always wanted to do it. To show willing, as she was regretting her irritation at her team, Clare jotted the idea down, but mentally dismissed it. No one knew anyone with a plane, and it sounded quite dangerous. She encouraged them to keep it simple.

Ivy's face lit up. 'Got it. Wine tasting at the Hall – that raised a thousand pounds for the organ.'

'Oh, I can see Magnus dispensing the wine now,' said Fred sarcastically.

'We could do our own wine tasting,' said Anna.

'The reason we raised so much money was because Richard donated the wine,' Ivy said.

The doorbell rang. Fred heaved himself up. 'Be right back,' he said.

Clare raised her eyes at Anna, then asked about the grounds for Richard to appeal. Ten minutes later, Fred hadn't returned. With a loud tut Clare got up. 'I'll go and see what's happened to Fred.'

The back door was open. She slipped inside and saw Fred slumped at the kitchen table with his head in his hands.

'Fred?' she said in a deep, low voice.

He raised his head. His tie was askew, as if he had yanked at it, his eyes were shut, and he was rubbing them with his fingers. Had he been crying? She stayed in the doorway, unsure if he would rather be alone. She knew nothing about his personal life. Had a relative been involved in an accident? Had that been the police at the door? No, they wouldn't leave him on his own after delivering a shock. She walked a little closer.

'Fred what's happened?'

He stood, swallowed, pushed something under a pile of gardening magazines and then sighed.

'Bad news?' she asked, lightly touching his arm.

'Forget it,' he said, 'Nothing I wasn't expecting.' He rubbed his eyes, gave her a thin smile then said, 'Let's get back to the meeting.'

She rested a hand on the table and looked at his face. His eyes were red and puffy – he *had* been crying. She asked, 'Anything I can help with?' He lifted his chair, placing it firmly back against the table as if signifying the matter was closed. 'Thank you, but no. Let's get on.'

Outside, Anna was scrolling through her phone and Ivy looked as if she'd fallen asleep. Fred perched on the edge of his deckchair. 'Tell us what to do next, Clare,' he said. There was a brittleness in his voice, making Clare hesitate. Was she ordering people about? Did people think she was dictating instead of chairing? Was that the explanation for their reluctance to engage?

'I just think there's no harm in planning for the worst,' she mumbled. 'If he doesn't appeal the decision—'

'Oh, he's going to appeal,' said Fred. 'No doubt about that.' He spoke with a bitterness Clare hadn't heard before. 'Tell us what we do,' he said for a second time.

Clare turned to Anna. 'Can you do some research? Get some quotes? Then let's meet again tomorrow evening and work out how we get our own EIA.'

'Fine by me,' said Fred forcefully.

Clare spent the day on a tractor mower, scooting up and down the avenues of apple trees, watching the machine shredding the long grass into tiny pieces. In the evening, as it was chilly, she decided to host the meeting in the kitchen by the Aga. She put out a few bottles of her mother's cider. It hadn't won a prize in the Brambleton show. Sam's cider came top, but she suspected he'd judged his own product – cheating was obviously a family trait.

Thinking about him brought a flush to her cheeks. Driving home on Monday afternoon, after Sam had offered her tea and then disappeared, she kept imagining the brothers laughing about her bumping into Richard. Those two were a team. She shouldn't have let Sam lull her into thinking otherwise.

The door opened and Ivy walked in carrying a lemon drizzle cake. Clare suspected it was a peace offering after yesterday's testy exchange. Anna arrived with a chilled bottle of Clare's favourite white wine and a tieless Fred brought nothing.

Clare poured four glasses of cider. Ivy didn't touch hers. Fred took a sip, Anna a gulp.

'Urgh,' said Anna, spitting back into her glass.

'Is it off?' asked Clare, sniffing at her own glass. It reminded her of drains. She took a sip. It was horrid, wincingly sharp, like lemon juice, and she was struggling to detect any apple flavour. What must the judges have thought at the show? She visualized Rose and Sam laughing as they spat out the ghastly drink. 'That's pretty nasty, isn't it. Let's have Anna's wine instead.'

Clare replaced the cider and took a small sip of wine. 'Shall we start with fundraising ideas?'

'Has he appealed?' asked Ivy.

'Save your breath,' said Fred coldly. 'That man . . . I'd like to wring his neck.' To Clare, his eyes seemed to bulge, and he was clutching at the sides of his armchair like she clung onto the seat arms in an aircraft when it went through turbulence.

'You been eating your Weetabix, Fred?' asked Ivy.

Clare glanced from Anna to Ivy. She couldn't look at Fred. She'd never heard him speak like that before.

'Before we discuss fundraising, I've had quotes from experts and chosen the cheapest,' said Anna.

Clare glanced across at her friend. Anna was twisting her wedding ring round and around her finger, making Clare feel queasy – how bad was the number going to be?

Anna reeled off a list of quotes. To comment on noise pollution would cost over £4,000; the water contamination expert was the most expensive at £6,000 and smell was another £3,000. Traffic, primarily from desktop assumptions, still demanded £2,000.

'Oh my god!' Clare whispered to herself. Anna was chewing her bottom lip. Clare totted up the numbers. 'Fifteen grand!' she said.

Fred whistled. 'That's a big number.'

It was a vast sum of money. Especially for a village in rural North Devon.

'We might all be worrying over nothing,' said Ivy. 'We don't know that he will appeal. He might decide to do the right thing.'

'We start fundraising,' said Clare.

Anna spoke. 'If he appeals—'

'*When* he appeals,' said Fred.

Clare was pleased to have a convert. Shuddering at the task ahead of them she chose her words carefully. 'We didn't firm up on any ideas yesterday. Has anyone had a brain wave?' asked Clare.

'Gina has offered to host a coffee morning and a cake sale. She says the others in the mothers and toddlers group all want to help.' Said Ivy.

'We need to try and tap money outside the village too.' said Anna.

Ivy offered to go on a sponsored slim, which Clare thought set the right tone, and Anna suggested asking the Smugglers Inn to donate a meal which they could auction.

Clare seized on the idea. 'Hastings is the landlord, so I'm not sure Rose will do that, but an auction is a great idea. Why not ask local businesses that aren't in Richard's pocket to donate prizes and have a grand auction?'

'Where do we hold an auction?' asked Fred.

'Village hall. He doesn't own that,' said Anna. 'Hang on. I've got an idea. A charity bridge evening with an auction at the end. Most of the Thursday players don't live in the village, a lot of retired doctors play bridge and they're all on gold-plated pensions.'

'Excellent,' said Clare.

'I don't know how to play bridge,' said Ivy. 'Do I have to learn?'

'No. I can organize the bridge evening,' said Anna. 'Let's provide food and wine, then we can charge more.'

'Can't offer wine. You'd need a licence,' said Ivy.

'A free glass of wine then. We're not selling it and can make that clear on the tickets. I think it will prove a sound investment. People are always more generous after a couple of drinks,' said Anna.

The meeting wrapped up. They only had two fundraising ideas, and watching Ivy eating the last slice of cake, Clare didn't think the sponsored slim would raise much money. Her hopes were pinned on the bridge evening.

Nineteen

It was Thursday afternoon, and Clare was on her knees in Prosecco and Prose helping Trish unpack books. Stop-it was scooting the empty boxes round the room with his nose. There was a delicious smell of cinnamon seeping out of the kitchen, which was both soothing and disturbing. It reminded Clare of the night in Sam's kitchen with the smell of spices. The two women were discussing the fundraising auction. A Barnstaple hair salon had donated a cut and blow dry, and someone else had offered a free manicure.

'I want to help too,' said Trish. 'I thought I could ask a local author to do a reading. If I throw in a glass of wine, I could charge a fiver and maybe the author would donate a portion of their book sales.'

'Fabulous idea,' said Clare. She looked outside at the crowded terrace. 'What's the sentiment?'

Trish pulled a face. 'Honestly?'

Clare nodded.

'People are nervous,' said Trish. 'They're thrilled the Council rejected the plans, but they expect him to win because he always does.'

Clare used a pair of scissors to slice open another box, then ripped it apart, the sound echoing her feeling of despair. She heard the door open and tutted, 'I just wish—'. Trish held a finger up to her mouth, then said, 'That cookery book you ordered is in, Sam.'

'Thanks. I'll stay for coffee and a slice of your fudge cake. Can I buy you two something? What about you, Stop-it?' The dog waggled a box at Sam.

Clare blushed, then glanced down at her T-shirt and slacks, remembering how smartly she always dressed in London. But she didn't think her current clients – Captain Hilts and his brood, plus the pigs – would bat an eyelid if she appeared stark naked, provided she fed them. She struggled upright with a pile of books in her arms, itching to ask him where he'd disappeared to on Bank Holiday Monday afternoon. Sam took them from her.

Not wanting to feel those eyes on hers, she leaned down for another batch.

'Where did you vanish to last Monday?' he whispered.

She looked up. He was smiling. 'Where did *I*? What happened to *you*?'

'I went to fetch some milk from my cottage fridge store and when I got back my brother was standing in the kitchen spitting feathers.'

She chewed her lip, wondering if he was telling the truth. A frown crossed his face, 'You didn't—. Richard didn't see you, did he?' His eyes widened. 'Is that why you left?'

She nodded.

'Ah. Awkward for both of you.'

Trish returned with a tray, saying excitedly, 'Can we tap you for a prize? There's going to be an auction and a charity bridge day.'

Clare shut her eyes. She wanted to scream. Alerted, the Hastings family would find a way to ruin the bridge tournament and with it, their hopes of funding an EIA.

When she wasn't helping Anna prepare for the bridge tournament, Clare was in the orchard. Using a strimmer secured by a strap over her shoulder, she worked her way up and down the rows of apple trees. She was clearing the grass and weeds that had grown through the mulch around the tree trunks, an area her mother's orchard books referred to as the 'sward'. When the last circle was bare, Clare hooked up the trailer, just as Sam had taught her nearly three months ago. She spent two days moving bark chippings from her mother's stores, scattering them liberally over each root zone. The book assured her that the fresh mulch would keep the weeds away and help to retain moisture round the roots. The branches above her were weighed down with fruit; she would be harvesting soon. All twelve acres. Flicking through her mother's records, she'd discovered that last year Cindy had harvested over forty tonnes. How had her mother picked all those apples? There must be a machine in one of the barns.

Clare traipsed round the farmyard, peering in at dusty spaces filled with cobwebs. One barn housed her mother's workshop, another stored the animal feed. In the old milking parlour next to the Rotovator she found a useful looking metal pole propped against the wall, beside which was a stack of rigid plastic baskets, like those used by supermarkets to deliver groceries. She concluded that her mother had harvested manually. That was going to take weeks. And Clare had no idea even what to do with the apples – her mother's cider was revolting.

Trish had offered to stock the juice, but Clare wouldn't sell forty tonnes of apples that way. What she needed was a neighbouring cider farm who wanted to buy her crop. But Sam Hastings was the only cider farmer she knew, and she wasn't going into business with him.

She had a more urgent challenge; whatever she ultimately did with the harvest, she had to juice the apples, and her mother's records also revealed that, for the last five years, she'd used Sam to press the apples! Clare had scoured the internet and found an alternative supplier, but he was near Bude, virtually an hour's drive away.

Whichever way she turned, her plans seemed to hit a Hastings roadblock.

That afternoon, while Clare was walking the dog, she ran into Anna trawling the village for auction prizes. Her friend confirmed what Clare suspected – most Brambleton businesses were Hastings' tenants. The pair fell into lockstep, working their way up the hill. Watching Stop-it investigate each lamp post and drop his nose into clumps of grass, Clare felt a sense of calm run through her. Brambleton offered a gentle way of life.

'Ivy says there's a steady stream of people offering to host cake sales and coffee mornings, and several are dropping off boxes of chocolates and books for raffle prizes,' said Anna.

Clare gave a soft groan. 'We need decent prizes to auction.'

'There's the dentist,' suggested Anna.

'That would make a terrifically exciting auction – a free trip to the hygienist.'

Clare's arm jerked sideways. Stop-it was straining to reach a discarded banana skin. 'This dog is interested in everything except kibble,' she grumbled, pulling the dog to heel. 'We're pinning a lot on the bridge evening. What do you think we can charge?'

Anna beamed at her. 'With food and a glass of wine, at least fifteen quid.'

Clare screwed up her face. 'Do you think we could get away with a teeny bit more? Say £17.50?'

'How many tables are we targeting?'

'I was hoping fifteen.'

Anna swallowed. 'That's sixty people. We could try. Let's play at the bridge club tonight and sound out our target market. I'll make up a flyer.'

Clare let out a deep sigh. It was kind of Anna to offer, but the notice had to be precisely worded to avoid a Hastings crying foul over the 'free' glass of wine. 'Let me have a look at your draft.'

'Come here,' said Anna, hugging her. Clare clung on to her friend, squeezing. She was worried she'd set herself up as a sort of mythical wonder worker, a 'prodigal daughter' returned from London to slay the monster threatening the village.

She'd never taken on a case unless convinced she would win, but this time she wasn't sure she could. And it was personal. Clare wasn't just fighting Richard's plans to save Brambleton, but also to protect her mother's legacy, the orchard.

As they released each other from the hug, Anna said brightly, 'Ivy may be right – he might not appeal.'

Clare shook her head, 'Sadly, I don't believe in Father Christmas anymore.

The next day, dressed in an old baggy sweatshirt and tracksuit bottoms, Clare was on her hands and knees picking windfall apples, and feeding them into long orange mesh sacks. The dew was still thick on the grass and her legs were wet and cold where the moisture had seeped through, but the sun was warm on her back, and she was finding the task unsettlingly enjoyable. Last night had gone well, with over twenty tickets sold for the BARS's bridge fundraiser, and several players offering to donate prizes for the raffle. Even Richard spitefully threatening to clamp any cars parked on his land that evening didn't dampen her mood. She scrambled upright, picked up the metal pole she'd found in the old milking parlour and whacked it against a branch. A handful of apples tumbled to the ground, and she bent to retrieve them.

An hour later, she dislodged the final apple clinging to a top branch of the first tree. She gazed down the rows. At this rate she would still be harvesting at Christmas. She stalked to the next tree, took hold of a thick low branch, closed her eyes and pumped it up and down as if she was using the battle rope in the gym. Apples rained down. She shut her eyes and winced as hard fruit thwacked her head. Something thumped into her arm. She peeked down; surrounding the tree was a carpet of apples. *This was the way to do it*, thought Clare. She used one hand to form her sweatshirt into a pouch and, kneeling, used the other to scoop apples into it.

After a lunch break, Clare modified her technique to arrange a blue plastic tarpaulin round the base of each tree before she shook it. She was giving a branch a good shake when she heard laughter and glanced up. Sam was striding through the orchard. By the time he reached Clare he was roaring with laughter, 'what the . . . what . . . on . . . what *are* you doing?' He chuckled, pointing at her head.

She giggled, peering through the metal colander she had taken to wearing before she shook each tree. She removed it, then the folded teacloth cushioning the makeshift helmet from her scalp. 'Improvised protection . . . Mum probably has a proper apple collecting helmet, but I must have thrown it out . . .'

He wiped his eyes, then spluttered. 'There's no such thing. Cindy didn't have a helmet; she had a tree shaker.'

She stared at him. *Was that a specialist or a machine?* She didn't want to show her ignorance, 'I suppose that would make it faster . . . I mean to get the apples down, but I don't know how she managed to collect them all, my knees are sore after just two days . . .'

He cut her off. 'Please tell me you aren't harvesting manually.'

Did Cindy used to borrow machinery from Sam, was he about to offer to lend it to her; if he was, she was going to accept. 'Yes.' She admitted.

'Why? Is the apple collector broken?'

'I think she must have sold it.'

'I doubt it.' he pointed to the orange baskets, 'those are part of the machine. Come on show me where you found them, and I reckon the collector will be there too.'

Walking to the old milking parlour, Clare was conscious of his proximity. He was so close she could hear him breathing. She imagined what it would be like feeling his arm around her waist or his hand grasping hers. She peeked down at Sam's hands; they were rough and weathered from years of working in his own orchard.

When they reached their destination, she pulled open the door.

'There it is' he said triumphantly pointing at the Rotovator, 'and that,' he said, indicating the anchor-shaped chunk of metal she had dismissed as a piece of old farm machinery, 'is the apple shaker.'

Clare spent the next week juggling preparations for the bridge competition with the competing demands of harvesting apples, keeping warm in the evenings, and feeding herself and Stop-it on her tiny weekly budget. Harvesting had become much quicker now she was using machinery. Hooked up to the tractor, the shaker neatly felled the fruit, allowing her to steer the collecting machine over the fallen apples and hoover them up. Listening to the fruit tumble into the two orange baskets secured to the back of the machine brought a smile to her face.

During the daytime, she was too active to notice the temperature, but the nights were chilly. In London, she never felt cold. Her flat was well-insulated, and the central heating run by cost-effective gas. The period farmhouse was draughty, North Devon wasn't on the gas grid, and she couldn't afford to fill up the oil tank. There was a pile of logs, mostly too big for the fire grates, but the thought of chopping wood sounded dangerous, and anyway, she didn't know how to lay a fire. Clare dragged an armchair next to the Aga, and in the evenings read a book with Stop-it curled up on her lap, thankful that its fuel tank registered 75 per cent full.

The freezer was empty and, bored with fried eggs, she rummaged through her mother's books, unearthing a copy of Delia Smith's *How to Cook* series. With Stop-it acting as chief sampler, one evening she made salmon fishcakes, and on the next she braised sausages in cider apples.

With a week to go before the fundraiser, Clare called a BARS meeting. Ready to tackle the temperature, she built a mountain of newspaper in the sitting room fireplace. She balanced a firelighter on top, a few small logs above that and then lit the paper. The flames burned brightly, devouring the newspaper; the firelighter caught, and the fire curled round the wood. For a few minutes Clare admired her handiwork. She sat on the sofa, snuggled into a corner in front of the roaring fire as she used to do so often as a child.

It was dusk, and the lamplight illuminated the shabby furnishings. Cotton throws covered the ancient sofa and both chairs, but there were muddy paw marks on them, and most of the cushions were at least six-sided, the extra angles added by Clare folding over corners and stitching them up after Stop-it's games. She pictured her pristine flat, but for the first time since she had arrived in Devon, she didn't miss it. Yes, it was warmer, but it didn't have as much character. Besides, she wasn't sure there would have been sufficient space to host tonight's meeting in her flat.

Her fellow activists arrived together. Anna and Clare sat on either end of the sofa, while Ivy and Fred took the armchairs.

'Were you burning some of your mother's old papers?' asked Ivy, gesticulating at the fire grate. There was a pile of black ashes, a scorched log, but no flames.

Clare threw her hands up in despair. 'I had that going. Why has it gone out?'

Anna rose, picked up a poker and stabbed at the wreckage. 'You need more kindling,'

'And more wood,' said Fred.

'I haven't got either.'

Anna and Ivy exchanged a glance. 'Let's sort this,' said Anna. 'Ivy, do you know where Cindy kept her wood store?'

While Clare stood by helplessly, Fred, Ivy and Anna bustled about, collecting kindling, logs and firelighters. She could hear wood being chopped outside. Anna laid a fire with the firelighter beneath a lattice framework of kindling, then a towering stack of logs, explaining, 'Fires burn upwards, so give the flames something to chase.'

'I'll come back in the morning and chop some more wood for you,' announced Fred as he dumped a full basket by the roaring fire.

'That's super kind, Fred, but please, just show me how to do it. If I'm going to be here for winter, I must learn.'

'How close are we to our target for ticket sales?' asked Ivy

'Still a dozen light,' said Anna.

Fred claimed he might be able to sell them.

'All twelve?' asked Ivy. 'My, my; God does move in mysterious ways.'

'Yup. Someone asked me this afternoon,' said Fred triumphantly.

'For *twelve* tickets?' said Anna.

Fred nodded.

Clare had a sudden unpleasant thought. 'It's not Hastings in disguise, is it? He'll find a way to scupper it. We can't let him play.'

'Oh, ye of little faith,' said Fred in a mocking tone. 'It's not Richard.'

If it wasn't Richard, Clare didn't care who played. They needed all the money they could get.

Twenty

On the last Saturday in September, BARS hosted its bridge tournament. Clare arrived at the village hall to discover a line of yellow and black striped hazard tape stretching from the side of the hall, across the field normally used for parking and all the way to the opposite fence. There was a stiff breeze, and the tape snapped angrily in the wind, as if mimicking the man responsible for putting it there.

With only five minutes to go before kick-off, the room buzzed with chatter and laughter, but twelve of the players were missing and Penny was beginning to question if the movement would still work with only thirteen tables. Clare was rushing about touting the raffle, ripping off tickets in exchange for £10 notes, then stuffing the money into a plastic bucket. The door opened to admit a group of strangers. Clare counted ten; they would still be a pair short. She gritted her teeth. The solution was obvious – she and Anna would have to make up numbers, which would prevent her from plugging the raffle.

She turned to look for Anna, but then heard giggling and spun back. Framed in the doorway was a young woman. She wore a bright pink trouser suit, with a white silk blouse. Her shoulder length strawberry-blonde hair and elegant, chiselled features gave off the air of a supermodel. The volume of background chatter lowered. Players shuffled in seats and gawped as the glamourous woman's partner walked in: Sam. Clare cast around for Fred, who had sold the last dozen tickets. When she didn't see him, she glared at Sam instead. She should have guessed that Richard would send his spy. That was probably why Sam was last to arrive. He'd been told to report on anyone illegally parked. Clare would have to keep her eyes on him, he wasn't here just to play bridge.

Watching Sam help his partner take off her jacket and then pull out her chair, Clare realized that this explained why Sam had orchestrated that run-in with his brother. He hadn't been fetching milk at all. He'd got cold feet about entertaining Clare in a cosy twosome, in case his girlfriend showed up, although she wasn't convinced that this glamorous woman would have felt threatened by Clare. Recognizing the insidious signs of jealousy stalking her thoughts, she told herself to accept Sam wasn't interested in her, and that was good news. He would have left her high and dry and crushed her heart, just like Guy. Her life would soon be back on track, in London, where she belonged.

Sam shot Clare a smile. She didn't return it. He reached for his cards and Clare scooted off to help in the kitchen, vowing to throw him out if he did anything to disrupt the evening.

By the time they stopped for food – with a warning from Penny not to discuss the boards, as half the room wouldn't have played them yet – it was obvious that both Sam and his stunning girlfriend were skilled players. Clare hoped they wouldn't win, as neither of them needed the money. She could see him now, turning up at Brambleton Hall with Ms Pink Trouser Suit for a nightcap with his brother, snickering over the evening they'd endured and plonking the prize money of £100 on the hall table – petty cash to them.

Dashing in and out of the kitchenette with trays of shepherd's pie, Clare spotted the enemy on manoeuvres. Sam was making his way from table to table, leaning in and chatting with people. She reminded herself that provided he didn't spike the auction, she didn't care. She heard him laugh, smiled and caught herself. Why did she still find that sound attractive?

Ivy said grace and then invited people to collect food. Anna served vegetables, Clare doled out shepherd's pie and Ivy was overseeing the vegetarian option. When the pink trouser suit stood in front of Clare, she told herself to act as if she was a client. 'Thanks for your support,' she said.

The woman leaned closer, giving Clare a blast of wine breath – it was supposed to be one glass each, but pink trouser suit had the breath of a wino. Clare's eyes darted round the room. There was a bottle of wine on every table. Where had they come from? BARS hadn't paid for those.

Sam's girlfriend was telling Clare she was down from London, saying she was staying at Sam's, 'I can never say no to bridge!'

Clare scraped the serving spoon against the tray. When Sam reached Clare, she kept her eyes on her job. 'Don't try anything,' she said, hammering her spoon against his plate.

'Smells delicious,' he said. 'Did Ivy cook this?'

Clare glanced up into his smiling face. 'I'm not sure you should be here.'

His smile slipped and he exhaled. He looked like he was about to get cross with her for being rude, but she didn't let him. 'Excuse me, we need to tidy up,' she announced, hurrying off, angry with herself for letting Sam rattle her.

While BARS did the washing-up, the remaining boards were played and then Anna announced the auction. Trying to ignore Sam, who was trotting from table to table acting as the wine waiter, Clare picked up a printed list of prizes. Written in Fred's neat handwriting was a couple of late additions, including a box of vintage claret that looked quite valuable.

Clare started with the wine. There were several bidders, but Sam's girlfriend was like an overenthusiastic schoolchild. Her hand seemed to be permanently waving at Clare, and the box of wine sold for nearly £2,000. The woman also bought a local artist's watercolour of the harbour and a hamper of local goodies. There was a fierce tussle over Ivy's home-baked Dundee cake. The pink trouser suit was once again in action, bidding against another stranger, who Sam was egging on, but who graciously bowed out at £120.

Sam and his girlfriend won the tournament. As he escorted his partner to collect the prize money, Clare clapped, a part of her pleased their chief supporter was clawing back a tiny portion of her donations. The woman leaned on Sam as they weaved their way towards Clare 'Wonderful evening for a marvellous cause. Thank you and good luck.'

Clare wanted to say she didn't think Sam would agree, but she didn't want to embarrass her generous benefactor, so, smiling, she handed over the envelope of money.

'What's this?' asked the woman, scrunching the envelope in her hand.

'Your prize money.'

'No, you keep it,' she said, thrusting the envelope back at Clare. 'I've had a fabulous time.'

Clare's smile broadened. Her hands tightened round the envelope. She didn't trust herself to look at Sam. He wouldn't enjoy reporting this to his brother.

When the last player had left, Fred, Anna, Clare and Ivy gathered round a table. Ivy upended the plastic bucket, and the raffle money tumbled out. They shuffled the notes and coins into piles, reminding Clare of counting savings from her piggybank the week before Christmas. She thought of her egg money jar and decided to keep that for a treat.

They counted the cash, then added the £1,120 from ticket sales and the money pledged from the auction. They'd raised nearly £5,000, £3,000 of which was from Sam's girlfriend. Anna gave a whoop of delight, Fred whistled, Ivy praised the Lord and Clare felt herself grinning. It was a staggering amount of money – a third of the target.

Outside, Fred celebrated by ripping down Richard's hazard tape. He rolled it into a ball, stomped onto the field and hurled it on to the grass.

'Fred Thompson, you make sure you dispose of that responsibly,' Ivy scolded. Fred picked it up. Ivy reached out a hand. 'It's soft plastic. Give it here. They recycle that at the supermarket.'

Walking home, the fizz of adrenalin fading, Clare felt like she used to as a youngster the morning after a wonderful party – the anticipation was gone, there was nothing to look forward to. The reality of BARS' finances was stark. It was fantastic to raise £5,000, and Gina and her gang of mothers were inching towards their target of £500, but they were out of ideas. Ivy's sponsored slim wouldn't raise the other £9,500, and Brambleton wasn't wall-to-wall with banking wealth and rich lawyers. Stopping to cross the road, Clare changed the angle of her torch and as she shone it sideways the beam fell on a barn owl. With a few unhurried rhythmic flaps, the bird sailed past into a nearby tree. She hadn't seen one since she'd worked in the pub. There weren't many of them in London. She heard the bird's low hoot, and a gentle peace settled over her.

There must be a solution. She would find it.

By mid-October the rich sweet smell of windfall apples made Clare feel nauseous. The bulk of the harvest had been collected mechanically, but for a second day Clare was crawling on her hands and knees collecting fruit. She imagined her mother scrabbling through the orchard. If Cindy could harvest alone, her daughter could. Wearily, she heaved up another basket, spilling the contents into an orange sack. Stop-it's nose was wedged through the gate, occasionally squeaking his desire to join the game. She leaned on the bonnet of the Land Rover and allowed the harvests from her childhood to wash over her: Clare sitting in a corner of the orchard playing on a picnic blanket while her parents collected apples. She tried to pinpoint which corner the blanket had been in. All four looked idyllic in the hazy autumnal sunshine. Gazing around the beautiful field, with its symmetrical rows of trees, she mused that it was no wonder they'd named the farm after it. She laughed, realizing she hadn't thought about where she should have been on her sabbatical adventure all week. She peeled off her gloves and went to check her emails.

On opening her laptop, her body went rigid. Her eyes darted, pausing briefly at the word 'appeal'. She groaned. 'Shit, shit, shit! Already.'

Bill had warned her this would happen. Richard had until the end of February but had acted quickly. BARS now only had weeks to raise nearly £10,000, commission an EIA and write their submission. The only local couple rich enough to donate that kind of money were Roger and Anna, and, given Roger's stance, that wouldn't happen. Maxed-out on debt and with her savings in a kitchen jar, Clare couldn't fund the shortfall. She couldn't think of anything to sell apart from the Land Rover, and she needed that to transport apples.

She turned towards Stop-it. 'Come on,' she said. 'Let's get you out. Life's always better after a walk, eh?'

Clare strode past the chicken enclosure. Hilts looked like he was scowling at her, and she glared back. Richard and his army of advisers would be crowing.

*

Clare dawdled along the Tarka Trail, past fields that for centuries had been home to Hetherington dairy cows. Rugged hills rose dramatically against the backdrop of the vast, grey estuary, and waves crashed against the rocks below. The breeze tousled her hair, which now reached her ears, and she sucked in a lungful of fresh, salty air. She loved this track. As a teenager during school holidays she, Trish and Anna used to cycle to Torrington and back – over fifty miles – just so that Trish could gaze at her teenage crush: a young gardener who worked at RHS Rosemoor.

Clare had stirred up a hornet's nest. Without an alternative EIA, Richard would win. And when he did, his challengers would be in his crosshairs. She wished she hadn't encouraged Fred and Ivy to fight. Richard could make them homeless. Stop-it seemed in tune with her mood: his leash was slack, and he nudged the side of her leg, copying her in staring morosely out to sea, at the people enjoying the water. She watched a paddle boarder glide gracefully, their silhouette serene against the sunlit waves, each stroke propelling them forward with quiet determination. In contrast, a kite surfer seemed to add a dash of exhilaration to the scene, their bright purple sail soaring high, tugging them across the ocean at speed. The surfer caught the wind, leapt and twisted, sending sprays of water sparkling into the air. The tourists were oblivious to the feeling of dread lodged in her stomach like a hard knot of despair.

She gnawed at a fingernail, debating whether to expel Ivy and Fred from BARS. Would that protect them? In her peripheral vision, she saw a man in the former Hetherington fields and recognized one of two people she didn't want to speak to.

'Hi there, you two,' called Sam.

'I expect your brother is pleased with himself.'

'He's enjoying the fight. He didn't expect the Council to turn him down, but this tussle was always going to end in an appeal.'

An appeal she couldn't fund. A guilty feeling clogged her throat.

Stop-it lunged after a passing rabbit. She staggered down the hill, both hands gripping the straining leash, dragging her arms virtually out of their sockets. Sam opened the gate. 'Give him here.'

'He's just excited. So many smells to investigate. I've been harvesting, so he hasn't been out much.'

'Why not let him off in here? Give him a chance to run around. There's no livestock.'

There used to be lots of animals, thought Clare, *and there still should be*. What would become of her family's former land? What would become of her mother's orchard if she couldn't protect the trees from Richard and his chicken run-off? Sam opened the gate wider, took the leash, then bent and unclipped the dog who shot off, kicking out his back legs like a horse released from stables after a long winter.

Clare walked beside Sam on a wide track, mown through the grass.

'I cut this so holidaymakers can get across to the coastal path.'

She couldn't think of a reply. These fields should be full of cows, not the occasional walker. But it was Hastings' land now.

They reached a copse which Clare recognized from her childhood. Her father had planted it as a cover for the dairy herd in hot summer months. It was a thin belt of holm oak and beech, both species hardy enough to absorb the salt thrown at them in winter storms. The saplings of Clare's youth now towered forty feet above her.

'I remember this wood as a child. My father planted it.' A dreamy look came over her face and she gave a little laugh. 'When I was at primary school, we used to play cowboys and Indians in here.' Sam had played here too, before he became too grand to mix with the local kids.

'I remember.' he said breezily. 'I used to nick Dad's Panama hat and Mum's Hermes scarves to dress up as a cowboy.'

She smiled despite her mood. 'Were you ever caught?'

He laughed. 'I've always been nimble-footed. I'm pretty good at sneaking round unobserved.'

They picked their way along a deer track, Clare walking behind Sam, talking about her harvest.

'What are you doing with your apples?' asked Sam.

'Not making cider, that's for sure! I finally tasted my mother's efforts.' She stopped. She wasn't sure if she wanted to talk about Cindy with a member of the family who had conned her out of her farm.

As if he could read her mind, he turned and looked at her, then said in a stern voice, 'I don't approve of what my brother did to your farm you know. Cindy didn't say anything to me and by the time I found out, it was too late to stop him.'

Clare sighed and shook her head. Nothing could have stopped Richard. Her mother had picked a fight with the wrong man, and he'd clobbered her. She must stop Ivy and Fred incurring his wrath; they were easy prey for Tricky Ricky. 'You were saying . . . you won't be following in your mother's cider-making footsteps?' Sam grinned.

Imagining Rose, Sam and the other Brambleton Show judges taking a mouthful of her mother's honking brew, Clare laughed, feeling the pent-up tension escape. When she spluttered to a halt, Sam told her he'd guessed the show had been the first time anyone had drunk Cindy's cider. He knew that being teetotal, Cindy wouldn't have tried it herself. And if Clare had tasted it, she would never have entered it. They walked on, and Clare told him she thought some of her mother's apples were dessert apples, not cider apples, and that might explain the disaster.

'No,' he said decisively. 'You can make cider from any sort of apple. The trend is moving away from traditional varieties like Dabinett, Foxwhelp and Kingston Black.'

She chuckled. 'Why do they have such odd names?'

'When someone discovered an apple, they named it. They must have wanted something memorable.'

'Tough for others to remember though.'

'Yes. The big commercial cider makers thought so too. One of them renamed them after women in the office – there's a variety called Meredith, and another called Frederika.'

'Those are a bit easier! Well, whatever Mum grew, she was doing something wrong.'

'Let an amateur make wine from the finest pinot noir grapes and you're unlikely to end up with something that will worry Burgundian vintners.'

'It really was awful, wasn't it!'

He barked a laugh. 'Yup. The word *rancid* springs to mind.'

The wood was thinning, giving a glimpse of Sam's orchards. Long straight rows of trees, their branches no longer weighed down by fruit. Beneath each tree canopy, the sward was punctuated with neat circular carpets of bark chippings. It looked as well tended as Fred's little garden.

Sam pointed at Stop-it a few yards ahead of them. The dog was bouncing in and out of the undergrowth, occasionally yelping in excitement. 'Look at him. He's having a marvellous time.' Clare interpreted Sam's comment as a subtle hint to get him under control before they reached the orchard, and the dog trampled over his windfalls. She stopped, patted her pocket, then took out a plastic packet, holding it up and rustling it noisily. 'Sit!' she said, then in a lower voice. 'Sit, good bully boy. Sit,' she said encouragingly. Sam gave her a sideways, puzzled look. She called out, this time in a high, excited voice. 'Sit. Oh, sit!'

Sam smiled. 'Why not use the more conventional "come" command?'

Stop-it appeared at her feet. She fed him a few biscuits, then hooked him onto the lead.

'Doesn't work,' she said. 'People think this breed is stupid, but he's actually smart, just stubborn. He understands "come" but associates it with a reprimand. *Sit* and he gets a biscuit. Which would you respond to?'

Out of the blue, he asked the question she'd been expecting since he appeared. 'I must ask this, Clare – can you really fund an EIA?'

Her head told her it might be an elegant moment to offer an olive branch, but her gut still told her to fight, and she wanted a defiant message to reach Richard. 'We'll get there,' she said, despite having no idea how they would. 'Yes.'

'So, you've got the money for an EIA?'

She blushed. She'd never been a good liar, so answered to her shoes. 'We've got enough to start with, and we'll raise the rest.'

'Good luck,' he said.

'Don't gloat.'

'I'm not. The Planning Inspector won't be swayed by local opposition like the Council was.'

'I'm a lawyer, Sam. I know how to present a decent case.'

And that was the problem. In her career, effort had been enough to win; the currency had been knowledge – how to use the law effectively – but that wouldn't be enough against Hastings. She needed money to pay for expert advice.

To do:

- Find someone local to juice apples
- Buy more chicken and pig feed
- Agenda for BARS meeting: Ivy and Fred to step back; fundraising
- Farmhouse renovations list

Another BARS meeting. Another lemon drizzle cake. This time the fire was kicking out a gentle warmth.

'Are you saying we're not pulling our weight?' demanded Fred.

'No,' said Clare, drawing out the word. 'You've been a huge asset, both of you. We'd never have managed the bridge evening without you. But I don't want you risking your homes. So far, we can blame it on the Council, but now it will be us, BARS, who will be on the front-line facing Richard. He's an evil monster.'

'I'm not running away from him,' spluttered Fred. 'Anyway, it's too late, he knows who's behind BARS.'

Ivy clasped the cross at her neck. 'God never sends me a challenge he doesn't think I'm able to face.'

Clare blew out a sigh. They were both behaving as if they were little children out playing an exciting game and she was Mum spoiling the fun, calling them in for bathtime. 'Richard is ruthless.' She bit her lip and looked at Anna. 'Help me,' she said.

Ivy reached out a hand and patted one of Clare's. 'I know you mean well, but we both know what we're doing. We're in the same position as other tenants reporting a broken boiler; we're just complaining about something different. We all run the risk of landlord revenge. I pray he doesn't do it, and I don't think he's that nasty.'

Clare tutted. Hastings was a Machiavellian monster, the nastiest man she'd ever known. Her instinct was to protect anyone vulnerable, but she counted Fred and Ivy as friends too. She wished they weren't so determined to remain on the front line.

'I've had an idea,' said Ivy. 'Villagers keep offering me donations, asking if there's a JustGiving page. Why don't I set one up?'

'Let's do it,' said Clare. She had an image of an old-fashioned paper bank statement, a page of BARS lines recording scores of donations. 'We can leave the details in all the places we left the leaflets. That's such a good idea.' Clare bounced up. 'Anyone for a glass of wine?'

'Sorry, but I told Roger I would only be an hour. Do you mind if we crack on?' said Anna.

'What's this on the agenda about drafting a submission?' asked Ivy.

Clare looked around at the blank faces. 'I'm not writing it alone,' she said, a note of desperation in her voice.

'Bit busy putting the dahlias to sleep for winter – got to dig them all up before the frosts start.'

'I'm covering for the interregnum of one of the Exmoor parishes. It's quite exhausting,' mumbled Ivy.

'Don't fortify yourself with food, Ivy,' warned Fred.

Clare looked at Anna and received an apologetic look.

'Bit flat out,' said Anna.

Clare sighed. She had the harvest to move. She'd calculated there were thirty trailer loads; it would take her more than a week to transport those to Bude. Her friends rose, shrugging on their coats – she understood why they expected her to draft the document. She was a lawyer. Just one with no spare time. How could she squash in a submission document? Of course, if she used Sam to juice the apples, instead of going to Bude, she would save days. She would swallow her pride and ask.

Later that week Clare was standing in Sam's Cider barn listening to the splash of water, the clatter of apples rolling along sorting belts and the occasional dull thud of an imperfect apple being tossed aside by Sam. It was a precise process, choosing the good and discarding the bad, and you needed to recognize which was which. Given the mess Clare had made of her life, she didn't think she'd be very good at it.

'Don't laugh,' she said, despite doing so herself, 'but I had no idea that the harvest needed washing and sorting before pressing.'

He grinned at her. 'You don't crush the apples themselves. You mill them into a pulp called a pomace, then crush that to release juice. You're welcome to watch but it might make more sense if you fetch me another trailer load.'

After delivering the final batch of apples, Clare rejoined Sam. Inside the barn there was now an overpowering smell of apples: it was rich and slightly tannic. She could hear the creaking of the press, the slow rhythmic squeezing, then the gush of juice as her mother's efforts were released. She caught herself – this wasn't just her mother's effort. Clare had cared for those apples in the crucial summer months, it was Clare who'd kept the sward low, Clare who'd harvested the crop. This was a joint enterprise of mother and daughter, just as her mother had always dreamed.

She shook the thought away and focused on helping Sam decant the apple juice into fifty litre containers. Using a sack truck, Sam wheeled them to the edge of Clare's trailer. He hefted each one as easily as if it was empty and loaded them onto the trailer.

'I think I'm busier in Devon than I used to be in London,' said Clare. 'You never get a day off as a farmer, do you?'

He turned, flashing her a smile that made her feel warm despite the autumnal chill. 'It's a way of life. You don't take days off from life,' he said.

'I'm supposed to be having a year off from life. It's my sabbatical year.'

'I heard you'd had to cancel your trip.' *That would be Fred*, thought Clare. It must be awkward for them being friends caught either side of a planning battle. 'Is someone helping you with these at the other end?' Sam asked.

She shook her head. 'I'll be fine. I used to deadlift fifty kilos at the gym.'

'Hmm. Borrow this,' he said, putting the sack truck onto the trailer. 'Do you miss London?' Clare thought about the question, picturing her small glass box of an office, then her neat tiny flat where nothing ever needed fixing. In London, she could walk to a supermarket or send out to dozens of local restaurants for food, and she used to have the income to fund both.

'I miss the restaurants. I'm not much of a cook and there's the most fabulous local Indian. I'm so flat out just now and am craving a tandoori paneer tikka masala.'

'As you may remember, I love cooking with spices,' said Sam, making Clare cringe. Did he think she was fishing for an invitation? 'Come for dinner tonight. We can discuss cider making. I can tell you what to do, and when, with that juice,' he said.

It was on the tip of her tongue to refuse, but her mouth was already watering at the thought of a proper curry. 'What can I bring?'

'Nothing. I enjoy cooking. No, you can bring something – you can bring Stop-it. I like having a dog around the house.'

At Orchard Farm, Clare backed the apple juice up to a barn. She climbed onto the trailer, pushed and jostled a container to the edge. She jumped off, hugged it and, tensing her stomach muscles, lowered it to the ground. She wiped a hand across her sweaty brow and limbered up to repeat the exercise. By the third container she was slick with sweat, her legs were trembling, and she was laughing – farmhands didn't need personal trainers. She moved the last container into the barn and collapsed on to her back on the floor, recovering her breath and feeling pleased with herself. Sam would tell her how to start cider making and she had found someone to finalize that process – if she could find the money to pay them.

She rolled onto her front and plucked out her phone. The first email she read dampened her mood. Richard's appeal had been validated. She wasn't surprised, but what did surprise her was the announcement of a public hearing. She sat up and read the details. The hearing would be in March and 'interested parties' had until the end of the year to submit their arguments to the Planning Inspectorate. Working backwards, BARS would need an EIA completed before Christmas, which meant site visits at least a week before then, giving them just six weeks to raise the money. Clare let the phone drop to her chest, feeling the enormity of the task weigh down on her.

She forwarded the message to Ivy, Fred and Anna, suggesting they meet tomorrow to discuss tactics in Prosecco and Prose. Clare checked her coffee jar and counted her egg money – £85. That wouldn't dent the BARS target. After showering and blow-drying her hair, Clare stood in front of her wardrobe, staring at the contents for inspiration. Jeans or a dress? She shut the door and slumped on the bed. What was she thinking? Learning about cider making with Sam in the barn today had been fun, but this wasn't a date; it was a business meeting. Even if she was interested in him, it was obvious his interest was purely professional – he'd made that clear decades ago, after that night in the Smugglers Inn.

It had been a busy night; she and Trish had felt like they'd run a marathon behind the bar. All evening her eyes kept meeting Sam's, each glance lingering a bit longer. When he leaned over to place his order, his fingertips brushed her arm, sending a spark up her spine. 'You've got a way of lighting up this place,' he murmured, his voice warm. She blushed, dropping her eyes to hide her smile, her pulse racing in reply.

Clare had taken a tray to clear a booth. Bending over to collect glasses, she felt arms encircle her waist and as she turned, she looked up into those startling blue eyes. Sam kissed her. It was deep, long and sensuous, and she melted into his arms. She pulled away, muttering, 'Sam, I'm working!' His warm breath was in her hair as he whispered, promising to meet her the following night after her shift, to go for a walk on the beach where they could be alone. The whole of the next day she had felt a bright glow of anticipation. She skipped into the pub and her boss handed her a note. The unfamiliar writing was neat and the message clear: Sam, a Hastings, could never be serious about a 'village girl'. Even now, thinking about the cruelty of his words caused her insides to shrivel with shame. Why would he be serious about someone like her, if he could date confident, outgoing, beautiful women like the Woman in Pink?

She should probably wear a suit tonight. Keep it professional. Except she wanted to dress comfortably, so she settled on her best jeans and a jumper, a light touch of make-up and the faintest spray of perfume. She dithered over taking Stop-it, but he was already waiting by the back door with a sort of 'I promise I won't be any trouble at all' expression on his face, so she grabbed a dozen eggs as a gift, hooked the dog to his seat harness and drove with a peculiar feeling of anticipation and dread.

Twenty-one

Clare arrived promptly at seven. The front door was open. 'Hello?' she called out from the entrance hall.

'In here,' came an answering call.

In the kitchen, Clare dropped Stop-it's lead, and he bounced over, planting his front paws on Sam's thighs. 'You did say to bring him,' she laughed. Sam spun around, showing his back to the dog. Stop-it jumped up, pawing at Sam's bottom, but he ignored the dog. Watching, Clare remembered her parents constantly telling her dogs were an excellent judge of character. Maybe Stop-it was an exception. He seemed remarkably keen on Sam.

After a few moments, the jumping stopped. Sam turned. 'Good boy,' he praised, reaching down and fondling the dog's ears.

'Wow, that was impressive,' said Clare.

'He just needs a firm hand,' said Sam. He pointed to a box on the counter. 'You said you were flat out, so that's a takeaway.' She lifted the lid and sniffed; it was something in a tikka masala sauce, and the smell transported her to London, back to a night shortly before Guy's accident, when she had returned late, exhausted from the office and found Guy slumped on the sofa. His shoes were kicked off and he was watching a movie. Empty takeaway cartons littered the floorboards, the tell-tale bright red of a tikka masala sauce coating one of them.

'Hi,' she had said, removing her coat and collapsing on the sofa. He didn't look up but moved his feet out of her way and grunted, his eyes glued to the movie.

'Is mine in the oven?' she asked.

'Didn't order you anything. Wasn't sure if you'd be hungry.'

She got up, her eyes smarting. 'I'm going to hit the sack.'

'Umm,' he said, staring at the screen, 'Could you lend me twenty quid?'

Thinking about it now, it wasn't the lack of food which had upset her; it was his indifference to her presence, other than as a cashpoint. Why hadn't she realized their relationship had changed from being symbiotic to parasitic? Her mother had been right. She blinked to force the memory away, realizing Sam was talking to her.

'I'm nearly done. You can either stay in here with a glass of wine and the smell of cooking, or I've lit a fire in the library.'

'The fire sounds enticing.'

'Come on Stop-it,' he called.

Following the sound of the dog's nails tapping on the floorboards, Clare was intrigued by the idea of a library in a farmhouse – only a Hastings would do that.

It was a cosy room with low ceilings, limed beams and linenfold panels. Ancient bookshelves covered two sides. As promised, there was a fire burning, kicking out heat and the sweet smell of apple wood. In front of it was a wicker dog basket. It had short stumpy legs raising it from the ground and a thick brown cushion, the sort of basket she imagined seeing a retired greyhound lounging elegantly in. She hoped Stop-it didn't chew the sides. The cushion had a handful of biscuits scattered on it.

'I'll fetch you that wine,' he said. 'Make yourself comfortable and don't fight to keep him off the furniture. I don't mind.'

'That's because you haven't seen what he does to cushions,'

Clare called after him. He returned smiling, with a glass of white wine and a wooden board of bruschetta.

'Last of my tomatoes from the greenhouse. You'd better have a few. I've already eaten several and there's quite a lot of garlic in them.'

She gave a faint smile, wondering if he considered the evening a date. But a mental picture of his beautiful girlfriend with her luscious strawberry-blonde hair soon dispelled that thought. He was just being polite, like when she used to brush her teeth before an afternoon meeting if she'd eaten something pungent for lunch.

She sipped her wine and nibbled. The bruschetta reminded her of holidays in Tuscany before she'd met Guy, and for a few minutes her thoughts vacillated between what the Hastings family had done to her and her mother, and how pleasant it was to have someone looking after her. The way her week was panning out, she was being catered for every day. If she stretched Sam's takeaway – Stop-it couldn't share it, it contained onion – it would be the weekend before she had to cook.

Her confidence buoyed by wine, she vowed she would raise the money, even if she had to borrow it from moneylenders. Then she thought of a cunning plan. She would pretend they couldn't afford an EIA. If they were careful, ensured the site visits took place when Richard, Sam and the other Hasting employees – AKA 'spies' – weren't around, they could add the report to their submission as a sting in the tail when it was too late for the opposition to react. It was worth a shot. She ate another canapé – damn, this man was good with seasoning.

After her third bruschetta, Clare got up to explore the room. With her wine glass in one hand, she ran her finger over the book spines, reading the titles. It was an eclectic selection, from the classics – Dickens and Shakespeare – to literary fiction and commercial novels. There was a wide section devoted to cookery books which made her smile. She'd never met anyone who kept those outside of their kitchen.

When Sam joined her, he brought a tray. She sauntered back and sat on the sofa. He held up a bottle, then sat next to her, so close she could smell his spicy scent. She shuffled herself into the corner of the seat.

'As a neighbouring apple grower, I must ask you to taste this.'

'Confession time. I don't drink cider. Bit too much scrumpy as a teenager.'

'This isn't anything like scrumpy,' he said, laughing. There was a pop and a hiss as she sat back and looked up. He was holding out a champagne glass full of a pale fizzy liquid. 'Go on. Try it.'

She dipped her nose and sniffed. There was a definite smell of apples, but it wasn't overpowering, it was enticing. She took a sip, feeling tiny bubbles explode on her tongue. It was like drinking apple flavoured champagne. She took another sip. It was delicious. How could Sam make something that tasted so divine when her mother's effort was so vile?

She looked at him over the rim of the glass. He was grinning at her. 'Enjoying?' he asked.

'Kind of different from my mother's brew!'

He chuckled. 'The secret is remembering it's a science. People approach it as an art, just like cooking, but the best cooks know that science lies behind their art and the same is true of making cider. I keep the alcohol level low and aim for 4.5 per cent.'

'How can I do that?'

'Dilute the fermented product with neat apple juice or you could use a pure Devon spring water. I can come and help you if you like?'

She let him talk about his craft, but lulled by the intimate atmosphere, her mind wandered back to her marriage. Guy had never approached his career as diligently. That was probably why he'd never made money; that and the fact money meant nothing to him. Provided he could drive cars, he would have been content living in a garden shed. Thoughts of sheds brought up a picture of Richard's 'shed', then one of Fred's, and she asked Sam if he knew what was bothering Fred.

He shrugged. 'No idea, he's quite a private soul, never shares his worries with me, but now I think of it, you're right – he has been out of sorts.'

'I think it's something to do with your brother.'

'Well, if it is, he hasn't told me,' said Sam.

When Clare walked into Prosecco and Prose at noon the next day, there was a heated debate taking place at the serving counter. Clare hung back, feeling like an uninvited guest. She couldn't hear the words, but Fred was speaking in a shrill voice at odds with the Fred that Clare knew, and Ivy was muttering in an equally unfamiliar shaky one. She walked closer; Trish's eyes met Clare's, then darted away. Her friend leaned forwards, her head twitching, 'Shush. Time out, you two.'

There was a collective shuffling of feet from Clare's side of the counter. The room fell silent. Clare felt a chill sweep through her: what were they talking about that Trish didn't think she should hear? From the expression on Trish's face, it wasn't a surprise birthday party.

'What can I get you, Clare?' asked Trish, rubbing a cloth over the counter.

'Well, I was going to ask for tea, but I think I might need a brandy. Is someone going to tell me what's going on?'

Ivy and Fred exchanged a charged look.

'Fred?' said Clare.

He raised his head. There was a bitter expression on it.

It was Ivy who spoke. 'Fred's had one of those Section 21 notices.'

Clare closed her eyes and reached for a stool to steady herself. This was her fault. She wished she'd expelled them from BARS. Richard was an evil monster, preying on a man who'd devoted his life to Brambleton. Her heart started pounding. What would happen if he couldn't find somewhere to rent? Would the Council help? Fred was fit and healthy, and there were others less fortunate needing homes. When she opened her eyes, she saw Anna had joined the group.

'He's given me three months to get out,' said Fred.

'What?' said Anna.

'Right, I'm going up and having it out with that man,' snarled Clare.

'*No!*' said Fred, clutching at her arm. 'Please, I know you mean well, but for now, it's just me. You go poking him in the eye and Ivy will get her packing orders too.'

Clare bit her lip. Fred was right. This needed a cool head, not a knee-jerk reaction.

'When did you get the letter?' asked Clare.

'That's what we were talking about,' said Ivy. 'Silly beggar has sat on this problem for two months already, thought he could sort it out himself.'

Trish revealed that Fred had spoken to Richard's agent, who'd refused to extend the notice period, and although Fred was registered with rental agencies, he had yet to view a single property.

'Why?' asked Anna.

Trish's hazel eyes flashed with anger. 'The agents claim the landlords are all inundated with applications from *more suitable* candidates.'

'What does that mean?' asked Ivy, her voice wavering.

'It means,' Clare said, struggling to control her temper, 'that Fred here, on a fixed and modest income, is more of a risk than people who are working.'

'Isn't that age discrimination?' asked Trish.

'No,' said Ivy, sighing. 'It's not just pensioners, it's anyone reliant on benefits. I come across families trying to raise children in a single room.'

Trish huffed, then said, 'I can't offer you a home, Fred, but I can offer you a free meal. In fact, if you all go for today's special, it's on the house.'

Clare and Ivy protested, but Trish insisted, saying there weren't many customers this month and she'd cooked far too much. They settled at a table; Ivy sat upright with a smile that buoyed Clare.

'We've had *lots* of donations,' said Ivy excitedly.

'See, I knew it,' said Anna, throwing Clare a triumphant look.

'Fantastic!' added Fred. 'How much have you got?'

Ivy's eyes sparkled. She leaned forward conspiratorially and whispered, 'Nearly £250!'

Clare forced a smile on to her face. Even ten times that amount wouldn't really help; they were nowhere near their target. Ivy seemed to sense Clare's true feelings and wagged a finger at her. 'Don't worry. There's still the sponsored slim – I've got pledges of over £100 already.'

Clare had a sudden thought, cupped a hand round Anna's ear and whispered, 'Do you think the experts would agree to start work now?'

Anna sat back, her eyes were wide.

'I never bill clients in advance, and I shouldn't think they do either,' said Clare.

'Nor do I,' said Anna.

Ivy leaned towards the other women. 'What's this?'

'We're being a bit precious raising all the money in advance,' said Clare excitedly 'Let's get the experts cracking and raise the shortfall while they do the work.'

Fred looked aghast. 'But what if we can't pay them?' he said.

'That's not very ethical, is it,' said Ivy, 'asking them to do the work when we aren't sure if we can pay.'

Anna tutted then said. 'Rest easy, Ivy. They'll want an undertaking that someone will settle their bills.'

'Give them my name,' said Clare. 'And here's the cunning part of this plan. The other side don't think we can afford an EIA, so let's keep it that way. We need the site visit to take place when the Hastings clan are busy. Any ideas?'

Fred leaned back in his seat, taking aim with an imaginary rifle and pulling the trigger.

'Of course,' said Anna. 'If we can get hold of Richard's shooting calendar, on those days all his lot will be tied up beating or picking up.'

'Leave that one to me,' said Fred, tapping a finger against his nose. His words conjured up an image of Sam – that's where Fred would snoop for intelligence – and she smiled, recalling their evening together. He may be a spy, but he was a very attentive one.

'Down to business,' she said firmly, ridding herself of the memory of Sam's attentiveness. 'Did everyone get my outline submission document? Who wants to tackle what?'

Clare looked from one blank face to the next. 'Don't all rush at once,' she said sarcastically. 'Anna?' she said, a note of desperation in her voice.

Anna gave her a beseeching look. 'I'll get back to you,' she said faintly.

Neither Fred nor Ivy spoke.

Surely, they didn't expect her to write it all. In her gut, she knew she would have to. Richard's experts would read every word of BARS's submission, and she wasn't putting her name to a shoddy piece of work.

Clare felt a blast of cold air and turned. At the door, a young couple, their faces flushed red from the cold were shrugging off coats and unlacing walking boots. Trish called out a greeting and rushed to take their order. Clare realized this custom was important to Trish; shoulder-season holidaymakers were especially thin on the ground this year. And that was when she had her idea.

Returning from the café, Clare was conscious of a rattling sound from the boot. It was Sam's sack truck tugging at her conscience, but she told herself if he needed it returned urgently, he would have said. She indicated to turn onto the main road, flicked a look in her wing mirror, and spotted a small blue car behind her. Driving slowly to avoid the noise of the sack truck, she expected the blue car to overtake, but it didn't. She turned off down the single-track lane to Orchard Farm. The blue car followed. Where was it going? She pulled over, switched off the engine, and glanced in the mirror. The car behind was stationary. After a couple of minutes Clare restarted the Land Rover; in the mirror she spotted the blue car behind her and she indicated to pull into a passing space, only to see the blue car stop too. There was a single occupant in the car, but it was too far away to tell if it was a man or a woman. Clare swallowed, feeling her heart thumping against her chest. Why was the driver mimicking her actions: were they following her? Why would someone tail her? She wanted the number plate. Clare put the Land Rover into reverse, gunned the engine and turned to look over her shoulder. The blue car was accelerating away backwards.

In the safety of the farmhouse kitchen, she told herself it must have been a tourist who was lost. The first thing she saw was

Sam's casserole dish soaking in the sink, next to the breakfast crockery. It would only take half an hour to wash up his things and take them back, but she didn't want to be distracted.

She threw a tea towel over the mess and, with the Aga warming her back, logged onto Airbnb. She searched for holiday cottages in Brambleton. There were several options, including both of Richard's, and she checked for availability in the last week of November. Smiling to herself, she closed the website, set up a new email address in the name of Clare Sanderson, and then contacted Richard's letting agency. She enquired about Jasmine Cottage, which was next door to Fred's. Within a few hours she had negotiated both a price reduction and a waiver of the security deposit – it was low season, and there would only be one guest. Clare transferred the fee and went to see Fred.

Feeling energized after her success, Clare decided to return Sam's things. She drove around hoping to leave them on the porch, but by the time she got out of the car, he was standing outside in his porch. He must have heard her car.

'Just returning your stuff,' she said. He walked over, in that loose-limbed, easy gait she found so attractive, and removed the sack truck from the boot. 'Time for tea?' he asked.

She had the submission to draft and all the farm chores, but she couldn't resist a hot cup of tea in his beautiful house. That would be lovely. He might throw in a slice of the delicious cake he'd served for dessert last night. She nodded and, carrying the casserole dish, followed him inside.

In his kitchen – unlike hers, irritatingly sparkling despite having entertained last night – Clare placed the dish on the kitchen island. She wondered if he cleaned or if there was a housekeeping team responsible for cottage changeovers that cleaned the farmhouse too.

Sam made proper tea using leaves, not bags. He moved about the room as if he had worked out the most time-effective way to complete the task. He picked up the teapot from a shelf next to the sink as he filled the kettle, before collecting cups, saucers and a milk jug. He then removed milk, and a saucer of lemon slices covered in cling film from the fridge, which made Clare question if she was the only person invited for tea today.

Pouring boiling water into the pot, he outlined his plans to graft apples, suggesting she did the same if she wanted to expand. 'Post Brexit, the cost of trees has shot up. Growing your own will save you a small fortune.'

'I wouldn't know how to do that.'

He raised an eyebrow, 'Smart girl like you? Cindy's got plenty of books about apples and I'm only five minutes away if you want a hand.'

Intrigued, she decided to spend an evening reading up on the subject. After she'd submitted the appeal document, of course.

'How's your brother's appeal going?'

'I dunno. Why not ask him yourself? I'm going for dinner at the Hall in December, and Cora has told me to invite a guest, preferably a woman, to even up numbers.'

Clare translated Sam's speech: Pink Trouser Suit had cancelled, forcing him to find someone locally. Although flattered, she wasn't sure she could be polite to Richard for a whole evening. Besides, she couldn't think of anything to wear, and her hair was a mess. Clare flexed her hands. Her nails were jagged, and scratch marks etched her wrists. She was on the cusp of saying no, then, thinking of it as another evening of free food, along with the chance to infiltrate the enemy, said 'OK then.'

She pictured a group of intrepid Second World War French Resistance fighters, scurrying around by moonlight, planting plastic explosives, then watching a German train loaded with tanks rumbling towards the bomb. If only she had a little more to hit back at her own enemy with, other than a dinner invitation and Ivy's sponsored slim.

When she got home, there was a handwritten note on her doormat, together with the post. The note was from Fred and set out Richard's shooting dates. It didn't explain how he'd come by them, but Clare wouldn't have cared if he'd burgled the shooting lodge. She scanned the dates then pushed the note into her back pocket and picked up her post.

There was another letter from Richard's lawyer. He was offering to settle the libel case out of court for £500,000. She shook her head. What planet did he live on? She didn't have a spare £500, and even if she did, she'd put it towards an EIA. She allowed herself a small laugh, thinking of him wasting money on London lawyers. She knew full well her leaflets were not libellous, and she would enjoy telling him so when she went for dinner in December. It would be good to see him lose at something.

Twenty-two

Clare checked the availability of the BARS's experts against Richard's shooting calendar and tasked Anna to reserve the matching days in December. They somehow needed to keep this a secret from Sam. By the end of the week, Fred had reported that Sam was helping at a two-day horse jumping event near Taunton in early December and would be staying there for the weekend.

Clare pulled up her diary, briefly wincing as she saw that she should have been on a flight to Bangkok today. Bingo. 8 December, a Friday. Richard would be shooting. She rang Anna, who promised to alert Ivy and the experts.

A month before Christmas, Fred moved house. By the time Clare reached the almshouses there was a white van parked outside, with the Smugglers Inn written on the side along with a picture of the pub depicted. The door was open, and, as she glanced inside saw the contents of Fred's sitting room along with some cardboard boxes stacked at one end. She clenched her fists – how would Richard feel if, out of the blue, someone gave him three months' notice to leave Brambleton Hall? Behind her she heard someone grunting, then Sam's voice: 'Steps coming up, George!'

Clare looked over her shoulder. George, Rose's husband, was backing out of Fred's front door, his arms cradling one end of a double mattress, his head pressed against a side. He staggered backwards a few steps, then the other end of the mattress appeared, with Sam straining under the weight. Clare scurried past and into the cottage, calling Fred's name.

'Up here.'

Upstairs, she found him unscrewing the headboard from the base of the bed. He was whistling and the cheerful noise made her want to cry. She should have refused to let him get involved with BARS. 'What's Sam doing here?' she asked.

'Grab a hold of the other side, then we can get this off,' he said. 'He's my best mate, of course he's going to help me move house.'

'You haven't told him where you're going, have you?' she hissed, lifting her side of the headboard, releasing it from its catches.

Footsteps rang out on the stairs just as George and Sam appeared. 'Can you two manage the headboard if we do the base?' asked Sam.

George grasped an end of the bed base. 'I thought you liked living here, Fred,' he said. 'I'm surprised to see you moving. Are you staying in the village?'

Clare shot Fred a warning look. 'Don't worry, you're not losing one of your best customers. He's not going far. Careful,' she added, 'mind those stairs.'

An hour later, the van was packed. George put Fred's suitcases into Clare's Land Rover. She gave Sam the keys to her barn – Fred would store his furniture there – and stood beside Fred as they watched the van leave.

'Check in time isn't until four o'clock,' she said, waving, 'but as we've no intention of sticking to many of his rules, I think we might as well get you settled in, Fred.'

She trotted round to the side of Jasmine Cottage, located the key safe and tapped in the code, thinking that if the cottage was hers, she'd chose something a bit more secure than '1234'. She extracted a key and handed it to Fred.

'You get yourself in and the kettle on, and I'll get the suitcases.'

Back at the farmhouse, she emptied the honesty pot and put out another tray of eggs. She was too upset from the morning with Fred to concentrate on drafting the BARS's submission, so instead exerted her temper by clearing away more of her mother's things. She tackled Cindy's clothes, separating them into two piles: charity shop and recycling.

Three recycling bags later – Cindy seemed to have lived in overalls, often stained with creosote, paint or what looked like oil – she spotted a suit carrier bag at the back of the wardrobe. Intrigued, she unzipped it. Inside was a vintage 1950s swing cocktail dress, with a fitted bodice and flared skirt. She pulled the dress out of the bag. It was stunning, a soft pink colour. She couldn't recall her mother ever wearing it; it was difficult to picture 'blue overall' Cindy in such a grand outfit.

Standing in front of the mirror, Clare held the dress up against her body. Given she was taller than her mother, the full skirt fell on the knee. She pulled it out, imagining dancing in the frock. In the Sixties, the family had been rich enough to buy the old almshouses. Before her father died, had her parents led a glitzy life? Had the farm been sufficiently successful to fund expensive dresses and a lifestyle to match? Did it all change once her mother was left to run it alone?

As a child, it had never occurred to Clare that the farm was losing money. Her mother must have hidden it, hoping things would improve, not realizing the losses weren't a result of farming going through a rough patch, but of her poor business skills. She felt tears prick at the corners of her eyes and let them spill over her cheeks. After her father died, her mother showed Clare how to pack away her grief and focus on the present. Task lists replaced memories, a process Clare would repeat again after Guy's death. Both women had lost their husbands tragically early, but unlike Clare, her mother had enjoyed a good marriage.

Letting go of the dress hem, Clare asked herself why her mother hadn't told her the farm was losing money. She could understand why Cindy had hidden the reality of farming when Clare was a child, but not once her daughter had become a successful lawyer. Or was it worse, that Cindy hadn't even realized? Had her mother made the classic business mistake of confusing cash with profit?

Clare hung the dress on the side of the wardrobe, wondering what she would have done if her mother had approached her for help when they were not on speaking terms. She sighed. She might not have loaned her the money, but she was sure she'd have found a better deal than Tricky Ricky's, or would have advised her mother to sell the entire farm, thus saving years of losses. She picked up the dress again, deciding to wear it for dinner at Brambleton Hall in memory of her mother; she would not look like the gawky villager dining at the posh house.

She had a sudden thought, dropped the dress on the bed and dashed into her own bedroom, rifling through the bags and cases she'd brought from London, finally unearthing an old shoe box. There was a lump in her throat as she lifted the lid. Inside was a vintage cream silk cocktail handbag with a diamante clasp – her last Christmas present from Guy. She'd chosen it and lent him the money. She'd never used it.

Her phone pinged. There was a WhatsApp message from someone called Helen. Clare didn't know a Helen. Then she realized she did; it was one of the trainee lawyers staying in her flat. Helen reported that both the sitters were going home for Christmas but would leave the heating on frost control. Clare replied thanking her, trying to recall when she'd last thought about London.

On the day Fred's weeklong 'holiday' ended, Clare and Stop-it walked into Brambleton.

Promptly at nine, Clare rang Jasmine Cottage's bell. Fred answered wearing a T-shirt and trousers. Kneeling to unhook the dog, she admired the room. 'Wow, this cottage is nice.' The exposed wooden beams were lime-washed, and the walls painted a soft lemon colour. There was no sign of peeling or blistering paint. 'Properly insulated too,' said Fred, grinning. 'Warm as toast in here.'

Checkout time was 10 a.m., but Clare suspected that out of season the changeover team might not be punctual. Shortly before noon, Clare heard a key in the lock. Stop-it barked and a woman's head wearing a bobble hat, appeared.

'I'm sorry, I thought you were leaving today,' she said.

'No,' said Clare smiling. 'Not today.'

'Righto. I'll change the linen and have a tidy up for you. Then I'll leave you to it.'

Fred rose. 'There's no need—'

'Thanks, that would be great.' said Clare, pushing Fred back down. 'We'll pop out for a coffee, walk the dog and be back in a couple of hours.' It was less than a month before Christmas. She didn't want to do the changeover team out of their wages.

When Clare returned to Orchard Farm – having seen Fred back into Jasmine Cottage – she found an email from Richard's letting agency, at her new 'Clare Sanderson' email address.

Dear Ms Sanderson,

We have been trying to contact you but have been unable to reach you via phone. We are delighted you wish to stay on at Jasmine cottage for another week, the cost is £500, and we would appreciate swift payment. Please let us know when you have transferred the money.

Clare hit delete and went to feed the pigs.

On the first Saturday in December, Clare completed her farm chores, despatched another email from Richard's letting agents to the trash, then emptied her savings jar and drove into Barnstaple. She spent over an hour at a beauty salon. Using rollers, the stylist shaped her hair into an iconic Fifties style, sweeping it off Clare's face in distinctive waves. Her nails were manicured and painted a pale ivory colour, then her make-up was done professionally with period thick arched eyebrows and exaggerated deep red lips.

Back at the farmhouse, she retouched her lipstick and stepped into the vintage dress. It accentuated her waist and on her tall frame looked stunning. With her hair swept off her face, she looked ready to audition for a part as Marilyn Monroe. She danced down the stairs and into the kitchen. The doorbell rang and Stop-it barked in response. Clare threw a chew at the dog's basket and stepped outside.

Sam stood beside his car with the passenger door open. As she walked towards him, his eyes popped wide – they really were the most alluring bright blue, and secretly she was pleased he'd noticed that she'd made an effort.

'Cora will be thrilled,' he said, taking her bag off her as she folded herself into the car. 'She's always ribbing me for not dressing up.' He pulled the seat belt out a length and passed it to her, then tucked in a fold of her dress which was dangling over the seat edge before carefully eased the door shut.

They drove in silence. It wasn't a strained silence. The atmosphere reminded her of sitting beside Guy in a London taxi, each content with their own thoughts about the upcoming treat – it was always something related to cars, but for her, just being with Guy was the pleasure. Sadly, discovering Hannah's postcard had soured her memories of happy times with Guy. Halfway down the drive, it began drizzling. Sam parked near the porch and hopped out, saying. 'Wait here.'

She did as she was told and a few moments later her door opened. The front door was ajar, and Sam stood in the rain holding an umbrella.

Carrying a brown paper bag tied together with a slip of yellow ribbon, Sam escorted Clare through to the reception room she had marvelled at when she'd last visited, trying in vain to persuade Richard to abandon the chicken factory. Tonight, the chandelier was alight, casting a warm glow over the guests, and the fire was crackling, kicking out a soothing heat. Clare felt like she'd entered a time warp. All the men except Sam wore black tie and the women were dressed as if attending a prom. Magnus and two smartly turned-out assistants were circulating with silver trays of canapés and bottles of champagne wrapped in white linen napkins.

Richard frowned at his brother and spoke frostily. 'You're late, and didn't you get my message? It's black tie - Cora's birthday.' He muttered something to the people standing close to him. The group turned, their eyes boring into Clare as if about to challenge her to a duel.

'Happy birthday, Cora. I brought you a present,' Sam said, handing over the paper bag. 'Made it myself.'

'That's sweet of you,' said Cora. Remembering her hostess's

outfit when delivering prizes at the agricultural show, Clare considered Cora's attire. Tonight, she was wearing equally vertiginous stilettos paired with a pale blue silk trouser suit. It would have been impractical for most hostesses, but then Cora wouldn't be dashing to and from the kitchen, carrying trays. There was a welcoming smile on Cora's face. 'Let me introduce you to my guests,' said the hostess, taking a sip of champagne. 'It's Clare, isn't it?'

Tucking her handbag under her arm, Clare accepted a coupe of champagne from Magnus, and tried to remember names as Cora spun her around the room, introducing her as 'Sam's friend from London'.

'Lovely dress,' murmured one of the other women. 'Is it vintage?'

'Yes. It's a family piece.'

'Very pretty on you. Excuse me,' said the woman, giving a tight nod. 'I must have a word with Cora' and she wandered off, leaving Clare alone.

Her hand felt clammy on the stem of the glass and for a few calming minutes Clare stood admiring the wallpaper. The section in front of her showed Chinese figures processing towards a temple. Although the colours were faded, the expressions on the faces showed a reverence for the ceremony, respect for a divine force, and she told herself not to be cowed by the opulence of the house or the glamour of her hostess. Magnus topped up her champagne and she took a glug. Sam came to stand beside her, and she listened to him talking about the wallpaper. She learned it was not the standard 'Chinese style' English paper, which was often found in bedrooms of National Trust houses, this had been painted in China in the early eighteenth century.

'It's like a tapestry,' she said, running a finger over the muted images.

'Good spot,' he said. 'That's what makes it so special. It's one big canvas, not a repeating pattern. This wallpaper has links with the Brighton Pavilion.' He explained that the paper dated from when the Prince Regent – later George IV – refurbished his Brighton royal residence in the exotic Indochinese style.

'Well, if Richard is ever short of money, he could always flog this!' she jested.

Sam gave a soft laugh. 'Unlikely. We're Grade I listed.'

It dawned on Clare that while Sam wouldn't benefit from the factory directly, the family estate was a permanent tie, which time couldn't sever. 'You said *we*. Is that how you think of the Hall, as if you still belong here?'

He furrowed his brows. 'It's complicated,' he said, downing his drink.

'More champagne, madam?' offered Magnus. 'I'll fetch you another cider, sir. Nice to see you here again.'

Two glasses of champagne later, Magnus announced dinner, and Cora shuffled her guests across the entrance hall and into the largest private dining room Clare had ever seen. She was staring up at the domed ceiling forty feet above her when she heard Sam's voice.

'It's the original medieval dining hall. Above that plasterwork are the roof rafters. One of our ancestors covered them up – I guess exposed beams came to be seen as a bit rural. They panelled the walls and created this spectacular room.'

Clare suppressed an urge to giggle – she should have bought a ticket; he was acting like a tour guide. She felt goose bumps on her arms. The room still retained the atmosphere of a Tudor dining hall. Clare felt an urge to scrape away the beautiful eau de nil wood panelling, to reveal what she was certain would be the original dark wood, to strip off the plasterwork and expose the rafters towering above. She could almost hear minstrels playing and wanted to roll back the vast rug beneath the table and replace it with herb-scented straw.

The party took their places, Clare with her back to the fire. Sam was on her left and Ivy's successor, Victor, was on her right. Cora asked Victor to say grace. Heads dipped, the vicar said a few words to which everyone responded 'Amen'.

'I'm glad I've got you to myself,' the vicar said, unfurling his napkin. She picked up her own, fashioned in a complicated pattern that looked like the Sydney Opera House. 'I wanted to talk to you about this little tussle over the chicken farm.'

She snorted, then replied, 'It's not a farm; it's a factory.'

Victor slathered butter on a roll and spoke softly: 'Is there any way we can stop this before it gets out of hand? I saw it in my last village. The dispute was over a farmer wanting a wind turbine. It split the village, and I can sense the same thing happening here.'

Had Richard put Victor up to this? 'Speak to your host. I've tried. He won't budge.'

'But it's just a few chickens. We're surrounded by farms. Will a couple more sheds really harm anyone?'

Clare felt her face flush. She was under attack. Inhaling, she caught her host's eye and said, 'Victor would like to discuss the chicken factory with you. He wants to stop the village fighting.'

'It's your fight, not mine,' snapped Richard.

'Now, now,' said Victor. 'She's entitled to her opinion.'

'But she's not entitled to spread libellous literature about me around my village.'

'It's not libellous,' said Clare, rolling her eyes at Richard, but pleased he had introduced the topic. She was certain he didn't have a case.

'But you don't deny writing it.'

'Of course I don't.'

'Enough, you two. Play nicely,' said Sam. He rose and walked away, saying, 'Cora, shall I ring for the first course.'

Richard was undeterred. He pulled something out of his jacket pocket, waving it at his guests. 'You don't deny writing this.'

'All my own words and I'm proud of every one of them.'

'See? You hear that? You are all witnesses to this treachery.' Richard rose and marched around the table, slapping the leaflet down in front of her. Victor was fumbling with his roll. He dumped it on his side plate and picked up the leaflet, wiping his greasy fingers on it.

'Hmm,' said the vicar. 'This is quite forceful, isn't it.'

Clare could see Sam by the fireplace pressing a bell she couldn't hear. He was scowling. She winced; she was his guest. If she created a scene, it would embarrass him, but she couldn't resist a parting shot. 'The village deserves to know the truth.'

Hastings was staring at her. She could see a vein throbbing above his bow tie and his face was a peculiar colour; she couldn't decide if it was red or purple, but she knew she was being rude and regretted it. Cora spoke in a pleading voice. 'Richard, it's my birthday. Can we stop this nonsense – you're frightening my friends.'

Hastings grunted. Clare felt her ears burning. She shouldn't have taken the bait. She snatched the leaflet from Victor, opened her handbag and shoved it in, snapping the clasp. Sam sat down and hissed, 'Let me see that.' He looked alarmed, making Clare regret what she'd done.

'No,' she said, dropping her bag on the floor by her feet. 'Let's forget all about it. I'm sorry I've caused a scene on your birthday Cora. I didn't mean to.'

The rest of the dinner passed uneventfully, and Clare found she was enjoying herself. Magnus topped up her water glass and cleared her plates without her noticing. By the time the last course was served, she was feeling light-headed and suspected Magnus had been as adept at refilling her wineglass as he had at clearing crockery. He'd served white wine with the starter, then a delicious claret with the main course, a different sweet wine with the dessert and then there was port with a cheese course.

Magnus announced coffee was waiting in the Chinese reception room.

Clare rose, pushing back her chair. Sam's leg brushed against hers. She pressed back, felt the answering pressure and a ripple of pleasure shot through her. For a few seconds, they stood like conjoined twins. She glanced up. He was staring at her with an intensity in those bright blue eyes. Victor's voice intruded on her dreams, offering to escort her to coffee. She stepped aside, trying to decide if there was something between her and Sam, or if it had just been wishful thinking.

Other than the roaring fire, there was nothing to suggest that anyone had set foot in the Chinese room all evening. The sofas were plump, cushions – all with only four sides and thick fringes which Clare suspected Stop-it would consider an amusing puzzle – rested equidistant from each other on pristine velvet sofas. There were no empty glasses and no crumbs. The host and his brother were last into the room, where they collected cups from Magnus before disappearing into Richard's study. Clare wondered if Sam was in for a dressing down for his guest's outburst.

She was on her second cup of mint tea, and enjoying a discussion about rare-breed pigs, when she felt Sam's hand on her bare arm. Clare froze, then felt a warm current shoot through her body and gazed upwards. Sam's lips parted slightly. She glanced around to see if anyone had noticed their interplay. He whispered he wanted to go. 'I've got an early start. Do you mind?'

Following Sam out of the room, Clare's body was fizzing with anticipation. Was he going to kiss her on the way home? For the past five years, kissing had been no more than an occasional peck on the cheek from friends. Would she disappoint him?

In the privacy of his car, she fiddled with her handbag. Sam got into the car and leaned close, bringing with him a smell of apples and spices, a heady mix that seemed to fill the car's intimate space. Sam gently brushed a strand of hair away from her face, his fingers lingering on her cheek and their eyes met. He cupped her face. His breath seemed to mingle with hers and slowly he closed the distance between them. Their lips met in a kiss that was gentle at first, then deepened, enveloping her, making her skin tingle.

He pulled away. She waited for him to start the car and drive off, then, replaying the sensation of his lips on hers, she apologized. 'I shouldn't have goaded your brother, especially as a guest in his house.' The car fell silent; Clare wondered if her words sounded too trite. His eyes turned on her. She could see anger in them and felt a rush of guilty shame.

He spoke slowly. 'I can't tell you how annoyed I am. Why the heck are you apologizing? And what for? He behaved abominably. But I need to see that leaflet,' he said, looking at her bag. She tried to think of a reason he would want the leaflet. Was something incriminating written on the back? Was this all part of a wider plan? Had he just kissed her to get her to relax? Was this a scheme cooked up over the port decanter in Richard's study? 'Please. I want to see it.' He spoke urgently, then lunged for the bag, snatching it off her lap.

How dare he? Even Guy had never looked in her handbag without asking. Anger coursed through her, and Sam's features seemed to blur with Richard's into one Hastings' face. His fingers were fiddling with the clasp. She wrenched the bag back. 'Leave my bag alone!'

'I'm trying to help you.'

She lashed out. All of the pent-up rage at what his family had done to hers; what it was doing to people they should protect, like Fred; and what it was planning to do to the village. It all came pouring out. 'You and your brother inherited everything you own. Didn't your parents ever teach you that with wealth comes responsibility?'

He was smiling at her, which was like pouring petrol on her fiery temper. 'You inherited Orchard Farm.'

Clare gasped. She was at a disadvantage. She'd had too much to drink and he was sober. 'No. I inherited *part* of Orchard Farm – the part your brother didn't steal,' she spat, then opened the car door. She didn't want to spend a single second longer with this man. He reached across her, his arm brushing against hers and a shiver of desire shot through her. She hated her body's disloyalty.

'It's raining,' he whispered.

'Then I'll get wet.'

For a few moments, they tussled over the door. The rain hammered against the windscreen, bouncing off the bonnet. If she succeeded in opening the door, her prize would be a drenching. She didn't care. Clare had to beat this family at something. She let her hand fall away from the handle, waited until his were firmly back on the steering wheel, then yanked the door open and shot outside, slamming it behind her.

The rain had softened to Devon mizzle. It was like walking through cold steam and she trudged towards a light shining from one of the lodge cottages. Behind her, she heard the engine start. Headlights illuminated the drive, and a cloud of insects flapped in the mist. As she walked, she took deep breaths to calm her racing heart. How had she ever thought Sam differed from his brother? They were both cut from the same arrogant Hastings' cloth of privilege. She'd made a huge mistake kissing Sam. It was all a game to him, just like it had been in her twenties. Her enemy was the entire Hastings family.

By the time she reached Orchard Farm, her anger had subsided. She opened the back door, listening to Sam's car reverse away – he'd crawled behind her all the way home. Looking down at Cindy's dress, now drenched, she burst into tears and slumped up the stairs, hearing Stop-it's paws thumping behind her. Clare threw her bag into the cupboard, slipped off the sodden dress and went to take off her make-up. She'd made a complete fool of herself. At least she'd avoided a one-night fling. Clare couldn't wait to get back to London where she could be anonymous again.

Back in the bedroom, the bright yellow walls failed to lift her spirits. She turned to shut the door but Stop-it's nose was wedged in the gap. She opened the door a little wider. The dog shot in, jumped onto the bed and sat with his head cocked on one side. She climbed into bed. He snuggled up to her and she cuddled him to her chest like a living hot water bottle.

On Monday there was another email from Richard's letting agents. This time they pointed to their terms and conditions, and threatened legal action if she didn't vacate the cottage or pay up immediately. She wasn't paying. She knew it was only a matter of time before they demanded her details from her bank and unmasked the fact that Clare had made the booking in her married name, but she suspected it would take a while for Richard and the holiday letting company to unravel the web she had woven.

That afternoon, Clare was enjoying a cup of tea and drafting BARS's appeal document when the doorbell rang. It was the postman.

'Recorded delivery for you,' he said cheerfully, holding out a machine. 'Sign here, please.' Clare scrawled her name and took the brown envelope. It didn't look like an early Christmas card. Using her thumbnail, she slit open the envelope and unfolded a letter.

> Dear Ms Hetherington,
> You have admitted responsibility for both writing and distributing the enclosed leaflet. With reference to our previous correspondence, the offer to settle this matter out of court is withdrawn. Our client, Mr Hastings has instructed us to pursue damages of £5 million for your libellous actions.

Oh, for heaven's sake! This was harassment.

Yes, the guests on Saturday had heard her admit she'd written the leaflet, but she'd never denied that she was the author. This time, she would ask Sally to draft a formal response.

She let the letter fall into her lap. Leaning over to take a sip of tea, it fell on the floor, the leaflet landing beside it. She spurted hot tea over her legs and gasped, the words spinning in front of her eyes. This wasn't her leaflet!

> Richard is corrupt; I reckon he's bribed officials to win planning permission.

Wow, that was strong.

> Do not believe what he says. He is a thief, a cheat and a liar.

The leaflet speculated about Richard's actual intentions:

> The purpose behind this application is pure greed. He doesn't care about the welfare of chickens or the village.

Clare wasn't an expert, but even she suspected this leaflet was textbook defamation.

She replayed Saturday evening in her mind. Had the Hastings brothers set her up? Was the whole evening carefully planned to trap her? Was the goal to elicit an admission that she had drafted this poisonous leaflet? Clare would lay odds Richard was its real author. Struggling to control her breathing, Clare sprang up and dashed upstairs. She was convinced the leaflet he'd brandished on Saturday night was not the poisonous one – that would have been too risky. Clare might have read it.

This explained why Sam was so desperate to get his hands on it. No doubt his mission had been to get hold of the innocent version and destroy it, allowing Richard and his chums to claim she confessed to writing the poisonous one. Sam had failed. Clare could now produce the innocent leaflet, complete with Victor's greasy fingerprint, proving she hadn't swapped it.

In her bedroom she dug through cupboards, in the same way Stop-it clawed his way through a border – clothes flew off the shelves, shoes landed on the bed, hats joined them, but no silk handbag. She had to find that bag and prove her innocence.

She pulled over a chair, clambered onto it, peering along the top shelf. Her heart skipped a beat. She could see the sparkle of the diamante clasp towards the back. Standing on tiptoes, she reached in, her index finger scrabbling at the bag. She scratched the silk with her fingernail, but she was pushing, not pulling, and with her next effort she clawed at air. Clare jumped off the chair and pushed it hard against the closet. She stepped up again, inched herself close to the shelves, reached in and nudged the bag towards her, then grabbed the prize with both hands and pulled it out. She took a breath, released the catch and pulled out the crumpled leaflet.

Twenty-three

With shaking hands, Clare unfolded the page, saw Victor's greasy fingerprints, and let out an audible groan. The same leaflet as downstairs. Why hadn't she looked at it on Saturday? The answer was simple: why would she, when she'd read it so many times so could virtually recite it? She reread the rude version, cringing at the words.

She took it downstairs, poured her lukewarm tea down the drain before making herself a fresh brew. She took a sip, peering at the leaflet. Something about it was resonating. She recognized some phrases. She had read them before. Where? She spluttered hot tea back into the mug. No! It couldn't be. It looked like the first draft she'd written as a joke. Had Richard paid a cyber expert to hack into her files and steal a copy?

Or had someone done this the old-fashioned way? The farmhouse was never locked. There wasn't anything worth stealing. Richard or one of his lackeys could have crept in when she was out walking Stop-it. Maybe that was what the person in the blue car had been doing; keeping an eye on her routine in case they needed to break in a second time. She wouldn't put it past Hastings to prowl round her home. Or ask his brother to. What was it Sam had said on that walk? *I'm pretty good at sneaking round unobserved.*

Richard had approached the planning application like a bowler at a skittle alley. With his first ball he'd shattered the village – most of the pins – and he was now picking off those still standing. Just like he'd threatened he would on that Bank Holiday Monday in his brother's kitchen. Fred, first; now, her. What would he do to fell Anna and Ivy?

She reread the poisonous leaflet, counting the libellous phrases. It accused Richard of theft, corruption, bribery . . . She might as well hand him the keys to Orchard Farm and head back to London with her tail between her legs. Then she remembered the sum he wanted. He would bankrupt her. She would lose her flat. Suddenly, she felt nauseous. Richard's goal wasn't to get money from her – it was to destroy her. An undischarged bankrupt couldn't practise law.

Clare slumped at the kitchen table. Was he that spiteful? She should never have agreed to spearhead the fight against him. She should have left it to Anna. Clare wasn't part of Brambleton, hadn't been part of it for years, but because she'd taken him on, raised the village against him, he was out to crush her.

Determined to check her facts, Clare pulled out her laptop and searched for the original draft of the leaflet but couldn't find it anywhere in her files. Had the thief stolen a copy, then deleted it? That made little sense. Why erase evidence of her authorship? Clare questioned why she couldn't find the first draft of the leaflet. There was only one logical answer, because she *had* deleted it. And she realized she could prove she had done. As a lawyer, and being cautious, she had not enabled the automatic delete function on her trashcan. To permanently delete files required manually emptying it. She clicked on that icon and found what she was looking for.

Clare chewed at her lip. She was already stretching the bounds of her imagination, envisaging Richard stealing files from her computer – but surely him rummaging in the digital trashcan on the off-chance there was something in there he could leverage was a step too far? So how did Richard get his hands on the deleted, unverified version? It had only existed for a few hours. Then she remembered that, for a laugh, she'd sent a copy to Anna, Ivy and Fred. But none of her friends would have given it to Richard, would they?

Back upstairs, Clare tidied away the mess, asking herself how she'd allowed this to happen. She folded a couple of sweaters, wishing she had just accepted that a canny man had bested her mother out of the farm. After their estrangement, Clare hadn't expected or wanted to inherit. When she'd discovered what Richard had done, she should have buried her mother, appointed an estate agent and gone straight back to London.

But after decades fighting for the underdogs, Clare was always going to try to right a wrong. When Anna alerted her to the planning application, Clare's automatic response had been to protect vulnerable people from a bully, especially when Richard's plans threatened her mother's orchard. That was naive – she should have realized how tenaciously Hastings would fight. It wasn't just her leading BARS which irked him. She suspected he was annoyed by the way she fought tooth and claw. That was her style, to keep going, determined to find a way to win.

Tidying away the last pair of shoes, Clare plodded downstairs, scanned the poisonous leaflet once more and sent it to Sally, asking her advice. But there was already the acrid taste of loss in her mouth. She received an instantaneous response informing her Sally was away on sick leave and not expected back until the new year. There were details of alternative contacts, but Clare didn't know any well enough to share her shame with them, and suspected there was no rush; from partners' meetings she knew defamation cases were slow.

As 8 December rolled around, the plan was for BARS and their experts to rendezvous at the Old Rectory. All except their lookout, Ivy, who was to text Clare when she spotted Sam's horsebox heading away from the village. Each BARS member chose an expert to accompany on the site visit. Ivy claimed smell and Clare water. For reasons that escaped Clare, Fred wanted to deal with noise, which left Anna with visual and traffic.

When Clare arrived, tingling with excitement, there were already several cars parked outside Anna's house. The front door was ajar, and Clare made her way to the kitchen where Anna introduced everyone by their names and specialisms.

Roger came in, trudged to the kettle and switched it on. Looking at his tight shoulders and the side of his pinched face, Clare questioned if she was relying on Anna too much. She didn't want to drive a stake through the heart of her friend's marriage. Clare cringed and looked away, telling herself it was safer meeting at Anna's. Someone might notice strange cars parked at Orchard Farm, or outside the old almshouses. Clare's phone buzzed.

Coast clear!

Clare's expert was a man called Walter. He was short and slim with sandy-coloured thinning hair and wire-rimmed spectacles. The first time he spoke, Clare liked his authoritative voice – it cast her back to university days listening to law lecturers – but not what he had to say.

'I've read their report. I was surprised, but you do realize it might be a fair assessment?'

She nodded but crossed her fingers.

Walter loaded his equipment silently into the boot of Clare's car and she drove him to the village hall where Ivy met them, a school girlish grin on her face. Anna unfurled a copy of the site plan and briefed the team.

'Can we pop up to the site and look for ourselves, I'd like to take some samples?' asked Walter.

Clare exchanged a glance with Anna, then huffed, 'Better not.'

'Shame,' said Walter, 'I expect the Inspector will want to visit the site as part of the public hearing.'

They split up. Walter used a small handheld machine to measure the distance from the village hall to the River Shire. Hugging her jacket around her, Clare joined him on the riverbank. As she stood listening to the gentle roar of the gushing stream, she tried to dispel the feeling that her hopes were being carried away like the water cascading out to sea. Walter pulled on thigh high rubber boots.

'You're not going in, are you?' she asked.

He nodded. 'I must test the water,' he said, and explained he would analyse the pH level to assess the baseline water quality.

'Right,' she said.

'You might as well leave me for a while. I want to take samples along the river; try and identify and quantify the different species of fish, invertebrates, algae and plants – assess the ecological health of the river. Fortunately, your opponent has conducted a hydrological study and set out the results, so I can critique his findings and check I agree with his conclusions on how, given surface water run-off patterns, those chickens would affect the water.'

Clare watched him wade off into the river, looking as content as she would be with her nose in an employment contract. Walter knew what he was doing. She hoped his conclusions matched her hopes.

It was two weeks before Christmas and the team were in the Smugglers Inn. The scent of mulled wine and pine needles filled the air, mingling with the comforting crackle of a roaring log fire.

Wrapped around the beams were branches of pine mixed with ivy and dotted with golden baubles. Candles flickered on every table, casting a soft glow on faces. Above the bar, strings of warm lights twinkled, their reflection bouncing off rows of polished glasses. At one end was a branch of mistletoe, waiting to catch unsuspecting couples, and in a corner, a Christmas tree decorated with what looked like ornaments handmade by the landlady's children. Clare listened to the fading bars of *Hark the Herald Angels* feeling nostalgic for past Christmases with her parents, and later just her mother, in this pub. She smiled, realizing that this time she hadn't moved the timeline of her memories to include Guy.

Ivy, Fred, Anna and Clare were in a booth close to the warmth, with Stop-it at their feet.

'How's Jasmine Cottage?' asked Anna, grinning.

'Eh?' said Fred, patting his pockets. 'I think I've left the damn hearing aids at home.'

Anna raised her voice. 'How's Jasmine?'

'Lovely and warm,' replied Fred. 'No need to turn the thermostat down when someone else foots the bill!' Ivy opened her mouth to speak. Clare braced herself – if Ivy suggested Fred was being unethical, she might hurl her copy of the submission document at the woman. How ethical had Hastings been in serving his Section 21 notice?

'There's something bothering me about Fred living in Jasmine Cottage,' said Ivy. Clare's hands curled round her document. 'How safe is he? Can he be evicted?' asked Ivy.

Clare gave Ivy a dazed look. The answer hinged on whether Fred was squatting. She didn't think he was. Fred hadn't broken into the cottage and, fortunately, despite their efforts, Richard's agents had made a mistake. They'd sent Clare an email, but hadn't twigged she wasn't the guest, and so a copy hadn't been sent to Jasmine Cottage itself. 'Don't worry about him, Ivy. He's not going anywhere anytime soon.'

'Good,' said Ivy, pulling open a packet of crisps. 'I've had another £700 in cash donations, Gina has transferred £825 and Trish another £282, and my sponsorship has grown – wait for it – I'm running at nearly £500.'

'Just when is this diet starting?' asked Fred.

Ivy paused mid-crisp. 'Umm, point taken,' she said, tipping the rest on to the floor. Stop-it lurched forwards.

'It's just if we're going to raise the money in time, you need to start soon,' said Fred.

Clare agreed with Fred, but she also felt sorry for Ivy. The woman enjoyed her food.

'Right, let's start,' said Clare, marking the date on the cover page. 'Comments?' She looked up and ranged her eyes over the others. No one met hers. 'Even if you don't have any suggestions, can't you look for grammatical errors?'

'Do we really care? It's not an English Literature A-level paper,' said Fred.

'I care. I want this to be as well written as Richard's.'

'Isn't what it says more important than how it's put?' said Fred. 'It doesn't need to be perfect.'

Clare realized that Fred had a point. It was the appendix with their own EIA which would win the appeal. Drafting the document was irrelevant – the group could compose Booker Prize winning prose, but what mattered to the Planning Inspector was professionals with credentials pulling apart Richard's biased EIA.

Ivy was shovelling in a handful of nuts.

'Didn't you just say you'd started dieting?' said Fred, knocking Ivy's hand with one of his, spilling nuts across the table. 'In fact, right now. Mineral water or diet drink, Ivy?' he offered. 'My round. Usual for everyone else?'

'Pint please, Fred,' said a male voice from the neighbouring booth.

Clare sat bolt upright. Anything they said in Sam's earshot was bound to be reported to Richard. Her mind clouded with a vision of their row in his car nearly two weeks ago. She wasn't having this. She rose, and with hands on hips, glared down into Sam's smiling face. 'You need to move. We're discussing something confidential.'

'Then do it somewhere private, not in the pub on a Friday evening,' reasoned Sam.

He slipped out of the booth and walked to the bar. Clare could hear him chattering to Fred, asking if he was comfortable in Jasmine Cottage. Then Sam casually asked, 'How short are you for the EIA?'

'Fred, no!' shouted Clare. Too late, she remembered he couldn't hear her, but she heard his reply, 'About seven grand.' Clare feigned outrage but was secretly pleased. When Richard heard the size of the shortfall, he would assume they could never reach their target. The experts had been and were typing up their reports; how she would pay them would be next year's problem.

Twenty-four

Clare woke up to a soft snuffling snoring sound. It was gentle and strangely soothing, not the rattling wheezing noise Guy used to make, which sounded like water gurgling down a plughole. She rolled on her side, gazing at the yellow wall, trying to push thoughts of Richard's defamation case from her mind. She must keep herself busy.

'Up we get Stop-it,' she said, jabbing the dog in the ribs.

Despite Hilts sleeping in now the sun didn't rise before 8 a.m., Clare still rose early to break the ice on the chicken's water tower. Huddled in one of her mother's old fleece-lined jackets, she used the edge of a shattered flowerpot, jabbing it into the ice, then pulling out the shards and tossing them aside to reveal the sweet pure Devon water beneath. Was that destined to be contaminated by Richard's run-off?

On the December morning the experts emailed their reports, the postman's arrival delayed her from reading them. She dropped the blanket she was wrapped in and answered the door, stepping outside and drawing it closed behind her to prevent the warmth escaping. It was another recorded delivery. She ripped it open and scanned it. She was becoming remarkably familiar with the letterhead of Richard's London lawyers.

It was a demand for payment for three weeks' rent for Jasmine Cottage. She had been expecting it. The contract was in her name, Fred was chewing his way through Richard's electricity and heating oil, and the website showed that the cottage was booked for Christmas and New Year – they were peak weeks each costing over £1,000.

Technically, Clare was not in breach of contract. She had only booked the cottage for a week, and she'd paid for that. The agents hadn't asked for the name of the guest, assuming it was her. Tossing the letter on the fire, she watched the flames engulf it and wondered how her life had reached this point. Technically she may not be in breach of contract, but if Ivy knew what Clare had done, she would call it unethical, and she would be right. Still, she felt no shame that Richard would be out of pocket after his cruel decision to evict Fred.

Wrapped once again in the blanket, Clare settled on the kitchen sofa and opened Walter's report. Her eyes danced over the sentences. When she saw the words 'scant regard has been paid to the proximity of the site to the River Shire,' she whooped and shouted, 'Yes, yes!'

Then slowly she read the rest of the report. In Walter's opinion, run-off would seep into the groundwater and from there into the river. Without stringent hygiene measures, the river would become contaminated, which was bad news; but good news for BARS, because if the Planning Inspector agreed with Walter, that would never happen.

With a mounting sense of hope, she read the noise report, learning it would be substantial – which was highlighted, so she assumed it was a technical assessment of the impact – for the residential properties closest to the birds. Except for Gina's house, all of the affected properties belonged to Richard. However, those inhabitants had precedent on their side, as previous planning cases had determined peace and quiet in the countryside was important. The expert concluded that there was a strong case for moving the site uphill or further along the coast. Clare didn't think that would help. It would just shift the problem to a different set of villagers.

Visual impact was disappointing. Although it would dramatically affect the views of several properties, no one had a right to a view. Apparently, the sort of visual impact a Planning Inspector got exercised about was one which risked disturbing a driver's concentration, such as the glare from a wind turbine blade, or coming across an object they weren't expecting. But the expert concluded that Richard's factory was far enough away that and drivers would be able to see it from a reasonable distance. Not good news either for BARS's case or for the Brambleton tourist trade if Hastings won.

Ignoring the stamp of *Draft, preliminary subject to review*, Clare read the last two reports. The traffic report buoyed her spirits: there would be material harm – the road to Brambleton Harbour was narrow, and deliveries already needed careful planning to prevent roadblocks. Adding regular heavy goods vehicles through that bottleneck without widening the road – which was impossible with the river on one side and the row of almshouses on the other – would cause problems.

The smell expert was also encouraging. Despite the prevailing wind being onshore, unless the applicant cleaned out the shed daily, it speculated that the smell of chicken manure would be overpowering as far as Prosecco and Prose. Clare's heart lurched thinking about how that would affect her friend's business. The terrace would be empty. The bottom section of the village wouldn't suffer significantly unless there was a northerly wind, when the smell might travel as far as the Smugglers' Arms.

Accompanying the experts' reports were their bills, all due within twenty-eight days. BARS were still £7,000 pounds short, and Ivy had lost less than a pound of her two stone target. Clare had already decided to take matters into her own hands, selling her engagement ring to raise £2,000 towards the bills. Now that the apple harvest was complete, she could sell the Land Rover too. She wanted the experts paid before Richard bankrupted her.

Three days before Christmas, Clare was in the kitchen wrapping a present for Anna when she felt a chill on her back. 'I've good news and bad news,' said Ivy, shutting the door behind her.

With a finger holding the package together, Clare turned in her chair. Ivy didn't look any slimmer. 'You've lost another few ounces?' she guessed.

Ivy slumped into a seat opposite Clare. 'I didn't think it would be so difficult, but everywhere I go there's a biscuit or a slice of cake.'

'It's not the best time of year to try and diet, is it,' said Clare, hoping this was the bad news. One-handed, she tore off a piece of tape and replaced her finger with it, then turned the parcel round and tucked in the other end of wrapping paper.

'The good news is, we don't need the money I'm raising,' said Ivy.

'We don't?' said Clare in a high-pitched voice.

'I've had a donation.'

'Umm,' said Clare, using her teeth to rip another piece of tape off. 'How much this time?' she mumbled through the tape.

'Seven grand.'

Clare spat the tape out. 'Seven grand? Where from?'

'God moves in mysterious ways.'

Clare coughed a laugh. 'Don't give me that bullshit!'

There was a pause. Ivy was chewing her lip. 'Anonymous donor.'

'Ivy, this is the single largest donation we've had by far. Who has that sort of money and where have they been hiding?'

Clare's mind whirred with possibilities of who it could be. Perhaps it was a rich, kind-hearted tourist down for Christmas. No one in Brambleton – except for Roger and Anna – had that sort of spare money and BARS had been fundraising for three months. Why wait until now? 'We must thank them.' She gave Ivy a penetrating look. '*I* must thank them. It's me on the hook for that money and I won't have to sell the Land Rover now!'

'You can't,' said Ivy firmly.

Clare stared at Ivy, who blushed under the gaze. Why wouldn't Ivy tell her? 'You know who it is, don't you?'

She nodded. 'But I'm sworn to secrecy.'

It didn't matter who their benefactor was. This called for a celebration.

An hour later, Clare put her credit card behind the bar in the Smugglers Inn. There was £2,000 from her engagement ring to spend. She wasn't leaving that for Richard. 'All BARS drinks on here, please, Rose. We'll start with a bottle of prosecco! Four glasses unless we can tempt you into a snifter too?'

Rose shook her head. 'Too busy, but thanks.'

There was an explosive *pop* and Rose poured four glasses. Clare clinked hers against Ivy's, Anna's, then Fred's. 'Well done everyone, and a special well done to Ivy!' She felt hands on her shoulders. 'What are you celebrating?' asked Sam.

It didn't matter now. It was too late for the Hastings camp to react. The deadline for submissions was the end of December and even if Richard offered to double their rates, his experts wouldn't sacrifice their festive holidays to help him. With a smug smile, she said, 'We've done it. We've raised the money, we've got our own EIA, and it blows crater-sized holes through yours!'

He spun her round and gave her a hug. Unthinkingly, she hugged him back. He smelt of apple juice, reminding Clare of her mother and bringing her to her senses. She pushed him away and grabbed Anna's arm. 'Come on, let's find a table. Oh, this is such good news.' At the table, Clare topped up their glasses. Ivy had hardly touched hers. Clare grinned at her. 'End of the sponsored slim Ivy. Drink up.'

Ivy gave her a faint smile.

'Ivy,' said Clare in a strained voice, 'is something wrong?'

'It's nothing, said Ivy, 'I'm just tired,' she raised her glass, clinking against Clare's, then Anna's and Fred's saying, 'Well done everyone.'

There was a thudding noise as a bottle of champagne in a plastic cooler was put down on their table. Clare glanced up. Sam. 'My contribution. Can I join you?'

Fred shuffled up to make room for his friend. Sam sat down and said, 'I've booked that cider making course I was telling you about. I'm off to Herefordshire for a week in January.'

'Always good to have something booked into the diary for January. Start the year with purpose,' said Ivy, smiling at Sam. It looked more genuine than the one Ivy had just given Clare, and she heaved a sigh of relief. This must be Ivy's busiest time of the year, helping overworked vicars. No wonder she was tired.

Thinking Fred looked glum too, Clare pulled him aside.

'What's up?' she asked

He handed her a letter. It was from the same London firm of lawyers who had written to Clare. It formally revoked his licence to occupy Jasmine cottage, warned him to vacate immediately, and threatened to get a court order to evict him if he didn't leave voluntarily.

'How long do you think it will take them to get this court order?' he whispered.

She tried to sound reassuring. 'Don't worry about this, Fred. It will probably come to nothing.'

His eyes narrowed. 'But if it does, if he does try and evict me again, how long will it take?'

Clare pursed her lips. She had to answer such a direct question honestly. 'At least a couple of months. The courts are rammed. If you get a summons, tell me and I'll go with you. He may have tripped up. They're complicated forms.' Clare spoke confidently, but Richard was using a lawyer; there would be no mistakes.

Sam charged everyone's glass, then poured himself one. Clare glared at him. How could he celebrate with them when his family was treating Fred so shabbily? Despite the champagne, she still suspected he was a spy. She was surprised that Ivy and Fred couldn't see that. But as his leg pressed against hers under the table, sending a shiver through her body, she wished the Hastings' spy was a little less attractive.

Clare didn't feel very Christmassy – she couldn't. Not with the multiple threats of Fred's eviction and her own bankruptcy in the new year – but she decorated a small tree and had invited Trish, Anna and Roger for Christmas lunch. She had bought a locally sourced free-range organic turkey but had never actually cooked the Christmas meal. Until she'd fallen out with her mother, she'd always come home; she and Guy used to go away to a hotel for Christmas, and since he died, she had eaten her Christmas lunch out, with other single colleagues.

Clare rifled through her mother's cookbooks. She found one devoted to Christmas and pulled that out, studying it as intently as she used to with her law books, scribbling down an extensive list of ingredients.

It was Christmas Eve and Clare was sharing a smoked salmon sandwich with Stop-it, while listening to Christmas carols. She was dreaming of winning the appeal, Hastings relenting and allowing Fred to move back into his old home, and then Sally solving her defamation case with a crafty defence that ChatGPT didn't know about. Life was so unpredictable – just last Christmas she'd been in London leading a professional woman's life.

She heard the back door open. It was Fred and from the look on his face, it wasn't good news.

'What's he done now?' she asked.

'It's Ivy.'

Clare swallowed. She should have guessed two nights earlier. Too intent on celebrating the good, she'd never asked Ivy what the bad news was.

'Section 21?' guessed Clare, the words almost clogging in her throat.

'Yup,' said Fred. 'March. Must have done it when he saw our EIA. And I've had another letter from that lawyer saying he's going for a court order.'

'Do you know, Fred, I can't think of a nasty enough word to describe how that man makes me feel. To do that, to Ivy of all people, just before Christmas – words fail me!' Ivy would be homeless. Except she wouldn't. No one would let that happen. People would put her up, but Ivy couldn't sofa-surf for the rest of her life. Clare racked her brains for a solution. Would the Church help?

'He's a nasty piece of work, isn't he,' said Fred.

She had a sudden thought and asked Fred if anyone was living in his old house.

Maybe Ivy could sneak in there?

'Nah, he's got the builders in. Nice set of blokes. Say they'll be at it for months, ripping it apart. Whoever's lucky enough to be the new tenant will have BARS to thank for the new boiler that's being installed.'

That was a non-starter then. Ivy couldn't squat in an unheated house. Clare must come up with a plan. Fast.

On Christmas morning, Clare followed the cookbook's instructions slavishly. She opted for an eighteenth-century stuffing, deviating slightly by using vacuum-packed, pre-cooked chestnuts. Her guests arrived promptly at 1 p.m. Stop-it was guarding the Aga, and the kitchen was filled with the pungent aroma of roasting turkey, just as it had during the Christmases of Clare's childhood. The three women promised Roger they wouldn't talk about Richard or the chicken factory, but they couldn't avoid the topic of Ivy, who had just weeks to find somewhere to live.

'Why doesn't she stay where she is?' asked Trish, pulling a green paper hat down over her ears. 'Come on, girls. Hats on!' she said grinning. 'Let's get this party started.'

'I suggested that' said Anna, unfurling her own hat. 'She says it's not ethical. There might be someone with a greater need than her.'

'Does that woman ever get angry?' asked Clare. 'If I hear her saying once more that this is God moving in a mysterious way . . .' She caught the strained expression on Roger's face, tailed off to prevent mentioning Richard and pulled her own hat on.

'She could move next door like Fred did!' laughed Anna.

'Richard won't fall for that twice,' said Clare.

'Something will come up,' said Trish cheerfully.

'Will it?' said Clare wistfully. 'In this village? Everyone does holiday lets; the yields are much higher. I don't blame people. Well,' she said, thinking of Sam's four cottages – he didn't need to make money – 'not all of them. They aren't second homes, they run them all year, employ people and it brings tourists here for other businesses.'

Conversation turned to village gossip and then to Clare's delicious food. Even Clare was impressed with herself – the turkey was tender and moist; the sprouts were crisp and the gravy lump-free.

After the meal they dragged themselves out for a bracing walk, then returned to flop in front of the fire, Stop-it hogging the best spot. Roger uncorked a bottle of port and suggested a game of charades. Clare offered to start, thought for a few moments, then gave him the Agatha Christie title *Evil under the Sun*. She flopped into a chair, sipping her port, wondering how he would tackle the challenge. Roger mimed it was a movie and a book with four words in the title, then held up a single finger showing the first word. He stalked to the window. Clare noticed his face was red from the lunchtime wine. He jerked the curtain back and jabbed his finger in the direction of Brambleton Hall.

Twenty-five

It rained on New Year's Day, and for almost a week afterwards the weather remained in sympathy with Clare's mood. She felt drowned by guilt at the mess she'd stirred up. Winter was pruning season, but her heart wasn't really in it. The orchard would soon belong to Richard. She flicked through her mother's books, taking in the theory of creating airflow. A section in the book on growing your own apple trees by grafting caught her attention.

Thinking positively, she decided to invest all of her remaining egg money into rootstock which she could graft the cuttings onto. However, even after rereading the pages, and studying the illustrations on cutting whips from apple trees, she realized she needed advice. It was such a dark and gloomy morning that Clare had to switch on the Land Rover's lights for the journey. Driving past the almshouses, she spotted Fred talking to a man wearing a builder's hard hat. She slowed and wound down her window. The front door of Fred's former home was open and cheerful music blasted out.

'Morning, Fred. Builders busy? I was thinking we should get together to discuss the planning hearing. We should work out how to play the Inspector's site visit.' He grunted and gave her a watery smile, which made her heart twinge.

'I've had a date for the court case,' he said.

She swallowed. What must he think of her, blithering on

about their planning battle, when within months he might not have a roof over his head. How she wished she could turn back the clock, prevent Fred and Ivy gambling with their homes. She should have known Tricky Ricky would take revenge.

'When?' she asked.

'Early February.'

She clenched her teeth together. Her ruse hadn't solved Fred's problem, just given him a reprieve. It was unlikely there were any more houses for long-term rent in January than in the autumn. In fact, it was more likely, that more people would be chasing them. Increased demand for an increasingly scarce asset was driving up rents as tenants scrambled desperately to secure a home, like medieval peasants sending bread prices rocketing as they strove to feed their starving families.

'I'll come with you,' she said brightly. 'That's the least I can do.'

She drove off, unable to dislodge a picture of the resigned look on Fred's face.

As she was driving through Sam's gates, Clare was still ruminating on Fred's plight.

There was a strange car in Sam's yard and a light on in the farmhouse kitchen. She sat for a few minutes, not wanting to intrude if he was entertaining. Telling herself she was just a fellow apple grower popping around for advice, she got out and walked to the door, lifted her hand to knock, then paused with her hand in mid-air. She stepped away, pacing in circles, like Stop-it did before settling in his basket. Clare took a breath, strode to the door and knocked.

The woman who opened it wore riding jodhpurs. Her dark hair fell in loose waves around her shoulders, and she had the dewy supple skin of youth. She looked every inch as attractive as the Woman in Pink. Clare crossed her arms, pulling the sides of her jacket tightly around her torso. She shouldn't have come.

The woman smiled at her. 'Hiya. If you're looking for Sam, he's not here. Can I help?'

Clare felt her cheeks flush. 'No, thank you.' She turned and sprinted from the door, vowing to work out how to graft apples herself.

Driving home, Clare examined her conscience – she hadn't really popped around to ask Sam about grafting. If she was honest, she'd wanted to see him. Apart from their row the night she'd been drunk, whenever she was with him, he lifted her spirits. But either he didn't feel the same way, or she'd been so horrible to him that he'd lost interest. The explanation was irrelevant – she needed to shut down her feelings for him. Sam wasn't interested in her.

The next morning, dressed in an old tatty sweatshirt, she flicked open one of her mother's books and read the section on grafting for a third time. Measuring nine inches from her index finger, she marked that with a felt-tip pen around her sweatshirt sleeve. She carried a ladder, a sharpened pair of secateurs and the book to the orchard. Shivering, she glanced at the horizon which was a soft blend of muted greys and blues, the colours bleeding into each other as if the sky itself was trying to shelter from the weight of winter. Clare chose a healthy-looking tree, propped the book against its trunk, examined the picture, then using her makeshift ruler, cut a pencil-thick length off a shoot, just above where it was budding. The ladder rattled as she climbed back down with her prize, as if applauding her success.

The air was crisp, biting at her skin, and soon Clare's exposed hands were white with cold. Nevertheless, each snip sent a shiver of pleasure through her, and every time she laid her cutting – which she started thinking of in its technical garb as a *scion* – carefully on the ground, she felt a happy jolt of triumph. Several hours and many trees later, there was a six-foot-long line of scions. She carried them to a corner of the orchard, dug a six-inch trench, then, bundling them together, she heeled them into the trench with just a few inches showing above the soil. According to her mother's book, they would be moist but dormant until spring. That was when she would tackle the tricky task of attaching them to the rootstock. Provided she hadn't given the house over to Richard by then.

Walking away from the trench, Clare calculated that she would discover if the grafts were successful at about the same time they would learn if their future would be blighted by run-off from a chicken factory. She sighed. Either way, when they were planted, the grafter would not be living here anymore.

In the damp dreary days which followed, Clare ignored Richard's regular threatening letters. Sally had returned to work and confirmed the leaflet was indeed defamatory. Her advice was to apologize, point out that this was a preliminary draft which was never distributed outside of BARS, and ask how he'd found the pre-verified version.

Clare asked Sally to reply, confirming receipt of Richard's legal letter and saying she was taking legal advice about his allegations. It was a stalling tactic. She was desperate to know which member of BARS had given the poisonous leaflet to Richard, but Clare needed to keep her team on side for the hearing. She couldn't start accusing anyone of treachery.

To keep her spirits up, Clare added another task to her morning ritual of breaking the ice on water troughs and feeding the animals – trekking to the corner of the orchard to check on her buried treasure. It was silly really. They were dormant, but each morning, seeing them poking up out of the ground like tiny beacons of hope, she felt reinvigorated.

It was the end of January and Clare was in the village shop chatting to Gina about preparations for the public hearing.

'I'm definitely coming, and so is my partner.' Gina said. 'I'm also rounding up support from my mothers and toddlers' group.'

Clare beamed at the other woman, 'Fabulous, we need a crowd. Show strength in numbers.'

Gina turned to leave; Clare heard a bell tinkle announcing the arrival of a customer. It was Sam. He held the door open for Gina, 'Hi. How's life at Orchard farm? Have you finished pruning?'

The word that sprang into Clare's mind was 'cold'. He lived in a well-insulated home like she used to. Sam wouldn't be huddling beneath a blanket or cuddling the Aga, but there was a warmth to his words, and she didn't want to be negative, 'All done,' she said, 'and you?'

'I love this time of year, still winter but all the promise of spring . . .'

'Yes, it's exciting thinking about new life around the corner.' She thought about what she had just said, realizing she meant those words. Farming was a slower pace of life, but she was finding it rewarding.

He put a hand on her arm, sending a fizzing sensation through her body, 'you will let me know if there's anything you need a hand with won't you.' He was looking at her with compassion radiating from his sparkling blue eyes, 'I don't think Stop-it is much good as a farmhand.'

She didn't move, enjoying the sensation of the pressure from his hand. 'Yes of course,' she whispered. 'Thank you.'

In early February, before buds appeared on the mature apple trees, Clare dug up the scions, sharpened the secateurs for a second time and, in the comparative warmth of her mother's small polytunnel, cut the top off each rootstock leaving them a foot proud of their pots. Consulting the precious book multiple times, she made 'upwards cuts' and 'downwards cuts', then carefully joined each scion to a rootstock, binding the two together with special grafting tape. By the end of the day, forty pots of apple grafts cowered in the warmth of the polytunnel. The tape was to be removed when a *callus* – the bulbous join attaching the two plants – was clearly visible, in about eight weeks' time. She noted the date in her diary – mid-April.

Later that afternoon, Sally phoned – Richard's lawyers had written to her. He was still claiming damages of £5 million. Sally's advice was to settle for £500,000, Richard's original proposal, but Clare suspected that Hastings wasn't really interested in the money. He wanted to destroy her, to bankrupt her. He wouldn't settle.

The pair debated tactics, deciding on Sally's original advice of apologizing and pointing out that the leaflet was not the version circulated publicly. Clare wasn't optimistic. She was the author and had circulated the defamatory leaflet to three people.

On the day of Fred's court case, Clare drove him into Barnstaple. Clare could barely look at him – this was her fault. She should have insisted he left BARS after the Council's decision. They travelled in silence, Clare rummaging around for topics which might distract him, but she didn't think he wanted to hear about her apple grafting, or how many eggs her hens had laid. And if she mentioned anything to do with BARS, they'd end up talking about Richard, a theme she was keen to avoid. She passed the time trying to prove Fred, Ivy and Anna's innocence by manufacturing explanations for how Richard had discovered that poisonous leaflet, but no rational explanation came to mind.

Having no idea how long they would be, Clare parked and paid for a whole day. Propping the ticket on her windscreen, she forced herself to glance Fred's way.

'Ready?' she asked. He rubbed his eyes, gave a slow nod then grunted.

It was a short distance to Barnstaple Court, a low, grey building from the 1960s. Inside was dark, which to Clare seemed appropriate. She suspected it reflected Fred's spirits, but hoped it wasn't a portent for his fate. Once through security, she checked in with the court staff and was told to wait. The pair sat side by side. Clare still couldn't think of anything to say. By the time they left this building, Fred would be on a conveyor belt to homelessness. Once a landlord was granted the legal right to evict a tenant, there was a series of hoops to jump through, delaying the process, but the culmination was inevitable. Unless the landlord changed their mind, even a model tenant inevitably lost their home.

Gazing around the unfamiliar space – employment tribunals weren't conducted in court – Clare diverted her mind from the reason she was there, by playing 'Spot the Lawyer'. It wasn't difficult; they were the ones in sober dark clothes, with an air of purpose. Some were on their own. A few accompanied smartly turned-out clients, but there didn't seem to be any accompanying the less well dressed, who sat alone or occasionally in couples, with hunched shoulders and furrowed brows. Those people all had one thing in common – a look of despair on their faces, which made Clare want to help them. But sadly, this wasn't her field. She felt like the proverbial chocolate teapot.

To Clare, it felt like landlords exploiting Section 21 'no-fault' evictions was the ultimate misuse of power; in a country that claims to safeguard its citizens, housing was slipping through the net. If they'd done nothing wrong, employees couldn't lose their jobs without compensation; in theory, the National Health Service took care of everyone, even patients who were not looking after themselves. Although not perfect either, benefits ensured people could afford necessities – food, clothes, heating. Provision of housing was neglected. A combination of decreasing supply – through right-to-buy and lack of new buildings, especially social housing – and rampant demand from a growing population had collapsed the system. A basic service had been outsourced to a private sector unfit to pick up the slack.

It wasn't like the NHS dipping into the professionally run private medical service to cope with backlogs. Private landlords included unscrupulous individuals like Richard, with a deaf ear to tenants' complaints about poor insulation and damp, but alive to every possibility to jack up the rent and upend tenants' lives on a whim.

There was no sign of Richard. No surprise there. Just like every other dirty task, he would outsource Fred's eviction. She was relieved; the superior expression on his florid face might ignite her temper.

In front of her, the courtroom door opened, releasing a scowling man followed by two women, both dressed in trousers and jumpers. The man stalked past, yanking at the exit door. The two women crossed in front of Clare. One wore a harassed expression on her face and said a rushed goodbye to her companion before dashing over to a man sitting near Clare. She overheard her leaning over and saying, 'Mr Harris, we're next. Let's go through that paperwork one more time, look for any errors.'

The man passed over a crumpled piece of paper while saying, 'Did you win that one?' The woman spoke while reading. 'The house is in their joint names and the Section 21 was filed in his alone. He'll be back when he's sorted it out. Come on, we're on. Leave this to me.' An hour later, a clerk announced Fred's case. Clare pasted on a confident look, and, feeling inspired, announced 'Leave this to me.'

Inside the courtroom, they sat away from Richard's three solicitors. His case was presented by a tall, slim man who seemed to like the sound of his own pompous voice. Clare labelled him as a wishful barrister, but his argument was compelling. Fred had no lease. He had been in the house for three months, preventing the owner renting the cottage over the lucrative Christmas season – he was squatting. All the paperwork was correct, and Mr Hastings was seeking a possession order with a short timeframe.

Privately, the judge might sympathize with their fate. He might prefer to be presiding over a technical dispute interpreting a dilapidations clause in a commercial lease, but he wasn't here to dispense charity. He was here to uphold the law. Clare begged for the maximum twenty-eight days' notice if the judge granted the possession order, then with a sense of foreboding sat again, the hard chair feeling uncomfortably plush compared to Fred's probable fate. Richard was granted an eviction order. That didn't entitle him to physically evict Fred, but in twenty-eight days Hastings could apply for a warrant for possession to allow bailiffs to do just that. Fred probably had until the end of May at the latest to find somewhere to live. If Richard won the planning appeal, of course, he might relent. Hastings was also awarded his legal costs. 'Don't worry about that, Fred,' muttered Clare. 'This was my idea. I'll pay those.'

Unless Richard dropped the defamation case, she'd be paying him with his own money.

The day of Ivy's eviction drew closer. There was a plan, but not a solution. For the first week, Ivy would stay with Trish, and former parishioners had also offered spare rooms. But Ivy needed a home, not a room.

Removals day dawned. Raindrops fell in steady streams, their rhythm a soft yet relentless patter against the already sodden earth. The horizon was barely visible, swallowed by mist and drizzle, while the wind swept the rain sideways, turning the cold air into a biting, wet chill. The Devon sky was dark and heavy with the promise of more rain. The clouds hung low, pressing down like a damp, suffocating blanket.

The Smugglers Inn van was once again parked outside the almshouses, this time ready to transport Ivy's possessions to Clare's barn. There was a dozen well-wishers wrapped in waterproof clothing, helping with removals. George backed out of the house, his arms under a sofa. 'Quickly now, it's pouring out here,' he said.

'Again!' shouted a male voice from within the cottage. 'There's hardly been a dry day all year!'

Standing next to Fred, Stop-it by her side, Clare hoped the weather cleared up before Easter – the start of the tourist season. That was only a few weeks away.

Ivy came out of her cottage, a stoic expression on her face. The informal removals team sent up a little cheer, then clapped as Ivy walked to the roadside, clutching the cross at her neck which sent a wave of pity through Clare. With rain trickling down her face, standing beside one former tenant and looking at another, Clare thought it was ironic that all four of the almshouses were now technically vacant yet couldn't be used by two people who needed them.

She passed Stop-it's lead to Fred. 'Hang onto him for me.'

'Where are you going?' demanded Fred. 'You've got that look on your face again. What are you plotting?'

Clare ran around the side of Rose Cottage, her eyes raking across the lemon-coloured render. There was a key safe attached to the wall, just like for Jasmine Cottage. She ran her fingers over the combination, lined up 1, 2, 3, 4, then pulled at the hinge. The flap fell and a key dropped into Clare's hand. She closed her fingers round it, a smile blossoming on her face. She was pretty sure she could spin this to Ivy as God moving in mysterious ways.

Twenty-six

Rain kept falling, breaking records. Newscasters reported it had been the wettest eighteen months for over a hundred years and farmers were bellyaching about not being able to plant crops or fertilize because the land was too soggy. For Clare, at least, it meant the end of breaking the ice on water troughs.

Wrapped up in waterproofs with rain pattering on her hood, Clare scooped out grain for the chickens. She felt sorry for her flock. She wished they would shelter inside the henhouse, but whenever she went to feed them, they were outside, looking a fraction of their usual size, with their feathers plastered against their sides. She added an extra measure of grain to the trough and ran back inside shivering – she would warm herself up with a hot cup of coffee.

'Blast.' She muttered peering into the empty tin.

Over by the door, Stop-it was wagging his tail expectantly, his eyes bright with the possibility of adventure. Clare paused, looking at him, then let out a resigned chuckle.

'All right, Stop-it, you win. Let's go get that coffee.'

With a quick tug, she hooked him up, pulled her coat back on, and braced herself as they stepped out together for the trek to the village shop.

Twenty minutes later the bell tinkled, and Clare stepped inside, her cheeks flushed from the winter chill. The scent of fresh bread hung in the air, warm and comforting. As she reached for a jar of coffee on the shelf, her fingers brushed against someone else's – a man's hand, rough yet gentle. Startled, she glanced up and locked eyes with Sam; there was a faint smile tugging at his lips.

'I'm sorry,' he murmured, his voice deep and soft. Their hands lingered for a moment.

'No problem,' she replied, her heart skipping unexpectedly.

He seemed to want to talk, so picking up the jar of coffee, she let him. 'I went on a cider making course last month and I'm going to start doing everything myself.'

'I tried grafting some apples,' she said. 'I think they've taken. I can see little green buds on the tops of the stems.'

'It's so rewarding isn't it . . . grafting,' he said, the enthusiasm clear in his voice. 'Knowing you created that new life. Keep the bases weed free and pot them on into larger tubs of quality compost.'

'And put them outside?' she asked.

'Not unless you want to take them all back in again in a cold snap. I'd leave them somewhere warm until the end of April at the earliest.'

'Thanks for the advice,' she said. Turning away, her eyes were drawn to a display of Valentine's cards still waiting to be cleared, and she quickly scooted to the counter with her jar.

The night before the planning hearing, Clare stayed up late writing her speech, listening to a storm rattle through the loose sitting room windows. She had an empty feeling in her stomach, which she attributed partly to her inability to eat more than half a sandwich, partly to worrying about Richard's defamation case, but mostly to the hearing. Although much more familiar with the nuances of planning law than she was nine months ago, compared to Hastings' experts, she was a novice, and tomorrow, they would all be there. Kindly, Walter, BARS's water expert, had halved his daily rate; and with Ivy's sponsorship money covered the cost of the experts, BARS wasn't entirely reliant on Clare.

She printed off her speech and stood up to practise. An hour later, she poured herself a glass of wine and took it outside onto the patio. It was already dark; the clocks were yet to go forward. She wrapped her jacket around her, gazing out at the black nothingness, feeling a sense of calm. There was no sign of another human. No lights, no noise from a neighbour's flat, no cars, no taxis, no buses. It was so peaceful. She was going to miss this.

There was a brisk onshore breeze, and she let it rustle through her hair, which now reached halfway down her neck. Clare sniffed. There was a sharp tang of ammonia coming from her chicken coup. She must have missed a cleaning day. Clare took a sip of wine, then heard a noise. She held the wine in her mouth, running her eyes around the silent farm, then swallowed slowly. She heard it again. It sounded like a wild animal stumbling through undergrowth. Clare sat up, peering round, expecting to see the yellowish green of a deer's eyes, but the meadows were empty. She glanced over towards her gate and saw a dark shadowy figure. Her heart started hammering against her ribcage. Her voice shaky, she cried out, 'Stop-it! Stop-it!' The figure turned and stumbled away.

Clare ran inside, collected the dog and retreated upstairs. Was this the same person she'd seen in the blue car? Was someone stalking her? Why?

Clare was awake before Captain Hilts. Deciding to shower after mucking out the chickens, she shot out of bed, scrambled into jeans and dashed into the kitchen, where she moved the kettle onto the hot plate. She pulled on thick rubber gloves and strode outside. The stench hit her as if she had walked straight into the henhouse.

Inside the pen, she unlatched the henhouse door, picked up the spade and a fifty-litre bucket and leaned inside. Sweet-smelling straw covered the floor, and the roosting bars were free of poo. Backing out of the hut, again the smell engulfed her. Where was it coming from? She sniffed, turning in a circle. Had someone been spreading muck? How? For weeks it had been raining. How had someone driven a tractor over a field without getting stuck in the mud? Who and why?

Suddenly it hit her that this pong was no coincidence – this was Hastings. He must have bribed a farmer to spread muck so that when the Inspector came for his site visit later today, he would think it always smelt like this. A hen shot past her, pursued by Captain Hilts, and she hurled her spade against the side of the hut.

Clare glared at the rooster, scooped up a portion of feed and stomped over to the cooler. He skulked after her, his head dipped and ducked into the small shed.

Dressed in the same trouser suit she'd worn to her mother's funeral, Clare parked at the Old Rectory, got out and slammed the car door shut. The suit had been chosen to remind her she was fighting for her mother's legacy, but also to remain professional, not biff Hastings' arrogant nose. Thoughts of his nose reminded her why she was cross, and she sniffed so loudly she could hear herself doing it. But the air smelt clean; she couldn't detect anything either pleasant or unpleasant.

Entering the sitting room, she heard the clinking of coffee cups and the animated conversations of her fellow activists. Clare crossed her fingers and raised her voice, 'How bad is the smell up at the almshouses?'

Anna stood, frowning. She shifted her long hair, so it hung over a single shoulder and asked, 'What smell?'

Clare thumped herself onto a seat with a loud tut. 'Someone's been spreading muck, and I think we all know who's behind it. That's a taster of what's to come if we don't win today.'

'It could be a dairy farmer,' said Anna.

'It probably is,' said Clare tersely, 'but he's been paid by Tricky Ricky to spread it the evening before the Planning Inspector visits the site.'

'Is it that bad?' asked Anna.

'Horrid,' said Fred, wrinkling his nose.

'Did anyone see the weather forecast this morning?' asked Anna. Clare scowled at her friend. How could Anna think about weather today?

'Chance of showers,' said Ivy. 'I didn't want to risk putting the laundry outside.'

'I don't know why you don't just use Richard's tumble dryer – it's his bill,' sniggered Fred.

'That's not ethical, Fred.'

'I meant the wind direction,' said Anna.

Clare felt a jolt of hope. A change of wind direction would blow the smell into the village. She pulled out her phone – four faces peered at the screen, scanning the hourly forecast. The wind was coming from the west, onshore. It would trap the smell right where they didn't want it.

'Not ideal,' she sighed, trying to keep the anger out of her voice. 'I wish we'd got the smell boffin coming today.'

'Do we have time to reach him, ask his advice on what to do at the site visit? It sounds like the Inspector will have to be nose-blind to miss this,' said Anna.

'I've got a call into him already,' said Clare. 'Ivy, do you want me to take over this section from you?'

'No, I have my notes somewhere in here,' said Ivy. She dug into her shoulder bag, taking out a cake tin, then her purse, followed by a phone. Clare closed her eyes, telling herself to keep calm. She would just have to take responsibility for smell as she was doing for so much else. 'Ivy, let me do it,' said Clare.

The rustling stopped.

'No,' said Fred, putting a restraining hand on Clare's. 'We've all got our parts to play.'

Clare ran her hands down her face, then answered with a small smile. 'You're right, Fred. I'm sure you'll do us proud, Ivy.'

'Everyone ready?' asked Anna.

'Let me at him,' said Fred, striding to the door.

The first face Clare saw at the hearing venue was Richard's. She tensed up, her fists bunching; she realized she had never hated someone before now – not even Guy, despite how he had betrayed her. Hastings was wearing a checked tweed suit, and next to him stood six people, all dressed in suits. She recognized the man she'd nicknamed 'the boffin' at the parish council meeting; despite wearing a suit, he also wore a V-neck jumper. There was no sign of Cora or Sam, but Magnus, looking incongruous in his uniform, stood stiffly like a soldier on guard duty. Clare didn't think she'd recognize Magnus casually dressed. She was pleased to see him – employing a butler was unlikely to endear the Inspector to Richard's cause. Magnus stood some distance away from his employer, beside four people Clare didn't know, who she suspected were also employed by Hastings.

A few minutes later, Ivy and Fred arrived together, and shortly afterwards, Anna.

'Roger's parking the car,' said Anna.

'Roger?' said Clare, giving her friend a dazed look.

'Yes. He drove. He's fully supportive of us now. He says he

won't sit on the sidelines after the way Richard has treated Fred and Ivy.'

Good for Roger, thought Clare. Hastings liked to project himself as the squire. In that privileged position, he owed a special duty of care to people like Fred and Ivy. Roger was a decent man, and as the saying went, all it took was for a few good men to stand aside to allow evil to flourish.

The doors opened and Trish strode in, followed by Rose, George and the entire Smugglers Inn team. Soon, there were over fifty people standing around BARS. The doors kept opening and the crowd swelled. Not a single person joined Richard's side of the room.

Two official-looking men walked in. Clare guessed it was the Planning Officer and his boss. One of them opened the chamber and switched on the lights. He let his colleague in, then turned and said, 'The Inspector is here. If you'd like to make yourselves comfortable, I'll go and fetch him.'

Clare felt like the doors to the exam hall had been opened. She let the opposition file in first. They took seats on the left of the chamber; the Planning Officer sat on the right, directly in front of a table and chair, where Clare presumed the Inspector would sit. She ushered her supporters in, now so numerous that behind the Planning Officer there was hardly a spare seat. The BARS team sat in the same row: Walter was in the aisle seat, Clare next to him, then Anna and Roger, Ivy, and furthest away from Clare, Fred.

Clare dumped her bag on the floor, fumbling to extract her speech. She crossed her legs, uncrossed them, recrossed them and started bouncing her top leg, jiggling that foot. Fred and Ivy were both used to presenting to a large audience. She hoped Anna didn't get stage fright.

A hush fell as a tall man with a long face strode in. He wasn't the sombre suited man Clare had expected. He wore a jumper, no tie and he had a slightly jolly air to him, like a head teacher about to award the prizes on Speech Day. Clare scraped her hands through her hair and told herself that they had a strong case. BARS would win.

The Inspector smiled at his audience and spoke in a reassuring voice. 'I'd like to outline the programme for today. For some this is a familiar experience, but for most of you it will be your first planning hearing.'

He explained he would invite all three parties to summarize their case, starting with the appellant, then the Council, and, lastly the opposition, BARS. Everyone who wanted to speak would get a chance, but there were to be no interruptions. He assured the audience that he had read the three submissions and would ask a few clarification questions, and then he wanted to visit the site.

Walter whispered in Clare's ear. 'This is perfectly normal; appellants always go first.' Same as a criminal trial, thought Clare. She shuddered at the analogy, but for the village, this was as serious as a criminal trial. If Richard won, life in Brambleton would change dramatically.

Richard's planning expert spoke first. Clare listened to him dismantle her submission, fighting the urge to hurl abuse. The expert waved a hand at the crowd of villagers. 'It is fear of change that is driving the opposition.'

'We're not frightened of change,' shouted Fred.

Clare cringed.

There was a wry smile on the expert's face and his client was beaming. Clare glanced at the Inspector. He was rubbing the back of his neck, a frown creasing his face. 'If I could be allowed to continue,' said the expert silkily. He spoke for another ten minutes, answering a few questions from the Inspector in exasperating detail.

Next the boffin spoke reassuringly about his client's plans to cope with the waste. He was followed by Richard. Clare suspected his advisers had written his speech. Hastings spoke crisply, bringing to mind how she used to rehearse her clients before their appearance at an employment tribunal. He spoke of needing to make the farm profitable, which made Clare want to scream. If he wanted to save money, Clare had a few ideas. How could he talk about a cost-of-living crisis with his butler sitting two rows behind him?

Hastings mentioned the chicken farm would provide local jobs and claimed there were several existing local chicken farmers. 'In fact,' he said, tossing her a supercilious smile, 'I believe the leader of BARS keeps chickens on her farm. Maybe she's frightened of competition.'

Clare sat on her hands. She felt a sudden rush of affection for her rooster. How dare Hastings compare Hilts and the Veras to what he wanted to do?

The Planning Officer spoke next, briefly, and then it was BARS's turn. Clare was first. Deliberately omitting the word 'farm', she argued that, if permitted, the factory would cause substantial harm to the environment, through contamination of the water, noxious smells and unreasonable levels of noise, and the visual impact of such a monstrous structure risked causing traffic accidents. 'This site has been deliberately chosen so it is as far away as possible from Mr Hastings' house. He's pushing the problem onto the village and destroying livelihoods.'

'And the environment,' shouted Fred. 'There's all sorts of wildlife on that field and in the river.'

The Inspector looked startled. 'Like what?' he asked.

'Newts,' shouted Fred.

The Inspector shifted in his chair. 'Have you conducted a survey?' he asked.

'I don't have to. I've seen them.'

Across the aisle, a woman rose. 'Sir, I *have* conducted a survey, which is summarized in our submission. No endangered species were detected.'

'You didn't look for any,' shouted Fred. 'There's newts.'

The Inspector gave Fred a hard look. 'Can you back up your allegation?'

Clare wanted to wring Fred's neck. She stood. 'Your honour . . .'

He smiled at her. 'I'm not a judge.'

'Our expert did find evidence of endangered species which are mentioned in his report in Appendix 1.'

'Yes, I saw that. Evidence of . . . but not the species themselves.'

'We only did one site visit.' Clare said, silently adding: *we could only afford to do one site visit.*

'They're in there,' said Fred firmly. 'And bats.'

'Bats?' said the Inspector, his eyes narrowing, 'Where?'

'I get bats,' said Fred defiantly, 'and I'm close to that site. You get bats don't you, Ivy?'

All eyes turned to Ivy who glanced around her. Her face and neck flushed red, she opened her mouth, closed it then cleared her throat. 'They're definitely in the church.'

'And that's not far away,' said Fred triumphantly.

Richard's expert was on her feet again. 'This is unhelpful. Even if there are bats in the church, that's where they live, not on this site.'

'What about the field mice?' asked Fred.

The Inspector held up his hands. 'Can we move on, please.'

Walter gave Clare an exasperated look, pointing down the row of packed chairs to Fred. 'Unhelpful,' he muttered. 'Can you shut him up?'

Clare leaned forwards and shot a dirty look Fred's way, but

he was facing forwards. In a shaky voice, she whispered to Walter, 'He's too far away.' Clare tore off a strip of paper from her speech and scribbled a note on the back. *Fred, please shut up*, then folded it in half, scrawled 'Fred' on the front, leaned across Anna and tossed it into Ivy's lap, jabbing a finger in Fred's direction.

Walter spoke next, challenging the boffin's claims. Walter explained how his modelling showed the run-off from the factory would leach into the groundwater. The Inspector was dismissive. 'But the proposed site is in an agricultural area. According to the appellant, there are several dairy farms close by. Presumably those farmers have mitigated the harm, and I note Mr Hastings intends to implement measures to minimize any contamination.'

'He's going to build a gas bomb,' said Fred.

Clare's heart sank.

'A what?' asked the Inspector scowling at Fred.

'He's going to build a digester. Once he's got this factory up and running, he's going to burn gas yards from where I live. It could explode any time, blow me and Ivy here to smithereens.'

Clare tried to block out the sound of snickering coming from across the aisle. Fred was undoing all their efforts. She questioned why Fred kept interrupting, trying to ignore the nagging voice in her mind – had Sam planted this idea with Fred?

'Let's stick to the planning application in front of us, shall we. If the appellant wants to install an anaerobic digester that would be the subject of a separate planning application, and you could raise your objections if and when it is lodged.'

Clare leaned over and tapped Ivy's arm. 'Get up and speak,' she hissed, 'before Fred does any more harm.'

Ivy made her case about noxious smells, but Clare had a sinking feeling. The Inspector clearly thought it was relevant that Richard's site was plum in the middle of a farming community.

One whiff of the pong currently permeating the upper half of the village would destroy Ivy's arguments, and it would take a gale to drive that stench away before the site visit.

The Inspector called a lunch break. Clare wasn't hungry, but she did want to put something large and immovable into Fred's mouth.

After a brief recess, Clare stood and apologized. 'I reminded my colleague Fred that he had offered to walk my dog, and he's taking him up to Exmoor so won't be able to join us for the rest of the hearing or be at the site visit.' There was a ripple of laughter, and she noticed a smile on the Inspector's face. Richard and his team didn't react, but she suspected they weren't pleased to see their secret weapon dismantled.

As she listened to each villager speak of the impact the factory would have on their business, Clare had a nasty premonition that they weren't landing any blows. The Inspector was listening, but not nodding sympathetically. When the third person claimed their holiday business would suffer, one of Richard's advisers stood and dismissed it as scaremongering, pointing out that his client owned the two holiday lets closest to the site.

Trish spoke last, then the Inspector announced the site visit. Watching her team troop out, Clare hung back. 'What do you think?' she asked Walter.

'You can never read these hearings. He may have made up his mind already, but my gut says a lot hinges on this site visit.'

'I was hoping you wouldn't say that. Richard's been playing dirty tricks,' she said, telling him about the recent muck spreading.

'Ah, not helpful.'

Roger had to get back to work, so Anna and Ivy clambered into the back of the battered Land Rover, and with Walter beside her in the front, the BARS team set off. As Clare accelerated out of Barnstaple, there wasn't much banter in the car. She looked out of her windscreen at the peaceful countryside sliding past, with a bitter taste of defeat in her mouth. Walter had as good as told her they were going to lose.

Although keeping to the speed limit, she was driving fast, and a mile outside Barnstaple the Land Rover pulled up behind a slow-moving flashy sports car. Clare instantly guessed who the single occupant was.

She trod down on the accelerator until her car was inches from Richard's. She could see the back of his head. Hastings sped up. Clare did the same, the Land Rover's engine roaring, a deep, guttural rumble, straining to keep up but managing to hug the bumper of the car in front as it tore around a corner and up a hill. Imagining she was Guy at a racetrack, Clare leaned forward over the steering wheel, foot hard on the pedal, the engine rattling, almost protesting, with Clare willing the ancient beast to surge forward just a little bit more.

Walter clutched at the dashboard. 'Hey, steady on,' he said querulously.

Clare released the pressure and the gap between the two vehicles grew. What was she doing? What had the Hastings family done to her? She was a lawyer; she shouldn't allow her frustration to translate into road rage.

As they drew closer to the village, Clare wound down her window, leaned out and inhaled, waiting for the stench to assault her nostrils. When she could see the almshouses, Clare's nostrils wrinkled. Beside her, Walter gave a loud sniff. 'Quite powerful, isn't it?'

Richard and his army of advisers were in front of the village hall. Hastings' face was flushed, and he was alternately jabbing fingers at his team and towards the site. Clare left the car on the street – she wasn't giving Tricky Ricky the opportunity to prevent her from parking in his field. As she was getting out the Inspector arrived. She glanced past the village hall and her brow furrowed. Magnus was running across the field. He ran flat-footed like a child, his blazer flapping at his waist. In hot pursuit was the boffin, followed by another adviser. With a face now a vivid shade of beetroot, arms windmilling above his head, Hastings was shouting after the runners. Clare looked beyond the waving Richard to the site. Slap bang where Richard wanted to build his factory, someone had parked a horsebox with a tall pole attached to the side. It looked as high as the letters on the iconic Hollywood sign in Los Angeles. Surrounding the lorry and, Clare assumed, illustrating the length and width of the proposed shed, a rope was stretched around four poles. The mock shed looked enormous, towering above the almshouses, making them look like dolls' houses. Clare didn't hide her grin.

The BARS team walked towards the Inspector, who was encircled by Richard's remaining experts like bodyguards protecting a pop star.

'That's not ethical,' muttered Ivy.

'No, it bloody well isn't, Ivy,' said Clare, grabbing Walter's arm and shooting off to join the party.

Magnus reached the horsebox and tugged at the driver's door, but evidently it was locked. His fellow assassin had reached one of the four poles and was rocking it back and forwards, trying to wrench it out of the ground.

'No, no, please leave it where it is. This is quite useful,' called out the Inspector.

Clare started laughing. Richard was standing in front of her, his hands on his hips. 'This is trespass. You've no right to come onto my land.'

'Oh, come on, Richard. This is a planning hearing. You can't stop me joining the Inspector on the site.'

'It's my land.'

'Well, can Walter please join the Inspector?'

'No.'

'Then play fair. Call your experts away.'

'Play fair, says the lady who's parked a horsebox on my land and staked out the site?' He looked over his shoulder. 'The Inspector looks quite content,' said Richard. 'I think we'll leave him to do his job.'

Clare stood impotently watching the Inspector stride around the roped-off section of land, an escort on either side of him. He stopped beside the horsebox, pointing at the pole, then turned and looked back down the field, first towards the almshouses, and then at the village hall. He took one more sweeping look, turned and walked towards Clare.

'Did a surveyor stake out the site?' asked the Inspector.

'I've no idea,' said Clare. 'I didn't arrange this.'

'Oh really!' snapped Richard. 'The local boy scout troop, was it?'

The boffin put a hand on his client's arm. 'I've already pointed out to the Inspector that this stunt isn't helpful. We've no idea how tall that pole is. The implication is this represents the proposed shed, but personally I don't think it's accurate.'

Clare suspected it was deadly accurate. It was an audacious move she wished she'd thought of and must have taken ages to set up. Fred had been with them all morning, so he couldn't have done this alone, and she couldn't think of another supporter who wasn't at the hearing.

'I'd love to take the credit, but it wasn't me.'

Richard snorted.

The Inspector was sniffing. Clare did the same and soon everyone was sniffing loudly.

'What the devil is that smell?' asked the Inspector. 'And where's it coming from?'

'Ah,' said the boffin. 'That's farm muck.'

The Inspector's eyes narrowed. 'I didn't notice any muck on the site.'

'Oh, it's probably just from one of the neighbouring dairy farms. It happens frequently. You get used to it,' said Richard.

'Actually, it's very rare,' said Ivy. 'Farmers only spread muck in the spring and autumn and they're very mindful that it's a tourist area, so they spread well before Easter and avoid October half-term week.'

'Pfft,' said Richard. 'I grew up here – good agricultural smell that.'

'Hmmm,' said the Inspector, taking another sniff. 'Interesting.'

Clare felt her heart sink. It smelt disgusting. If the Inspector thought the air normally smelt like this, they were sunk.

Anna offered to come home with Clare, but she suspected her friend would want to come in for a glass of wine and Clare wanted to lick her wounds in private. She dropped Anna at the Old Rectory and crawled back up the hill.

Stop-it was waiting for her, his paws on the top rung of the farm gate. She pushed it open, knelt and dropped her head on to his furry neck, inhaling the doggy smell of him. The look on Richard's face when the group sniff had occurred said it all – BARS had lost.

Stop-it wriggled free and dashed off, twirling round in circles, his eyes searching, then he pounced on the recycling bin, dashing back with an empty milk carton.

She lunged for it, and he backed off, trotting away.

'And just what am I going to do with you, you little rascal? I don't think you'd like London very much.' But she'd miss him. He was such a cheerful soul. For ten minutes she played chase the milk carton with the dog, laughing as he dodged round her, circling then darting forwards and backwards. She leaned over, resting her hands on her thighs. 'You're much better at this game than me.'

Clare fed the pigs, then the chickens, smiling at Captain Hilts with his wings out, forcing the hens to gather at either end of the feeding trough. He was a tyrant, but he had an excuse. He was a rooster, and she'd miss him, too.

Twenty-seven

As a trainee lawyer, Clare had taught herself never to scroll through emails in meetings; but a couple of weeks after the hearing, she found herself constantly fidgeting with her phone like a teenager waiting for a Snapchat message.

One evening, as she was upstairs tidying her bedroom, sipping a calming mug of camomile tea and trying not to dwell on her probable fate at the hand of the Hastings family, she heard Stop-it barking. He was bored. It had been hours since they'd last played together and they hadn't gone for their evening walk. She glanced outside. It was dark, that sort of eerie blackness that comes in the countryside where you can't see anything beyond your feet. She didn't want to walk him now. She picked up her mug and took a swallow, but the tea was tepid.

Stop-it growled. A chill shot through her. It wasn't his usual playful sound. Questions fizzed in her brain: was someone outside again? Who? Had Richard sent someone to hurt her? Why? Did he have those sorts of contacts?

An owl hooted, sending a shiver down her spine, then she heard a knock at the back door.

Clare crept downstairs. Halfway down, she realized she was carrying her mug and stopped. It wasn't much of a weapon. Richard's heavies would not be deterred if she hurled lukewarm tea at them. In the kitchen Stop-it was jumping up and down as if on springs, snapping at the door handle. Someone was outside. She swapped the mug for a poker.

Clare opened her mouth to speak, but no sound came out. Her heart was racing, and she could feel the hairs standing up on her arms, mirroring Stop-it's hackles. Who was at the back door and why hadn't they come to the front?

With trembling fingers, she put down her weapon and called Anna. Her friend answered cheerfully, 'Hiya, how's—?'

Clare gasped. Her breath was rasping, her throat almost too tight for the words to squeeze through. Her voice came out in a croak. 'There's someone at the back door.'

'Clare!'

The dog's snarls were echoing round the room. As he pounced at the door, his paws were creating a thunderous rhythm against the wood. In between the bursts of noise, she heard someone knocking at the door. Clare couldn't breathe. 'Help me, what should I do?' she wailed.

Stop-it crouched. His tail was bolt upright, rigid and his nose was wedged into the crack between the floor and the door. His growling was persistent, a noisy reminder of the threat. Clare felt like she was suffocating, incapable of thinking straight.

'I'm calling the police,' said Anna. 'Stay where you are and *do not* open that door. I'll call you straight back.'

The line went dead. Clare's heart was hammering so loudly it sounded like it was about to break free. There was another knock on the door. Stop-it went berserk. Then she heard a faint voice; it probably wasn't faint but just sounded that way above the cacophony coming from the dog.

'Please, can I just come in.' It was a soft voice, respectful and calm; neither it nor the words sounded like those of a hit man.

'Tell me who you are and what you want.' Her voice sounded confident, although she didn't feel that way. 'The police are on their way.' That sounded brave. The police had to come from Barnstaple. It could be twenty minutes, and that was if there was a patrol car free. 'Come to the side window where I can see you.'

She heard footsteps cross the patio, and a face squashed up against the window. The man wore jeans and a dark jumper. She didn't recognize him, but he was smiling.

'Madam, please let me in.'

It was Magnus. Out of uniform, but definitely Richard's butler. She wasn't sure of a butler's job specifications but was pretty sure that it would not include duffing people up who upset Richard. 'Please,' said Magnus.

Clare grabbed Stop-it's collar and opened the door a crack. Her hand felt like it was being torn off her arm. The dog was still growling. She wasn't in a hurry to shut him up. 'Just say what you've been told to come and say, then leave me alone.'

He looked puzzled. 'Please, can I come in? I've only got half an hour, any longer and Mr Hastings might miss me.'

Her brow wrinkled. 'He doesn't know you're here?'

'No, but I have something to say which may help you.' His eyes fell on Stop-it. 'Do you mind doing something with that dog? He's making me somewhat nervous.'

With his feet scrabbling in protest, Clare dragged Stop-it up to her bedroom, threw a chew on the floor, closed the door and rushed back downstairs. Magnus was standing where she'd left him. She picked up her abandoned mug of tea and ushered him into the sitting room. 'Would you like . . .?' She offered, indicating the mug.

He was still standing, and it occurred to Clare he wouldn't sit without being invited. 'Please, take a seat,' she said, getting up and removing a ball and a frayed rope from an armchair, then shaking the covering throw in the air, dispersing a cloud of white dog hairs.

'I'm all ears.'

'I've worked for Mr Hastings for nearly ten years. It was a tough decision to come here tonight, and if he finds out, it might cost me my job.'

She was aware of the sort of confidentiality clause likely to be in Magnus's employment contract. She'd drafted plenty herself. Discussing anything that went on at Brambleton Hall would constitute gross misconduct and enable Richard to fire him. And the chance of Magnus finding alternative employment was slim – people who hired private staff were unforgiving of breaches of confidence. Telling herself not to spook him, she gave a slow, encouraging nod.

An eerie high-pitched scream sounded. Clare jumped. Magnus shuddered. Quiet fell, and he swallowed twice, as if summoning his courage. 'It was a fox,' she said reassuringly.

A wailing police siren shattered the quiet. Magnus opened his mouth to speak. The siren got louder, and then Clare heard tyres screeching and her front gate slammed against the brickwork. Captain Hilts was squawking and upstairs Stop-it was barking.

Magnus stood, his eyes popping wide.

'Oh shit!' said Clare. 'Anna . . . the police . . .'

Magnus was staring at her, his body trembling.

Fists pounded on the back door. 'Police, open up!' shouted a female voice.

Magnus wrung his hands. His eyes were darting round the room as if looking for somewhere to hide. 'I can't be seen here. Please, help me.'

'Coming,' she shouted out to the kitchen. She shot upright. 'That way,' she hissed, pointing at the stairs. Magnus ran up the stairs in the flat-footed way that she recalled from the site inspection. She hurtled up after him, following his heavy footsteps. 'In there,' she directed, pointing at her bedroom. Hearing

Stop-it's delighted squeals, she scrambled downstairs, hoping Magnus would cope with the dog.

In the kitchen, she took a breath, then opened the door. Outside was a crowd. There were two policewomen, Anna, Roger, Ivy and Fred.

'Hi,' she said. 'Sorry.' She waved a dismissive hand. 'I was just . . .'

'Thank goodness you're okay,' said Roger.

'Madam, we've had reports of an intruder,' said one of the policewomen.

'Ah yes,' she mumbled. What was she going to do? What if the police offered to search the house and discovered Magnus? 'May we come in?' asked a policewoman.

Clare opened the door, and the crowd spilled into her kitchen.

'What happened?' asked Anna, in a breathless rush. 'Who was it? Did you see them?'

Clare envisaged Magnus trapped upstairs with the dog.

'Would you like us to search, make sure no one's inside?' said Roger.

'Outside. He was outside,' said Clare.

'Did you see him?' asked Roger. 'Could you give a description? Did he threaten you in any way, try to force his way in?'

'I'm fine. I think I overacted. Panicked. A bit of Londonitus.' She gave a short laugh.

'But there was someone at your back door? Were they trying to force it? Do you want us to record this?' asked an officer.

'No,' she shook her head. 'Thanks for coming out, but I'm fine.'

'Well, we're stopping here with you,' said Anna, taking hold of Roger's hand.

'And me,' said Ivy.

'Sounds like a party,' said Fred, opening Clare's fridge.

Clare had a sinking feeling. She wouldn't expect Magnus to

open up in front of an audience. Somehow, she had to smuggle him out without her friends seeing. Any moment now, Tricky Ricky would ring a bell summoning his evening decanter of port.

As soon as the officers left, Clare opened a bottle of wine, plonked five glasses and several bags of crisps on the kitchen table, then excused herself. 'Help yourself. I'll be right back.'

Walking up the stairs, she heard a strange squeaking noise. She opened her bedroom door. A peculiar version of a push-me-pull-you stood on her bed. Magnus was at one end, Stop-it formed the other, and the middle was a pillow. Magnus moved, the bed squeaked, Stop-it tugged backwards.

'He's terrifically strong, isn't he!' said Magnus.

'It's a game. Everything is a game to this dog,' said Clare. 'I'm desperate to hear what you've got to say, but sadly I've got an impromptu party downstairs. I'll take the dog with me, shut us all in the kitchen. I suggest you sneak out the front door. You should get home before you're missed.'

'Right.' He said, dropping the pillow. Stop-it bounced off the bed clutching the prize.

Magnus clambered off and turned to straighten the linen.

'Leave it, please,' mumbled Clare.

'I must speak to you. What about tomorrow evening?' Magnus suggested.

They arranged to meet the following night in the upstairs section of the local supermarket. Clare thought it was an odd spot for a rendezvous but had to admit that Magnus was unlikely to be seen there by anyone who knew him.

Using a pillow as bait, she coaxed Stop-it out of the room. In the kitchen Roger and Anna were sitting at the table. Fred and Ivy were at opposite ends of the sofa, a metal bowl of crisps between them. Stop-it leapt up. Fred picked up the bowl, lifting it above his head muttering, 'No you don't. Not for you.'

Anna passed Clare a glass of wine, then took a gulp from her own before asking, 'Who was it? You clearly didn't want to tell the police, but there was genuine fear in your voice when you called me. Was it Richard?'

Clare sipped her wine and mumbled that she couldn't say.

Ivy craned her head around. 'Even to us?'

'It's nothing for you to worry about. Someone came to visit, and I wasn't expecting them.'

'And that's all you're going to tell us?' said Anna.

Clare nodded. The room fell silent, but it wasn't a comfortable silence. Clare sensed her friends were upset she wouldn't confide. She had cried help, and everyone had rushed to her rescue and instead of being grateful, she wouldn't share what the threat was.

Suddenly, Stop-it barked, leapt off the sofa and shot off to the door.

Fred shouted, 'Let him out. He'll catch the sod.'

Picturing Stop-it's jaws clamping onto Magnus's leg as he scurried to the front door, Clare held up her hands. 'Enough. I'm very grateful for your concern, but this is *my* problem.'

'We're a team,' said Fred, 'and your friends,' he added, shaking his shock of white hair. 'Your problems are ours. What's going on?'

She wasn't used to people helping her, instead of her helping them. These four people had fixed her shower, paid for her Wi-Fi and even mended the kitchen floor tiles. No one had done anything like that for her in London. 'Okay guys, here's my real problem,' said Clare. She opened a drawer and pulled out the latest letter from Richard's lawyers with the offending leaflet. Speaking to Sally, they had unearthed an escape route: find the person responsible for giving Hastings the leaflet and get them to confirm Clare's instructions to destroy it. That might make her offer of a public apology more attractive. At the very least, it would limit his compensation claim to a manageable number. She didn't show the legal letter to her friends. She couldn't. Clare would not humiliate herself by admitting the mess she was in.

She passed the leaflet to Anna.

Anna's brow furrowed. 'It's quite strong, isn't it? I never saw your first draft; I didn't realize it was so rude.'

That puzzled Clare, making her question Anna's innocence. Why pretend this was the first time she had seen the leaflet?

'What is it?' asked Fred. Anna tossed the leaflet onto the sofa and Fred and Ivy read it together before casting it aside. Roger got up and grabbed the page, his eyes bulging as he read. 'Wow, no wonder the village sprang up to support you. Quite punchy, Clare.'

'Did one of you gave this to Richard?'

Everyone wore a vacant expression. Or did they? Clare peered at Ivy, asking herself if her mother's best friend had just blushed. Surely it couldn't be Ivy. That wasn't ethical.

The following night, Clare was standing on the travelator in the supermarket listening to its repeated warnings to push the trolley off the end of the conveyor belt. If only someone had warned her to push off instead of taking Tricky Ricky on.

Alighting at the top, Clare scanned the aisles. She wasn't expecting to learn anything useful, but Magnus was risking his job to meet her. The least she could do was turn up. It took her ten minutes to find Richard's butler. On her first circuit, she assumed he was late; on her second, she thought something had prevented him from coming – he had no way of contacting her. She was doing a final scan when she spotted him, crouched down, hiding at the end of the 'sales' section. She laughed inwardly – there was no chance of designer-clad Cora browsing the supermarket sales aisles like Clare did.

The café was close by, and she suggested they sit down. He shook his head. 'So, what's this about?' asked Clare.

'I've been trying to contact you. I need to advise you about something.'

'Was it you that night by my gate, and in the blue car?'

Magnus admitted that he'd tried to speak to her several times before, but every time he'd got close he caught fright. What did he want to tell her?

'I need to advise you; Mr Hastings is very cross about a leaflet that's circulating in the village.'

She held up a hand. 'I know all about it. It's a bit of a mix-up. I didn't distribute the offensive one. I circulated a much tamer one, but . . .' she tailed off, realizing there was no point explaining this to Magnus.

'It was the night you came for dinner. He was thrilled. When I cleared the port glasses, I heard him boasting to two of his friends that he'd set you up for a fall.'

Magnus was watching her, looking pleased with himself. She didn't want to tell him he'd risked so much to tell her something she couldn't use. How had someone as lovely as Magnus ended up working for someone as ghastly as Richard? 'I should have known he was up to no good. Thanks for alerting me. The thing is, all of his guests witnessed me admit that I wrote the leaflet. No one is going to support my side of the story.'

'Mr Hastings Junior will.'

The mention of his name conjured up a picture of them together in his car before she'd ruined things. She shook her head. Sam was in on the scam too. 'No, he won't.'

'He will. You can trust him.'

'I can't trust Sam,' she said, shaking her head. 'He's Richard's brother. The two are in this together.'

Magnus spluttered. 'No, you're wrong. They try and keep it

hidden, and Mrs Hastings does her best to keep things smooth, but Mr Hastings loathes his younger brother for splitting up the estate. That cider farm used to be part of the estate, and when his father left it to Sam, Mr Hastings tried to dissuade him from taking it. He's never forgiven his brother for not agreeing. Says it deprives the estate of crucial income.'

Despite the earnest expression on Magnus's face, Clare wasn't convinced. It would be great to think she could trust Sam, but it didn't ring true. Why would Magnus be privy to such an intimate family secret? Had the Hastings brothers sent him to persuade her to trust Sam? Why? What more did Richard want from her?

Driving back from her meeting with Magnus, Clare challenged herself to work out if she'd learned anything useful. Even if she could trust Sam, it didn't help. He was unlikely to tell her who had given the offensive leaflet to his brother. But what Magnus *had* done was give her an excuse to call on Sam. She drove to his farm but stopped at the gate, wondering if the dashing divorcee was alone.

Clare pulled up in front of the kitchen. There was a light on. Evidently Sam was comfortable entertaining in there. Before she got out of the Land Rover the front door opened. Sam. For a few moments, she watched him from the safety of the car.

He walked towards her, moving his long legs as elegantly as a dancer. It would be much easier to cast him as a villain like his brother if he, too, had a florid face and a paunch. He was reaching for her door handle when she realized that if Sam was part of the entrapment party, he would know about the Magnus meeting. If he wasn't, then the butler must be telling the truth, and she could trust this man.

The door opened. Sam smiled and Clare felt her face flush.

'Hello.' Her voice sounded high-pitched, and she tried to get control of it. 'I've just come from the strangest meeting,' she said.

He held her door wide. 'Come in and tell me about it. Glass of cider? Wine?'

She shook her head. 'I'm driving.'

He led the way to the kitchen, flicked the kettle on, then offered her a cup of tea. 'I've a decent selection of herbals.'

Yes, he would have with his coterie of women friends, thought Clare. He crossed to a shelf, reading out the options.

'You choose,' she said.

'So, tell me about this meeting. Who was there?'

She waited until she could see his eyes before saying, 'Magnus.'

'Ah,' said Sam, a thoughtful expression crossing his face. The news didn't surprise him. 'And what did he have to say?' he asked.

She told him about the leaflets. The one she'd circulated and the rude version she'd deleted, all the while assessing his reaction to her story. She was pretty sure she wasn't telling him anything he didn't already know. He passed her a mug, the tag of the tea bag secured around the handle. 'Richard played you like a fiddle that evening. I tried my best to stop you, but you wouldn't listen.'

She took the mug from him and, trying to control the tone of her voice, muttered 'Why did you walk me into the trap?'

'You walked yourself in. I took you because you wanted a meeting with Richard. You're the one that had to take credit for writing the leaflet.'

She eyed him over the rim of her mug. 'Did Richard break into my house and steal it?' He shook his head. 'How can you be so sure?' she asked.

'He didn't have to. Someone sent it to him . . . and I know who.'

Twenty-eight

Clare felt giddy. Sam could save her, *if* he told her.

'Tell me, please. He's suing me for defamation. I admitted I wrote those leaflets.'

He pursed his lips. 'I reckon he's banking on you not fighting. Someone knows who's responsible, and I bet it's someone close to you.'

Who did he mean by that? 'Who knows?' she asked.

'Try asking your friends.'

'I have!'

'Then you haven't been honest. You have to explain why you want to know. You have to admit you made a mistake and you need help.'

She winced. She couldn't admit the extent of her plight. 'They don't need to know.'

'They bloody well do.'

'No.' She shook her head, then drank some of her tea. 'I don't want to make them feel they're to blame.' Even as she said the words, she knew it didn't sound convincing.

'You can keep saying that if it makes you feel better,' he said, a lazy smile playing at the corner of his lips, 'but we both know it isn't true.' He leaned across the counter. He was so close she could smell him, a spicy scent so different from Guy who never wore cologne. 'Now, do you want my help or not?' he asked.

Clare gave a nervous laugh, the thrill of his closeness denting her confidence. 'Could I have that glass of wine first?'

In the morning, exhausted by a lengthy game of chase the empty milk container with Stop-it, Clare arranged to meet her friends at Prosecco and Prose. She put the phone down, and to divert her thoughts, checked her emails. There was nothing interesting. Stop-it was standing next to the recycling bin – his new toy box. She dashed over, pulled out a plastic bottle and hurled it for him, smiling as he charged back and dropped the toy at her feet. She threw it once more, then collected Richard's legal letter and copies of both leaflets.

Outside the café she dithered, casting her eyes over the terrace where brightly patterned blankets decorated chair backs. The sun was a mere smudge of light struggling to pierce thick layers of clouds, casting a dull silvery hue across the terrace. A few hardy tourists were huddling in thick coats, sipping steaming mugs of coffee, their breath forming small clouds in the crisp air. She spotted her friends and swallowed, wanting to retrace her steps. For a few moments she took deep breaths, then pushed open the door. Trish was behind the bar. She would start with her.

'Trish, you know those leaflets I gave you, the ones about the chicken factory?'

'Yes.'

'Did you keep any?'

Trish screwed up her face. 'Hang on a tick, I might just.' She wandered into a back room. Clare listened to drawers being opened and then slammed shut, followed by doors banging. A few minutes later, her friend was back, holding a bunch of leaflets. 'Here you go,' she said.

The leaflet fluttered in Clare's wavering hands. She gasped. 'Where did you get these?'

'From you,' said Trish indignantly.

Clare shook her head. 'No, you didn't. These aren't the ones I left for you just before meeting Bill Matthews.'

'No, of course not,' said Trish pulling an exasperated face, 'I threw those away like you instructed. These are the updated ones.'

Clare shook the leaflet at Trish. 'Who told you there were updated ones?'

Trish hesitated, a look of confusion spreading over her face. 'I thought *you* did. I just found an envelope full of them with a typewritten message saying that these were the updated version. You asked me to destroy the previous lot and replace them with these. Do you want them back or not?'

Clare felt like someone was smothering her. Someone had circulated the poisonous leaflet, and even Trish seemed to think that Clare had been responsible. How widely had the culprit circulated the defamatory leaflets? No wonder Richard was angry. Clearly, Trish wasn't the friend in the know.

Clare turned to face the terrace. Ivy was waving. Clare took baby steps towards her friends.

'Any news from the Inspector?' called out Fred.

Clare checked her emails again. 'No. But that's not why I asked to meet you all.' She sat down next to Fred, swallowed, then blurted out, 'I've screwed up.'

She told them about the night at Brambleton Hall and showed them the letter from Richard's lawyer.

'Five million quid?' said Fred. 'His reputation wasn't worth a fiver before he applied for that factory.'

'Or threw me and Fred out of our homes,' said Ivy.

'If you asked people round here to value his reputation,' said Anna, 'he'd be lucky to get fifty pence.'

Clare felt a warmth spreading through her chest. She wished

she'd told them sooner. They were so supportive; she wanted to hug them. 'Sadly, his reputation is worth a lot of money in the eyes of the law. It's my mistake and I might have to pay for it.'

'No. There's been a simple mistake,' said Ivy.

Clare held her breath. Ivy knew something. She was exchanging a glance with Anna. Did they both know? While Ivy tussled with her conscience, Clare checked her emails. She dropped her phone. There was one from the Planning Inspectorate.

'Clare, are you okay? You've gone white,' said Anna.

She looked at her shaky hands, then at her friends. Clare pointed at the phone. 'There's an email from the Planning Inspector.'

Fred leaned across her. Chairs scraped on tiles and all three crowded around her as she fiddled to download the attachment, scrolling through the formal details naming the parties and the background to the case. 'Yup, it's the decision.'

'What does it say?' demanded Anna.

Clare read aloud, her tongue tripping over words, desperate to skip to the conclusion. 'Impact on landscape . . .' she said, then muttered a few lines to herself. She raised her voice, saying excitedly, 'After careful consideration of visual evidence, and taking into account the plans to mitigate the impact by screening, it was determined that the proposed development . . .' She swallowed, then continued flatly, ' . . . would not significantly detract from the rural character of the area.' Clare's heart was racing. This was a disaster. Hastings was going to win.

'It's not the shed that's the problem. It's what's going *in* it that matters,' said Ivy.

'I don't like the shed either,' said Fred.

Clare tried to concentrate on the next paragraph while in the background Ivy and Fred continued to squabble. She blanked out their voices and read on. She felt a surge of adrenalin.

'Hey, shush,' she cried. 'Listen to this next bit. In terms of noise and traffic . . . it was concluded that the proposed measures to mitigate adverse effects were inadequate.' She looked up a smile stretched across her face. 'It's suggesting the factory should be a minimum distance of a kilometre from the almshouses.'

'That'll push it pretty close to the Hall!' cried Anna.

'See how he likes that!' chortled Fred. 'See if the need to make his *farm* profitable overrides a view of his park!'

She heard her friends laughing and chuckling. Someone slapped her on the back, and she could feel her smile broadening. She read on and cried out. 'It's a no!'

She looked round. Fred's jaw had dropped open. Ivy was clutching the cross at her neck and Anna had a pained expression on her face. But Clare was still smiling. 'It's a no – that means the appeal is dismissed. We've won!'

'Can you forward it to us!' demanded Anna.

'Is that it? Is it over?' asked Ivy.

'Let me call Walter,' said Clare.

Walter had received the same email and confirmed the Inspector's findings were quite damning. Too excited to think straight, Clare tried to concentrate on what Walter was saying. He told her that if he were advising Richard, he would suggest moving the site, so it was nowhere near the village, and to come up with a better plan for managing waste. Better still, he'd be advising Richard to farm something radically different and undertake proper community consultation before submitting a revised proposal.

'Do you think that's the last we'll hear of the chicken farm?' asked Clare.

'Don't crow about it, but yes.'

She forgave Walter for his feeble joke. 'You did it, guys. Oh, this is fabulous news.' She got up and hugged everyone in turn.

Squashing them against her, she was oblivious to the startled expressions on other customers' faces. It was only noon, but Trish insisted on opening a bottle of prosecco. 'On the house,' she said, pouring five frothy glasses. 'To BARS, and from the bottom of my heart . . . thank you!'

Thinking at least all her sacrifices had been worth it, Clare took a gulp of bubbles.

'I'm going to send Richard a present,' said Fred.

'What?' asked Ivy.

'A box of battery farm eggs!'

Anna spluttered over her prosecco.

'No, I've a better idea,' said Clare. 'Let me take some of my proper free-range ones, from my rescue hens.' She would finish her drink, then go straight over there.

Clare walked home with a sense of urgency in her step. She imagined what would be happening at Brambleton Hall. Richard would be having a tantrum. She hoped he wasn't taking it out on Magnus.

Buoyed by two small glasses of fizz, Clare drove to Brambleton Hall. She reached the turning circle and spun the car around, so it was pointing the way she'd come, enjoying the scrunching noise of the tyres on the gravel. Clare turned off her engine and checked her appearance in the mirror.

It was Richard himself who met her at the front door. Maybe Magnus did have days off. He didn't invite her in, just stood in the open doorway with his arms crossed, the splendour of the entrance hall seeming to magnify his presence.

'What do *you* want?' he asked.

'I came to tell you the truth about that leaflet.'

'You came to try and wriggle off the hook. I don't discuss legal matters without my lawyers present.' His bottom lip curled into a sneer. 'Now, if that's all . . .'

'Wait,' she said. 'I know you're angry about the decision . . .' Why had she just said that? She shouldn't have come here after drinking. What a stupid thing to say to someone like Richard.

'Angry? Why should I be angry? This is just a little setback. I'll find something else to put in that shed.'

Shit, of course. Walter had warned her. The Inspector didn't have a problem with the shed, provided it wasn't full of chickens. Richard's advisers would have spotted the same loophole. Two thoughts vied for attention in her mind. What would Richard substitute for chickens? And could she persuade him to tell her?

Taking in his smug smile, Clare's chest tightened.

'Can't we talk about this?' she cried, hating the note of desperation in her voice. 'There must be a compromise we can reach, something which will give you what you want without destroying the village.'

'No.' His eyes narrowed to little slits, and he spat his next words: 'I. Will. Destroy. You.' He walked backwards into the hallway. 'When I'm finished, you won't have a penny to your name. Oh, and you can tell Fred and Ivy to start packing. Their little holiday jaunts are over. The bailiffs won't be long now. When they've gone, I'll be running all four cottages as holiday lets. That much I do think my brother has got right.' Then he shut the door in her face, leaving Clare listening to his shoes ringing on the flagstones.

She should never have come after having a drink, and certainly not without planning her speech. This time, she really *had* screwed up.

Later that afternoon Clare received a three-word message that sent her into a tailspin. She pushed the disastrous encounter with Richard to the back of her mind, took a shower, then pulled on a dress. Standing in front of the mirror, she ran her hands over her hips, turning left, then right. She did a little twirl before pulling the dress off and tossing it on to the bed.

Ten minutes later, Clare was still only wearing her knickers and bra. Stop-it lay on her bed nosing through each discarded outfit. She finally decided on a pair of white jeans, a green silk blouse, jade-green cowboy boots and liberal amounts of perfume. Tonight, she wanted to be festive and bold. Smiling to herself, she collected two dozen of her eggs, Stop-it's uneaten bowl of kibble, a bottle of wine, and set off with the dog in tow.

Sam met her at his front door. He flashed her a smile. Tonight, she felt confident enough to return it. He had invited her over to celebrate. Magnus must be right – she really could trust this man. He was holding two glasses of champagne.

'Congratulations.' He said taking exchanging a glass for Stop-it's bowl.

Tucking the bottle of wine under her arm, Clare unhooked the dog. He clinked his glass against hers and then she took a large gulp, the bubbles fizzing as they slid down her throat, making her almost dizzy with delight.

'It was the right decision,' she said.

She stepped inside. 'There's no way a monstrous chicken factory belongs on the outskirts of a village. He was bargaining on people whingeing but not getting organized enough to fight back.'

'Well, he met his match in you.'

Sam hadn't moved very far, forcing her to stand close to him. For a few moments, their eyes locked and she felt an overwhelming desire to kiss him. She tore her eyes away, hiding her embarrassment with another gulp of champagne.

'I'm glad we won.' Sam arched his eyes at her. 'Come through, I've got a plate of nibbles for us; thought we'd have them outside as it's such a lovely evening.'

She followed him out onto the patio, where he put down a tray loaded with champagne – in an ice bucket – a platter of canapés and a red and blue plastic flying saucer the size of a dinner plate. Sam teased Stop-it with the toy, then hurled it as far as he could. The dog hurtled after it, his legs seeming to skim over the grass. For a few pleasurable minutes Clare and Sam sipped champagne, laughing at Stop-it devouring his new toy.

'I hope he's not a sore loser.' Said Clare.

'What do you think?' said Sam mockingly. 'He's not had much experience of losing, and don't count on this being over, Clare.' His words dragged her back to her earlier encounter with Richard. She feared Sam was right. Wanting to avoid dampening the mood she gave a small laugh. 'Fred was all for getting a supermarket to deliver him a case of battery farm eggs.'

'My advice would be not to gloat. He may come up with an even worse idea. His real goal was the anaerobic digester. He needs to cut his utility bills.'

Clare felt a chill run through her. Was that Richard's plan? Walter had said if he were advising Richard, he would recommend a very different sort of farming. Waste to energy would fit the bill. She dismissed her fears. Tonight was for celebrating. She could worry about the future tomorrow.

She took a bite from a filo parcel, using one hand to catch the flaking pastry, her mouth filled with a mixture of creamy spinach and salty feta cheese. Wow, this man could cook. It was delicious. 'Nope,' she said, pushing the remains of the food into her mouth. 'We won. Battle over.'

'Don't be so sure. I've read the judgement. The Inspector didn't have a problem with the shed, only what was going in it. Personally, I'd prefer chickens to gas. I wouldn't fancy being Fred or Ivy, living in the almshouses, going to bed each night, wondering if there was going to be an explosion yards away.'

'Except Fred and Ivy don't live in the almshouses.'

Sam stroked his chin. 'What?'

For a few moments she stared at him, then she spoke slowly. 'You don't know, do you?'

He gave her a glassy look. 'Know what?'

'Richard evicted them.' She looked at Sam's ashen face. 'Under Section 21.'

'But only while he renovates their cottages,' said Sam defiantly. 'They won't be in his holiday lets for much longer.'

'Hang on . . . has your brother suggested he's *allowing* them to stay in those holiday lets?'

'Isn't he?'

'You'd better take a deep breath before I tell you the truth.'

She told him what his brother had done. Sam shook his head. 'Why didn't Fred tell me, I'd have put a stop to that!' His eyes narrowed, 'Does the whole village know, am I the only . . .' Clare winced then nodded. 'I guess that explains why I've been feeling a bit cold-shouldered these last few months. Everyone must be assuming I know what he's done and that I condone it . . . thank goodness Fred had your scheming mind helping behind the scenes.' When she mentioned how she'd got Ivy into Rose Cottage, he roared with laughter. 'You little minx. No wonder Richard didn't tell me any of this. I love it!'

Sam leaned over to top up her glass and his hand grazed her skin. Her whole body seemed to fizz. She glanced up and saw his mouth lower towards hers, felt his breath warm against her face. His lips hovered just above hers. The anticipation making her heart race.

She closed her eyes and then he kissed her softly. His hand cupped her face, his fingers gently tracing her jawline as his mouth moved against hers with a slow, sensual rhythm that made her melt into him.

Clare wished the kiss could continue but she reluctantly pulled away, a flicker of doubt rising. She refused to be just another conquest, no matter how pleasant the experience.

His hands stroked her shoulders. 'Relax, dinner will keep. Unless you're not enjoying yourself? Am I going too fast?' His eyes were steady on hers, and there was a look of love, not lust, in them. Had she misjudged him?

'I'm more of a one-man, one-woman sort of girl.'

A look of astonishment crossed his face. 'The implication being I'm not?'

She blushed. Did she have to spell it out? 'What about your London girlfriend; the savvy bridge player in pink?'

He laughed, and it sent a pulse of desire through her. 'Hang on, you didn't think that gorgeous woman was my girlfriend, did you? She's very happily married and not in the least bit interested in me. She books one of my cottages for a girls' weekend every year. She just happens to be a shit-hot bridge player, very rich, and passionate about the environment. I thought she was just the sort of supporter your fundraiser needed.'

Clare found herself laughing, then remembered the young woman who'd answered the door when she came round to ask Sam's advice about grafting. 'But there was another woman in your house, in January . . .'

'Blonde hair or dark?'

He was teasing her. He must know who she meant. 'Dark.'

'Dark is Carol. Blonde would have been Lucy. Neither are interested in men. They've been partners for five years. They both work for me, helping with the cottages and they housesit if I'm away, so there's someone here if a holidaymaker has a problem. If you remember I was on my cider making course.'

Relief flooded through her. But then she asked herself why

would Sam be interested in her? She had assumed those women were linked to him because they looked and acted like the sort of women he would date. They spoke with the same accent he did. Carol rode. She didn't do either.

'Clare,' he said, sitting beside her and taking one of her hands in his. 'I'm a rebel at heart, but this is not an act of rebellion. I've always admired you, but you've never given the remotest sign you were interested in me. I even tried to date you when you were at university.'

Clare frowned. He hadn't tried very hard. That letter he'd written was dismissive and cold, calculated to hurt and mock her:

> Last night was just a bit of fun, a dare to see if I could snare a village girl before my real life begins. Thanks for being a willing participant and for making it so enjoyable. Sam.

He'd never apologized, not in that note, nor when he had the temerity to show his face in the pub a week later. He'd just smiled that lovely smile of his and asked if she'd got his note. If anything showed he wasn't serious tonight, it was mentioning his 'non-interest' when they were younger.

'You never tried to date me.'

'I distinctly recall kissing you. I thought you enjoyed it as much as me, that's why I wrote and apologized when I couldn't meet you the next evening.'

'Yes, I got your note thank you.' She said tersely, 'Who was the dare with?'

He looked puzzled. 'What dare?'

How could he have forgotten? She frowned. 'You explained in your note – the one where you told me you'd made a mistake – that someone had dared you to kiss me.'

His jaw dropped. He shuffled in his chair and sat upright. 'I said what?'

She repeated the lines he'd written, chiselled indelibly on her heart, as surely as if he'd etched them himself.

'I never wrote that. I liked you, Clare. I wanted to see you again. Anyway, I would never do that to anyone – I was twenty-one, not twelve. But I think I know who wrote that note and swapped it for the one I did write, explaining I had to go to London on business with my father. No wonder you froze me out when I got back a week later.'

'Who wrote it then?'

'Does it matter?'

She could guess anyway. And did it matter? She could love this man, with his gorgeous eyes and his shock of grey hair. He had a zest for life and the same winning spirit she had. Maybe, just maybe, it was worth trying.

'Could we start again?' she asked.

'Do you want to eat first, or afterwards?'

She picked up her glass and looked into his eyes. 'I'm not that hungry for food.'

They ate at midnight on the terrace. Sam lit candles and wrapped up in one of his fleece jackets, Clare ate greedily. Sam flash-fried fillets of white fish he'd bought that morning in the harbour and laid them on a bed of celeriac and potato, with a splash of lemony sauce on the side.

'How come you cook so well?' she asked, savouring the mash. It was so well seasoned, with a hint of smoky truffle in it, offset perfectly by the lemon sauce.

'My wife wasn't interested in cooking, so I did it all.'

'My husband couldn't manage anything more exotic than to keep a takeaway warm for me.'

She gave a half-laugh. In the last few months Guy hadn't even bothered with that. Sam put down his plate. 'Tell me about him.'

Clare recalled the ugly scene with her mother in the orchard. Cindy had been right about Guy. If he had lived, he would have broken her heart.

'My husband was very different from me. He did make me happy, at first,' – and for the first few months Guy did – 'but we were only married a short while.'

'They say opposites attract.'

She smiled. 'Not always a good thing.'

'That's what caused the rift between you and your mother? She didn't think he was right for you?' said Sam.

Clare inhaled sharply 'Who told you that?'

'She did.'

'When.'

'Just before she told you.'

'Why did she tell *you*?'

'My marriage was failing, Laura had left me by then, gone back to London. I went to see Cindy to ask her if she thought I stood any chance with you, if you'd ever indicated you might be interested in me. I didn't want to pester you directly, since you'd made your feelings clear when we were twenty-one.'

Clare's eyes started to water. She screwed them shut. Her mother had known who would make her daughter truly happy. There was an underlying reason she had tried to stop Clare marrying Guy. But Clare didn't want to talk about that now.

'Does your brother know you helped BARS?'

'He's probably guessed. He knew I was against his plans, but he also knew I'd never fight him in public, and he thought he'd neutralized me by putting the shed somewhere it wouldn't affect me. But I care more for the village than myself. I know the estate needs more income and if he'd put it up next to me, he might have got away with it.'

'He nearly did get away with it. We struggled to pay for the competing EIA.'

He grinned at her.

'You helped us?' she said, pointing her fork at him. She counted up the occasions this man had helped defeat his brother. It was Sam who'd goaded her into fighting back, Sam who'd brought the wealthy punters to the bridge tournament.

'Did you donate that case of wine that went for so much money at the auction?'

'Not entirely. I brought it, but I didn't buy it. It was a village fundraiser, and I thought Richard should make a donation, so I got Magnus to open up his cellar. He won't miss it. He's got more wine than he can possibly drink in a lifetime.'

'And that final donation of seven grand . . . Was that you too?'

'We've both known Ivy for long enough to know her heart's in the right place, but she wasn't going to lose that much weight.'

He'd been on their side all along; she'd lay odds it was Sam behind the horsebox stunt at the site visit. And Clare had assumed he was a spy. 'How come we never guessed?'

'I couldn't risk splitting my family by making it public. And as I said, I've always been good at sneaking around.'

'Tell me, you must have some idea what Richard will do next. What do you think I should do to try and finish this drama?'

'I was hoping you'd ask me that. Here's what I would do . . .'

Twenty-nine

In the morning, Clare woke with a strange sensation in her tummy. She rolled over and looked at Sam. He was flat on his back, his head tilted to one side. Grey stubble covered his cheeks, and he was breathing softly. He didn't even snore. She didn't want to disturb him, so slipped out of bed, gathered her clothes and went in search of Stop-it.

The dog was asleep in a basket in front of the Aga, his untouched bowl of kibble next to him. She prodded his side. An eyelid slipped open, then he snuffled and dug his nose under his front paws. Clare found a scrap of paper and wrote a note for Sam, then, throwing a last look at her dog, left. She had a lot to do, and it would be quicker without Stop-it in tow. Sam could try and persuade the dog to eat kibble.

Back at Orchard Farm, she showered, slipped on overalls and went to complete the morning chores. There wasn't a cloud in the sky and the wind was barely a whisper, heralding a gorgeous spring day – a perfect day for new love.

She sprinkled food into the trough and stood watching the hens. Hilts was at the centre of the trough, guzzling. If anything happened to her cockerel, she knew she would name a new one Richard. Walking past the orchard, she pictured her mother, that last day she'd seen her alive. It must have taken a great deal of love to risk losing touch with her only daughter. It was soothing to understand what had prompted her mother's speech that day.

Today, she had her own speech to make. She collected another dozen eggs and drove the short distance to the Hall, tossing phrases around in her mind. How could she persuade him to stop trying to force industrial scale schemes on the village? Sam was certain she could, but she didn't share his conviction.

Halfway down the drive, she passed one of the Hastings' gardening team on a mower so large it wouldn't have looked out of place on a golf course. Further down Clare saw another man trimming a hedge. She pulled up in front of the house behind a trailer filled with bedding plants. There were two gardeners wearing Brambleton Estate overalls: one was using a Rotavator, the other sprinkling fertilizer in front of the machine's path.

Clare switched off the engine and sat looking at the vast house. Richard's electricity bill must be stratospheric, on a par with her mother's when she'd been dairy farming; but that was to run the milking parlour, not keep the lights on. Scaffolding hugged the sides of the west wing like ivy – three floors of it. She counted the windows she could see. There were over thirty. How much did it cost to keep the woodwork in order?

She heard someone crunch over the gravel. Her wing mirror showed it was Magnus. He opened her door, and with his back to the house, whispered, 'Tread carefully. He's in a foul temper.'

She picked up the eggs and handed them to the butler. 'These are free-range, from my own chickens this morning. Thank you for what you did. Coming to see me took a lot of courage.'

Magnus swallowed several times, blinking rapidly, making Clare wonder if he had welled up. 'It's not often anyone thanks me for anything,' he mumbled.

'I'm curious, why do you work for him?'

He gave her a weak smile. 'Do you like everyone you work with?'

Clare imagined Hilts crowing at five-thirty in the morning,

laughed and shook her head, then pictured herself planting out the saplings with Stop-it pawing at the ground near her feet. She reached over to the passenger seat for her handbag, asking herself why she hadn't thought about her London job instead.

'It's a way of life, being a butler . . . not a job.' *Just like farming*, thought Clare. 'And there's no one else in these parts who would allow me to live as I do.'

She got out and walked beside him. She could see Richard framed by the porch pilasters; his arms were crossed. Behind him stood Sam.

The meeting took place in Richard's study, beneath the elegant birds, cherubs and sheaves of wheat. Wearing a scowl, Richard lounged in a chair with his feet on the desk; Sam sat on the fire fender. Clare remained standing. She glanced at Sam. His eyes were smiling at her, sending a mixture of adrenalin and lust through her body. This was Sam's scheme, not hers. Would his brother accept? 'I've got a proposition for you,' she said.

'I'm listening,' said Richard, but his tone suggested otherwise.

'Why not go for solar?'

He sat up, removed his feet, and leaned across his desk. 'Solar? In a shed?'

'No shed. I'm thinking small scale, well screened and undetectable from the village. For most of the year, the panels – if you backed them up with batteries – would generate enough electricity to power the estate. You might have surplus.'

'And no doubt you're going to tell me what I can do with that,' sneered Richard.

'Any surplus could provide the almshouses with free power.'

Richard threw back his head and laughed. 'Are you for real? You come here to suggest I run a cooperative energy scheme. Next, you're going to ask me to let Fred and Ivy move back into the cottages I've spent a fortune renovating. Thanks for the advice, but I know exactly what's going in that shed - an anaerobic digester.'

Her mind went blank. She'd warned Sam that she didn't think his brother would be receptive. A black fog of rage filled her head, and she battled to stop herself from picking something up and hurling it at Richard's smug face. Richard rose and spoke in a low voice. 'Get out.' Then he shut his eyes.

She was being dismissed with no discussion. Sam was right. He was a very sore loser. Richard opened his eyes. 'Why are you still here?' he asked.

Sam pushed himself off the fender. 'Because she's not going anywhere, Richard. You are.'

Richards's jaw dropped. 'You don't mean that.'

'Yes, unfortunately for you, I do.'

'Not after what you promised Pa.'

'I promised Pa I would look after you, protect you. I have, but you've gone too far this time. You can't compromise with a bully. I've tried. Clare just tried. The entire village has tried. Enough. Go!'

Clare gasped. Impressive speech, but how was Sam proposing to get Richard to comply?

'You will live to regret this, Sam,' snarled Richard.

'I probably will,' said Sam.

Richard stormed out of the room. Sam got up and followed him, leaving Clare scrambling to make sense of what she'd just witnessed. Richard wouldn't compromise on the contents of that shed, nor would he back away from the defamation case. She'd lit the fuse on a powder keg and there was nowhere to hide from it.

Ten minutes later, Sam returned with two glasses of red wine and handed one to her.

'It's a bit early for me, but I think I need it,' said Clare, taking a gulp. 'Well, that went well, didn't it! I wonder what Machiavelli's next move will be.'

Sam laughed, then said, 'If he'd been smart enough to follow that sixteenth-century philosopher's golden rule, Richard wouldn't be pondering his next move.'

'What do you mean?'

'Richard sees Brambleton Hall as a fortress, but as Machiavelli said, "The best fortress to be found is in the love of the people . . . No fortress will save you if you are hated by the people."'

How true, thought Clare. The villagers had united against Hastings because he treated them with contempt. None of them felt that way about Sam.

She took a gulp of wine. They needed to get away before Richard returned, but first she had to defuse that defamation time bomb.

'Before your brother bankrupts me, you told me you know who sent him that draft leaflet. Who was it?'

He smiled, and Clare remembered the strange look in Ivy's eyes that day she'd confronted BARS on the terrace. 'Was it Ivy?'

He shook his head. 'No, but Ivy worked out who did.'

So that explained Ivy's expression that day. 'Why didn't she tell me?'

'Because she thought you knew but didn't want to admit it.'

'What? Who sent it?'

'It was you.'

'I did not!'

'You did. Richard showed me. I think you might have been a bit tipsy. It was clear from the covering note you meant to send it to Anna – *Rianna*? I can only assume your email bar inserted Richard's email address instead of Rianna's.'

She gasped, then spluttered into laughter. That was why Anna had looked so shocked when she'd read the poisonous leaflet. It *was* the first time she'd seen it.

'Ivy worked it out. When she saw how shocked Anna was

reading that leaflet, she checked the original email you sent, spotted Anna wasn't included, guessed you'd tried to send it to Anna separately, and by mistake sent it to Richard instead.'

'So, it was Richard who circulated those rude leaflets? He set out to trap me?'

This time, Sam was smiling as he shook his head. 'Do you really think such a proud man would circulate something which ridiculed him? That was me. No one knows Richard like me, and he was behaving like a medieval squire complaining the peasants were about to storm his grain stores. I thought I'd stir things up a bit, give him something to worry about.'

She let out a huge breath, her eyes locking onto his. Clare felt light-headed. She put down her glass and reached out for him. He held her, murmuring into her hair. 'I didn't think he'd launch a lawsuit against you. I'll get him to drop it. You might have to apologize for emailing it to Fred and Ivy, but he can't claim compensation. You didn't circulate the leaflet, I did.'

'What did you mean earlier, about protecting your brother?'

'I promised our father I would look after Richard, and I have tried. But I can't forgive him for writing you that spiteful note all those years ago. And after the way he just treated you, I've had enough.'

Clare paused, letting his words sink in. Her life could have turned out very differently if Richard hadn't meddled in it. 'I must get out of here before he comes back. I'd rather not be in in his study when he returns.'

'I told you – he's not coming back. Can you keep a secret?' asked Sam.

'I'm a lawyer. I'll take many secrets to my grave.'

'The reason Richard and I don't get on is because of my father's will.'

She swallowed a final mouthful of wine, remembering the bizarre meeting with Magnus in the supermarket. 'Magnus told me, about your farm; how Richard tried to talk you out of splitting up the estate.'

'That's not quite right. That's the story we agreed to circulate, but it's not the truth. The truth is our father left everything to me.'

Her mouth went slack. She cleared her throat, then said, 'But you're the younger son.'

'Pa was free to leave everything to whomever he wanted to. Traditionally, the estate would be left to the eldest son, but he could see how much I loved the village, how in tune I was with it, and how out of tune Richard was. I think he foresaw the kind of battle we've just had; that Richard would expect the village to doff the proverbial cap like it did in the nineteenth century, whereas I wouldn't. That's why I promised to look after Richard. I was always the favourite son, the one who would inherit everything, and Pa knew how much that hurt Richard.'

'Wow. So why don't you live here instead of Richard?'

'Because I didn't want to, and Richard did. It's lovely to visit, but I didn't want the responsibility. I'm much freer to live the life I want where I am. But I think it's time I faced up to my responsibilities. My father chose me for a good reason and now I must fulfil his wishes.'

'You swapped the Hall for your cider farm?'

'Yes. But it's an informal arrangement. Richard has no legal right to live here. He won't be homeless, I'll find him somewhere on the estate, maybe the shoot lodge, or my house.'

'Somehow I'm having difficulty picturing Richard and Cora in a farmhouse.'

'Why? This is a farmhouse right here. The perfect Devon farmhouse.'

Thirty

Four months later

Wearing a dress with one of her mother's aprons tied over it, Clare scattered chopped basil leaves over her homemade tapenade. She sliced a baguette, and heaped pieces round the bowl, dropping the crusty ends onto the floor, where Stop-it efficiently cleared them up. She heard a tooting car horn, Hilts crowed in response, and as his squawking tailed off, an engine replaced the sound. Her guest. The engine died and she wiped her hands on her apron, reaching round to untie it.

She felt a gust of wind and smiled. 'Doesn't anyone ever ring the bell in Brambleton?' she asked, spinning round to the open door.

Sam beamed at her. 'Didn't want to waste the time. Quite opinionated that cockerel of yours.'

'Remind you of anyone?'

'Yes,' he said, taking her in his arms. She laughed. 'Who?' she asked. But he didn't answer, instead closing his mouth over hers. She pulled away and repeated her question.

'You,' he said.

'Me?'

'Yes. He's as feisty and opinionated as his owner.' He released her and stooped to stroke Stop-it. She slipped off the apron and tossed it over the back of a chair.

'I've brought something for you,' he said.

'What's that?'

He tapped the side of his nose.

'Curiouser and curiouser,' she said.

He disappeared, returning with a large cardboard box. There were no markings on it. 'What's this?' she asked, wanting to claw her way inside. She gave a throaty laugh. 'Are you going to tell me?'

He was grinning at her. 'Why not take a look?'

She peeled back the folds, revealing twelve bottles. There were no labels, but she guessed what was inside. 'The four corner ones are chilled,' he said. 'Come on, let's try it.' He pulled two bottles free. Clare rummaged in a drawer, found a bottle opener and took it into the sitting room along with the tapenade and a bowl of kibble. There was a log fire burning and the room smelt of apple wood. In front of the hearth, Stop-it was stretched out, with his belly facing the warmth. She popped the bowl of food beside his muzzle. He gave it a desultory look.

Clare's eyes flickered to the corner where her mother's Georgian writing desk used to sit. Ivy had collected it a month ago, along with the furniture stored in the old milking parlour. Yesterday, her mother's best friend had returned to Orchard Farm clutching an envelope. Written on the front, in her mother's spidery handwriting were two words: *For Clare.*

'Wh— What's this?' stammered Clare fingering the envelope.

'It was in the secret drawer of the writing desk,' said Ivy. She pursed her lips. 'Do you want me to leave you alone?'

Clare shook her head, sat down and ripped at the seal. With twitchy fingers she removed a single sheet of paper from the envelope, took a deep breath and read.

Dearest Clare,
I have wanted to write to you so many times but honouring your request to leave you alone, I have resisted. I hope one day Ivy will persuade you to read this letter.

I wish I had explained why I said what I did in the orchard so many years ago. There was a reason, a person I thought you would be so much happier with than the man you chose, but it was wrong of me to try and inflict my choice on you. It's your life and I wish with all my heart I had accepted your decision and supported you in your brief marriage. I hope I was wrong, and Guy did make you happy and didn't break your heart.

I have missed you so much and have never stopped loving you. I only hope in time you may be able to forgive my foolish words which were said in love but in haste.

With all my love
Mum.

Clare had burst into tears. She felt Ivy's arms around her shoulders and, still sobbing, had passed her the letter. She hadn't realized how much she had needed to hear those words. All that compartmentalizing, all those task lists had been a distraction, a sticking plaster for the gaping wound of believing her mother had died feeling out of love with her daughter. She felt revitalised, knowing that Cindy had wanted to heal their rift as much as Clare did, and although cruelly robbed of the opportunity to do so, had never stopped loving her.

Now, watching Sam pour two glasses of cider, she felt her mother's love wrap around her. Sam passed her a glass. If he noticed she seemed happier, more carefree since they last met, he didn't mention it but knowing her mother would approve of their relationship made it feel even more special, as if they were truly meant to be together.

'You try it first,' she said, sniffing her own. There was a strong apple scent, making her think of spring and summer in the orchard, and then of her mother in her blue overalls, arms threaded through the blossom, busy thinning apples. Sam swirled the contents round his glass, held it up to the light, then wafted it under his nose. He sniffed, wrinkled his nose – Clare couldn't decide if that was in approval or jest – then he took a long swallow. Clare held her breath. He wasn't wincing, nor were his eyes screwed up, but he wasn't smiling either.

'Drinkable?' she asked.

He took another gulp and flushed it round his cheeks.

'I can improve on the flavour, if you'll let me, but not bad for a maiden vintage. Go on. Try it yourself.'

She let out a long, noisy breath, unable to speak. Nothing could convey her relief. She took a sip herself. Not bad!

Her sabbatical had finished months ago, and it had been a huge gamble to stay in Devon. She had an image of that day in the Managing Partner's book-lined office, with its framed *Punch* cartoons and a view of the open-plan office. 'I love this job,' she'd said, and she really meant those words, 'but I love Devon life more.'

The senior partner spoke in a soft Welsh purring voice that Clare would miss. 'Can't we explore you working flexitime, so we can still keep you?'

Clare shook her head. An image of the apple orchard popped into her mind, the grass cut short, the swards' neat brown circles of mulch, every branch covered with tiny fruit. 'Farming is a way of life, and it's the life I want.'

'What a waste – you are such a brilliant lawyer.'

Smiling, Clare replied, 'That's kind. Don't worry, I'm not abandoning the law entirely, I'll still take on a few pro bono cases.'

She'd only been back to London once since, to pack up her flat when it sold. Severing her past life was tough, but selling the property was a simple decision. She couldn't become a landlord. She accepted they weren't all as bad as Richard, but she preferred to leave it to the professionals.

Feeling Sam's arms wrap around her waist, she leaned into him. 'If the Devon man wants to help me do a proper job,' she said, enunciating the last two words in a North-Devonian accent, 'I think I could accept.'

For a few minutes they sat eating the homemade tapenade, listening to the crackling logs, Sam teasing Stop-it with hunks of baguette. She kicked off her shoes and wriggled her toes close to the fire, thinking how often her mother used to do this, how often the pair of them used to do this when Clare was a child. She realized this is what her mother had wanted for her; she'd known it was what would make her daughter happy. Her mother had always hoped Clare's law career would be a stepping stone to returning to the farm. Sadly, Clare had left it too late. There wasn't much of the farm to return to, but if she planted the remaining acres of fallow land with the right apple trees, she could have a viable cider business.

'I've been thinking, and I've got an idea for you,' said Sam. He leaned over and kissed her on the cheek. 'We could merge the two farms, plant trees on the fields between us.'

She had an image of a farm that stretched from her farmhouse to his. Two orchards joined by her mother's former fields. 'Would apples grow on those fields between us? They face the sea.'

'You're not thinking big enough. You've got the wrong farmhouse. I meant join up with Brambleton Hall.'

'The fields where Richard wanted the shed?'

'It would give the tenants in the almshouses a marvellous view.'

All the tenants thought Clare. Ivy and Fred were still living in Rose and Jasmine Cottages respectively, and new families had moved into their former, now refurbished, houses. Everyone had a new landlord – Sam – and they all had five-year leases. Although it was a wrench, Sam was planning to move out of his house and into Brambleton Hall explaining that was what his father would have wanted him to do.

'I've been thinking . . . isn't it a bit selfish us living in two big houses?' said Sam.

'I come with my animals.'

'Stop-it and I get on well, don't we, boy,' he said.

'What about Captain Hilts and the Veras?'

Sam laughed. 'I suppose they can come too, but only provided the flock doesn't grow too large – I don't want to become a chicken farmer.'

Clare laughed and laid her head on his shoulder. As her laughter died, she realized there was a strange crunching noise. She gasped. Over by the fire, Stop-it was contentedly munching his kibble.

Dear Reader,

As you close the final page of this story, I want to take a moment to say thank you. Sharing these stories with you is a privilege, and knowing you've spent your time with my characters truly means the world to me.

At the heart of every story are people – flawed, wonderful, and utterly human. I love exploring relationships, whether romantic, familial, or friendship, and watching how they change under pressure. My hope is that these characters stay with you long after the story ends.

While I start these stories with a plan, I leave space for inspiration to strike. Often, the best twists and emotional moments come unexpectedly, and weaving them in keeps the story alive. I also enjoy adding little insights – quirky details, interesting facts, or a glimpse into an unusual job – that bring depth and texture to the world my characters inhabit.

Finally, can I ask a tiny favour? If you enjoyed *A Perfect Devon Farmhouse*, would you mind leaving a quick review online? It doesn't have to be Shakespeare – just say how you feel. I read all my reviews and I am grateful for every single one (yes, even the bad ones!). Writing can sometimes feel solitary, but knowing you're out there connecting with these stories makes it the most rewarding thing I could ever do.

Thank you for being part of this journey – I can't wait to share the next one with you.

With love,
Debbie x

Did you love A Perfect Devon Farmhouse?

Welcome to Brambleton!

Nestled along North Devon's rugged coastline, Brambleton, although of course fictional, is everything you'd hope for in a village – picturesque cottages, winding lanes, and a community where everyone knows your name, even if they don't know your secrets. And trust me, there are plenty more of those hiding behind its pretty stone walls!

The Brambleton books aim to take you right into the heart of this little haven, where friendships are lifelong, love is full of twists and turns, and surprises have a habit of appearing as often as the wildflowers in the hedgerows. It's a place where life isn't always perfect, but it is always full of heart.

Each story brings a new cast of characters, from the hilariously endearing to the quietly courageous. While each book stands alone, you'll spot familiar faces and places as you explore Brambleton's nooks and crannies, making it feel like coming home to old friends.

So make yourself a cuppa, grab a blanket, and lose yourself in one of these feel-good, light-hearted tales. They're brimming with warmth, laughter, and the kind of moments that remind us that even when life feels a bit off the tracks, love and community can see us through.

The next book in the series is *A Perfect Devon Pub*, starring one of my favourite characters yet. Fiona is a sommelier who arrives in the sleepy village of Brambleton to rest and re-charge after a sad breakup with her boyfriend, a celebrity chef. She ends up working at the Smugglers' Inn, where she becomes embroiled in an investigation involving stolen bottles of high-end wine. Poor Fiona! I've really put her through the wringer in this one.

Here's an exclusive extract to introduce you to *A Perfect Devon Pub* . . .

I hope you enjoy it!

Love, Debbie x

One

Amid the vibrant bustle of London's Portobello Road Market, an unassuming restaurant lay ensconced between antique dealers and vintage clothing stalls. In perfect harmony with the market's spirit – equal parts tradition, innovation, and authenticity – it beckoned with understated charm, a quiet steady presence amid the ever-shifting crowds.

The Fork & Cork – the name painted in crisp white letters on a modest green awning – was a place where the market's energy spilled over into every plate and every conversation. It had quickly become the neighbourhood's worst-kept secret. Seating just thirty, the intimate space had drawn a steady stream of devotees over the last eighteen months, lured by TikTok clips showcasing the fluid grace of the open-plan kitchen and reviews exalting the aromas that swirled through the air: rosemary's earthiness mingled with bright zesty lemon and the rich warmth of melting butter.

On this August evening, through its windows, a passerby could glimpse the choreographed dance of the four junior chefs, hands flying between chopping boards and pans, knives scattering light into the steam that spiralled up from copper pots. In the centre of it all, conducting this symphony of flavours, stood London's latest culinary sensation: the head chef, Ruben Nkosi. His broad-shouldered frame pivoted between stations, each movement precise and purposeful as he tasted sauces, adjusted seasoning, and issued commands with a quiet authority. The stark white of his chef's jacket emphasized his athletic build, while the kitchen's warm lighting caught the waves in his dark, closely cropped hair. When he turned to inspect a dish, his high cheekbones caught the light, and his square jaw would tense in concentration before relaxing into an easy, confident smile that seemed to energize his team.

At one end of the gleaming kitchen counter was the Chef's Table. Here, four privileged diners perched on leather-topped barstools, leaning forward as if tethered by an unseen string, following each flick of Ruben's wrist, each subtle nod of approval. The occasional sizzle or burst of flame drew soft gasps, and when aromatic steam billowed up from a pan, they inhaled deeply, unconsciously running their tongues across their lips in anticipation of the feast to come.

Behind them, in the restaurant, a soft and curvy woman named Fiona was weaving between the cramped tables, pouring wine, uncorking bottles, recommending pairings for the food. Fiona was the kind of woman who usually radiated an infectious energy that can light up a room. Her dark blonde hair was cut in a style that framed her round, freckled face and drew attention to her usually bright eyes. Today though, those eyes were clouded, and the spark had dimmed. When the restaurant had opened its doors at 6.30, Fiona had painted a bright smile on her face. Now, nearly two hours later, she wasn't sure how much longer she could keep up the good cheer. As she explained the differences between Champagne and Crémant to a couple celebrating their wedding anniversary, the ghastliness of the last three days kept intruding on her thoughts. No, not the last three days: the first two had been invigorating; even most of the third had been stimulating. But the sixty seconds between 4:30 and

4:31 yesterday had lodged in her mind like a splinter buried too deep to remove. Now it was throbbing painfully with the memory of something she could neither forget nor face.

Fiona's eyes flicked towards the master of ceremonies; Ruben was laughing and posing for selfies at the Chef's Table. Further along the polished stainless-steel bar, two middle-aged women, wide-eyed with excitement, were eagerly trying to catch his eye. 'Chef! We've seen your videos!' called out one, waving her phone in the air. He turned, grinned, and walked over with the poise of someone well-used to being the centre of attention. Resting his hands on the counter, he smiled at the customer. 'Glad to hear it. What are you having this evening? We had a wonderful delivery of fresh fish this morning.'

The women swooned as the celebrity chef started talking them through the evening's specials, his deep voice describing the lemon sole with thyme and brown butter sauce with such enthusiasm Fiona felt her mouth watering, and her irritation with his showboating melt away. She helped one of her team clear and relay a table, then, spotting empty glasses, fetched the correct wine from the central chilling bucket, wiped off the moisture with a cloth, and poured it out expertly, to the widest part of the glass. When she replaced the bottle in the cooling bucket, the satisfying clink of glass against ice felt oddly final, like locking away a secret in an impregnable vault. But no matter how deep she tried to bury the memory, those sixty seconds kept floating back up.

Fiona shook her head to clear her mind, pulled out her notepad and manoeuvred between the cramped tables towards the Chef's table, her movements graceful, but her shoulders tense. The stainless-steel counter – Ruben's culinary stage – gleamed beneath the spotlights. Upon it, were the well-orchestrated props: heirloom tomatoes in earthenware bowls; baskets of garlic bulbs, both black and white, each one the size of a tennis ball. Along the counter's edge, freshly made sauces stood sentinel in labelled bottles, their ranks as precise as soldiers awaiting inspection, transforming the counter into an alchemist's workbench.

'Ah, Fiona,' Ruben said as she arrived, 'perfect timing.' He gestured at the two women, both still wearing the eager expression of the dedicated fan. 'We need some advice on the ideal wine to match tonight's scallop dish. What about a New Zealand Sauvignon Blanc?'

Fiona's face twitched, her eyes narrowing for just a moment. Tonight, she wanted to forget all about new world wines. Telling herself to be professional, she chewed at her lip, then managed a weak smile. 'Of course. It's an excellent choice – bright, crisp, with a mineral finish that will really lift the seafood.' She looked up at Ruben, hoping to catch a glimpse of recognition for her skills, but he was already diverted; another customer was calling his name. Fiona wondered if he caught the flash of frustration in her expression before she refocused on the guests in front of her, advising them of the price of their wine choice.

'Service!' cried a junior chef. Plates clattered onto the serving counter, and Fiona swivelled to collect them. The hiss of a hot pan filled the room, steam rising as Ru seared a fillet of fish, the aroma of butter and thyme enveloping the air. The diners at the kitchen counter hunched forward, captivated by his cooking, hanging on every word as he explained the dish.

'You're amazing, Chef! Can we take a photo?' a young woman asked eagerly, phone already in hand.

Ru flashed his trademark smile and obliged, leaning in for the snap. Fiona turned her back on the flurry of activity. She approached a table of regulars who had been coming here for months, knowing the service they would receive from Fiona and her team would always be personal, attentive, full of expertise.

'Your usual bottle of white burgundy?' she asked with a knowing smile, pouring expertly into each of their glasses. On the cusp of engaging them in conversation, another burst of laughter erupted from Ruben's station, drowning out her words. Fiona glanced over to see the chef with a group of men, signing autographs on napkins as if he were a rock star. Ruben was basking in the attention, his focus seemingly more on the camera flashes than on their shared passion for creating something special together. Fiona bit back her irritation, knowing it was unfair of her to blame Ru for enjoying his newfound celebrity. He was a wonderful chef, and a brilliant promoter of their restaurant; it was Ru who had made it so successful. It was churlish of her to begrudge him his moment in the sun, when he had worked so hard for it.

As the night wore on, the energy in the restaurant swelled. Plates arrived at tables with bursts of colour – grilled sea bass with bright green herbs freshly picked that morning, warm, crusty bread with golden extra-virgin olive oil, and vibrant salads topped with edible orange flowers. The smells of roasted vegetables, caramelized onions, and grilling meat intermingled, making the space almost alive with flavour. Ruben, still centre stage, seemed animated by the buzzing atmosphere, chatting with customers between cooking, throwing in witty remarks that drew chuckles and applause.

At the Chef's table, Fiona was pouring another glass of wine for a couple. 'You're so lucky to work with him,' commented the man. 'He's incredibly talented, isn't he?'

Fiona's smile was polite, her tone light, but there was a knowing look in her eyes. 'Yes, he's very talented. But it's not all glitz and glamour. There's a lot more to running a restaurant than what you see on social media.'

As the door shut behind the last diners, Ruben took off his

apron, mopped his brow and approached Fiona, his usually loose-limbed gait a little stiff, likely still fizzing from the evening's adrenalin. 'Busy night, the team did well,' he said with a grin.

Fiona gave him a small smile and kept her voice soft. She didn't want him to feel bad, but she had to say something. 'Yes, they did do well. But what about you? You're not just cooking anymore, Ru. You're performing. And I wonder how long you can keep that up.'

'Hey, come here.' He pulled her into his arms. Being a foot shorter enabled her head to rest on his chest and she breathed in the comforting smell of him. Her nose, fine-tuned to detect the subtle aromas of different wines, picked up top-notes of lemon, rosemary, thyme and mint, over the not-unpleasant base notes of cooked oil and fried fish. She inhaled deeply and felt a small lump form in her throat. 'Sorry, Ru. I shouldn't deny your success just because I'm a failure.'

'Forget it, Fi,' he whispered.

Her voice thick with emotion, she muttered, 'I can't.'

He spoke firmly. 'You *must*. You can't be like this tomorrow morning. Come on – let's go home and leave the team to do the final clear up for once. Their future depends on us. We need to prepare.'

She suspected his current preparation plans wouldn't address their most crucial blind spot. 'Ru, face it, things have changed. They won't back us now.'

He laughed. It was a wonderful sound, throaty and self-assured, filling her with courage, and despite herself the corners of her mouth started twitching upward. He had never let her stay down for long. She questioned if he was right. Was she being too negative? Or was Ru just blustering, to boost her confidence? His was unshakable. He believed he would always succeed; on the rare occasions someone said no, Ru interpreted the word as a challenge, convinced that with time and effort, he would persuade them to change their mind. This time, though, his confidence was misplaced. Fiona was certain that the investors would still back Ru, but there was no way they'd back her. Not now that she'd failed to prove her worth.

Using a finger, he tipped her head gently off his chest. 'Don't dwell on it, Fi,' he whispered, 'you'll get another chance, and the investors will understand. I will make them understand. We're partners. If they want me, they must want you too.' Then he kissed her, and all thoughts of her failure were temporarily quenched. She pulled away, giving a soft laugh. 'Don't do that when we meet the investors! We don't want them suspecting we're more than business partners, that we would let romance cloud our professional judgement.'

He chuckled, then took both her hands in his. 'Well, that might be tricky . . . after all, it will be a breakfast meeting.'

That made her snicker; for them, breakfasts were like dates: the only moment in the day when it was just the two of them, and they could relax together away from the constant drumbeat of work deadlines or the steady buzz of the restaurant kitchen.

A voice called out from the stoves. 'Good luck tomorrow chef!'

Ru turned to wave at his team. 'Thanks! And guys . . . thanks for everything tonight, you all did brilliantly. See you tomorrow.'

They slipped outside, and walked hand in hand through the empty market, a warm summer breeze brushing against their skin. The low hum of trucks collecting the day's discarded rubbish and the clatter of bottles being emptied into metal bins replaced the usual noise of vendors and tourists.

'I spoke to your aunt Ivy today,' said Ru. I thought we should get away this weekend, to celebrate.'

'Ru! Don't tempt fate,' she scolded; sometimes Fiona thought his confidence bordered on cocky. Nevertheless, she would love to see her aunt Ivy, who had hung up her clerical collar just months ago and had time on her hands these days to spend with her favourite niece. They shared the same diminutive height and round freckled face, but that's where the similarities ended. Unlike Fiona, Aunt Ivy didn't give a fig for the trappings of success, and she rarely worried about the future. She had been Fiona's sanctuary when her parents' cold silence echoed through her childhood home, her steady lighthouse through the stormy waters of adolescence, and a font of wisdom through the maze of early adulthood. Perhaps now, Ivy's presence would be the familiar balm it had always been, a gentle hand smoothing the ragged edges of her thoughts.

Ru squeezed her hand. 'No . . . hear me out. We both need a break. We haven't had a holiday for over a year. The team can manage without us for a week. They'll have to get used to it once the new restaurant opens, in any case. I've taken a decision. We are going down to Devon to stay with Ivy for a week. I've hired a car, and we can drive down after Friday night service. It will be fun, walks on the beach, dips in the sea . . .'

Listening to his enthusiasm, she warmed to his plans; just being with Ru and Ivy for a week would recharge her batteries. Allow her to get yesterday in perspective. She took a breath, inhaling the mixture of scents in the market – mouldy wood from abandoned crates, and the sour tang of overripe vegetables left rotting in the bins. She wouldn't miss those if they spent a week by the sea.

They walked in silence, the kind that settles between people who've known each other long enough to be comfortable with their own thoughts. The sounds of metal lids clanging shut, and the rumble of engines faded behind them, leaving only the soft shuffling of their steps. A stray newspaper page tumbled across the ground, rustling against Fiona's bare ankles before skittering away into the shadows, carrying yesterday's headlines into tomorrow.

She sighed. 'What are we going to say to them tomorrow? You know . . . about . . .'

He grasped her hand. 'Leave that one to me, pardner.'

His voice was so reassuringly firm that she felt the stirrings of hope. Maybe her failure wasn't such a big problem after all? Perhaps she was overthinking things, as usual.

Two

With her sandals in one hand and Ru's warm fingers intertwined in the other, Fiona walked steadily along Brambleton Beach. The soft sand felt silky and warm between her toes, yielding gently beneath each step. Under the intense summer sun, the grains sparkled as if someone had scattered crushed glass along the shore, forming a glimmering path above the waterline.

It was Saturday, and the beach seemed to pulse with energy. Locals and tourists alike were lounging in canvas beach chairs under colourful umbrellas or sprawling on towels behind striped windbreaks. Some were absorbed in books, others napping. Near the water's edge, children were building sandcastles, wet sand slipping through their fingers as they shaped towers and moats, their giggles drifting up over the steady rhythm of waves breaking on the sand.

The air carried a medley of scents: the salt-laden sea breeze, coconut-scented sunscreen, and the earthy tang of damp seaweed. Fiona smiled to herself; at least today, no one would ask her which wines those scents might evoke. It was a perfect, sunlit morning; everyone seemed at ease. She looked around at the kaleidoscope of relaxation and contentment. Swimsuit styles may have changed over the years, but the scene was reminiscent of Fiona's childhood summer holiday walks on this very beach. She could almost hear the soft hum of her aunt Ivy's favourite hymn, the one she used to sing under her breath when they strolled toward the ice cream shack, their traditional destination.

It felt fitting, somehow, that Ivy was the first to learn the investors had agreed to back her and Ru's new restaurant. Earlier that morning, Ru had delivered the news while whipping up a fluffy soufflé omelette in Ivy's kitchen.

'Well done, love!' Ivy exclaimed, pulling Fiona into a warm embrace. Her arms were strong and reassuring, and Fiona couldn't help but melt into them. 'Hopefully that's the last exam you ever have to put yourself through.'

Fiona hesitated before mumbling, 'No. I didn't pass.'

The words hung in the air for a moment as she glanced up at her aunt, whose face softened instantly with a gentle smile of understanding.

'Well, you tried your best, and that's all anyone can do,' Ivy said, her tone filled with quiet encouragement. 'Besides, didn't you tell me that only 25% of people pass the sommelier exam first time?'

Ivy didn't say any more, and Fiona felt a wave of relief. Ivy's unspoken acceptance was as comforting as the summer sun streaming through the window. It reminded Fiona why this place – and this person – always felt like home. Still, she was disappointed in herself to have messed up the exam. She really *had* tried her best, yet she'd still failed. Wasn't that the worst possible outcome? Was it any surprise that a little worm of doubt had now wriggled into her mind, whispering that she simply wasn't good enough? She shook the thought away and tugged her shoulder bag closer, feeling the reassuring sharp edge of the books inside. She would soon be studying again – and if she passed next time, she would feel a lot better.

'And the good news is,' said Ru, sliding a perfect omelette onto a warm plate, 'it doesn't matter.' Giving Fiona a pointed look, he put down the frying pan and bounded across the room, scooping her into his arms, lifting her off her feet and kissing her. He set her down, saying, 'The investors are still stumping up the money for the new restaurant.'

That was a careful choice of words, thought Fiona.

At the kitchen table, Ru sliced the omelette. 'Come on, let's eat; Ivy has a meeting to get to, and' he said, excitement clear in his voice, 'you and I have a date with a beach. Ivy, do me a favour and pass me that shoulder bag. *That* is not going with us.' Ivy chuckled, and Fiona managed a smile. One day off wouldn't matter.

Ru's voice brought her back from her worries about the exam. 'Happy?' he asked.

She told herself it felt good to be on holiday, with the sun on her back and the man she adored beside her, not toiling in the fuggy heat of the cramped London restaurant. But she dodged his question.

'Fancy an ice cream?' she suggested.

He wrinkled his nose. 'Real ice cream? Or hydrogenated trans fats?'

She punched him playfully on the arm. 'Proper Devon dairy ice cream made with real milk from local cows, of course. They've been selling it here for nearly a hundred years.'

'Well, how can I turn down the chance of that!'

They reached the ice-cream kiosk, a shack painted in mint green and pale pink. It had a weathered wooden exterior, and white slatted shutters pinned back to let the cooling sea breeze inside. Above the entrance, on a large board, someone had written the flavours and prices in pink chalk: classic varieties like vanilla, strawberry, rum n' raisin and caramel, alongside local specialties like Devon clotted cream and elderflower.

Inside, vintage glass jars stuffed with toppings lined the shelves. The staff wore striped aprons just like the ones Ru's team wore in London, and she gave her head a tight shake to dislodge the association. She didn't want to ruin today by constantly thinking about work.

'Two scoops of caramel, please!' she called cheerfully to an attendant, forcing a smile that didn't quite reach her eyes. She wanted to enjoy this moment with Ru, to bask in the sun's warmth and the sweet innocence of ice cream. She glanced sideways at him, his face a mask of quiet determination, though she sensed an underlying anxiety.

When their ice creams arrived, they took them outside. Ru chose the table furthest from the shack, and they slumped into deck chairs, digging their feet into the sand. Fiona took a tentative lick, the ice-cream melting into her mouth, sweet and silky smooth. As she savoured the moment, she reached for his spare hand, feeling the warmth of his skin against hers. She could tell that something was bothering him. This was rare – he was usually so easy-going and confident – but she decided not to ask, certain he would tell her when he was ready.

'I spoke to Ben this morning,' said Ru.

Ah, thought Fiona, Ru's troubles must be work related. Ben, Ru's sous chef and best friend, was running the Fork & Cork while the couple were in Brambleton. Fiona suspected despite Ru's bravado at breakfast, he was regretting this holiday already, leaving his team at such a sensitive point. He would probably rather be in London nurturing them. Trying to keep the tension out of her voice, she asked, 'has he handed in his notice yet?'

Ru squeezed her hand. 'Relax, the entire team is moving with us, and everything is under control at the Fork & Cork.'

So, Ru's anxiety wasn't related to business – neither the new venture nor the existing one. A family of four flopped down at the table next to them. The two children, both in bright swimsuits and flip-flops, swung their legs eagerly beneath the table, while their parents, dressed in light summer clothes and sunglasses, eyed the chalkboard menu.

Ru frowned and slipped his hand into his pocket as if feeling for his wallet.

'We're not in London, no pickpockets in Brambleton!' Fiona joked reassuringly.

'Sorry,' Ru mumbled, withdrawing his hand, but his eyes darted around as if he was expecting someone to jump out from the shadows. He glanced down at the ground before casting a quick, wary look over his shoulder. Even as he forced a small smile, his fingers twitched at his sides, betraying a nervous energy.

Fiona couldn't understand what was wrong. Perhaps he was just finding it difficult to relax away from the restaurant. 'It's lovely to be here with you,' she said, stroking his arm. His muscle was tense, but as she stroked, she felt it relax, and a smile creased his face.

'It's going to be a magical week. Let's just chill, we've earned it,' said Ru.

He hadn't chosen his words so carefully this time. Fiona was reminded that while Ru may have earned a week off, she hadn't.

'What do you fancy doing tomorrow? How about a day trip to Lundy?' asked Ru. She loved the rugged, windswept beauty of Lundy Island out in the Bristol Channel, but she wrinkled her nose. She couldn't spare another whole day away from her books.

'I think I should be revising.'

'Nope. Forbidden! You are on holiday. This is a celebration.'

'Except it's your celebration, not mine.'

He spoke forcefully. 'Fi, this is *our* celebration; the investors are backing *our* business.'

Except they weren't. The message from the investors was clear; they would back Ru, but not Fiona, claiming she didn't carry the same weight as him. Ru was now officially the owner of the new restaurant. Just like Ben and the rest of the team, Fiona would be his employee, not his partner. That wouldn't have happened if she had passed her advanced sommelier exam.

'Fi, please, don't dwell on that exam.' He pushed his sunglasses off his face and his eyes sparkled with his enthusiasm. 'We're a team, and an amazing one, that's what the investors saw and that's what they're backing. We are equal in this venture, what's mine is yours. Anyway, come on, you don't need a piece of paper to say you're the best sommelier in town.'

'The investors think I do.' Fiona wasn't surprised – in fact, she agreed with them. Certificates were there to prove one's worth. To separate the successful from failures like her. Her mother and father had proved that with their own careers, gradually accumulating more letters after their names as they advanced in the field of neurogenetic research. They hadn't taken much notice of her as a child, finding discussions of amyloid plaques much more alluring than reading bedtime stories, but they'd always been proud when she came home from school waving a certificate.

'Are you really going to pour yourself into study? You'll never have time to enjoy life.'

Fiona sighed. Hadn't he realised she'd been doing that all her life? In fact, it was Ivy who suggested a teenage Fiona channel her efforts into academia. Whether she did so to keep her niece busy, or because she knew it was the only way she could earn the sporadic attention of her parents, Fiona wasn't sure. Either way, it was addictive. Her parents applauded each exam passed, every qualification she achieved, but like brief rays of sunshine in a dreary summer, they withdrew their affection once the triumph was celebrated and buried themselves back in their own work.

On turning eighteen, when Fiona left home to study for sommelier exams in London, her parents emigrated to Australia to take up a research post at the Florey Institute, a global leader in neurodegenerative diseases. Fiona couldn't help but feel they'd been waiting for the opportunity ever since she was born. Communication dwindled to a text on her birthday, and a phone call to congratulate her on each academic milestone: passing her levels 1, 2, 3 and 4 WSET Wine exams, and later her Introductory, and Certified, sommelier exams. With no more progress to report, Fiona realised she hadn't heard from them in nearly a year.

A football thudded in front of Fiona, startling her and bringing her back to Brambleton bay. She watched fondly as a boy in faded knee-length swimming trunks traipsed through the sand towards his toy. The child looked about ten, with gangly limbs, and a skinny chest. Behind him, his mother was following, dressed in a pink bikini and stepping gingerly on the hot sand.

Ru bent and picked up the ball, handing it to the boy.

'What do you say Mark?' instructed the mother. She looked from her child to Ru, then did a double take. 'Oh, my goodness . . . it's you, isn't it? From the Fork & Cork? Wow! Are you on holiday here too?' She smiled coyly. 'Wait until I tell my girlfriends. I only live in Shepherds Bush, you're local for me.' She batted her eyes at him. 'Could I be frightfully rude, and ask for your autograph?'

Ru stood. He was smiling at his admirer, who was twirling a lock of hair between her fingers. Involuntarily Fiona pressed her lips together, her fingers fidgeting with the edge of her sleeve. *Come on,* she wanted to say to the woman. *We're on holiday!* She hoped he'd refuse.

'It's flattering to be asked,' said Ru, giving a self-deprecating laugh. 'I'd be happy to, provided you've got the pen and paper?'

The woman ran off, her feet sinking into the sand with each step.

Fiona tutted. 'Did you have to say yes?'

'It will only take a second, and you heard her, she lives

locally, both to the Fork & Cork and the new restaurant,' he said, flashing a smile at the returning fan. 'She and her friends are our new customers!'

She told herself Ru was right. It was vital to cultivate support, especially now they were setting up their own business. Except it wasn't theirs, it was his. If only she'd passed that wretched exam, it would have been theirs. She watched Ru sign with a flourish, saying, 'I hope to see you in my restaurant when we get back to London.'

The word 'My' tore into her soul like a jagged shard of glass.

Watching Ru's latest fan walk away, Fiona spoke wistfully. 'Your restaurant?'

'Fi, stop this,' he said. He took her hand in his, stroking it gently. 'I'm sorry, I didn't think. You are my equal in the new restaurant, just as we are equal in life.' He smiled at her, and it was a playful smile that made her think he was holding onto a delicious secret, like he had something exciting up his sleeve. Had he thought of a way to make her his business partner like they always planned?

Ru let go of her hand and pointed over to the cliffs. 'Come run with me to the end of the beach where we can be more private.'

Keen to get away before anyone else accosted Ru, she ran, letting the wind ripple through her hair, and the salty air fill her lungs. They sprinted along the shoreline, Fiona's feet skimming across the damp sand. The waves were breaking beside them, and she let out a childlike whoop as cold water swept up over her feet. Beside her, the soft thud of Ru's footsteps blended with her own, their laughter rising and falling with the roar of incoming waves.

At the far end of the beach, Ru steered her towards the cliffs, where, sheltered from the sun, the sand was empty of tourists.

He stopped and removed his sunglasses. His chest was heaving, and exhilarated from the run, Fiona bent over panting. 'That . . . was such . . . good fun,' she said, gulping air into her lungs. She straightened, laughing.

In front of her, Ru dropped onto one knee. Fiona felt her insides quiver. There was a passion shining in his dark eyes.

'Fi, I love you. Please, say you will marry me.' In his hands was a tiny blue box. He flipped it open. Nestling on a cream velvet cushion was an art deco ring. A stunning elongated emerald, set in platinum, the sparkling green gem surrounded by tiny glittering diamonds. Thoughts rushed through her mind. Why now? They had never discussed marriage before. Was this really what he wanted, or was this him taking pity on her?

Grinning, he rose. He evidently hadn't detected her doubts. Her heart started fluttering. He passed her the small box. Despite the size, it felt lead-like in her hands: this box represented his offer of marriage. She adored him, but she wasn't ready to change their relationship. Not now. Not while he was on a high and she was on a low. She slipped the box into the pocket of her shorts.

He was still grinning at her. 'Fi, I love you, and I want to look after you for ever. I know you want to marry me. I've reserved a slot at Chelsea Registry office for when we get home, and I've got a surprise for you.'

She stuttered into laughter. 'You proposing is already a surprise . . .'

'I've booked the honeymoon too! You're going to love it. We're off to Melbourne, so you can visit your folks, and I can finally meet them!'

Her head shot forwards. She never talked about her parents, not even with Ivy. Fiona had only told Ru where they lived to stop his incessant questions. What gave him the crazy idea of visiting them? Didn't he understand that they didn't want to see her? This was him all over— confident that he knew best, booking the wedding and honeymoon without consulting her, assuming a leadership role and expecting her to acquiesce. In a flash, she realized that much as she loved him, she couldn't marry him. Marriage should be a partnership of equals, and she could never be his equal. He was so much surer of himself, so much more capable. Better.

She swallowed, feeling the quake in her voice.

'No. I'm very sorry . . . but I can't marry you, Ru.'

His face seemed frozen, the beautiful jaw she loved to kiss went taut, then he took a step aside, slanting his body away from hers and staring at the ground.

'Why not?' he said, the words sharp and clipped.

She blinked, shaking her head slowly. How could she find the words to explain? She couldn't marry him, but she loved him and didn't want to lose him.

'Tell me,' he insisted, his voice rising as though the sheer force of his personality could break her silence. He turned to face her fully, his glare cutting into her. His jaw worked furiously, muscles still taut with disbelief. His brows drew together in a confused expression, his hands trembling as though barely able to contain the storm of emotions bubbling inside him.

The combination struck Fiona mute. She couldn't find the words to explain; he wouldn't understand. He wouldn't believe her. He would assume she wanted to hurt him, and she didn't want to do that.

'Why?!' he demanded, and there was a hint of despair in his voice now, which sent a chill through her body. 'Why won't you marry me?'

Silence hung between them, a chasm too wide to breach.

Ru was the one to break it. 'If you can't even explain yourself to me, don't bother coming back to my restaurant.' His lip curled, distorting his lovely features, as he channelled his pain into anger. 'And yes, you heard right. It's *my* restaurant. As you keep reminding me, you're just the wine waiter.'

Fiona gasped and burst into tears. She tried to swallow, but her throat felt too dry. How could he be so cruel? Yes, she'd said she couldn't marry him, but she'd expected him to row back from the proposal, revert to their easy, relaxed relationship, perhaps make a joke of it all. The taste of her tears was a salty reminder of her failure and her sorrow. Ru reached out a hand for her, but she pushed him away, evading his encircling arms, like a wild animal desperate to break free of its captor. Fiona tore up the beach, still sobbing, her chest heaving with each step. She heard him calling out to her to stop, to come back, to talk to him, but she raced on, her eyes swollen with tears. The damage was done. He'd finally spoken the truth, and he couldn't take that back.

Above her, seagulls cried out as if in sympathy with the lonely figure below them. Her chest ached with the weight of her decision, her heart torn between love for him still, and the unbearable truth she couldn't escape. But she had said *no*. Their relationship was finished.

Listening to the waves crashing against the shore, she felt as though the sea itself was mourning her loss, the pull of the tide mirroring the emptiness inside her. She had given him up – given *them* up – every footfall in the sand was another step further from a life she didn't want to lose.

Somewhere in the distance, a ship's horn sounded, deep and mournful, and she collapsed to her knees on the sand, sobbing into her hands. She would never see the man she loved again, feel his arms around her, his lips on hers.

What had she done?

Acknowledgments

Writing *A Perfect Devon Farmhouse* has been an absolute delight – though I suspect some of my neighbours are still wondering why I spent so much time lurking around farms and agricultural shows with a notebook and snapping endless photos on my phone! Living in Devon, of course, made it easy to find inspiration, whether it was in the beautiful landscapes, the charming people, or the occasional amusing mishap.

First, the biggest thank you to Laura Palmer – Your wisdom, encouragement, and brilliant editorial input have been a guiding light throughout this process. This book wouldn't be half the story it is without your expertise.

Hannah George and the Meiklejohn team – you geniuses! The cover illustration couldn't be more perfect if it tried. Honestly, it's like you peeked inside my head and painted Brambleton exactly as I imagined it, and I'm still in awe of the gorgeous little details. Also a huge thank you to Amanda Rennie for the illustration of Sir Frederick.

Jessie Sullivan, my social media star – what a gift you've been! Your creativity, flair, and ability to make online platforms feel a little less daunting have been so helpful. You've helped bring *A Perfect Devon Farmhouse* to readers in ways I couldn't have dreamed of doing on my own.

Gale Winskill and Katherine Biggs, my editorial dream team

– you've kept me on track when I was at risk of wandering off into the wilds of Devon entirely. Your insight, attention to detail, and encouragement have brought this book to life in ways I never could have managed alone.

To everyone who's played a part in bringing *A Perfect Devon Farmhouse* to life: you have my endless gratitude. Thank You.

About the Author

Debbie Morrison was always meant to write, but real life held her back. She studied law, then qualified as an accountant, and went on to work for twenty years in the City. Now, finally freed from the shackles of the day job, she has moved from London to rural Devon to pursue her childhood passion and become an author, writing the kind of books she loves to read: fast-paced, escapist and visual with credible and relatable characters.

When Debbie is not writing, she can be found playing tennis (badly), bridge (a little better), walking her dogs, or tending to her garden. She also loves cooking her own home-grown produce for friends and family. She lives on the edge of Exmoor with her husband, miniature bull terriers and small flock of free-range hens.

Visit debbiemorrison.co.uk to find out more.

Printed in Dunstable, United Kingdom

79578413R00201